VELVET ANGEL

A RUSSIAN MAFIA ROMANCE (VOROBEV BRATVA DUET BOOK 1)

NICOLE FOX

Copyright © 2021 by Nicole Fox

All rights reserved.

No part of this book may be reproduced in any form or by any electronic or mechanical means, including information storage and retrieval systems, without written permission from the author, except for the use of brief quotations in a book review.

✽ Created with Vellum

MAILING LIST

Sign up to my mailing list!
New subscribers receive a FREE steamy bad boy romance novel.

Click the link below to join.
https://sendfox.com/nicolefox

ALSO BY NICOLE FOX

Vorobev Bratva

Velvet Devil

Velvet Angel

Romanoff Bratva

Immaculate Deception

Immaculate Corruption

Kovalyov Bratva

Gilded Cage

Gilded Tears

Jaded Soul

Jaded Devil

Ripped Veil

Ripped Lace

Mazzeo Mafia Duet

Liar's Lullaby (Book 1)

Sinner's Lullaby (Book 2)

Bratva Crime Syndicate

Can be read in any order!

Lies He Told Me

Scars He Gave Me

Sins He Taught Me

Belluci Mafia Trilogy

Corrupted Angel (Book 1)

Corrupted Queen (Book 2)

Corrupted Empire (Book 3)

De Maggio Mafia Duet

Devil in a Suit (Book 1)

Devil at the Altar (Book 2)

Kornilov Bratva Duet

Married to the Don (Book 1)

Til Death Do Us Part (Book 2)

Heirs to the Bratva Empire

Can be read in any order!

Kostya

Maksim

Andrei

Princes of Ravenlake Academy (Bully Romance)

Can be read as standalones!

Cruel Prep

Cruel Academy

Cruel Elite

Tsezar Bratva

Nightfall (Book 1)

Daybreak (Book 2)

Russian Crime Brotherhood

Can be read in any order!

Owned by the Mob Boss

Unprotected with the Mob Boss

Knocked Up by the Mob Boss
Sold to the Mob Boss
Stolen by the Mob Boss
Trapped with the Mob Boss

Volkov Bratva
Broken Vows (Book 1)
Broken Hope (Book 2)
Broken Sins *(standalone)*

Other Standalones
Vin: A Mafia Romance

Box Sets
Bratva Mob Bosses (Russian Crime Brotherhood Books 1-6)
Tsezar Bratva (Tsezar Bratva Duet Books 1-2)
Heirs to the Bratva Empire
The Mafia Dons Collection
The Don's Corruption

VELVET ANGEL
BOOK 2 OF THE VOROBEV BRATVA DUET

Tomorrow is the first day of the rest of my life.

I'll have my daughter back in my arms and we can start over.

Spoiler alert: tomorrow never comes.

At midnight, there's a tap on my window.

And who should burst in but the devil himself?

Isaak Vorobev never intended to let me go.

He made me his fake wife.

He made me his Bratva queen.

Now, he has one more request…

And this time, he won't take no for an answer.

VELVET ANGEL is Book Two of the Vorobev Bratva duet. Isaak and Cami's story begins in Book One, **VELVET DEVIL**.

1

CAMILA

THREE WEEKS LATER

"I want to speak to Eric."

"I don't give a fuck what you want," Andrew snaps, his dark eyes flashing dangerously.

He's got severe features and an intense gaze. Not the good kind of intense, though. More like the kind of intense that makes me want to hide underneath a rock until he's gone.

"Don't I get a say in the agent assigned to me?" I demand.

"Clearly not, or Eric would be dealing with your bullshit instead of me," Andrew replies sourly.

Honestly, hasn't this guy had any professional training? He's blocking the doorway of my tiny little tinder box room. If the thought of brushing up against him didn't have my stomach turning, I'd have stormed out the second he showed up here.

"I want to request a change," I say stubbornly.

He rolls his eyes. "Not possible."

"You're an asshole."

His mouth twitches with irritation. "I've been called worse."

"Imagine my surprise."

He takes a step back, clearly dying to end this conversation as soon as possible. I would feel the same—but, asshole or not, he's my only link to the outside world. A world that includes my sister and, most importantly, my daughter.

For the first time in over two years, I'm back on U.S. soil. It feels both surreal and slightly overwhelming. Or at least, I imagine it would—if I ever get to leave this depressing little safehouse nestled in the middle of God knows where.

"When do I get to leave?"

"Leave?" Andrew asks, his eyes bulging slightly with disbelief. "Leave the safehouse?"

"And your delightful company," I add, unable to help myself.

"Are you high? You do realize that the fucking Vorobev Bratva is after you, right?"

"I've already told all the agents that spoke to me: Isaak rescued me from Maxim. I was with him of my own free will. Which is why I was able to walk out of his manor the day Eric showed up outside his gates."

"Whatever. Isaak Vorobev may not be after you, but Maxim Vorobev sure as fuck is."

I bite down on my tongue, desperate to argue. But the truth is, I'm pretty sure I won't be convincing.

I know that Maxim is looking for me. I know that he won't stop until he finds me.

What I don't know is what he'll do if that ever comes to pass.

"He'll be looking in England," I say, without any real evidence that that's true.

"How do you know?"

"Because... well, why wouldn't he?"

"Do you know just how fucking powerful the Vorobevs are?" Andrew says. "They have eyes everywhere. The States are where their main operations live."

"So why bring me back here?"

"Beats the fuck out of me," Andrew says with clear annoyance. "It wasn't my decision."

I grit my teeth. We're getting off track. "Well, who decides things then? I need to see my... sister."

He gives a frustrated sigh. "It's not a good time."

"When will it be?"

Instead of answering me, he turns around and walks away. I consider letting him go, but I'm a little starved for human attention right now—plus, I need answers. So, huffing angrily, I lurch forward and follow him downstairs.

The house is a small and old, but there's a decent-sized backyard where I spend most of my time during the day. Except when Andrew's around, in which case I stick to my room to avoid seeing his sourpuss expression and hideous combover.

As I reach the bottom of the stairs, Andrew is pushing his way through the front door.

"You can't just walk away from me!" I cry out after him.

"Watch me."

He stops at the gate and turns around so fast that I almost stumble into his chest. I back off with disgust as he fixes his dark eyes on me.

"You are not to leave this goddamn house, you understand me?" he says. "In a few days, you'll be moved to a new location. Until then, you need to lie low."

"I'm not going anywhere without first speaking to Eric."

Andrew doesn't respond to that at all. He just clambers into his truck and drives off. I flip him the bird. I'm pretty sure he sees the gesture through his rearview mirror. At least, I hope he does. If not, I'm happy to repeat myself.

Alone again, I stand in the yard, looking around at the drying grass and the dying leaves. My soul screams for some relief from this constant onslaught of setbacks.

There's no relief in sight.

Sighing, I walk back into the house. Rudy sits at his usual spot by the window. It's obvious he's watched most of the unpleasant exchange I just had with Andrew.

"Sorry about that, Rudy," I mumble, trying to hide my exasperation.

He gives me a smile. His luxurious graying beard flashes in the lamp light. "Sit down and have some coffee."

That's one of the only good things about staying here: the constant supply of coffee. I take a seat and pour myself a mug, careful to sip slow.

Rudy likes his coffee strong. His wife obliges by brewing him pot after pot of stuff that could strip paint off the walls or fuel a nuclear reactor. The first time I had a mug, I was up the entire night vibrating from head to toe.

I wasn't too upset about that, though. Not sleeping meant I got to avoid the constant dreams that've been plaguing me. Dreams that all star a certain blue-eyed Adonis with a heart of ice.

"Where's Lillian?"

"Shop."

Given that Lillian and Rudy have been operating a safehouse for the U.S. Marshals' Witness Protection for well over two decades, you'd think they'd be a little chattier.

Or maybe that's exactly the reason they're not.

"Need somethin'?"

I shake my head and wrap my hands around the hot mug. "I'm good."

"You don't eat a lot, do you?" he asks, raising an eyebrow at me.

I smile and blush. "If you're going to lecture me, don't bother; I've already heard it. Lillian told me I could hide behind a grain of rice."

He nods. "She's right. The woman isn't always right, but she's right about that."

He eyes me again, but there's nothing salacious or offensive about his gaze. It's almost professional, as though he's studying the strength and speed of a horse before purchase.

"Drink your coffee."

He's gruff but fatherly. It's reassuring, in the oddest way. I take a sip, but the bitterness scalds my tongue.

"That agent's a piece of work," Rudy adds after a long silence.

I roll my eyes. "You have no idea."

"These young fellas have no idea what's what. They've got egos like hot air balloons."

"Again, tell me something I don't know." We both chuckle quietly for a moment. Then I look up at him again. "How have you done this for so long?" I ask.

He shrugs. "Lil and I retired early 'cause of it. Didn't see the point of working 'til we conked."

It's not the noblest of reasons for getting involved in the Program, but I appreciate his blunt honesty. Makes me like him a little bit more.

"Thanks for the coffee. I'm gonna head up to my room now."

"Wait a moment," he says unexpectedly with a glance outside. "Looks like you might have another visitor."

Frowning, I peer through the window as a blue Chevy rolls up outside the gate. When I see Eric climb out, I almost scream with joy.

I abandon my barely touched cup of coffee and fly out down the front drive before Eric has even walked through the gate.

"Eric!"

"Hey, kiddo," he croons, pushing open the white gate. "How've you been?"

"Better now that you're here. You missed Andrew by ten minutes."

"Thank the fucking Lord for that."

I laugh and launch myself at him. He hugs me tightly, but releases me before I'm ready to let go.

"I brought you a Big Mac," he says, offering me the bag. "There's fries in there, too, and a six-pack of chicken nuggets. Spicy, of course."

"Bless you," I say, accepting the bag even though I'm not even remotely hungry.

Eric glances towards the window and gives Rudy a wave. Rudy dips his head down low and keeps sipping his coffee without ever taking his gaze off us.

"They're a strange couple."

Eric laughs. He's gotten so much grayer in the months that I've been away. There are more lines on his face, deeper wrinkles around his eyes.

"You have no idea. They're trustworthy, though."

"Is that why you placed me here?"

"Well, that, and the location is just remote enough that it's the last place that the Vorobevs will think to look."

I never know who he's talking about when he says "Vorobev" like that. Does he mean Maxim? Or Isaak?

"Come on," he says, gesturing for me to follow him into the backyard. We take seats on either side of the little picnic table parked out in the grass.

I'm fidgety for some reason. Pent-up energy from the not-so-pleasant visit with Andrew, maybe. Eric doesn't miss it.

"Eat," he says, nodding at the bag he's just handed to me. "You're too skinny."

"Why does everyone keep telling me that? I'm not hungry."

"Camila." He seems like such a parent when he uses that tone on me. It feels so familiar that I actually welcome the sound. A little piece of normalcy in my chaotic world.

"Fine," I concede, pulling out the burger.

I have to admit, it does smell delicious. The first bite is heaven. And not just any heaven, but a familiar one. It's so alarmingly comforting that I actually close my eyes and savor the sweet, spicy notes in between the hits of saltiness.

"I didn't think McDonald's would be something I missed about America, but damn, that's good."

Eric laughs. "I don't remember Lillian being a very good cook."

"I haven't really noticed."

"Because you're not eating," Eric points out sternly. I take another bite and he shakes his head at me.

"Do you bring Big Macs to all the wayward souls you manage?"

"Just the ones I like."

"Lucky me."

Eric rifles around in the bag and pulls out a Big Gulp. He pushes it towards me and I take a long drink before my stomach settles.

Maybe I was hungry after all. I've just gotten used to the gnawing feeling in the pit of my stomach.

"Did Andrew come to tell you you'd be moved to a new location in a few days?"

"Yes."

Eric nods. "He's been kicking up a fuss at the agency."

"What do you mean?"

"He's filed a complaint against me."

I drop the burger. "What?!"

"He thinks I'm too emotionally invested in your case and that I should be barred from having any contact with you."

"That motherfucker—"

"He has a point, Cami," Eric says with a drawn-out sigh. "I'm not your agent. I haven't been for years."

"Then you should be," I retort. "I don't want Andrew dealing with me."

"I don't have a say in that. Neither does he, for that matter."

"Something's off about him."

Eric smiles. "You just don't like him."

"True, but that doesn't mean I'm wrong."

"He's a rookie. He'll learn."

"Learn what? To be less of a puckered-up asshole all the time?"

"Cami…"

I look at the new lines around Eric's eyes and realize with a jolt that they might have something to do with me. He's genuinely worried about my safety.

"What is it?" I ask softly.

"Rudy called me last night."

I frown. "Okay?"

"He told me you've been having nightmares."

"What the hell is he doing in my room? I lock the damn door."

"He can hear you through the walls, Cami," Eric says calmly. "They both can. Rudy says you scream in your sleep."

I wince. *Well, fuck.* "That's… embarrassing."

"It's concerning."

I try to wave it away. "I'm fine, Eric. I'm holding up."

"Are you? Because from what I can tell, you're enduring at best. Not exactly thriving."

"That's a pretty minute distinction."

"Not really. One implies suffering; the other implies strength."

"Did you bring the Big Mac to butter me up before you punch me in the gut or something?" I ask, only half-joking.

"Like I keep saying, I'm worried about you."

"Don't be. I'm fine."

"That's what *you* keep saying."

"Because I mean it."

He shrugs. "Questionable, but okay, I'll let it go. Then let me ask you another question: why did you protect him?"

I wince again. We've been skirting around this topic for the entire three weeks since I've been here. But I can tell he's not going to be put off anymore.

"Eric—"

"And don't feed me a lie, Cami," he says sternly with a finger in my face. "I deserve better than that. I happen to know that you were abducted by Isaak Vorobev. So why then make a statement that you were with him of your own free will?"

I don't know how to give him what he wants without stripping my soul bare in the process. Hell, I'm not even sure I have a good answer to the question. "I was… it… it's complicated."

He stares at me, his eyes searching hard. It makes me want to hide my face behind my hands.

"Try explaining it to me."

I take a deep breath. He's been kind and understanding since I got back. Respectful of my space. But he's not backing down now. "Well, it's true that it started out… forced."

"He abducted you," Eric clarifies.

I cringe a little, but I don't refute it. "I don't like that word, but okay. But towards the end, I was there more by choice than anything else."

"Jesus Christ," Eric says with a heavy sigh.

"What?"

"You're in love with him."

I bristle immediately, but it's all false bravado and unnecessary defensiveness. "That... that's ridiculous."

"Look at me and say that again."

Frowning, I try to make my expression convincing, but somehow, I can't make it fit onto my face. I decide to concentrate on my Big Mac instead.

"Stop staring at me," I mumble.

"Cami, you're a smart girl. And he's a very dangerous man."

I sigh deeply. "He treated me well, Eric."

"You do hear the irony in those words, right?"

"I'm not deaf, am I?"

He stares at me, and then a slow smile breaks across his face. "So why did you leave then?"

Why did I leave?

The echoes of the last conversation Isaak and I had resound in my head. No, it wasn't a conversation; it was a fight. An all-out brawl. And I'd let it get to me. I'd thrown myself at his mercy by being so damn transparent about everything.

Including Jo.

I'd been chipping away at that impenetrable exterior of his, and in order to prove to me just how strong I was, he gave me a choice. Gave me *the* choice.

And he did it for only one reason: to prove that he didn't care either way what I chose.

It worked, obviously. Of course it did. Pride was the only thing I had left; he'd taken everything else from me. So if he took that, too… then I'd truly have nothing.

I couldn't let Isaak Vorobev do that to me.

"I left because I had to make a point," I say finally.

Eric runs a tired hand over his face. "Is that right?"

"Like I said, it's complicated."

"You're telling me. Do you think the feeling is mutual?"

"Jesus, Eric," I say, grabbing my drink. "You should have brought me liquor instead of McDonald's for this conversation."

He chuckles. "Next time." He waits until the drink has run dry before he adds, "Still waiting on an answer."

"I'm not a mind-reader. You'll have to ask him."

"I'm asking you."

"You're such a dad," I complain.

"I *am* a dad," he points out.

I sigh and rest my forehead on the table. It's easier to say these things when I don't have to look Eric in the eye. "There was a point that I thought the feelings were mutual. But I don't know anymore."

"Because he let you walk?"

"Maybe."

Eric takes a moment to process this. "He treated you well?" he asks, as though he needs to make doubly sure.

"He did."

"Jesus."

I smile and look up at him. "Have I shocked you, old man?"

"Not for the first time," Eric admits.

"Probably not the last, either," I laugh. Then my expression turns serious. "Will this complaint Andrew filed be a big problem for you?"

He gives me a reassuring smile. "I've been in the agency for three decades. I have friends and colleagues who know me, respect me. Don't you worry—it won't amount to anything."

I give him a tight smile. He seems confident enough to put my fears at ease.

"I want to see Jo, Eric," I tell him, lowering my voice automatically.

It infuriates me that I'm back to talking about my daughter in whispers. But it's par for the course at this point. At least I can talk about her with Eric.

"I'm not sure that's a good idea right now, Cami."

I frown. "You sound like Andrew."

"Andrew knows about Jo?" he asks in a panicked voice.

"No, no," I clarify quickly. "I just mentioned that I wanted to visit my sister before I was moved to a permanent safehouse. He didn't exactly jump to arrange it."

"Cami, I swear I'll try and organize a visit for you later. But right now, things are volatile."

"Why do you say that?"

"Because there's been lots of movement in the city lately. Bratva movement."

"Isaak or Maxim?" I ask immediately.

"It's hard to tell."

Not for the first time, I think about Isaak and what he's doing now. Has he moved on with life like I was never a part of it? Will he do something to annul our marriage and marry a woman more suited to the role of Bratva wife?

Will he forget the fact that Jo is his daughter… or will he do something about it?

And which one of those would I prefer?

That's just a sliver of the thoughts that have been plaguing my nightmares lately. And I don't know how to make any of it stop. Which is why I've been pushing so hard to see my sister.

Bree always has a way of slicing neatly through the chaos in my head.

"When can you organize a visit for me?"

"I can't promise you a time frame, Cami."

I get to my feet, feeling the panic start to rise. "Eric, I… I have to see her… She needs me. She needs her mother."

"I know," he says, standing up along with me. "But—"

"What if I choose to leave the program?"

"I'm afraid that option has been taken off the table."

"Why?"

"Because you need protection, Cami. Now more than ever."

"The agency was willing to release me before," I remind him.

"Because you were marrying a man powerful enough to be able to protect you with his own resources."

"Don't even get me started on that. The agency had no idea that the man I was involved with was Maxim fucking Vorobev! Now, I'm just supposed to trust their sterling judgment?"

"The Bratva has resources, Cami. Maxim was able to conceal his identity from everyone, not just you."

I roll my eyes. I know I'm acting like a spoiled child right now, but I can't help it. I'm pissed.

"I'm going up to my room," I tell him. "Sun's going down anyway."

"Cami…"

I wave away his concern. "I'm fine. I can handle this."

I say it like I mean it. But the truth is, I'm having a hard time believing that myself.

2

CAMILA

It starts raining almost immediately after Eric leaves. I gather up the fast food trash and toss it in the bin before heading into the house. Lillian is unpacking the groceries and Rudy is still sitting in the same spot by the window—with a fresh pot of coffee in front of him, I note.

"Is Eric gone already?" Lillian asks me, looking up over a huge box of Captain Crunch. Apparently, it's the only cereal Rudy deigns to eat.

"Yeah, he just left."

"Shame. He could have stayed for dinner."

"Ah, I actually just had my dinner, Lillian," I tell her. "Eric bought me a big Mac."

She wrinkles up her nose in distaste. "Why would anyone eat that?"

"Because it's delicious," Rudy interjects, even though he doesn't turn his gaze from the window.

Lillian throws him an annoyed glance. "I'm going to make chili. Sure you don't want a bowl?"

"I'm sure," I say. "I think I'm just going to turn in early, actually."

"Oh, honey, you're too damn skinny. You gotta eat."

"Trust me, that Big Mac did a lot of damage."

"I don't think—"

"Lillian!"

Rudy's voice can really boom when he decides to make himself heard. Lillian drops off instantly and even I jerk a little as we both turn to him.

"Leave the girl alone," he mutters.

Lillian gives a big, frustrated sigh and continues with her grocery unpacking. I go slump on the couch near Rudy.

"Thanks," I tell him.

He gives me a wink. "I'll be getting an earful about that later, I'm sure. Don't be alarmed if you find me sleeping on the couch tonight."

That reminds me: "I'm sorry if my nightmares have been keeping you and Lillian up, by the way," I say with a wince.

It's not the easiest or the most comfortable thing to bring up, but I don't feel like I can ignore it, either. Not after the concern led Rudy to call Eric.

"That's not why I called him, you know," Rudy says. "I was concerned about you."

"I'm touched, but it's not a big deal."

"Seems like a big deal to me."

"It's not, though. I promise. Anyway, I'll... say goodnight now."

He nods. "Goodnight."

I head up to my room, feeling strangely untethered. The last time I was in WPP temporary housing was more than five years ago, right after I joined the program. Being back in another one feels... regressive.

Maybe that's another reason for the nightmares, the restlessness, the sinking feeling that I'm repeating a cycle that I can't escape.

Because I am.

My room is simple and sparse. A bed, a chest of drawers, a cheap mirror on the wall. The bathroom is small enough that I have to mind my elbows when I turn around.

Then again, after the expansiveness of the Vorobev Manor, everything was bound to feel a little cramped.

I'm glad for my window, though. I can see the front garden and part of the street from my bed.

Sighing, I flop onto the mattress. I'm wearing grey sweats and a white t-shirt that's at least two sizes too big for me.

Eric had one of the female agents put together a small selection of clothes from Target. The stuff she brought was fine—a decent pair of jeans, some simple graphic tees, a soft hoodie. I prefer the sweats, though. It's been my uniform for the past three weeks.

I wear it to sleep. I wear it downstairs. I even wear it in the garden when I pretend to I know what I'm doing with the pruning.

I'm on the way to the bathroom when I notice my reflection in the mirror above the dressing table.

And I don't know whether it's everybody telling me I'm too thin or my own paranoias catching up to me, but I stop in my tracks and examine myself.

It's not that my appearance has changed all that drastically. I don't look like a different person—I'm still Camila Ferrara. *Camila Ferrara Vorobev,* I correct bitterly in my head.

But I do look a little, I dunno… drawn? Gaunt? My cheeks didn't used to seem so hollowed-out like they do now.

My hair's looking a little wispy too, but that probably has more to do with the fact that I haven't washed it in a few days.

I try to give myself an objective once-over. Maybe I'm wrong. Maybe the Cami looking back at me is not the Cami I've always been. Parts of her are recognizable, yes.

But other parts, not so much.

Like the way her eyes have dulled. There's a listlessness in them that's hard to reconcile with the determination I feel inside.

I have no intention of giving up on my quest for freedom, for autonomy, for the life I deserve with my daughter at my side. And yet, the woman staring back at me from the mirror definitely looks like she's given up.

On her appearance, if nothing else.

"Come on, Camila," I whisper softly to my reflection. "You can do better than this. Do it for Jo."

The words come out hollow and robotic, though. Like a prayer that used to be comforting, but now you've repeated it so many times that the words don't sound like words anymore. Just meaningless babble.

I turn from the mirror and pick out a fresh, foam green t-shirt that's a little closer to my size than the one I have on now. Then I head into my tiny bathroom.

I strip out of my clothes and discard them regretfully in the hamper underneath the sink. Then I turn on the water, wait until it warms up, and step inside.

The tiles are a sallow yellow that doesn't exactly help my mood. There's a pattern of white daisies across each tile. It just feels so unnecessarily bright that it comes across as disingenuous.

Of course, I might be reading too much into bathroom tile. "Projecting," as they say.

I spend fifteen minutes in the shower, hunting for some kind of meditative peace in the hot flow of water. I don't find anything, and after a while, I give up.

It strikes me as I'm rinsing off the soap that I may be depressed.

Can you be depressed and not even know it?

I step out of the shower and scrape my elbow against the door. It leaves a pretty noticeable scratch, but there's no blood. Annoyed with myself and with the cheery daisies alike, I dry off and put on the clean t-shirt.

I have to wipe off the foggy mirror above the sink before I can see myself in it. I don't look any happier, but I certainly look a little less Walking Dead. That's improvement, I guess.

I trudge back into my room and slide under the covers. It's early, but I've taken to going to bed as early as possible. God only knows how much sleep is awaiting me on any given night.

And the devil only knows what I'll find in my dreams.

I toss and turn for an hour before I drift off into a troubled slumber. I dream about Eric and Andrew. Locked in a strange kind of fight that almost looks like a dance.

"Stop!" I find myself screaming. I try to push them apart, but they both burst into flame and burn my fingertips off.

I fall to my knees, tears pouring. I'm struggling to differentiate Eric's ashes from Andrew's when I feel the ground cave in from underneath me. A second later, I'm engulfed by the familiar and terrifying sensation of falling.

"Help! Help!"

I try to find something to cling to as I plummet through nothingness. My hands swipe again and again through empty air—until suddenly, I find something rock solid and entirely too… real. Too tangible.

I gasp awake, my eyes darting open, trying to keep hold of the shadows slinking away into the corners of my vision, but they're gone before I can stop them.

It takes a hazy second for the fog of sleep to clear.

And when it does, I realize two things:

One, the window above my bed is open. I'm a thousand percent certain it was firmly closed when I went to sleep.

Two, there's someone in my room.

3

CAMILA

My body goes cold with dread. I'm on the verge of screaming when the silhouette separates itself from the cluster of darkness in the corner and lunges forward, quick as a flash, to clamp a hand down over my mouth.

"Now, now, little *kiska*—don't make any noise."

I stare at Isaak Vorobev with wide eyes. Surely I'm still dreaming. Surely this isn't real.

But his cologne smells real. His hand feels real. His voice sounds real.

"I'm going to let you go now. Don't scream. Nod if you understand me."

I nod slowly. True to his word, he removes his hand from my mouth. I try to form the words that will help me understand what's happening.

"Isaak?"

The rain has ceased, but it's left behind an inky grey sky. The moonlight can't get past the shadows, so the room stays shrouded in darkness.

Still, my eyes are adjusting fast. I can see the sharp lines of his face now. The power of his square jaw and the light stubble that covers it.

"You're growing a beard?"

That takes him by surprise. He gives a dark chuckle. "Hardly. I've just neglected to shave the last couple of days."

"You and me both," I joke. As soon as the words come out of my mouth, I shake my head in amazement. I went from a sleeping nightmare to a waking one to making cracks about my hairy legs? Who the hell am I?

Isaak doesn't respond to it, though. Not so much as a smile. "That's not the only thing you've been neglecting," he murmurs.

He reaches out to brush his knuckles against my cheek. I stiffen and try to look away, but he pushes my face up, forcing me to meet his eyes.

"You've lost weight."

"What are you doing here?" I ask, starting to work myself up to the appropriate level of anger.

He looks around nonchalantly and shrugs. "Thought I'd drop in. See how you're doing."

I slap his hand away from me and look towards the open window. "How did you find me? How did you get in?"

"Does any of that matter, Camila?" he asks.

It's been a while since I've heard him say my name. It's strange how familiar it sounds coming from his lips. That, too, helps my current level of anger rise a little higher.

He has no fucking right.

No right to be here. No right to look at me. No right to say my goddamn name.

"I should scream."

"But you won't."

"Still a cocky prick, I see."

He laughs quietly. "Did you really think three short weeks would change me?"

Three weeks. He's right, but I can't reconcile with that. Time is a funny thing. Days can feel like years and years can feel like days.

Being away from him has felt like eternity.

Not that I'd ever admit that to the smug bastard.

"What do you want?" I say.

He doesn't hesitate. "Information."

I'm expecting something along those lines, but the disappointment that spools inside me is pathetic. "Of course," I snarl. "How silly of me. That's all you ever wanted from me."

"You have a right to be pissed about certain things," Isaak growls. "But so do I."

"What the fuck have *you* got to be angry about?"

He sits on the edge of my bed, taking up all my space, all my breathing room. We're only inches apart, forced together by the limitations of the room.

A part of me is already starting to feel claustrophobic.

But the second, slightly bigger, significantly stupider part of me is thrilled by the proximity.

He smells of musk, wood, and oak. He smells of the old English manor that had come to feel like home. The irony was that I'd had the realization only after I left it.

"Are you seriously asking me that?" he asks, leaning in a little closer.

I can see the blue in his eyes now. They look as dark and stormy as the skies outside.

"You hid my daughter from me for six fucking years."

Right.

That.

"I didn't exactly have a name or a forwarding address to write to," I point out sarcastically.

His eyes narrow at my tone. "And what about months ago, when you didn't need a forwarding address—because you fucking *lived* in my house?"

"We've had this argument before."

"And I'm still not satisfied with the result."

"That makes two of us."

His breath tickles my nose. I should move away. I should want to put as much distance between our bodies as possible.

But the sad truth is that… I've fucking *missed* him.

And from the hungry, almost predatory way he's looking at me, I'm starting to wonder if the feeling might be mutual. Though with Isaak, I can never really tell.

Every time I've started to feel like I'm on solid footing, he's ripped the rug out from underneath me and I'm left staring at the ceiling, wondering how I've landed myself on the floor.

"She's my daughter, Camila, every bit as much as yours."

"You don't even know what she looks like. I hardly think you have that kind of claim to her."

"Is that what you think?"

"What I think is that you need to stay the hell away from her," I tell him fiercely.

"What power do you have to stop me?"

I freeze and gulp. "What… what are you planning to do?"

"I want to know more about my daughter."

"Is that your way of threatening me?" I ask. "I give you information or else you'll get it yourself?"

"I always get what I want, Camila. How that happens is up to you."

My hand lashes out to slap him, but he grabs my wrist just before my palm makes contact with his face. Our eyes lock together and he gives me a smile I recognize all too well.

It's the smile that ignites a slow-burning fire in my belly and spreads across my entire body.

"How much have you missed doing that?" he asks.

"Still an asshole."

"Isn't that what you like most about me?"

I try to rip my hand free, but his grip is too tight. He doesn't even look like he's trying. As usual, I feel my own sense of power deflate in the face of his.

"I don't like you," I snap. "I hate you."

"Yeah?" he asks, leaning in a little closer. "Make me believe it."

I don't know what exactly happens in the next two seconds. Chalk it up to a combination of desperation and urgency. Or maybe just temporary insanity.

I can't even say who initiates it.

All I know is that suddenly, we're locked in the most heated, most thrilling kiss I've ever experienced in my life.

His lips scour mine as he dips his tongue forward, parting my lips with an aggressive thrust that has the heat crawling down between my legs.

My hands are on his chest, trying to find even the tiniest chink in his rock-hard armor.

It strikes me that it's entirely possible he has no chink. No weakness. I've been searching for months—no, years—and still haven't found one. So why would tonight be the night that I do?

Unfortunately, I can't say the same about myself. Maybe it's that realization that has me switching gears and shoving him away from me.

I've given him all of me.

He's given me nothing.

I break the kiss, trying to equalize my ragged breathing. For some reason, I barely recognize my own voice when I speak. "Stop, Isaak. Just stop."

Then I realize why it sounds so strange: I sound alive again.

4

ISAAK

Her hands flutter half-heartedly at my chest. She's trying to resist me, but it's obvious to both of us that she's slowly losing the battle.

I wrap my fingers around her wrist to keep her locked in. Her eyes go wide as she realizes just how close we are.

There's no place for her to go.

"Stop."

"Why?"

She narrows her eyes. "Why are you really here?"

She's not wrong in assuming I have an ulterior motive for my sudden arrival. But I'm too consumed with her presence to get into all that just yet.

"I was missing you terribly," I drawl.

"Bullshit," she snaps. "You kicked me out."

She struggles to remove her hand from my grip, but I hold fast. "I gave you the choice," I remind her. "You're the one who chose to leave."

"I was there, Isaak. I remember what happened," she says softly. "I remember everything you said to me."

The hurt is still there, holding pride of place behind all her rage and resentment. But it doesn't escape my notice that she's gotten stronger in the last few weeks.

Not physically, clearly—she looks like she's wasting away.

But mentally.

Emotionally.

Something's driving her forward, giving her a purpose that she's determined to see through to the end. And I have every confidence that purpose has to do with our daughter.

Daughter. The word still feels strange to me sometimes. It's like I'm trying to force on a pair of boots that don't fit quite right. But I know it's just a matter of breaking them in.

"I chose to leave because I realized something: we were playing make believe, you and I."

Her eyes flutter towards the window. She looks at the sky, but I know she's reliving that last day in London. The day she walked out of the manor and chose to accept the protection of the United States government instead of mine.

"Is that what we were doing?"

"Stop talking to me like I'm a child," she snaps, finally ripping her hand out from underneath mine. "You want honesty from me, but you're not willing to make any concessions of your own."

"What kind of concessions would you like?"

"You're not willing to give up control. You're not even willing to share it."

"For me to share power, I would need to find someone who's my equal."

A flicker of irritation flits across her eyes, but it's tempered by the knowledge that I'm actively trying to get a rise out of her.

"You can talk all the shit you want, but your actions speak otherwise. You're here. That proves I'm something to you."

I lean back and regard her. "You overestimate your own importance," I say coldly. "I'm here for information about my daughter."

I feel that same surge of discomfort in my chest when I say the word aloud. Not least of which is because I'm still wrapping my head around the seismic shift it represents.

But also because said daughter is currently occupying the largest room on the third floor of my New York mansion.

Of course, Cami doesn't know that. And I haven't met her yet. She's been on my property for almost twenty-four hours and I haven't even seen the child.

I told myself that I was occupied. Other things required my attention. But those justifications sounded hollow and ill-conceived, even to my ears.

So before I was forced to give them to Bogdan or my mother, I'd left the mansion and come straight here. To the woman who hates me with a burning passion—and can't stop loving me in spite of it.

"You have dozens of men whose job it is to find information," she says. "Why would you need me?"

"Because my team might be able to tell me when Jo was born, which hospital, which ward, and every other insignificant detail that comes along with a person's biography. But I don't want to know those things. What I want to know, only you can tell me."

She looks angry, but more with herself than anyone else.

Then she raises her eyes and I'm forced to correct myself: she's definitely angrier with me.

"Not only did you take my freedom that night, you also took away my ability to be a mother to Jo."

"But I gave you Jo," I point out.

She's on the verge of softening at that when she catches herself. "Jo was never meant to happen," she says. "That whole night was never meant to happen. It was just a giant mistake."

"Sometimes, what looks like a mistake can be an opportunity."

Her eyes seem to wrinkle as she considers my words. "Are you meant to be the opportunity in this analogy?"

"You think too much."

She grimaces. "The whole reason I didn't tell you about Jo is because I knew you'd try to… involve her in all this. And I didn't want that."

"Involve her in what exactly?"

"The Bratva, your life… All the risks that this world involves."

"Life is risky, Camila."

"Exactly—so why add fuel to the flames? I sacrificed a life with my daughter to ensure she grew up like a normal child. With friends and playdates and trips to the beach and the zoo. Somehow, I can't imagine you doing any one of those things."

"Should I be flattered or insulted?"

"It doesn't matter," she says with a wave of her hand. "It doesn't change the bottom line. I want Jo to grow up normal."

"What am I if not normal?"

She surprises me when she grabs my right wrist suddenly and flips it over to reveal the line of silver scars that stretches from my wrist to my elbow.

"Is this normal, Isaak?" she demands softly.

I'm quiet for a long time. "I am not my father."

"Aren't you?" she asks. "Because from where I'm sitting, you two seem awfully similar."

"I don't think you're qualified enough to make that assessment."

"Why? Because I didn't know him?" she asks dismissively. "It doesn't really matter. Because I know *you*. I don't believe you would ever hurt Jo. But I don't think you'd love her, either. I don't think you know how."

I curl an angry fist in the sheets. Goddammit, this woman has a way of rattling my cool that drives me fucking insane. But I won't give her the satisfaction of seeing that her words are finding their mark.

Stay calm. Stay focused.

"Love has many different expressions."

"She's five. She deserves to be loved. Tenderly. Affectionately. If that's love," she says, nodding at my scarred arm, "then I want my daughter to be far the fuck away from it." Her green eyes are bright emeralds in all this darkness. The room is hot and thick with our breathing now, despite the breeze through the open window.

"It doesn't matter," I tell her. "The decision was made the moment I found out I had a child."

Her eyes go wide. Her jaw clenches tight. I've seen that expression before and I know what is coming next: her completely losing it. "You—"

Before she can continue her tirade, we hear footsteps clomping down the hall. Camila straightens immediately, spine stiff with panic.

She mouths something to me, but I don't hear a sound. A second later, there's a light knock at the door.

"Cami?"

She mouths something again. *Ruby,* I think. *Rudy? Rue me?*

She jumps off the bed, bumping her knees against mine as she struggles to right herself. The t-shirt she's wearing is green. It also happens to be short, so the moment she bends over to pick up a pair of discarded white shorts, I'm offered a clear view of her perfect ass.

My cock stiffens at once.

Fighting the urge to reach out and take hold of her body, I stay on the bed, amused by her panic. Once her shorts are on, she turns to me with an expression that suggests she's shocked that I'm still here.

"Camila, is everything alright?" says the man at the door.

She gestures for me to stand up. The moment I do, she herds me into her bathroom.

"Jesus," I growl, knocking into at least three things as I turn on the spot.

She leaves the bathroom door cracked as she runs over to answer the knocking. Her hair hangs long and thick down her back. I'm struck by a sudden flashback—my hand wound in all that hair, wrenching her head back while I thrusted into her from behind, and the noises she made with every collision of our hips…

"Hey, Rudy," she says, unable to completely cover the slight edge of breathlessness in her tone.

"Is everything alright?" the man asks in a gruff voice. "I thought I heard voices."

She raises her eyebrows. "Um, well, it didn't come from my room." She's placed herself squarely in front of the door, preventing him from coming in to check.

"Hm. I was just worried about you…"

"Don't be," she says with a smile that's a little too bright to be real. "I'm fine."

"Another nightmare?" he asks.

Nightmare? She tenses slightly. I can tell she's doing her best to keep her gaze from sliding in the direction of the bathroom. "Maybe. I was sleeping…"

"You should talk to someone. A shrink."

"God knows I don't have the money for that," she says with a chuckle. "And I don't think Uncle Sam will pick up the bill."

"Oh, you never know."

"Thanks for checking up on me, Rudy."

"Let me know if you need anything," he mumbles.

The fondness in his voice is obvious. I don't trust it, though. Then again, I don't trust anything.

That lesson was carved into my skin a long time ago.

"How the fuck do you do anything in there?" I growl as I step out of the bathroom.

She glares at me. "Not everyone lives in sprawling English manors," she snaps. "Keep your voice down."

I move closer to her. She's wary, but she stays put until the moment my hand finds her hip. "You've been having nightmares?"

"What do you care?" she asks, trying to turn away from me.

But I don't want to let her go now that I've touched her. I hook her back around so that she smashes right into my body. "I'm getting tired of you turning away from me."

She jerks her chin out. "Then stop forcing me away."

"How am I doing that?"

"By being an asshole."

"Would you believe me if I said that's who I am?"

She tries to struggle out of my hold, but now that her body is flush against mine, I'm even less willing to release her.

"Let me go," she hisses, bringing her face an inch from mine so that she can deliver the same level of fervency without shouting.

I ignore her. "You need to learn to lie better."

"I don't like lying at all."

"You did pretty well with me for months on end."

"That's different."

"How?"

"Because protecting my daughter is more important than telling the truth."

"I'm no danger to her."

"You told me the same thing once, remember?" she says, her eyes growing hazy with the old memory. "You told me that, of all the people in the world, I was the only one who didn't need to be scared of you."

"It's still true."

"No, it's not. Because I was scared of you then and I was right to be."

"When have I ever fucking hurt you?" I growl.

"You hurt me every time you open your mouth," she says softly.

Her eyes say what her words can't quite capture: sometimes, the scars that stay with you forever are the ones you can't see. The ones that linger underneath your skin, masquerading under the pretense of strength.

I pull her forward and crash my lips into hers.

She groans at the sudden contact, but it takes several long seconds before she starts trying to shove me off her. Even when she manages to tear her lips from mine, her eyes betray her.

"Get off me!"

"Make me believe that's what you want."

She shakes her head. "I left. I walked out. It's unfair of you to come back now. And for what? For what?"

What the hell do I tell her?

That meeting Jo doesn't feel right unless she's there, too? If I tell her that now, she will rage and storm and topple all my plans.

She hit the nail on the head before: I am my father's son, no matter what I say out loud. He trained me to be hard, ruthless, uncompromising. He trained me to never lose focus. To never change the plan based on emotion.

"I want you to leave me alone," she says when I don't answer. "I want you to leave my daughter alone, too."

"*My* daughter," I correct.

She slams her fist into my chest with a grunt of frustration. I shrug off the hit and walk her backwards towards the door until her ass is pressed against the old wood. "You keep forgetting, Camila: this is my world, and you're in it now. So is she. You may have walked away, you may try to run and hide, but it doesn't matter, because I will find you. You know why? Because you are mine. As much as Jo is."

Her eyes spark with rage, but there's desire there, too. Just like there always has been.

This time, when I capture her mouth in mine, her lips part for me. I force my way in deeper. Her tongue doesn't participate for the first two seconds, and then, as though she can't help it, she meets me.

My hand lands on her left breast and I squeeze hard, drawing out a loud moan. I pull back as I roll her nipple between two fingers.

"You have to be quiet," I tell her. "Unless you need me to gag you."

Annoyance flickers across her eyes as she leans in and grabs my bottom lip between her teeth. She bites down, hard enough to draw blood.

I don't jerk back, though. I revel in her sudden depravity, the burst of wildness I always knew was in her.

"How do I taste, *kiska*?"

"Like sin."

Smirking, my hands travel down to her beautiful ass. I shove the shorts off her. Then I cup her and hoist her up around my waist.

She hooks her legs around me and starts fumbling with my shirt. I grind my hard cock against her pussy and she moans again, louder than the first time.

Shaking my head at her in disapproval, I shove two of my fingers into her mouth, forcing her to suck them as I keep grinding against her.

Her saliva coats my fingers and nearly makes me lose it right there. But I've been without her too long. I need to be buried inside of her sweet little pussy before I let myself go.

She's trembling faster now, damn near vibrating. I pin her against the wall and use a free hand to free my cock from my pants.

I ought to take her slowly. Make her feel my every fucking thrust, if only to prove what I said: that I own her now; that I'm in charge.

But that goes out the window the moment my cock lines up with her slit. I shove myself inside her in one long thrust and she bites down on my fingers.

She's fucking heaven.

Three weeks felt like nothing in some senses. But this? This feels like I've never had it before. As good as the first time—better, even. Pure fucking bliss.

Her wetness. Her moans. Her hair flowing over both of us as she pants and grinds and whimpers like she's already on the verge of coming undone.

Her body moves in rhythm with mine. I fuck her relentlessly against the wall, muffling her cries with my palm over her mouth.

Her orgasm takes a while to build, but when it breaks, her body spasms with long-suppressed desire. "Isaak…" she sputters. She clings to me like she's scared she'll soar away if she doesn't stay anchored.

I keep fucking her until I can't hold myself back any longer.

I come the exact way I envisioned: all the way inside of her. Then I pull out and set her back on her feet.

She puts a hand on the dresser to steady herself. Her legs tremble and her breath comes hard. I stand and watch as the light leaves her eyes.

Then the transformation is complete. The unrestrained Cami disappears.

The one who hates me is back.

She brushes past me and heads to the bathroom. I turn to watch her mop my juices up from between her thighs. She glances at me in the mirror. Her eyes are hard, cold, distant.

"Do you know where they're moving you?" I ask.

She frowns. "No, but you probably do."

"For a change, I don't."

"Does that mean, once I'm gone, you won't be able to find me?" It's hard to read her face. To know if the thought of severing this connection forever makes her happy or frightened or something else altogether.

"Most likely."

She nods. "That's probably for the best," she says—though it sounds like she's trying to convince herself more than anything.

It's time for me to go. I've already lingered too long.

Before I head for the window, I pull out a small piece of paper from my pocket. There's nothing but a phone number printed on the face.

"What's this?" she asks when I offer it to her.

"A lifeline. Just in case."

She stares at my outstretched hand for a long time before she accepts the paper. The moment it's delivered, I turn around.

And then, despite every instinct in my body…

I leave.

5

CAMILA
TWO DAYS LATER

"Cami? You okay?" Lillian asks, looking at me over her newspaper.

She and Rudy are probably the last people in the world who still buy and read newspapers. She likes the advice columns and the recipe section. Rudy reads world news and politics. It's stereotypical, but also kind of comforting in an antiquated way that reminds me a little bit of my own parents.

"I'm fine," I say, plastering a smile on my face. "Just a little… nervous about the move."

"Andrew will set you up someplace nice," Rudy says without taking his eyes off his paper.

I give them both a distracted nod.

In all honesty, I should be worried about my next move. Any other given time, and I would be. But since his visit two nights ago, my thoughts have been dominated by Isaak.

Isaak Vorobev and his sinful fucking body.

His heartbreaking blue eyes.

I feel like a naïve idiot. Like he took advantage of me. Though of course, he hadn't exactly had to fight to take much of anything. Not when I'd given in so fucking easily.

"The move's not for another two days," Lillian says, forcing me from my hole of self-loathing. "I wouldn't think about it until you have to."

"I just wish they would tell me where I'm going. I hope it's not too far."

"They'll keep you in the States, I'm sure," Lillian says. "No reason to fret."

"That's what they said the last time. And they sent me to England."

"Well, I suppose there are worse places to be."

She's not wrong. But it's not like I can explain why I want to stay in New York. Because no matter where I go, or who I meet, I can't own the fact that I have a child. People look at me and see a nobody. A ghost.

What I want them to see is a mother. A mother who's desperate to fix some of her mistakes and show up for her daughter.

Jo will be six soon. Some days, it boggles my mind how that happened so fast. Life is what happens when you're waiting for things to start.

"Eat something," Rudy says, pushing the plate of bacon and eggs towards me.

I stare at the meal and my stomach turns. "I'm not hungry right now. I'll just have a cup of coffee and head up to my room."

I'm washing my mug in the sink when I notice the blue Chevy pull up again. "Eric?" I say to myself. Weird that he would show up unannounced like this.

I do a half-assed job with my coffee mug and run outside to meet him as he walks in through the little white fence gate.

"Hey," I say, hoping he has some good news for me. "I wasn't expecting you today."

"I came to give you a heads up," he tells me somberly. "Andrew will be arriving in the evening to prep you for the coming move."

I frown. "Why today? We've got plenty of time before…

He sighs. "Cami…"

"No," I say, shaking my head in disbelief. "No. I'm leaving tomorrow?"

"I'm afraid so."

"Why?"

"Bratva movement in the city has seen an uptick in the last few days. My superiors think it's best to speed things up a little."

"What about Jo?" I ask. "I have to see her. At least before I leave."

"Camila…"

"I hate when you say my name like that," I say desperately. "I know what's coming."

"It's too dangerous. We have reason to believe that you're in imminent danger."

"From whom?"

"From the Vorobevs."

There it is again: the lack of distinction between Isaak and Maxim. It makes me uncomfortable, even though neither man deserves my loyalty.

"Isaak Vorobev has returned to the city," Eric says gently, like he's trying to break the news to me as softly as possible.

"Yeah," I say, rolling my eyes. "I know."

He goes ramrod straight. "You know?"

I nod. "He broke into my room the night before last."

Eric stares at me for a long moment that's prickly with tension. "Jesus Christ."

"It's fine," I say, trying to alleviate some of the stress on his face. "I've told you before: Isaak would never hurt me."

Physically, at least. I add that caveat in my head.

"How did he even locate you?" Eric asks.

I shrug. "He's Bratva. They have resources, as you yourself keep telling me."

"What did he want with you? What did he say?"

I move forward and put my hand on Eric's shoulder. "Hey, calm down, old man. We just talked."

I decide to leave out the part where I'd spread my legs for Isaak and let him fuck the hell out of me. Somehow, I don't think Eric's going to take that very well.

"Calm down?" Eric repeats. "Cami, he was in your bedroom."

"Not the first time."

He wrinkles his nose. "Spare me the details."

I almost laugh. "Oh, grow up, you old prude."

I glance towards the house. Of course, Rudy's sitting by the window like he always is. The difference is that Lillian is standing by his shoulder. They're both watching us.

"I'm assuming they don't have a clue?" Eric asks.

"Rudy heard voices," I admit. "He checked on me, but I assured him everything was fine."

Eric's expression grows still.

"What?" I ask.

"That's the second time you've lied to protect him."

"Have you seen the size of Isaak? I lied to protect Rudy."

"You're playing with fire, Camila."

Camila. Full name again. He means business.

"I don't know what you want from me. It wasn't like I asked Isaak to climb into my window. He came of his own accord."

"What did he say to you?"

Before I can answer, I hear the screech of tires. Eric looks up, immediately alert.

"It's just some idiot speeding," I say dismissively.

But when I look towards the window, Lillian has disappeared and Rudy is rising to his feet. He never leaves that seat if he can help it.

"Cami, get—"

Then the glass window separating us from Rudy explodes. I feel wind hit my face and immediately after, Eric's sweaty hand clamps around my arm as he pulls me backwards.

"What the hell is—"

The gun in Eric's hand is what forces me into silence. I don't look back as I follow Eric into the neighbor's backyard. The two German shepherds tied to their kennel post jump onto all fours as we rush across their lawn.

Luckily, we're in the adjoining neighbor's yard by the time the dogs have made a run for us.

Then I hear the sound of a gunshot.

Then another.

I freeze, my entire body descending into shock. I pivot on the spot and stare in the direction of Rudy and Lillian's house.

"No! No, Eric, we have to go back."

He doesn't say a word. Instead, he grabs my arm again and steers me in the opposite direction.

"What are you doing?" I cry hysterically. "Rudy and Lillian. Rudy and Lillian…"

"We don't have time now, Cami," he whispers. "It may be too late anyway."

After that, I follow Eric blindly. Mostly because I can't really see through the veil of tears that blurs everything in front of me.

I don't know how long we keep going. Left after right after right after left, never stopping or slowing down or looking back.

Until, finally, Eric sighs and lets go of my hand.

If I weren't so fucking destroyed on the inside, I would have been seriously impressed with his stamina. He moves fast for an old man.

We duck into a gas station and head to the back of the store so that we're not standing by any of the windows. Eric walks down one of the back aisles and stops next to the slushie machine by the racks of candy.

"Want one?" he asks.

"Want what?"

"A slushie?"

I stare at him incredulously. "I… I don't think I can eat or drink right now."

"It's a prop, honey. We gotta buy something now that we're in here."

He heads down from the aisle and lands at a display rack that holds a bunch of sad grey sweatshirts and baseball caps. "Pick one."

I take the first one on the rack and check to make sure it has a hoodie.

"Let's look around," Eric says, nudging me forward.

I turn and plant myself squarely in front of him. "Eric," I say, trying to breathe through the panic, "what just happened?"

"He found you."

"He?"

"Maxim," Eric says, looking around as though he's genuinely searching for stuff on the shelves. "Maxim Vorobev. Well, I mean, it could also have been—"

"It's not Isaak," I interrupt immediately. "He knows where I am, Eric. He's known for days, if not longer. He could have just taken me anytime. Not to mention the fact that he wouldn't have let me walk out of his manor if he was just planning on recapturing me again."

"The Bratva is complicated, Camila," he says heavily. "Plans change, and men like Isaak and Maxim change accordingly."

I shake my head. "Isaak is… I'm not saying he's a saint or a hero. But he's not like Maxim, either."

"You're hoping," Eric says pointedly.

I run my hands over my face. "Those were gunshots we heard as we were running," I say. "Gunshots, Eric."

"I know."

My breath catches on a sob. "Lillian and… R… Rudy…"

"Hey, we don't know anything yet."

"There were fucking gunshots, Eric. Who else were they aiming for?"

"Stop," Eric says in a voice I've never heard before. "Stop it. You're spinning out and that's not helpful right now."

I take a gulp and stare into his worried eyes. He reaches into his pocket, pulls out a phone, and starts to dial. "Wait here," he tells me. "Stay away from the windows."

I stay behind the shelves as Eric starts talking to someone on the phone. I probably should be paying attention, but his words keep slipping out of my ears and I can't hold onto them no matter how hard I try.

There are three cars at the gas pumps outside. Beyond them, I can see the street and a couple of people walking their dogs past that. No one seems to be aware that a few blocks away, a couple might be bleeding out on their embroidered yellow carpet.

"Okay," Eric says, coming towards me again. "Backup's heading to the house now."

"Rudy and Lillian?"

"The moment I know anything, you'll be the first to know."

It's not much of a consolation, but I'm forced to accept it. "What do we do, Eric?"

He hesitates.

"What is it?" I ask. "Tell me."

"The guy I just called is an old friend. I trust him."

"Okay?"

"But once I inform the agency that you're with me, they'll tell the relevant department. That includes Andrew."

That's when it dawns on me. "You don't trust him, do you?"

"I… I don't like making accusations," he says. "It's just a hunch and I might be wrong—"

"I don't trust him, either."

Eric nods. "The point is that if my hunch is right, and Andrew knows where you are, then Maxim does, too."

He looks around as though he's hoping a solution will drop out of the skies and into our laps. When it doesn't, he grabs a can of Coke and a packet of chips and heads to the cashier.

Once he's purchased everything, we leave the gas station through the side exit. The neighborhood is pretty suburban. It's far enough away from the city to be peaceful, but close enough to allow us to blend into the crowd.

"What are we doing?"

"Getting out of here," Eric replies. "We're too close to the house." He stops outside a broad street lined with crumbling houses.

"Wait here for me."

I frown. "Where are you going?"

"Give me five minutes."

Without offering me much else, he heads down the road and turns the corner. I stand on the curb, feeling extremely exposed and very much on edge.

I slip on the grey hoodie and zip it up. I start pacing along the pavement, wondering if every person who looks my way is concealing a weapon they're about to whip out all of a sudden.

All I can think is: how am I ever going to get to Jo now?

∼

What feels like an hour later, a white car comes to a stop right in front of me. I'm about to make a dash in the opposite direction when I realize Eric's sitting in the driver's seat.

"Get in."

I don't wait to be asked twice. "Where'd you get the car?"

"The less you know, the better."

I give him a raised eyebrow. "Wow, Eric Keller, car thief."

"A car thief doesn't return the car after the fact."

I smile. "You gonna leave a note, too?"

"Shouldn't you be in shock or something?"

Still smiling, I stare out at the road ahead. If I think back, I'll lose any semblance of composure I've currently got. And now's no time to break down.

We drive for at least an hour before Eric comes to a stop some feet away from a small intersection up ahead. I can see people milling around, most with shopping bags in tow. After we park, he leads me into a little ice cream shop tucked between a music store and a tattoo parlor.

"Are we really getting ice cream?"

"You need to get something in your system," he tells me. "Sugar's the best way to do that. Pick a flavor."

"I need to sit down first."

We take a table adjacent to the window, more comfortable now with being seen. Eric sits down opposite me, his eyes darting around the parlor every few seconds.

"So we can't rely on the agency, can we?" I ask.

"I don't think so."

"Then who do I rely on?"

The moment I voice the question out loud, Isaak's face pops into my head. I reach into my jeans pocket and pull out the slip of white paper.

"What's that?" Eric asks.

I look up at him, my eyes wide with resigned acceptance.

"A lifeline."

6

ISAAK

I stare at the two of them from the driver's seat of my understated black Audi.

Camila's got her blonde hair hidden underneath the ugly grey hoodie she's wearing. It's so big that it pools around her wrists, but she hasn't bothered pushing up the sleeves.

With her face free of makeup, her adolescent clothes, and the bowl of ice cream in front of her, she looks so young.

I get out of the car and walk around to the passenger side door. I lean back against it, and almost immediately, Camila looks up.

Like she's sensed my presence.

The half-smile on her face slides off, and she switches her gaze to Eric. I focus on her lips.

"He's here," she tells him.

I have a picture of Eric Keller on file. He looks just as ordinary, just as unimpressive as his photograph suggested. But I've never believed you could get the full measure of a man without meeting him in person.

Without looking him in the eye.

Eric heads towards the counter to pay. Camila leaves her half-eaten ice cream on the table and makes her way outside to me.

Considering it's midday and most people are inside having their lunch, the street is relatively peaceful. Camila comes to a stop two feet away from me. As if she's afraid of getting too close. I cock my head to the side and wait for her to break the fragile silence.

"Hey."

I raise my eyebrows. "Hey?"

She sighs. "You gave me the number."

"I'm aware."

"So… I called it."

"Why?"

Her eyes dart around the street. She doesn't answer for a long time. "The house was attacked," she says finally. Her eyes land on me, but they're filled with worry and stress. "Rudy and Lillian were in there when the shooting started."

I tense. "Maxim?"

"I can't think who else it could be."

"How the fuck did he know where you were?"

"You did," she points out.

I snort. "Did you really think I was just going to hand you over to the fucking cops without some insurance?"

She frowns. "What are you talking about?"

"I had a team track you after you left with them. There have been eyes on you since the second you left the manor."

She narrows her eyes at me. "That's a violation of my privacy."

I push myself off the car and take a step towards her. "Fuck your privacy. I knew I needed to keep an eye on you. And I was right."

"Is that why you were so unconcerned about my move?" she asks. "Because you never planned on letting me disappear into the system, did you?"

I don't answer her. I'm too busy watching the agent she cares so much about step out of the parlor and up towards us. He looks wary.

"Mr. Vorobev," he says formally.

"You can call him Isaak," Camila says.

I shoot her a look. "Mr. Vorobev is fine, actually."

I've never been a fan of cops. Or the government. And it has nothing to do with who I am or the world I was born into. If I were born a totally ordinary citizen with a nine to five cubicle job and a 401K, I'd still feel the same way.

Camila glares at me. I have to suppress a smile.

"You failed to protect her," I say to Eric bluntly.

He bristles at first, but then slumps his shoulders forward and sighs. "I think the agency might have a breach."

"You have a mole."

Eric nods uncomfortably. "It's only a hunch—"

I snort. "Maxim decided to attack Camila's safehouse days before her permanent placement elsewhere," I say. "You definitely have a mole in the agency."

He sighs. I can tell that no matter how true my words may be, he still doesn't like hearing them. Especially not from me.

"Say your goodbyes, Camila. You're under my protection now."

It's meant as a reprimand. I know Eric will get the subtext. Camila turns and wraps her arms around him. She prolongs the hug longer than necessary.

"Thank you, Eric," she says. "For everything."

He gives her a smile that can only be described as genuine. Then he kisses her on the forehead. There's a familiarity between them that transcends the relationship between agent and charge. In fact, it looks more like a father giving his daughter away at the altar.

"Don't worry," she tells him, lowering her voice in the hopes that I won't be able to hear. "I know what I'm doing."

Eric's expression is worried when he pulls away. "I got a text while I was in there, by the way," he tells her. "Lillian and Rudy are both alright."

Her eyes go wide with relief. "Really?"

"Lillian took cover when the shooting started, so she wasn't hurt at all—barring the trauma of the attack of course. And Rudy…"

"Oh God."

"He was shot," Eric says gently. "But they performed emergency surgery on him and he's stable now."

"He'll be alright?"

"He'll be alright," Eric confirms.

It's very possible that he's lying to her to ease her mind, but I understand the instinct to want to shield the people you care about. It makes me respect him a little bit more. Despite the badge he's probably got concealed somewhere on his person.

"Go on," Eric tells her, pushing her towards the car. "You don't have time to waste ogling me."

She gives him a small smile and gets into the car. I wait. The moment the door closes on her, Eric looks at me with barely concealed distaste.

"She thinks she can trust you."

"She can."

"I would never have allowed her to call you if I didn't think you were the best chance she had of getting through this."

Interesting. "Are you saying you don't trust your own department?"

"Not the way I used to," he says irritably. "Trust and loyalty are rare commodities these days."

"Not in my Bratva."

"Then you're lucky," he says, glancing towards Cami in the passenger's seat of my Audi. "Not everyone is that confident."

"What are you going to tell the agency?" I ask curiously.

"That Camila chose to leave my custody of her own free will. That she chose to go back to you. She told them that she stayed with you once before, so it tracks."

"Does that mean you and your people will leave me alone?"

"So long as you keep your business to yourself."

I smirk. "I'll do my best, old man."

He glares at me suspiciously. I'm surprised to find I like him more than I thought I would.

"She has feelings for you," he says abruptly.

I wait for him to continue. He shuffles on his feet awkwardly, reminding me of the way older generations balk when they're confronted with uncomfortable topics.

"I hope your feelings for her are as sincere."

"My feelings are my own concern," I say brusquely.

"I don't want her hurt."

"Then we have the same goal."

Eric sighs. "I just hope I'm not making a mistake."

"It wasn't your decision," I point out. "Camila is the one who called me."

"I didn't discourage her," he says, and he almost sounds regretful.

"You were right not to. I'm the only one who can protect her. The Bratva is not something you can go up against easily, no matter your resources."

Eric nods, resigned to the truth of what I'm saying. I head to the car and get in the driver's seat.

"What were you two talking about?" Camila asks, giving Eric a parting wave as I pull out onto the street.

"Ice cream."

I can feel the intensity of her glare boring into the side of my face. "Can you not be an asshole for two seconds and answer the question, please?"

"His favorite flavor is chocolate. I prefer hazelnut."

"Jesus," she groans. "Forget it."

Smirking, I turn onto a main road that leads away from the town and its people. Within a minute, I'm flooring it at a hundred and fifty.

"Thank you for coming," she says in a small voice.

I glance towards her. "Gratitude sounds strange coming from you."

"It shouldn't. I'm not a condescending prick like you are."

I smile. "How quickly that ended."

She sighs, and I feel the air prickle between us. Our energy has always been combative. Maybe it's just the natural clash of our personalities. Or maybe it has to do with the circumstances under which we came together.

Either way, it always feels like we're a stone's throw away from a brawl.

I've fucking missed that.

"You could slow down, you know," she says, white-knuckling the door handle.

"No."

"And you could have been nicer to Eric."

"Also no. Why would I do that?"

"Why?" she repeats. "Because why the hell not?"

"He's a cop."

"So?"

"So I don't trust them."

"Are you being serious right now?"

"When am I ever not serious?"

"Isaak, you're a Bratva Don who's been on the wrong side of the law since you were born."

"Your point…?"

"Eric's not the one who deserves distrust."

I give her a pointed glance. "And yet when you needed protection, you called me."

"Are you going to rub that in my face?"

"Probably."

"For how long?"

"For as long as I need to."

She crosses her hands over her chest and I notice her chin jut out. I can't help it—I start laughing. Of course, that only causes her to double down and pout a little harder.

"Why the hell are you laughing?" she snaps.

"Because, *kiska,* you look like a bratty teenager in that get-up, especially with such a stubborn look on your face."

"You make me feel like a teenager," she responds. Then she adds, "And not in a good way."

I roll my eyes. She rolls her eyes right back at me.

And for a moment, everything is as it should be.

∼

The drive to my mansion takes almost an hour. It's a mostly silent experience. Camila sits as far away from me as she can manage, her body angled towards the window. She stares out of it the entire time, and the only times she glances at me is when she thinks I'm not paying attention.

When we approach the gates, she sits up a little straighter. "Jesus," she says. "A manor in England. A castle in Scotland. And now this?"

The black brass gates part slowly and open up onto the paved private driveway that leads towards the main house. The Vorobev properties that Cami has seen were both respectful of the past, of tradition, of legacy.

This mansion, on the other hand, is a fuck-you to the past.

It's gleaming glass, sharp angles, cruel and modern and impossible to look away from. It looks fucking expensive—because it is.

"Don't let the façade deceive you; it's comfortable inside."

"Really?"

"No," I laugh. "Not really."

"How much money do you have?" she asks, staring up at the mansion's jaw-dropping façade.

"A lot."

"If I divorce you, do I get half of everything?"

I smirk. "Unlikely."

"How come?"

"I have the best lawyers alive."

She sighs. "Of course you do."

We get out of the car at the same time and I lead her into the house. The inside is massive, ten thousand square feet of granite and steel. Black glass shines as far as the eye can see. It's spartan. Functional. But there's no mistaking the craftsmanship bleeding from every inch of detail.

"Your room is on the third floor. Third door on your right. You can't miss it."

She glances towards the staircase. "Thanks."

"And I expect you to join me for dinner this evening."

She's on the first step when she turns to me with the same pouty expression she was wearing for most of the drive over here.

"Isaak, I've had a hell of a day, and I'm not interested in doing a whole song and dance—"

I raise up a hand to cut her off. "I don't really give a fuck what you're interested in."

She slams her mouth shut, but I can see the building anger in her face. It's entertaining, not to mention strangely comforting.

"Dinner will be at eight," I add. "Wear something nice."

"Fine," she snaps. "Is there a phone in my room?"

"You're not calling your sister," I say dismissively, noticing Bogdan approach from the door right under the staircase. He stops short, clearly not wanting to put himself in the middle of an argument.

"Why the hell not?"

"Because I said so."

"Isaak!"

I meet her gaze coolly. "Camila."

"I have to speak to Bree. I… I need to talk to Jo. You know that."

"I do. And you'll get a chance to. Just not right now."

"Why?"

"I have my reasons."

"If I'm going to suffer for them, then I deserve to know what those reasons are."

"Have you always been this dramatic, or do you save that shit for me?"

She grinds her teeth together and I can tell she wants to stomp over to me and fight like she usually does. But she's also wary of being too close to me.

The math with us is always the same: proximity plus anger equals explosive sexual tension. She thinks she can change that calculus. That she can set boundaries for herself to prevent the inevitable from happening.

Or maybe those boundaries for me.

It doesn't really matter, I suppose. Either way, they won't last long.

"Go upstairs and get some rest."

"Stop bossing me around."

"If you didn't want to be bossed around, *kiska,* I was the wrong person to call."

"Fuck you," she says huffily. Wisely, she doesn't wait around for me to retaliate. She turns her back on me and hurries up the stairs.

I wait until she's turned the corner before I glance towards Bogdan.

He saunters forward with an amused smile. "So, you two are off to another great start."

"What do you have for me?"

The smile slides right off Bogdan's face. "A message," he says. "From Maxim."

"Are you fucking serious?" I growl. "What does he want from me now?"

"Actually, the message is not for you," Bogdan clarifies. "It's for… Camila."

I frown. "He knows she's with me?"

"Apparently. It makes sense that he would assume she was with you."

"But so soon?" I ask. "The only person who knows for sure where Camila is… is Eric Keller."

Bogdan reads my expression. "You think we should keep an eye on him?"

"Two eyes. The whole 'concerned old bloke' routine might just be for show."

"I'm on it," Bogdan assures me.

"Good."

"Are you going to tell her?" he asks, scouring my expression.

"We're having dinner tonight. I might tell her… depending on how that conversation goes."

"Maybe we shouldn't put any sharp cutlery out."

I snort. "I can handle her."

"Oh, I don't know," Bogdan says. "She gives you a run for your money." I roll my eyes as he tries to stifle a laugh. "But you know that's not what I meant when I asked if you've told her. You should do it sooner rather than later, brother. Some things can't be kept under wraps forever."

I tense. There are secrets in these walls. But contrary to what Bogdan may think, I intend on keeping them hidden until the time is right.

"How are things?" I ask instead of engaging.

"Fine at the moment, I think," Bogdan says. "Mama's taking care of stuff."

For once, I'm glad she's around. And apparently, so is Bogdan, judging from the relief in his eyes.

"It's a pretty big thing to keep from her," Bogdan points out.

I give him an annoyed glare. "You're like a dog with a bone. I know what it is and what it means, *sobrat*." I turn into the corridor and head to my office.

Bogdan follows, falling into step beside me. "Hey, you know I'm on your side. Always. But this situation is… unique."

"I'm aware."

"I don't want shit to hit the fan."

"Don't you know me at all?" I ask. "Since when have I ever lost control?"

"It only takes one time, big brother," he says gently.

I shake my head impatiently. "Not with me."

7

CAMILA

My heart is beating fast as I press my back against the wall. I can hear Bogdan's voice, but I can't see either one of them. I'm hoping that means they can't see me, either.

Maxim knows I'm here. That thought runs through my head again and again like the beating of a drum. The fact that he knows where I am concerns me less than the fact that Isaak might decide to keep his message from me.

It's not really about what the message contains as much as the principle of the thing. I just don't want to be a pawn again. I refuse to let myself be controlled and manipulated.

It's ironic that, despite that, Isaak is the one I chose to call.

But now, I'm wondering if I haven't made a horrible mistake.

"… not what I meant when I asked if you've told her."

My ears strain to pick up every little breath between each word. What else is he keeping from me?

I'm disappointed the moment Isaak responds. "How are things?" he asks, evading the question.

I inch a little closer, hoping that the sleek wooden floorboards under my feet won't creak and give me away.

"Fine at the moment, I think… taking care…"

I catch only the last part of that sentence, but I can't risk moving any closer. If I do, they'll definitely spot me hanging over them.

"It's a pretty big thing to keep from her…"

Bogdan's voice is deep, but not as deep as Isaak's. I'm not totally sure, but I could swear I detect a small amount of concern in his tone.

I lose Isaak's next sentence as they move away, deeper into the house, leaving me scrambling for more.

I risk moving forward—and I'm rewarded with a few words thrown by the wind. "…This situation is… unique…"

It's not exactly a significant clue. But I know one thing for sure: Maxim's letter is not the only thing Isaak is keeping from me.

That naïve, hopeful, infatuated voice inside my head tells me to hold on. Maybe Isaak is just waiting for the right time to tell me. Maybe he's planning on telling me tonight at dinner.

That's it. That must be it.

Sighing, I leave them behind and follow his directions to my room on the third floor. My first thought when I enter is, *This is too much.*

After three weeks in a tiny little shoebox with Rudy and Lillian, I don't even know what to do with myself in all this space.

Whereas the Vorobev Manor in London was lush and richly detailed, this place is color-sparse and brutally minimalistic. Just like in the foyer, black glass and neutral colors gleam like diamonds. I feel like I've crash-landed in the capital of an alien kingdom.

Weirdly, I don't see any closets or wardrobes. I frown and do a slow walk around the perimeter of the room, letting my fingertips trail over the cold granite walls.

Suddenly, my finger catches on something. The tiniest little lip. I peer closer—then, acting on a hunch, I press into it.

I nearly shriek when the button depresses. I leap backwards as a rectangular hairline crack appears in the seemingly seamless stone wall, and all of a sudden, there's a door where before there was nothing.

Still moving cautiously, I push the door with the flat of my palm. It swings inward silently, to reveal a walk-in closet the size of Bree's college apartment.

The lighting is austere and professional. Rack after rack of clothes and shoes and purses sit patiently along the walls.

"Whoa."

I'm only slightly surprised to find that some of the items hanging up look familiar—the clothes I bought in England when I'd been forced to go on that shopping spree with Lachlan as my bodyguard.

I feel a little stab of heartache when I think of the bright-eyed Scotsman who'd managed to charm his way past my veneer of dislike. He was a good man. One of the few I've met in a long time. He deserved better.

With a heartfelt sigh, I turn my attention back to the clothes on display. The ones I recognize quickly give way to an endless succession of designer labels. I fondle each of them, savoring the feel of the luxurious fabric.

I come to a stop in front of a separate closet that's set apart from the rest. There are a bunch of dresses hanging there that I definitely didn't pick.

They're all beautiful, formal, and clearly absurdly expensive. And, weirdly enough, each dress has a distinct scent. As though they've been daubed in perfume first. Is that some rich person thing I didn't know about? Perfume individualized by outfit?

I finish my circuit of the room. In the center, there's a sprawling dressing table oriented around a huge, bulb-lined mirror. The shelves are packed with makeup.

There's more, of course. Shoes. Luggage. Jewelry. All of it seemingly looking at me and saying, *Do you want us?*

And part of me wants to say yes. What woman would want anything else? This is *Sex and the City*; this is *Princess Diaries*; this is *Pretty Woman*. It's a fantasy wrapped in a daydream.

But it's all wrapped around a lie.

It's just another play in Isaak's seduction. His manipulation.

"Fucking hell," I breathe. I need to get my shit together.

I turn and step up onto the dressing room dais. Six different Camilas look back at me, reflected from each of the mirrors. Eyeing myself sternly, I say, "Focus, girl."

I'd made the decision to come to Isaak. Demanding and pleading doesn't work with him; I know that as well as anyone. So I decide to try a different tack.

I'll play into his hands and see what he does with that.

To that end, I head into the bathroom. It's as obnoxiously big as my bedroom, and it also boasts a breathtaking view of the gardens. I'm tempted to use the tub, but I change my mind and step into the shower instead. The slanted skylight on the ceiling lets sunbeams radiate into the massive, echoing space. A living wall of plants greedily soaks up the humidity from the hot water.

It's enough to make me feel as though I'm outside the whole time I'm showering. Which I suspect is exactly the point.

Once I've scrubbed my body clean with all the essential oils and perfumed soaps on offer, I towel off and pad into the walk-in closet.

It takes me a while to find the underwear drawer. Although, "lingerie drawer" would be a more appropriate way to describe it. Everything in there is lacy and sexy as hell.

But tonight, it suits my purpose. So I pick out a black thong and a strapless bra to match. Once they're on, I move to the fancy dresses I saw before.

It takes me a while to pick the right one. They're all beautiful, but I need to make the right choice. I want to look sexy tonight, but I don't want it to appear as though I'm trying too hard.

It has to come off natural.

In the end, I decide on a pale blush mini. Its' corseted bodice highlights a decent amount of cleavage without being overly generous, and the hemline is just short enough to be young, sexy, and flirty.

Given that it's a strapless dress with a tight corset, it takes me almost fifteen minutes to get myself into it. There's probably a maid somewhere who'll help me if I ask, but I'm not about to head out into the corridor to search for one.

I don't exactly feel sexy when I'm trying to force the zipper up my back, but I get it done somehow. And when I'm staring at my reflection in the mirror, I feel oddly triumphant.

I look good.

Good enough to stand next to a man like Isaak Vorobev and not feel completely insecure.

I decide to rev up the look with a little makeup. It's been a minute, but there is a certain paper courage that comes over me as I apply some blush and eyeliner.

I stick to neutrals, only colors that compliment my skin tone. I want to look as natural as possible. Just... turned up a little. More me than me.

Once my foundation is done, I apply a nude lip liner and then I paint my lips with a light rouge-brown that makes the green in my eyes pop.

I dust eyeshadow on the base of my eyelids and then give myself an understated but effective winged eyeline. I give myself an objective once-over when I'm done, and I actually feel quite... pretty.

Sexy, even, if I do say so myself.

I get up and head over to the shoe rack. It takes me a minute to pick out the right pair of shoes. Mostly because I'm spoiled for choice.

I narrow it down to three pairs. I let myself be a girl for five minutes and I try on each pair and strut around the room, checking myself out in the mirror.

I settle on the champagne stilettos with a tiny little strap over my toes. Feeling confident and ready for the first time since meeting Isaak, I head into the room and check the time.

8:15.

Fuck. Cinderella got a little too swept away playing dress-up.

I rush out of the room. I'm halfway down the stairs and I hear someone clear their throat behind me. A petite woman standing by the foot of the stairs, dressed in a maid's uniform.

It's only marginally different from the uniform that Edith wore in the manor. Like the house itself, her uniform is more modern.

She smiles. "Pardon me, Mrs. Vorobev," she says. "But dinner will be on the rooftop tonight."

"Oh. Okay."

I'm slightly thrown by the way she addresses me. Three weeks apart was long enough to bury the memory of my wedding to Isaak, I guess.

I climb back up to the top of the staircase and let her show me the way to the rooftop.

"I thought this was the highest floor?"

"And it is. But there's a rooftop patio that Mr. Vorobev likes to use when he entertains."

I raise my eyebrows. "Does he entertain often?"

She completely misses the insinuation in my question. That, or she just chooses to ignore it. "He does, Mrs. Vorobev."

I frown. "My name is Camila," I tell her. "Camila Ferrara."

"Would you prefer I call you Mrs. Ferrara?"

"I'd prefer you call me Camila."

"That wouldn't be appropriate, ma'am."

She's a slight little thing, but her features are mature. She's probably in her thirties, maybe even older. But her stature gives the appearance of youth.

"Ms. Camila, then?" I suggest with a suppressed sigh.

"If you wish."

"What's your name?"

"Cindy."

Her accent is super American, but she has the formality of old English tradition. It's confusing.

"Through that staircase, Ms. Camila," she says, pointing the way to a narrow circular stairway that forms a perfect spiral ascent all the way to the top.

"I'm going to get vertigo climbing this thing."

She smiles. "I'm afraid there's no other way up."

"I'll manage," I mutter, holding my skirt down as I start the climb.

I'm regretting the heels as I head up. Thankfully, Cindy doesn't stand right underneath me, so I'm hoping that I'll avoid flashing her. The thong I'm wearing isn't exactly conservative.

The steps stop directly in front of a narrow white door that's been left slightly ajar. I pause at the threshold for a moment to collect myself.

Isaak is on the other side of this door.

My future is on the other side of this door.

If I want things to go according to my plan… I have to play my cards right.

8

CAMILA

When I'm ready—or as ready as I'm ever gonna be, I guess—I push through the door. My first thought is… have I entered another world?

I'm not sure what I was expecting, but it certainly wasn't this.

The rooftop looks like the Garden of Eden, filled with plants and flowers and vines that curl along every surface they can find. The path I'm on points in one direction.

So I follow it… directly to Isaak.

He's dressed in dark pants and a white shirt and he has his back to me. I have no doubt that he knows I'm here, though. I've long since accepted that the man seems to know everything. I ignore the set table in the center of the roof and head over to him.

He turns to me, and I feel a thrill of satisfaction when his impassive expression gives way to surprise.

Then admiration.

Then desire.

"You look beautiful," he growls.

I raise my eyebrows. Somehow, I'd expected a different choice of words. Something less... touching. More generic, offhand, inconsequential. But the way he says the word makes my skin prickle with heat.

"Thank you."

He reaches out and cups the side of my face. He stares at me so long that I can't stop the blush creeping up my cheeks. I'm the one who has to break away from him.

And just like that, the self-consciousness is back.

"This... is not what I expected," I say, gesturing to the garden we're surrounded by.

"That's exactly the point," he says. "I wanted to do something different with the space, something that clashes with the house."

"You succeeded," I tell him. "It's breathtaking."

"Hungry?"

"Not really."

He ignores that and leads me to the table anyway. There's already warm bread in the basket between us and two small silver cloches on either side of the table.

I sit down, and Isaak pulls off the cloches and sets them on the empty trolley beside the table.

The smell of pumpkin and garlic wafts up to me, and suddenly, I am ravenous.

"You haven't eaten anything but ice cream all day," he says with a knowing smirk. "So dig in."

"Can you go an hour without bossing me around?" I snap, putting my spoon back down automatically.

"It's not bossiness when I know what's best for you."

I glare at him. "Wow."

He gives me a cool smile that makes my ovaries do a little dance. *Jesus, woman*, I chastise myself, get ahold of yourself. My only solace is that he can't read my mind… I hope.

"It's true."

"You can't honestly be that arrogant."

"Is that a challenge?"

I want to refrain from eating even a morsel just to spite him, but the soup smells too damn good. And he's right—I haven't eaten all day.

Plus, playing nice is the whole point of tonight. I need to be my most agreeable self, to see if that'll make the difference between him hiding things from me and being honest.

I spoon a mouth of soup into my mouth and sigh. "Damn, that's good."

He smiles, and only then does he taste the soup himself. "A little salty."

"You have impossible standards."

"Always."

I finish half my soup, waiting for him to say something. But he doesn't. He just observes me in that calm, thoughtful way that makes me feel both flattered and self-conscious at the same time.

No one else in my life has ever looked at me like that.

"So… what's new?" I ask. It's an odd question and it lands wrong, but I can't take it back now.

"What's new?" he repeats.

"Er, yeah. It's been a few weeks since we last saw each other," I say, trying to force some normalcy into the conversation. "I was just wondering if there were any new, I dunno… developments."

He considers that for a moment. I can't tell if he's suspicious or just confused.

"Is there something specific you'd like to ask me, Camila?"

I grit my teeth and remind myself to play nice. I should have known that Isaak's not the type of man to be steered into anything against his will. Conversation included.

"No," I mumble, focusing on my soup. "Forget it."

Once we're done, two waiters materialize suddenly and whisk away our soup bowls.

"Where'd they even come from?"

"Same place you did."

I frown. "Carrying all those trays and plates up the spiral staircase seems a little impractical."

Isaak smiles. "There's a dumbwaiter on the other side of the wall."

"Oh. That makes sense. How did they know to come at just the right time, though?"

"I have a button I press when I need them."

"Jesus," I breathe. "What a life."

He cocks his head to the side. "You sound envious."

"No," I respond immediately. "Not envious at all. Just trying to wrap my head around the way some people live."

"You seemed quite comfortable in the manor," he points out.

"You know, if you're going to be an obnoxious ass the whole night, I'd rather eat alone in my room."

He smirks at that one and moves his hand as fresh cloches are set in front of both of us. I can smell the meaty scents rising from the crack beneath the silver lid and my mouth waters instantly.

The waiters pull off the cloches a moment later to reveal veal shank with roasted vegetables, caramelized onions, and a red wine reduction on the side.

"Thank you," I say to the waiters as they disappear down an aisle of daffodils.

They don't respond.

"Friendly lot," I mumble sarcastically when they're gone.

"They're professionals," Isaak replies.

"Is it true that you entertain up here a lot?" I ask, cutting into my shank. It falls off the bone like warm butter.

"Sometimes," he says with a shrug. "I wouldn't say often."

"Seems like a strange place to have a business meeting."

"Why is that?"

"It just seems very… feminine."

He cocks his head to the side. "Because of the flowers?"

"Well…"

He gives me a crooked smile that makes him seem boyish. "I'm surprised at you, Camila. Flowers don't necessarily equate to femininity. And even if they do, it's just a man-made construct meant to reinforce gender stereotypes that shouldn't have a place in a modern, progressive society."

I actually blush. Because, apart from teasing me, he's also completely right.

"All I meant was that it seems more suited for seduction than business deals."

"Seduction?" he repeats. I regret my words instantly. "You think I bring women up here to seduce them?"

"Never mind. Forget I said anything."

"I'm a married man," he points out.

I glare at him. "Stop that."

He chuckles. "Is this worrying you?"

Idiot. Why had I opened my mouth at all? "Not at all. You can fuck whoever you want."

There's nothing but pride fueling that sentence. Inside, I'm screaming at myself because even picturing Isaak with another woman makes me want to pull out my hair in chunks.

"I have your permission then?"

I'm ninety percent sure he's still teasing, or calling my bluff rather. But I'm not sure if I'm willing to make that assumption and take the risk.

"Can we please just eat dinner?" I say irritably. "Talking in circles with you gives me a migraine sometimes."

"You've made an effort today," Isaak says by way of changing the conversation. He juts his chin at my dress. "Should I be flattered?"

I roll my eyes. "I just liked the dress, okay?"

"I thought it might suit you when I picked it out."

So he had chosen it himself. I can't help but be impressed by his taste. But then again, I've been in three of his homes now, and every single one has been tasteful, elegant, and extremely sophisticated.

It makes me feel intimidated… and incredibly lacking.

Maybe that's why I get defensive.

"I don't need you to shop for me," I tell him.

He shrugs. "I just thought I'd give you options."

"If you could extend that to life choices, I'd appreciate that," I say sarcastically.

His eyes flash with annoyance. "Are we back to this again?" he asks.

My mood change has taken me by surprise too. But I understand myself a little better now. Those weeks of near isolation had given me a lot to reflect on.

Including the person I thought I was, versus the person I want to be, versus the person I actually am.

Within the span of months, Isaak has taken over my entire life—again. I should be railing against him, desperate to regain my autonomy. But instead, I find myself more and more drawn to him.

And when I was in trouble, he was the first person I turned to.

How can I call myself a true feminist if the moment shit hits the fan, I run to a man to save me?

Even now, I'm aware of all the secrets he holds. Secrets concerning me and my life that he's purposefully keeping from me. And even then, I find myself desperate to touch him. Desperate for him to touch me.

"Back to *what?*" I ask dangerously, feeling my anger rise to meet his. "You seriously expect a clean slate?"

He leans in a little. "Need I remind you that you called me, Camila?"

It stings, but I refuse to let it show. "Yes, I called you. But let's face it: it's not like you let me go," I point out. "You were having me followed. From the first moment I left the manor, you had your men tail me."

"And for good reason."

"To control me?"

"To fucking protect you," he says impatiently.

"That's a convenient perspective."

"Is there a reason you're acting like a brat?" he asks in his cool, measured way.

"Same reason you're acting like a bastard, probably."

So much for playing nice.

Isaak's eyes darken. His finger tightens around his cutlery. "You need to be careful what you say to me, *kiska*."

"You're not going to tell me, are you?" I demand.

He arches a surprised eyebrow. "Tell you what?"

I push back my chair and it scrapes the floor, making an ear-piercing screech. "About the message Maxim sent for me."

9

ISAAK

I've never wanted to kill Maxim so much in my life.

No matter how we start, it always ends up here—in a fight. With that fucking blowhard in the middle of every argument.

It's hard to concentrate on my arguments, though, because she looks like a fucking Amazonian princess tonight. The dress she's wearing is feminine in color and composition.

But the silhouette and the bodice are strong. Powerful.

She looks like every fucking fantasy I've had since I was a boy. Her green eyes flash with anger as she gets to her feet, her blonde hair blowing back softly in the light breeze that crosses through the patio.

I'm pissed, too. But that doesn't stop me from imagining her bent over this very table with her ass in the air, wet and desperate to receive me.

"You were listening to my conversation," I say, wondering how much else she's heard, how much else she's pieced together.

"I had to. I already know I can't trust you."

"You're here," I tell her shortly. "What does that say about your level of trust?"

Regret flickers across her face. "I shouldn't be. I should never have called you."

Low blow, but I let it roll off my back as I get to my feet. She has to crane her neck up a little to compensate for my height. I walk around the table towards her.

She takes a tiny step back, but we both know she's not going to back down. Not yet.

"Then why did you?"

"You did this," she says, trying to line up her accusations. "You're the one who made sure I was powerless, so that when I needed help, I'd have no one but you to go to."

"Is that what I did?"

"Stop it. Don't treat me like I'm a child or an idiot. I'm neither."

"You realize that you called me in order to escape Maxim," I remind her.

"What's your logic?" she retorts. "I ran from him, so I won't want to hear a message he's sent to me? Don't you think you should have given me the choice?"

"No."

Her green eyes glow a little brighter. Honestly, it would be so fucking easy to grab her now and pull her against my body.

All I want to do is rip that little dress right off her and fuck her right now, against the table, on the floor, in the grass beds, up against the wall.

Every-fucking-where I can.

"I want to hear his message."

"Why?"

"Because I have a right to."

"What rights you have are those I choose to give you," I tell her, knowing it's only going to infuriate her further. But fuck it—I've never been the conciliator.

If anything, I'm more pyromaniac. At least with her.

And I'm willing to set the whole fucking world on fire just to see the flames reflected in her eyes.

"I can't believe I willingly put myself back under your thumb. You're nothing but a control freak who gets off on the power high of controlling me."

I say nothing. That only pisses her off further.

"You're not even going to defend yourself?" she asks, pushing at my chest.

I was hoping she'd touch me first. It gives me the excuse I need to return the favor.

I grab her arm and yank her against my body. Her cheeks flush pink when I stare down at her, our noses almost touching.

"I don't have to fucking defend myself. Everything I do is for a reason. I don't give a fuck if you understand those reasons or not."

She struggles to get out from under my grasp, but there's no way she's moving unless I release her.

"Let me go."

I smile coldly. "Is this why you dressed up for me?" I ask. "You were trying to manipulate me into telling you about Maxim's message?"

"I only wanted you to be honest with me," she hisses. "I was hoping that if I gave you time, you'd tell me."

"Miscalculated, didn't you?" I growl, the rage building steadily inside me.

I should throw her down right now and fuck her until she forgets Maxim's fucking name all over again. I should teach her a lesson about trust, about hope, about control.

"That's not the only thing I miscalculated," she snaps. "I thought you were a decent man."

I snort. "No, what you thought is that I was a convenient contact."

She freezes a little, her eyes going wide. "W… what?"

"You want to keep us both, don't you?" I ask. "Keep both Maxim and me on the hook, and weigh which one will be the better investment in the long run."

Her eyes turn hazy instantly. It's so fast, that I have to look a little closely to make sure. Something about that accusation has hit a nerve.

"You think… I'm using you?" she asks, a sob dancing on the edge of her voice.

I glance down at her body. "That's a sexy look you've got going on. Did you dress like this for Maxim when there was something you wanted?"

Tears jump to the surface and run down her cheek.

I didn't expect that. In surprise, I drop her hand. Cami steps back immediately as more tears come. One after another, like a downpour without warning.

"You really are an insensitive asshole," she chokes out.

Then she turns and runs.

I watch her go, because I'm still trying to figure out her exact trigger. Had I stumbled across the truth, or a deep-seated insecurity?

I press the button to call for the waiters, but I leave the rooftop before they can get there. I head to the bar room instead and pour myself a strong drink.

The glass is almost empty when Bogdan walks in. And he's not alone.

My mother's eyes linger on the near empty glass in front of me. Just to give her something to bite her tongue about, I pour myself another glass.

"How about one for your little brother, too?" Bogdan asks, sitting down next to me.

Mama walks around the bar and sits opposite the two of us. To my surprise, she takes the whiskey bottle and pours Bogdan a round, and then she fills up a glass for herself.

"You don't drink," I say.

"Maybe I'll start," she says, taking a sip of the whiskey. Her face gives nothing away as she tastes the liquor. Not so much as a twitch of the eyelid.

She's a Vorobev through and through.

"I take it dinner didn't go well?" Bogdan asks.

"Why do you assume that?"

"Well, you're sitting at the bar drinking," he says with a small laugh. "And it's 9:30."

I take a large sip of my own whiskey. "She overheard us talking about Maxim's message."

"Fuck. Really?"

I nod. "She demanded to hear it. I said no. The inevitable fight ensued."

Bogdan punches me lightly on the arm. "Just focus on the make-up sex."

"Isaak," Mama says, her tone serious as she shuts down Bogdan's attempt to keep things light, "you need to meet the child."

I sigh, knowing they'd come in here together for a reason. I glance at Bogdan. "You ganging up on me, little brother?"

"What did I say before?" he reminds me. "I've always on your side. But, c'mon, *sobrat*: she's five years old and she's been ripped away from everything familiar."

"She's scared, Isaak," Mama adds. "She keeps asking for her aunt and uncle. She's been here almost twenty-four hours now and you still haven't even seen her."

"Don't you think I'm fucking aware of that?"

"Are you planning on telling Cami?" Bogdan asks.

"I'll tell her when I'm ready to. For now, she stays in the dark. Their rooms are on opposite ends of the house, so that will buy me some time."

Bogdan looks slightly uncertain.

"What?"

"Cami's not exactly the kind of girl who listens or stays in her corner."

"I can handle her."

Mama and Bogdan exchange a look that I definitely don't like. But I decide to ignore it and focus on my drink. The bitterness of the whiskey is helping to clear my thoughts a little.

It's not exactly helping my erection go down, though. Every time I calm down a little, I see Camila in that sexy little dress, her green eyes flashing angrily, her lips pouting, and I get hard all over again.

"She looks like you, you know," Bogdan says. "She's even got some of your mannerisms."

"Yeah?"

Mama smiles. Bittersweet regret pools around the corners of her eyes. "She's a beautiful child, Isaak. Sweet and lovely. She's just scared…"

"Seeing me is not going to change that," I say. "I may be her father, but she has no idea. To her, I'm just going to be this giant—"

"Monster?" Bogdan offers.

I glare at him. "Giant man she doesn't know," I finish.

"It'll take time," Mama says. "But building any relationship takes time. You have to start now."

I know she's right. They both are. The only problem is that I have a feeling that Jo is going to be one more thing I won't be able to control.

Children are unpredictable. And they're honest in a way that adults have forgotten how to be. I have no idea how to be a father. The only thing I've ever been is a don.

Somehow, I don't think that's going to help me here.

"It's okay to be scared," Mama says.

It's like the woman doesn't know me at all. "I'm not scared," I snap. "I just have other shit I need to deal with first. Camila being one."

Bogdan gives a snort that he tries to hide behind a cough. I glare at him and he looks down at his whiskey glass pointedly.

"If you go any deeper you're going to get whiskey on your nose," I drawl.

He gives me a sheepish grin when he looks back up.

"You don't think I can get her in line?" I press.

"Actually, I do," he says. "I just don't think she'll be happy about it."

"When I'm done, she will be."

Mama gives such a loud sigh that both Bogdan and I turn to her simultaneously. "Something wrong?" I ask.

"Both of you," she says, shaking her head. "You have it all wrong."

"Me?" Bogdan asks, as though he's insulted by the notion that he's been included in Mama's summation. "What did I do?"

"Camila's not one of your men, Isaak. She's not a business deal you can manipulate or a lieutenant you can order around. She's a woman with opinions, beliefs, and feelings of her own. And until you start acknowledging them, you're never going to be able to tame her. You're just going to drive a wedge between the two of you. Keep it up long enough and that distance will become too hard to bridge."

I consider her words carefully. "How would you know?"

She takes another sip of whiskey. "It's what happened to your father and me."

It stings a little—the knowledge that I'm more like my father than I care to admit. Every time I compartmentalize my personality, I fail to take into account that more and more of myself has been built on who he was.

Or at least, who I thought he was.

"Maxim is a real problem, and until his Bratva has been taken out, I don't have the luxury of listening to other people's opinions."

"Even your wife's?" Mama asks.

"Especially not hers. Besides," I add, "she's not really my wife."

"Isn't she?"

Mama's eyes are steely as she poses the question that I've been avoiding myself for a long time: how real is my marriage to Camila?

It started as nothing more than a political tool, a way to gain the upper hand and force Maxim's. But somewhere along the way, things got complicated.

And it has nothing to do with my cousin.

"I need to get some sleep," I say, downing the last of my whiskey.

"You could go and see her now," Mama suggests. "She's sleeping. There's no risk of any interaction. Just look at her, Isaak."

I growl as I stand up, "Not tonight."

"Isaak—"

"Enough," I say gruffly. "I will see the child when I decide it's best. Until then, you and Bogdan can tend to her."

Bogdan knows me well enough to keep his mouth shut. But Mama either hasn't read the signs, or she just doesn't care to.

"You brought her here, Isaak. You uprooted that girl and pulled her away from everything that's safe and familiar to her. The least you can do is look her in the eye and reassure her that everything is going to be alright."

"Yeah… and what makes you think she'll believe me?"

"You're her father," Mama says softly.

I make for the door without a word. Refusing to say out loud what I'm thinking…

If I am really a father, why don't I feel like one?

10

CAMILA

I'm sitting by the window the next morning with a book in my hands, when my door swings open. I know it's him without even having to look up.

"I want to speak to my sister," I say without turning my gaze from the window. "I want to speak to my daughter."

"I thought we already established last night that that's not going to happen."

I slam the book shut and throw it onto the little coffee table in front of me. I get to my feet, completely unconcerned about the baggy sweats and oversized shirt I'm wearing.

I'm done trying to make myself look good for him. What's the fucking point? He just sees me as some evil manipulative bitch who's trying to have her cake and eat it too. I don't need the fucking grief.

I've had all night to stew over my mistakes. I've combed over all the little regrets that have piled up over the years; I've tried to unravel the complexities of my psyche.

And all that's done is driven me into a rage-induced frenzy.

"You can't do this!" I cry out in frustration.

"Oh, I think you'll find that I can," he says, with all the confidence of a man who knows he can make the sun retreat if he decrees it. "Easily."

I want to fight back, even though I know I won't win. I want to lash out, even though I know I won't get any satisfaction from the attempt.

He's more powerful than I am. He holds all the cards and I have none. On top of which, I've gone and admitted as much to him by asking for his help when I was most vulnerable.

I've been a fool, and I'm not sure I can stop being one.

Because no matter which way I come at my problems…

I hit the same freaking roadblock every single time.

I am hopelessly infatuated with this man. If I were a braver woman, I might even use the word "love." But since I can't say the word without feeling like I'm compromising some small part of myself, I decide to cling to denial for a little while longer.

"What do I need to do?" I plead. "Since compassion doesn't work with you, maybe bargaining will. What do you want from me?"

"Obedience."

"Anything but that."

"It is possible, *kiska*. You just have to bend."

"I've bent plenty," I snap. "Now, it's time for you to take a stab at it."

He smiles coldly. "You must be confusing me with someone else."

"Have you never compromised for anyone in your entire loveless life?"

"Loveless?"

"It's clear you've never loved anyone in your life, Isaak. If you did, you'd understand that love means putting someone else's feelings above your own. But you're not capable of that. Because you live for yourself and no one else. Why do you think I kept Jo's existence from you even after I got to know you? I was trying to protect her from you. I'd rather she had no father at all than a monster like you."

I'm bringing out the big guns, the kind that you can't put away. But I don't fucking care. What else do I have left to lose?

Isaak's face looks like thunder. His natural calm exists only as a menacing afterthought. He steps towards me, his blue eyes burning with contempt.

"You were never going to tell me about her, were you?" he seethes.

Even I don't know the answer to that. But I'm not interested in being honest today. I'm interested in lashing out. I need an outlet for my frustration.

"No, I wasn't. Because I have to protect my daughter—no matter what."

"Protect her from me?"

"Yes."

The darkness in his eyes recedes for a moment. I have no idea what that might mean.

"Don't you have any humanity?" I whisper. "Almost six years and I've barely been with my child through any of it."

"I'm supposed to sympathize with you now, am I?"

I narrow my eyes at him. "You were never meant to be a parent, Isaak. You chased power, not family. But me? I'd give up every ounce of power I have if it means I can keep Jo safe and happy."

"Would you?" Isaak asks.

"Yes," I say, without hesitation.

"What if I could guarantee that for you?"

"No one can guarantee that. Not even you."

"Suspend reality for a moment. Let's speak hypothetically. If I could guarantee that, you would give up every ounce of power you have?"

I don't hesitate. "Of course."

"And if I asked you for obedience then?"

I tense, realizing belatedly where this is leading. But if I back out now, I'm blowing up my entire argument. And I truly mean what I'm saying: Jo is all that matters.

"I would give it to you."

"Even if I asked you to get down on your knees in front of me?"

My entire body flushes with heat. There's anger underneath the desire, but I'm more determined than I've ever been. So I move forward, locking my eyes onto his.

Then I lower myself to the ground in front of him.

He's not expecting it. Surprise flashes across his eyes when my knees hit the floor. I keep my eyes on his and hold my position.

"What do you want now?" I ask in a hoarse whisper.

He stares at me wordlessly for a moment. I can see reluctant admiration in the upward tilt of his mouth. "You're really doing this?"

"You asked me if I would give up power to make sure my daughter was safe," I say. "Well, here I am, proving that I would. Go ahead. Tell me what you want."

I already know what he wants. I'm at eye level with his crotch and his erection is very visible from where I'm kneeling. I try not to look directly at it, but it's hard.

Isaak's eyes flash. There's definitely lust there, but there's something else along with it. Reluctance? Uncertainty? Regret? I can't quite tell. He's a master at covering his emotions.

"Come on," I say challengingly. "You're the one who wanted obedience. Don't you have a command ready for me, Don Vorobev?"

"I'm not sure you want to go there."

"Shall I tell you what you want then?" I taunt. "Shall I read your mind?"

"Camila..." he warns. There's a growl in his voice that makes me so wet so fast that the intellectual part of me shuts down, and my animal brain awakens.

I reach out and start unbuttoning his pants. Within seconds, I have them down around his ankles. His cock is huge and swollen, pushing out against the soft fabric of his boxer briefs.

My mouth fills with saliva, and the moment I've teased the fabric down around his ass, my lips lock down around the tip of his cock.

"Is it this?" I whisper with his dick in my mouth. "Is this what you want?"

"Fuck," he rumbles.

I let my tongue circle the head of his cock. I can feel his body tense against me with every lash, so I keep going.

Little by little, I draw him in deeper. I suck him off slowly, building momentum as I keep going. I play with his balls, sucking and stroking, using one hand at first and then both.

I resist the urge to touch myself, even though I desperately want to. I need his cock inside me, but I won't let myself ask for it.

When his cock hits the back of my throat, he growls. It's a guttural, menacing sound that I feel all the way down in my pussy.

Desire pulses through me in waves as I practically choke on his cock. I'm gagging on him, but the tremors of pleasure rumbling from him into me and back again make it all worthwhile.

He won't last much longer.

He stiffens.

Groans.

And when he comes, he empties into the back of my throat.

I force myself to hold my position until he finishes. Then, when there's nothing left in him, I fall back against the floor with a gasp. I'm wheezing for air. My eyes remain fixed on Isaak's cock.

It's fucking beautiful. Even in my state of half-crazed anger, I can appreciate it.

It looks huge, like it's still hard and in need of more satisfaction. I'm almost tempted to give it to him, but that would undermine the point I'm trying to make.

He pulls his boxer briefs and his pants up and buttons himself in again. The bulge is still there, but it's a little less obvious now.

Slowly, I get back to my feet. He doesn't try to help me, and I'm glad for that. I don't know what would happen if I let him touch me right now.

When the silence stretches on longer than I expect, though, I can't help but break it.

"Did I prove my point?" I say. "Did I show you the lengths I would go to for my daughter?"

A shadow flickers across his face and stays there. He doesn't say a word.

"I want to speak to her."

The shadow on his face only gets darker. "And I've already said no."

I'm almost too angry to speak. I'm definitely too angry to think about my word choice. "Fine," I snap. "You won't let me speak to my sister or my daughter? Then I want to speak to Maxim."

"Maxim?" he growls.

I keep my expression impassive. "Yes, that's right. I want to speak to him. And it's clear he wants to speak to me."

"To what end?"

I shrug. "Closure, curiosity… whatever you want to call it. He hijacked my life, a lot like you did. I deserve the right to look at his face and ask him why."

Isaak considers that for a moment. I can tell he's pissed. Extremely. But he doesn't want to give me the satisfaction of putting it on display.

"He was a part of my life for a long time, Isaak. I agreed to marry the man. You say it was a fake version of him. But I refuse to believe that in all those months, I only ever saw a mask."

"You're going to be severely disappointed."

"Well, that would serve your purpose, wouldn't it?" I ask.

I know he'll refuse me. That's the whole point of the request. He'll refuse me; he'll get angry. Maybe if I'm lucky, he'll even get jealous.

I'm searching for just that in his eyes, but his mask is perfectly placed and refuses to budge.

"What's the matter, Isaak?" I ask, with the taste of his seed still on my tongue. "Insecure about something?"

He snorts, but he doesn't even bother to answer. He doesn't get defensive, either, which annoys the hell out of me. What will it take to get a rise out of this man?

I move closer to him. "So what do you say?"

He doesn't flinch away. "I think you already know the answer to that."

"What are you so scared of?" I demand. "I'm legally your wife, remember? So unless you plan on divorcing me, we're stuck together for the foreseeable future. Are you so intimidated by your cousin that you wouldn't allow me one conversation with him?"

"Intimidated?" Isaak scoffs. "By Maxim? You're stretching, Camila."

"Then prove me wrong."

His blue eyes flash steel. "I don't have to prove a fucking thing."

"If you expect me to fall in line and obey you, you're going to have to make some concessions. Otherwise, I'm going to be the most difficult wife in the history of the Bratva. You're going to be begging me for a divorce."

His face breaks into a smile that forces a shiver down my spine. He takes a step forward, and I know I've pushed him too far. And I'm stupid enough not to have even realized it…

Until now.

"I never beg for anything. When I'm done with you, you'll know it."

We've done this song and dance before. We fight, I insult him, accuse him, blame him, and he maintains calm the entire time so that he can deliver a blow at the last moment.

A blow that inevitably leaves me reeling with hurt.

This time is no different. But I refuse to let him see just how much he scalds me with his sharp words. I push past him and head to the door.

"Where are you going?"

"For a walk," I spit. "I asked for one small thing, and you refused. There's nothing more we have to say to one another."

He doesn't stop me as I storm out, taking what's left of my dignity with me.

I stride towards the library, but then I stop short, realizing that I'm not in the manor anymore. I don't know where the library is. In fact, I don't even know if there is one in the first place.

Feeling deflated and a little more upset, I head outside to the gardens. The Manor's gardens were like the house: gorgeously overwrought, bursting with life and color and scent.

This mansion's gardens are equally impressive, but much like the building itself, everything is heartbreakingly modern. So neat, so brutal, so alien. There's nowhere out here to hide—from Isaak or from myself.

So I just walk. I barely notice the flowers, the stone sculptures, any of it. I just watch one foot go in front of the other.

I do my best not to think. For a little bit, I succeed.

When I've been walking for a while, I turn and look up at the house again. I'm on the far side now, putting as much distance as possible between Isaak and me.

This house is just like him, I realize. So viciously cold that it almost hurts to look at. But so beautiful that you can't look away in spite of that.

And I'm trapped here.

With him.

How fucking fitting.

I'm about to turn away when I notice someone walk across the window of a room in the west wing of the house. I do a double take.

It looked like a child.

It was just a glimpse. Only a small little silhouette and a head of dark hair. But the more I think about it, the fuzzier the details become.

Could it be...?

No. I dismiss the thought immediately.

It's not Jo. How can it be? She's safe at home with my sister.

Isaak may be a monster. But there's no way he would keep something as huge as this from me. There's cruel and then there's inhuman. Isaak dances on the edge of those two; I just have to believe there's enough of a soul left in him that some things remain forbidden. Harming my daughter is certainly on that list.

I turn from the window and chalk it all up to a figment of my imagination. I've been without Jo too long. It's natural that I would start to hallucinate her into existence.

I'll keep walking, I tell myself.

I'll just keep walking.

11

ISAAK

I'm still reliving the moment Cami's plump pink lips engulfed my cock.

The moment she'd gotten on her knees in front of me, I'd gone stiff as a board. I knew this was the kind of erection that wasn't going down without a release.

I was prepared for blue balls.

What I wasn't prepared for was the way she had assumed control of the situation. It didn't last long, but she'd held her own. She'd been a worthy adversary.

And while she'd been sucking on my cock like it was her last fucking meal, I'd actually considered letting her have control… and letting her keep it.

Of course, once I'd come down from the high of that face-melting orgasm, I'd gotten hold of myself and salvaged the situation.

But just barely.

Now I'm walking towards the west wing, feeling a heavy sense of responsibility—not just to Jo, but also to the woman who's literally willing to do anything for her child.

I stop outside the door of Jo's room. I can hear voices. The raspy melody of Mama's voice, and a higher tone, youthful and innocent.

I feel something stir inside me. But instead of giving me the courage to walk through that door, it makes me want to turn around and head downstairs to my office.

"Fuck," I growl to myself.

I don't miss the irony of the moment. I've walked into rooms with armed men who I knew for certain wanted me dead. But somehow, the thought of facing down a frightened five-year-old under my own roof gives me pause.

I spent the entire night thinking over Mama and Bogdan's words. They were right in the end: I'd brought the child here. Made her my responsibility.

And now, I needed to walk through that door.

I knock first, a gesture that's completely unfamiliar to me.

A few seconds later, it swings open. My mother is staring at me with a shocked expression. "Isaak?"

I look past her into the massive room. The moment Bogdan had gotten on the plane, I'd had a team down here within the hour to convert it into a space fit for a child.

They'd procured everything necessary, from furniture to clothes to toys.

A white wardrobe pushed to the side has been painted with a pattern of rockets and planets. A canopy bed sits in the corner with a whole zoo's worth of stuffed animals lounging on top of the sheets.

In the center of the room looms an elaborate dollhouse, all pointed turrets and shutter windows thrown wide open to reveal the exquisitely detailed dioramas inside.

But Jo's not playing with any of it. She's standing in front of the ivory bookshelves, running her fingers over the spines as though she's trying to make an important decision.

Of course she goes right for the books.

Just like her fucking mother.

Mama pushes me out of the room before Jo catches sight of me. She pulls the door closed a little without shutting it fully.

"Are you sure you're up for this?" she whispers.

"You're the one who encouraged me to be here."

"I know, and I'm glad you came… But she has to be handled delicately."

"Is she upset?"

"She veers between moments of panic," Mama admits. "Not that you can blame her."

I push past her and walk into the room. Jo turns around and the moment her eyes land on me, they go wide with new panic.

Mama walks around me and goes straight for her. "Darling…"

She says it with so much affection that I find myself holding back, letting her take the lead.

"This is Isaak," she finishes. "Will you come and meet him?"

Jo stares at me for a moment longer, and then she shakes her head.

No.

I've never been very concerned about that word. I don't hear it often. When I do, it usually ends with somebody bleeding out at my feet.

But this time, it means something to me.

There's no bulldozing over Jo. No weapon I can muster. I can't throw my weight around and expect her to yield.

She's a child who's looking for comfort and security. Not a mark I can manipulate.

And even if I could do that to her, I wouldn't.

"Peter Rabbit, huh?" I say, spying the top cover of the book she's holding. "That's a good book."

She looks down at it as though she's forgotten what she's holding. She sidles closer to Mama and hides behind her. But I can still see her big, almond-shaped eyes peering at me from behind Mama's hips.

They're bright blue. Not quite the same hue as mine, but close enough to make me shiver.

"It's okay," Mama tells her, patting her head. "He's really not as scary as he looks."

I shoot Mama a glare. *Helpful*, I mouth to her.

She gives me a smile I don't quite recognize. It looks so… open. So unreserved and sincere. It hits me that maybe Jo has something to do with that.

Jo looks up at Mama. Her little fingers curl around the folds of Mama's flowing white pants.

"Jo," I say. Her eyes snap to mine automatically. "I'm a friend of your mother's."

That seems to get her attention. Her eyes go a little wider, and she steps out from Mama's shadow a little. "You know my mommy?"

"Yes, I do," I reply. "You wanna come over here and sit with me for a bit?"

Her expression turns wary again. She shakes her head.

"That's okay," I say with a shrug. "I'm just gonna sit here by myself then."

I go to the fluffy teal carpet and sit down cross-legged on it. She watches my every movement, and every so often, she glances up at Mama for reassurance.

I make myself comfortable on the carpet, spreading out and groaning when my muscles crack. I can't remember the last time I sat down during the day just for the hell of it.

"Fuck, this carpet is soft."

"Isaak!" Mama scolds instantly.

Almost immediately, I hear a little giggle that forces me upright again. Did I just make the kid laugh?

I look at her to see she's standing beside Mama now, with a smile on her face and the threat of a giggle on her tongue.

"You said a bad word," she says, clearly amused by my slip.

"Yeah," I admit, "I did. It was an accident though."

She edges a little closer. "Aunt Bree says naughty people use that word."

I smirk. "Maybe. But frustrated people use that word, too."

She considers that for a moment. "Are you... frus... frussated?"

I can't help but smile. I'm not sure if it's a biased biological instinct or if Jo is really that cute.

At the moment, I'm leaning towards the latter.

"Sometimes, other people can frustrate me," I tell her honestly.

She smiles. "Aunty Bree gets frussated all the time," Jo tells me. "But mostly at the boys because they're dirty and don't clean up before dinner."

It's almost heartwarming, the way she offers me little snippets into her life without questioning it, without holding back. The purity. The honesty. No qualms or hesitation or second-guessing.

That doesn't exist in my world.

"I bet she doesn't get frustrated with you, though."

Jo edges closer still. Her curiosity is winning out over her fear. "Only one time, when I went out in the rain even though she told me not to."

"You did that?"

Her eyes go wide with remnant guilt. "I like the rain. But Aunty Bree said it was too cold."

"She was probably right, huh?"

She sits down on the carpet opposite me. In the background, I notice Mama edge away from us. She doesn't leave the room, just moves to the window seat to give us some space.

"I got a cold the next day," Jo informs me. I laugh, and she laughs with me. "But I got better."

"I'm glad to hear that."

"And Uncle Jake bought me a stuffed teddy bear to cheer me up."

It strikes me suddenly that another man has taken my place in the last six years. I feel a pang of anger, but not at him. On the contrary, I feel a strange sort of comradery with the man who's been a father figure to Jo all these years.

"That was nice of him."

Jo nods. "I miss him. I miss my Aunt Bree too. And the boys… but not Sam so much."

I balk with laughter. "Why not Sam?"

"He likes to tease me."

"Sounds like typical cousin behavior."

She gives me a long-suffering sigh. "Peter always takes care of me. But Sam likes to jump out of corners and scare me."

"I can have a word with him, if you like."

Her eyes go wide with delight. "Really?"

"Sure."

She nods vigorously, causing her hair to bob up and down. "Yeah! He'll be super scared. You're so tall and scary."

I chuckle. She's got a little bit of mischief in her, it seems. "Do you really think I'm scary?"

She looks hard at my face and cocks her head to the side. It's such a mature gesture that I see myself in it, and I feel that inexplicable something stir in my chest again.

"A little bit," she admits, at last. Then she adds, "Your eyes are blue."

"So are yours."

She nudges forward on her knees and leans in to take a better look at my eyes. "I like your eyes," she says. "They look like the sea."

"You like the sea?"

She nods in her fervent way. "I love making sandcastles. But the last time I made one, Sam knocked it down."

I frown. "Sam's a real problem, huh?"

"Oh yeah," she says seriously. "Uncle Jake made him apologize, and then Sam hugged me and helped me build it again. That was fun."

Quick to anger and quick to forgive. At least she inherited one of those qualities from her mother.

"Do you know Aunt Bree and Uncle Jake, too?"

"Not really. I'm more your mommy's friend."

She considers that for a moment, but then her little cheeks start to droop. "Have you seen my Mommy?" she asks. "Because I haven't. She hasn't called."

I move a little closer to her. But I do it slow so that I don't spook her. "Your mom is trying to get to you, Jo," I tell her. "She's doing her best."

"I know," she says with a little sigh. "But there's a monster keeping her in a tower."

I raise my eyebrows. "Who told you that?"

"Aunt Bree."

Flattering.

"What else did Aunt Bree tell you?"

"That Mommy loves me very much and she's going to come back home soon. I just need to be brave… and patent."

"Patient?"

"That's what I said!" she says with annoyance. "I hate being patient."

I suppress a chuckle. "Hey, you want me to read you that book?"

Jo looks down at the Peter Rabbit book in her hand. The way she's holding it—reverently, like it's the most important and delicate thing in the world—reminds me of Camila. In fact, there's a lot of Camila in her.

The shape of the eyes and the face.

The delicate bone structure and dimpled smile.

But as much as she looks like Camila, she looks like me, too. I can see both of us in Jo, and somehow, it feels like I've come full circle.

I never expected to be a father. It wasn't something I chased.

But now, faced with this sweet little girl with big, curious eyes, I can't help but feel as though life turned out exactly the way it was meant to.

I try and push away the uncharacteristic sentimentality. I accept the book she hands to me.

She sidles closer, but she's shy. She keeps glancing at me out of the corner of her eyes. I resist the urge to wrap an arm around her.

Baby steps, I tell myself.

I read her the entire story, cover to cover. Once I finish the book, Jo takes it back possessively.

"Thank you," she says, so polite that my chest throbs. "That was a nice story. Can you read me another one?"

I nod, not sure if I trust my voice right now.

She runs over to the bookshelf. I turn to my mother, who's still sitting on the window seat. She hasn't said a word since I sat down, but now, she's giving me a knowing smile.

"What?" I snap.

She shrugs. "The things you do for them…"

"*Tak tebe prikhodilos' chitat' kuchu skuchnogo der'ma, kogda my byli molody?*"

Translation: *So you had to read a bunch of boring shit when we were young?*

Mama laughs. "*Konechno. I ya s radost'yu eto sdelal.*"

Of course. And I did it happily.

I turn to find Jo standing off to the side watching me intently. "What's that language?" she asks.

"Russian."

She raises her little eyebrows thoughtfully. "It's pretty."

I smirk, knowing that's not how very many people would describe Russian. It's a cold language. It can be harsh in certain people's mouths—mine, for instance.

But it doesn't frighten her, it seems.

"Can you teach me?"

I grin. "Of course."

"Jo, darling, how about we have our bath now?" Mama suggests.

"Okay," she says agreeably. Then she turns to me. "Will you come and read to me again?"

"Of course."

"And teach me Russian, too?"

"Definitely."

She smiles from ear to ear. "Okay. Bye-bye."

Then she turns and skips into the bathroom without so much as a backward glance at me. Laughing, Mama leaves the window seat and walks up to me.

"Well?"

"That went… fine."

"Fine?" Mama repeats. "That went spectacularly. She took to you so easily."

I nod solemnly as I stand. "I'll come by to see her again later."

Mama reaches out and touches my arm. It's a gesture she hasn't made in years. On another day it would have felt out of place.

But we have a commonality tying us together now: we're both parents.

I slip out of the room and head down the hall. I haven't even reached the end when Camila comes around the side of it and nearly bumps into me.

"Camila?"

Her eyes dart past me and down the hall. I pull my mask into place. The only reason she might be in this part of the house is if she suspects something.

I'm not ready to unveil the secrets of the west wing just yet.

"Isaak," she says coolly.

"What are you doing here?"

She shrugs. "Just… exploring."

Her tone is clipped. On edge. Something's spooked her just now, and I sense it's only partly to do with me.

"There's nothing much on this side of the house," I lie. "Just a bunch of empty rooms I haven't gotten around to furnishing."

"Oh." She frowns. "Right."

But I can see it in her eyes: she doesn't believe me for a fucking second.

12

CAMILA

Something's up with him.

There's an expression on his face that I can't quite put my finger on. A softness there that I've never seen before.

"Are you alright?" I ask.

I expect him to dismiss the question and revert to his old combative and jerky self. Par for the course in Isaak World.

But instead, his features twist into thoughtfulness. "When did you first feel like a mother?"

I have no idea what's brought on the question, but it leaves me unexpectedly reeling. I realize that I haven't allowed myself to think of the early days of Jo's birth. I've deliberately stayed away from those memories because it was too painful to venture there.

The only way to survive my present was to disassociate from my past.

It's worked—thus far.

But God only knows what it's cost me.

Isaak is still looking at me. His usually stormy blue eyes seem smoother. Contemplative.

"Why are you asking now? After all this time?"

"Well, I recently found out I'm a father. Maybe that has something to do with it."

I decide to ignore the sarcasm. "I… it's a hard story for me to talk about."

"I don't doubt it. But tell me anyway."

I snort.

"What?" he demands.

"Bossing people around just comes naturally to you, doesn't it? Sometimes, I don't even think you realize what you're doing."

He rolls his eyes and steers me in the opposite direction. His hand is on the small of my back, and every part of my body tingles immediately.

I shrug out from under his touch, but I keep pace with him as he leads me to the main body of the mansion.

"You might as well get used to it."

I give him some major side-eye. "I'm never going to get used to it, Isaak. So stop asking and stop expecting it."

He sighs. "Things will be a lot easier if you do."

"For you."

"Exactly."

"Have you ever considered that compromising with me might be the smartest way to avoid an argument?"

His face breaks into a sexy smile, but he doesn't say anything.

"What?"

He shrugs. "I was just thinking… it would be a pity if we stopped fighting completely."

A blush creeps up my cheeks. He chooses that moment to look at me. I try to hide behind my curtain of hair, but his low chuckle tells me that he knows exactly how self-conscious he's just made me.

"Shut up," I snap irritably.

He laughs and leads me into the garden through a door I missed earlier when I'd passed through this foyer.

"I've already seen this part of the gardens," I tell him.

"Trust me" is all he says.

He leads me through a familiar path I'd taken only an hour ago. Then he makes a left that takes us down a relatively narrow path. One I definitely haven't been down before.

"Where are you taking me?"

"Somewhere special."

"Oh God, you're going to kill me and dispose of my body, aren't you?"

His only response is an annoyed glare. I suppress my laugh and follow him. The path we're on opens out into an intimate, circular clearing.

A rock wall rises up on one side. Water cascades like a veil down the dappled stone and collects into a skinny water feature that wraps around the perimeter of the circle.

Topiary sculptures stand opposite the wall, staring it down across the open space. Each has a light at its base illuminating the faces carved into the hedges with an artful touch.

The trees above are strung with fairy lights and it feels like every flower in the world has been bred in this tiny space to jostle with one another for the soft sunlight.

"Wow… this is amazing," I breathe.

"Yeah," Isaak agrees. "My gardener is somewhat of an artist."

"You didn't design this?"

"Gardening isn't exactly a hobby of mine," he drawls. "I gave him free rein and an endless budget. He gave me this."

I sit down on the ornate bench that faces the water wall. Isaak joins me there. He doesn't sit too close, but I can still feel the heat radiating off him.

The air between us is charged, just like it always is, but it's not tense in the way I'm used to.

Of course, I know from experience that it only takes the one word or one look to blow up the relative peace between us. I decide not to worry about that until I have to.

"Are you going to answer my question?" he asks.

So he hasn't forgotten.

I take a moment. I let myself fall into the headspace I was in six and a half years ago, when I first found out I was pregnant.

"I think I felt like a mother the day I knew for certain she was real," I admit shyly. "It was the day I found out she was a girl. I was about five months pregnant."

"What did it feel like before then?"

"Honestly, I don't remember a lot of those first few months. I was scared and alone and I had this big decision to make. I think I blocked most of it out."

"Self-preservation?"

I nod. "When I found out I was pregnant, I was already almost three months along."

"That far in?"

"I know; it sounds really stupid," I say. "But I was put in the Witness Protection Program after… after everything, and I was moved to England shortly after that. I was trying to get my bearings and I was trying to accept my new reality. I was also trying to recover from the trauma of my kidnapping. The fact that I hadn't gotten a period in three months just didn't factor high on my list of priorities."

"How'd you realize you were pregnant?"

"Scarily," I say with a nervous laugh. "I had this sharp pain in my stomach and I assumed I'd caught a bug of some sort. I visited the doctor and he ran some tests. Then he came back and dropped the bomb."

"That must have been some revelation."

"It's a little embarrassing to think about now," I tell him. "But when the doctor told me, I laughed. Straight up laughed, right in his face. I told him it wasn't possible that I was pregnant because I hadn't had sex in over a year."

He gives me a mock offended look. "Wow, you'd forgotten about me already?"

"I was in shock," I clarify.

I stop short of telling him that I thought about him every day back then. Even before I knew I was carrying his baby.

"Then when it sunk in, I felt…"

"Pissed?"

"That," I agree. "And sad and happy and emotional and relieved and every feeling in the book. I took another two months to process it. I think it only really sunk in when they told me I was having a girl." I pause for breath. "It took me another few months to make the decision to give her up."

He's watching me carefully, but I'm so lost in my story that I don't feel self-conscious at all.

"Feeling her kick for the first time was pretty amazing, too, though."

He nods. "It must have been."

His responses strike me as strange. Every time I expect an accusation or a lash of anger, he does the opposite and gives me sympathy instead.

It's unsettling. Too tempting to trust in his calm. I'm nervous to get overly comfortable with Isaak, and jaded enough to anticipate that this pleasant conversation might be a trick that lands us right back to our usual state of play.

Which is, of course, anger, resentment, and a whole heap of sexual tension.

"I used to talk to her a lot," I continue. "But that was also because she was the only one I had to talk to for a lot of the time. She couldn't talk back, obviously, but I just wanted to tell her things. I told her about her aunt and uncle. Her cousins. I talked about my parents and what life was like growing up in the Midwest. I gave her my entire life story and hoped that some small part of her would retain the memory of my voice when I wasn't with her."

"She was listening," he murmurs, almost to himself more than me. "They're always listening."

I give him an odd look. He shakes his head and the moment passes.

"She was born in England?" he asks, a little more brusquely.

I shake my head. "Eric managed to move me back to the States when I was six months pregnant, so I got to spend my last trimester with my sister and her family."

It's oddly cathartic to tell Isaak my story. Not only because he's the kind of listener that doesn't interrupt or react apart from a nod here and there. But also because I've never really told anyone the whole thing start to finish before.

Bree knows a lot. Eric does, too. But they were there for a lot of it. The experience of explaining what I went through to someone who was removed from it feels like releasing a breath after long, agonizing minutes of holding it in.

"Those months were both wonderful and horrible in equal measure. I was wrestling with my decision to leave Jo with Bree. But I was also trying to soak up every little moment. It was amazing having Bree with me. It was amazing to have people I could wake up to every morning. I wasn't just talking to myself anymore."

I take a deep breath, reliving that final month of my pregnancy. I used to read to the boys at night. And after they were sleeping, I'd struggle to my feet and go downstairs, where Bree would be waiting with a mug of hot chocolate.

Still to this day, I can't resist a cup of hot chocolate. It has a lot to do with the fact that I associate the drink with her.

With safety.

With the comfort of family.

"Was your sister with you when you gave birth?" Isaak asks, breaking through my reverie.

"She was," I say with a nod. "She was right there in the delivery room, holding my hand and telling me to breathe through the pain. You know, it's funny… I remember that labor was painful, but I can't pinpoint the exact kind of pain anymore. It feels fleeting now. I know I screamed and cried and squeezed Bree's hand so hard that I gave her bruises and I'm fairly certain I swore that it was the worst mistake of life. But now… I think I could do it again."

The moment the words are out of my mouth, I realize the implication.

Blushing, I turn away. "What I mean is…"

"I know what you mean," Isaak says, graciously saving me from muddling through an explanation I'm not even sure I have handy.

Still fighting the rush of blood to my cheeks, I launch back into my story.

"I was in labor for seven hours," I tell him. "She was born in the middle of the night. Three-forty-three in the morning. That's what they wrote on her birth certificate."

Isaak's cerulean eyes are gentle. His voice is, too. "What did she look like as she was born?"

I smile inwardly. "I know I'm supposed to say she looked like the most beautiful thing in the world. But the truth is, she looked like a mushy-faced alien with gross gunk all over her body."

He snorts with laughter, and I find myself angling my body in his direction. Instinctively opening up to him like a flower to the sun.

"They cleaned her up right after, though, and the second time I saw her—"

"She looked human?"

"I wouldn't go that far," I chuckle. "But she looked… like she belonged to me."

He doesn't say anything. I feel a strange bout of sympathy wash over me. I'd been robbed of so much of my time with Jo. But at least I had *some* moments to cling to.

When I miss her, I can close my eyes and go back to those first six months and imagine breastfeeding her to sleep. Or singing her awake. Or watching her smile for the first time.

I've gone over those memories so often, that they still stand out, as fresh and bright as if they were brand new.

Isaak has none of that.

"After they cleaned her up and put her into my arms, my first thought was… she looks like you."

Isaak's eyes meet mine and I feel the air around us prick up again. The tension tightens a notch, but it's not aggressive or bitter.

There's a bond that connects the two of us now. Jo connects us and it's the first time we're both acknowledging that. In some ways, it's hard to say all this to Isaak.

In other ways, it's the easiest thing I've ever done.

"She had a head full of dark hair. And the moment she opened her eyes, all I could see was blue."

"How did that make you feel?"

I understand why he's asking, but for a moment, I don't know what to say. The truth is too personal and he'd be able to spot a lie.

"It made me feel… overwhelmed," I say.

It's true enough, without giving away too much.

But I still remember almost tangibly what it felt like to realize how much my daughter looked like her father. It felt like that one night with Isaak became concrete in that moment. It was meaningful.

And in some strange way, I was glad that I had such a vibrant and beautiful memento of our time together.

"I think I appreciated those sleepless nights in a way most new mothers don't."

"Because you knew you'd have plenty of uninterrupted nights of sleep soon?" Isaak guesses.

I nod. "I knew I'd be alone and far away, longing to be woken up by my baby's cry."

"It must have been hard… leaving her behind."

The separation was the worst the first few months. Especially when my body reminded me at every turn of the baby I'd pushed into the world.

"It was the hardest thing I ever had to do. The only reason I was able to do it at all is because I was convinced it was the right thing for her. And because I knew that Bree and Jake would take care of her like she was their own."

"How did you explain it to Jo as she got older?"

"She's never known anything else," I explain. "She's always lived with her aunt and uncle and cousins. She knows she has a mother who she can't see all the time. It's her version of normal. Which is not to say she has struggles with it. She went through this period of nightmares that involved me. She had anxiety attacks when she first started going to school. It hasn't been easy, and I feel guilty every day that I'm not there for her. I also feel guilty for making it Bree's problem."

"I wish you had come to me then."

"How?" I ask. "I had no idea how to contact you. And honestly, even if I did, I wouldn't have. The agency told me all about the Bratva and what they—you—were involved in. I was terrified that the Bratva would get their hands on my child."

He stiffens a little when I say that, but I refuse to take back my words. They're the truth. He must see that.

"I wanted to give her a normal life, far from all the politics of the underworld."

"Underworld?" Isaak asks, raising his eyebrows.

I shrug. "It's how the agency refers to… your world."

I brace myself for the anger, the defensiveness. But neither come.

"Do you want to keep walking?" Isaak asks abruptly.

I don't know what has happened to change his demeanor so drastically, but I can't resist it. I can't resist him.

And that, at the moment, is my greatest fear.

Despite that, though, there's only one answer I can give. Only one answer I've *ever* been able to give to Isaak Vorobev.

"Yes," I say.

And when he offers me his hand to help me up onto my feet…

I take it.

13

ISAAK

She walks beside me. Her shoulders are straight and eyes forward, but she's still lost in old memories.

I want to crack her open and sift through each one like I'm hunting for diamonds.

"Where are we going?" she asks once we're walked a few minutes in silence.

"The hangar."

"The hangar?" she says, gaping at me. "You actually have an airplane on the property."

I smile. "It's just the name I use for my garage."

"Good Lord. How big is it?"

"You'll see."

I don't know why I'm taking her there in the first place. I think I'm just trying to prolong this moment. I have a feeling it'll be fleeting.

And not only because of the secret I'm keeping from her.

"Tell me about your childhood," she says as come up on the garage.

I frown. "What do you want to know?"

Her eyes flicker to the scars on my arm. "I know you had a complicated relationship with your father. But were you ever close with him? At any point?"

"No," I answer without hesitation.

She snorts. "Well, that was definitive."

"He was not really a man who understood how to connect with my brother or me. And honestly, I don't think he really wanted to."

"He didn't want to connect with his own sons?"

"The connection he was looking for was forged from blood and sweat and strength. He wanted Bogdan and me to be strong, to be powerful, to be so independent that we could handle everything the Bratva's enemies would ever throw at us."

"It sounds like he treated you both like projects."

I feel the instinct to be defensive, but I rein it in. My father doesn't deserve my devotion. Not after the lies and hypocrisy. It's still hard for me to reconcile the fact that he had killed his own brother after everything he had taught us about loyalty.

"We were his possessions," I say simply.

"That checks out."

I throw her a sharp glance and arch a questioning eyebrow. "Does it?"

She shrugs. "It just explains a lot."

"Like what?"

"The way you treat me sometimes," she says. Not angrily or sadly—just matter of fact. The way things are. I'm surprised by how physically those simple little words affect me.

"I may have some… control issues," I admit gruffly.

She snorts with laughter. *"May?"*

I roll my eyes and gesture towards the hangar. It really does resemble an industrial warehouse from the outside. Camila hasn't even registered it until now.

"Jesus," she says when she takes in the sight of all that metal arcing above us.

"Come on."

I lead her inside. As soon as our eyes adjust to the lowkey lighting, her eyes go wide with shock. "How many cars do you own?"

"Fifty-four in total. I'm acquiring another couple at the end of this month."

"Is there a reason you have so many?" she asks with a wry smile in the corner of her mouth. "Or is it an overcompensation thing?"

I give her a warning smile. "Careful. Keep talking about my dick and I might think you're trying to seduce me."

She stops the blush on her cheeks by biting down on her bottom lip. But all that does is get me stiff as a board.

Turning, I meander with her down the long aisle. She stares at the cars in awe.

"The north side of the hangar houses all the vehicles that we use often. The south side, though… that's where the special cars are kept."

"Special cars?"

"Convertibles from the 60s. First edition from the 1920s. Some have been restored and others have been preserved in their original condition."

She stops in front of one of my most expensive purchases from a few years ago. The woman has taste, I'll give her that.

"This one's a beauty," she says, running her hand along the nose of the car.

"It's a Bugatti Royale Kellner Coupe," I say. "Type 41."

She throws me a look over her shoulder. "Am I supposed to know what any of that means?"

"It's just the name of the car. This one was actually manufactured in the Great Depression. I was lucky to get my hands on it at all."

"How did you get it?" she asks. "Whacked someone for it?"

I glare at her. "Surprising as this may be, not everything I have has been built illegally."

She narrows her eyes at me. "But some things have?"

I shrug. "No one's perfect."

Chuckling, she runs a finger down the curving length of the car frame and observes the black canopy that hoods the passenger compartment. "Have you driven it?"

"Only once, when I first purchased it."

"How does it drive?"

"Better than you'd expect," I reply. "But nothing beats modern engines."

"If you say so."

I move closer to her and when she turns around, I can tell she's taken aback by my proximity. But she doesn't back away.

"Do you think about him?" she murmurs.

"Who?"

"Your father."

"Are we still talking about that?"

"You haven't really given me much," she points out.

"Because there's nothing much to tell."

"Isaak, c'mon…"

I sigh. "You want to know what he was really like? The truth was, he was an asshole. A fucking monster. He only had one shade to his personality, and that was alpha. I suppose it was fitting that he was murdered. Now that I think about it, there was no other way he could have gone."

When I look at Camila, she's staring at me with her mouth hanging open. "You think it was *fitting* that your father was murdered?"

"The stakes are always high in the Bratva. He knew the risks. We all did."

Of course, there's much more to the story, but I'm not prepared to get into all of it now. Especially not with Camila. She'd never understand, no matter how much I explained.

My world and hers are not the same.

"Did it hurt?" she asks. "When he punished you?"

"You can get used to pain."

"No," she says, shaking her head. "I'm not talking about physical pain."

I stiffen. "It was the only reality I knew. I started training when I was five years old. This life chose me."

"If you had a choice, would you stay in the Bratva or would you leave it?"

I shake my head and sigh. "You're not getting it. That's not a question I can even answer—because the Bratva is not a thing you can take or leave. I *am* Bratva. There's no other reality but this one."

She nods like she expected me to say that, and her shoulders slump. I wonder how much hope she had pinned on my answer to that question.

Because it's clear that I've disappointed her.

"I suppose I can relate," she says at last.

"Do tell."

"I am Jo's mother," she says softly. "I can't imagine an alternate version of life where I'm anything else but that."

She's looking down when she speaks, so I can't pick out the nuances of her expression. When she raises her eyes to mine, though, I'm surprised to see they're shining with tears.

"Camila…"

It's blindingly obvious how much it's hurting her to be so close to Jo and feel so far removed all the same. The years have taken a toll on her. She's reaching her breaking point.

But if I tell her where her daughter is right now, it'll undo all the progress we've made in the last hour. And selfishly, I want to hold onto that peace a little longer.

It may be an illusion, but it's one I want to bask in.

Even if that makes me a monster or a fucking masochist.

"I get it, Isaak," she says. "The Bratva is your life. But Jo is mine. I may not have been the best mother to her all these years, but I want to be. God, I want to be that so bad. I want at least the chance to be."

Almost unconsciously, my hand nestles along the curve of her neck, against her jaw. She looks up at me with tears swimming in her pearly green eyes.

"I don't want her to hate me," Camila whispers, unable to suppress her sob. "And I'm running out of time to convince her that I'm not just some absentee mom who's chasing freedom instead of providing for her."

"That's not what you're doing."

"But how is she going to know that?" Camila demands. "She's young now. She doesn't know any better. But one day, her questions are going to get harder to answer."

"Stop. You're only—"

She shakes her head. "My parents weren't the best all the time, but at least they were around. That's all a kid really wants, you know. For their parents to be there."

Her hand curls around my wrist. The same wrist that's locked against her neck. She looks up at me with those fucking devastated eyes.

And when she does, I can't stop myself.

My lips fall against hers. Heavily, desperately, hungrily. She gasps and her lips part instantly.

I open the door to the Bugatti and push her inside. She lands silently on the cushioned back seat, but her hooded eyes are fixed on me, burning with the same desire that I'm feeling.

She balances on her elbows as she straightens up. There's a second of hesitation that flashes across her eyes like a shooting star. Then, in the next second, it's gone.

She starts fumbling with the zipper of my pants as she struggles to get them off as fast as she can. With some help, she manages to push my pants down around my ass.

I push her further into the car and climb in after her. It's a fucking spacious vehicle, but I'm a big man, and it feels like every time I move, I hit something.

I don't give a flying fuck, though. The only thing I'm concerned with is being inside her.

I claw at Cami, parting her clothes without removing them completely. I crush her against my chest as I pepper her neck with kisses.

"Fuck, Isaak… Isaak… Wait."

I break away for a moment and look down at her. "What?" I growl.

"I… I'm so confused right now… I don't know if we should be doing this…"

"Then tell me to stop. Tell me to get off you."

If that's what she really wants, she has to be willing to say the fucking words. Her eyes flash with regret. She's weak to this and I know it. She knows it. The whole goddamn world knows it.

There's no turning back for us.

I grind the head of my cock against her glistening pussy and she moans, her eyes rolling back into her skull.

"You want me to stop, *kiska*? You've got to make me believe it."

My lips come back down against her neck and she moans again as she rubs her pussy against the hard length of my cock. Her fingertips run down my abs.

I make quick work of her bra. The moment her tits pop free, I grab one taut nipple in my mouth and suck hard.

"Fuck… ah… God…"

She gasps in successive bursts of adrenaline, as though she's not quite sure how to express the full intensity of what she's experiencing.

"Stop" isn't even in her vocabulary anymore. The only way forward is through.

So, unable to contain myself any longer, I push her panties aside and ram myself into her.

She cries out. It's loud and desperate and the hottest fucking thing I've ever heard.

She clenches around me and I revel in how tight she is. I fuck her slow at first as she adapts to me, but it takes only a handful of strokes before she's cupping my hip and urging me into her harder and faster.

She bites at her own wrist as she tries to stifle her cries. But two, three, four thrusts later, that won't work anymore, and her hand falls to her side as her moans echo louder and louder around the cabin of the car.

Her orgasm is loud and messy and has her writhing underneath me like some wild animal struggling to get free. As soon as it hits her, she grabs hold of me and refuses to let go until it's done with her.

I keep fucking her the whole time until I'm right on the edge, too. I explode with a guttural roar. She doesn't let me go for even a second.

My body is like one raw nerve ending exploding in sensation. But nothing can compare to the look in her eyes when I erupt inside of her.

I thrust into her a few more times before finally going limp.

Her body is damp with sweat. I'm not sure if it's hers or mine.

I slide backwards out of the car and cool air hits me from all sides. I zip myself back up. In the backseat, Camila scrambles to pull her clothes back into place.

"Will that increase the value of the car or decrease it?" she asks suddenly.

I snort with laughter. She offers me a sly smile that threatens to get me hard all over again. Chuckling, she slides down the length of the seat and throws her legs out of the car.

But then she hesitates for a moment, looking up at me. The hangar is quiet, no one else in sight. Just a pair of green eyes, gazing into mine and hoping to find things in there that may not even exist.

I could tell her right now. I could tell her the truth and be done with it.

But I can't give her that concession just yet. So I decide to give her something else. Something that will buy me a little more time.

Until I can figure out how to best package the secret that I must tell her one day.

"Camila."

"Yes?" she asks, looking at me cautiously.

"I will allow a conversation between you and Maxim."

Her eyebrows hit the roof. "You… you will?"

I nod. "But there's going to be rules and conditions. If you want this meeting to happen, you're going to agree to my terms."

She looks at me with a dumbfounded expression. "But… why would you allow it?" she asks.

"Think of it as a peace offering."

14

ISAAK

SOMETIME LATER

She's sitting on the lawn surrounded by a bunch of books.

She probably has no idea that I have a bird's eye view of her. And I'm glad that's the case. She's lying flat on her belly, with her bare feet crossed at the ankles and thrust up into the air.

Her blonde hair cascades down either shoulder in soft waves. She's wearing a white cotton dress that clings to her body. But what she doesn't know is that the sunlight streaming down on her has turned her skirt see-through.

I can see the pale blue of the underwear she's wearing. As well as the perfect apple of her left ass cheek.

She has this way of keeping a finger against her bottom lip, as though she's thinking deeply about every single thing she reads.

Add it all up, and I'm hard as a fucking rock. Have been since I noticed her lying out there.

Before I can give into my animalistic desire for Camila and jerk off while watching her, there's a knock on the door.

"*Blyat'*," I growl, turning from the window. "What is it?"

The door swings open and Mama walks in. She looks wary, even a little panicked, as she strides up to my desk, ignoring both chairs in front of it.

"Is it true?" she demands.

I sigh inwardly. "Am I supposed to know what you're talking about?"

"Maxim," she says. "Is it true that you're going to let him walk in here?"

I sit down and lean back in my chair so that I can still keep an eye on Camila in my peripheral vision. "Yeah, it's true," I reply with a curt nod.

"Why on earth would you allow that?" she asks. "Did the last time teach you nothing?"

I narrow my eyes at her. "Last time was necessary."

"He nearly killed you!"

I snort. "Killed me? Don't be silly. He didn't even get close. I was the one who had him under my fucking thumb."

"Yet he's still alive, isn't he?" Mama retorts. "He's still around, still posing a problem."

I narrow my eyes and lean in a little. "He's still alive because I had a blood debt to repay. One that was not mine to take on."

She tenses instantly, her eyes sliding away from me guiltily. "I didn't tell you because—"

"You were being selfish."

"Selfish?" she repeats, recoiling with insult. "It wasn't selfishness that made me hide the truth from you boys all these years."

"Then what was it?" I demand sardonically. "I'm dying to know."

She's quiet for a long moment. The look in her eyes hints at a trauma that she's still not fully worked through.

"Do you know how long I've kept your father's secrets?" she asks finally, an uncharacteristic shiver in her voice.

"Otets has been dead for a long fucking time," I remind her coldly. "You're going to hide behind a corpse now?"

Her back straightens. "You're my son, Isaak. And I will always love you. But sometimes… you remind me so much of him."

She spits out the last word, turning it into a blade. A killing blow.

Unfortunately for her, I'm well-versed in sparring. Both verbally and physically.

"Why do you sound so surprised?" I ask. "I am his son. I am what you allowed him to make me."

She does a double take, her eyes flooding with hurt and guilt. The wording had been deliberate on my part, but now I regret it.

Not because it's a lie, but because this is not a conversation I'm willing to have.

"I was powerless to stop him," she whispers. Now, there's an audible tremble in her voice. "I tried… It may have seemed like I had power on the outside. But whatever authority I had was only what he allowed me to have. I was not a person while Vitaly lived, Isaak. I was his tool, his pawn, his possession. I was whatever he needed me to be whenever he needed it."

Her eyes are misty. I'm frowning. I can't remember the last time I saw my mother so distraught.

"Maybe I should have fought harder. But I was so young when I married him. And he made sure I would fear him. That fear exists inside me, even to this day."

"And that fear is why you didn't tell Bogdan or me the truth?"

"In part. And just… habit. Inertia. I had kept the secret for so long. When he died, I just… I continued on."

"Then why tell us when you did?"

"Because you deserved to know," she says with a tired sigh. "And because I have so much guilt built up inside me that I wanted to alleviate some of the weight of carrying so much."

It's an honest answer. Enough to make me back down—just a little.

"Sit," I tell her sharply.

She hesitates for a moment. Then she lets out a long breath and sinks into the chair right behind her.

"Want a drink?"

Her eyebrows go up. "That was a one-time thing," she says, blushing. "I'm not a drinker."

"You used to be."

"Because your father wanted me to appear a certain way in front of his colleagues. He wanted me to be confident and witty with them. But docile and obedient with him. I was constantly terrified of mixing personalities. Sometimes, it happened. If I decided to talk back to him, he'd punish me. If I turned submissive at one of his gatherings, he misinterpreted it as coyness. And he'd punish me for that, too. I was constantly walking a tightrope with him."

I can appreciate what she went through, but even I can admit that I can't relate. I've never been anything but in control.

I've felt pain, insult, and injury, but I learned over time to manage them all.

Until I mastered them.

But my mother never had that option. She was bound by the restrictions her sex placed on her. I glance automatically towards the window.

Camila's still on the grass, but she's turned around now so that she's on her back, facing the sky. She's holding a book up with one hand, two fingers balancing the spine.

"I want it to be different with you, Isaak," Mama says, forcing my eyes back to her. "I want you to have more than just a marriage of convenience. I want you to have a true partnership. And I think you can, too."

My immediate instinct is to change the subject. "The only true partnership I have is with myself."

She sighs. "You might be Vitaly's son in name," she says gently. "But you don't have to try and mimic the man at every turn."

I bristle instantly. I'm pretty sure Mama knows she's gone too far. "I'm not fucking mimicking anyone. I am what I am. I was always meant to be this way."

"I suppose we'll never know now," she murmurs. She stares off into the corner for a moment, lost in her thoughts and her regrets.

I scowl and watch Camila lying motionless and blissful on the lawn. Even now, it's a stark reminder that her world and mine are lightyears apart.

She still has the capacity to lie in a meadow and lose herself in a book. To be happy.

If I ever had that power, it's long gone now.

"Can you tell me why you're allowing Maxim into this house?" Mama says.

"Because it's my house," I growl. "And I make the decisions here."

She sighs. "Fine. No one is questioning that; you make the decisions. Can I at least know why?"

"Because Camila needs closure," I growl. "And I want to give her that before I kill the motherfucker once and for all."

"Have you extended the invitation?"

"Not yet."

"I'm assuming he has to walk in alone, unarmed?"

"Yes."

"And you think he'll agree to that?"

"He will," I say confidently. "It's the only way for him to get to Camila."

She frowns.

"I know Maxim," I explain. "He's going to risk walking in here if it means getting the upper hand. He'll try to convince Camila to come with him, to choose him."

Mama's frown deepens. "You're working off a lot of assumptions," she points out. "What if Camila does choose to be with him over you?"

I smirk. "I know her, too."

Mama looks troubled. "She's in love with you."

Excitement and adrenaline snake down my spine. I wouldn't have put it that way, but the words make me feel infinitely powerful.

And not in the way I'm accustomed to.

It's a different power, love. It's softer. But maybe more durable for it.

"She'll never choose Maxim over me. Even her request to talk to him was an attempt at making me jealous."

She considers that. "You could kill him afterwards, when he's walking out," she says slowly.

I raise my eyebrows. "But I won't."

"It would be so easy…"

"Despite what you and Camila seem to think, I'm not so egotistical that I assume I'm completely unpredictable to Maxim. If I was, he'd never accept my invitation here. He knows I'd never go back on my word of safe passage."

"He's broken his word to you," Mama reminds me. "Your last appointment with him was supposed to be a gentleman's meeting. He voided the agreement by concealing a weapon and attacking you."

"All true. But I will not stoop to his level. I'm a better man than he is."

"I have no doubt of that—"

"Then why ask me to do something that will prove otherwise?" I interrupt harshly.

She sighs. "Because I don't want things to backfire again. What if this time, he manages to really hurt you?"

"Is this maternal concern, or tactical?"

She glares at me. "Can't it be both? Is that so hard to believe?"

I know I'm being unfair to her. Just because she didn't stand between us and Otets when we were boys doesn't mean she doesn't care about us at all.

But I'm not sure how to undo a feeling that I've built up over a lifetime.

"No," I grumble. "No, it's not."

"I just…" She taps her nails on the armrest of the chair. "I don't trust Maxim. Or his mother."

"His mother?" I ask. "When did she become a part of this?"

"Make no mistake: she has always been. She is the hand guiding Maxim into all his decisions. You don't know Svetlana like I do."

"What happened between the two of you?" I ask.

She hesitates—just like I expect her to.

There's something hidden here.

"You were sisters-in-law, living under the same roof, working towards the same goal. Even if you weren't friends, you should have been allies."

"I don't think you're in a position to be lecturing me about allies, Isaak."

I didn't expect her to bite back. It's almost refreshing to see the steel in her eyes. Maybe I haven't inherited all my fight from Otets alone.

I'm surprised by how comforting that is.

"Well, well. I bet that's an interesting story," I say. "Care to share it with me?"

"Not today."

"Why am I not surprised?"

She sighs. "I don't want you exposed to them."

I frown. "Mama, are you forgetting who I am?"

"You are my son."

"And that's the problem," I say with a nod. "You're thinking of me as your son. You're seeing a boy, a four-year-old who still needs you. I'm not that kid anymore. I haven't been for a long time. I am a don first, second, and third. And then come the other roles. Son, brother, friend."

"And what about husband?" Mama asks pointedly. "What about father?"

"Being both of those things are dependent on being a good don. A strong don."

She shakes her head. "If you want a family, Isaak—a real family—then you're going to have to make concessions. You're going to have to prioritize."

I frown, wondering how much Mama has been talking to Camila. My wife had used the same words on me not long ago.

"I don't have to do anything of the sort."

"I feel the distance between us, son. I have since the moment your father wrestled you from the nursery and put you in that training ring. But that doesn't mean I don't still know you. You want a family—"

"You are delusional," I snap before she can finish her sentence. "The only thing I want right now is to deal with Maxim, and remove him from the board. That is my only priority."

Mama regards me carefully and sighs. "Denial may seem convenient in the moment, Isaak. But in the long run, it causes more damage than is necessary. Trust me—I wish sometimes I hadn't lived such a lie."

I narrow my eyes at her. "If that's what you wanted, then you shouldn't have turned a blind eye while Otets killed his own brother."

Her eyes go wide with hurt. She rises to her feet.

"You think I knew Vitaly was going to kill Yakov?"

"Didn't you?"

"Of course not. Of course not!"

The very insinuation seems to cause her grave insult. I take note of that as I watch her fingers twitch involuntarily. She takes a breath after a moment.

"Don't assume, Isaak. You don't know the whole story."

"Whose fault is that?"

"Your father's," she says immediately. Then she sags forward. "And partly… mine."

"I'm glad you can recognize that."

"I only want what's best for you. For your future."

"The future is what I make it, Mama. Nothing more. Nothing less."

Her shoulders slump a little when she realizes I haven't changed my mind about anything. "Just remember, son: you are the rightful don."

"I know that already," I tell her dismissively. "Despite what Otets did to Yakov. I know I'm the right person to lead this Bratva. Maxim would have been as aimless a leader as his father."

Mama drops her eyes for a moment.

And in that moment, it becomes clear to me. "Svetlana knows, doesn't she?"

She meets my eyes again. "Knows what?"

"That Otets killed Yakov. She has proof. That's why the rumor spread so quickly. She knows what happened. That's why she hates you so much."

Her silence is confirmation enough.

But Mama's eyes are troubled when she replies.

"She knows some things. She suspects others. It's enough reason for her to hate me."

Secrets on secrets.

I'm not the only one in this house hiding things from the light.

15

CAMILA

The shower is hot as hell. Hot enough to scald. But for some reason, I'm finding a twisted kind of comfort in that right now.

Maybe I'm more masochistic than I realized.

Or maybe not. After a few minutes, I reduce the heat. But it takes a long time before the steam dissipates and I can see the rest of the bathroom again.

I've spent the entire morning thinking about all the transitory relationships in my life. Every time I form a connection, no matter how strong, it breaks. Then the vestiges of those relationships are blown away almost immediately, giving me no chance to grieve.

I've lost so much so soon, and I realize that I've grown accustomed to it. I run through the list of people I'd allowed myself to form attachments to over the last six years.

Elise and Harper, my first temporary caretakers before I was moved to London for the first time.

Alba. She was the woman who first hired me at the bookstore in Chelsea. Kind old lady with a glass eye—she loved popping it out to shock people.

Miguel, the building super who invited me to dinner with his wife and kids a few times, because apparently, I looked lonely.

Rudy and Lillian, of course.

Then the heavy hitters: Isaak, Eric, Maxim, Jake, Bree, their sons Peter and Sam.

And Jo. Always and forever Jo.

It's a long list, and at the same time, it strikes me as glaringly short. Have I opened myself up to so few? Have I lost the ability to trust and love and let people into my life?

"You should stop thinking so much."

"Aargh!"

I whip around in fright to discover that Isaak is standing in the bathroom, leaning against the closed bathroom door. He's got his hands crossed over his chest and one leg bent. He looks so damn calm, so damn confident.

His eyes scour my body unapologetically. They linger on my breasts and between my thighs, and everywhere they look, I feel a soft kind of heat spread through me.

By the time I unfreeze, it feels much too late to attempt to cover myself. In any case, I don't want to seem ridiculous by making the attempt at all.

He's seen me naked plenty of times. He was inside me literally yesterday. The memory heats up my cheeks, but I hope that Isaak is far enough away that he assumes my color has to do with the hot water, and not him.

"Why are you blushing?"

Goddamn him.

"How long have you been standing there?" I say instead.

He checks his watch. "About ten minutes," he says without any self-consciousness whatsoever. "You were so lost in your own head you didn't notice."

"A gentleman would have knocked."

He smirks. "I think we've already established that I'm no gentleman."

I roll my eyes and try to continue my shower. But no matter how hard I try, my body is too aware of him. I move stiffly, intent on washing off the soap quickly so that I can grab a towel and hide behind it.

"Introspection can be dangerous, you know," he warns teasingly. "Especially when you do it too much."

"What can I say? I like quiet self-reflection."

I try hard not to turn my back on him, but it happens inevitably. I swing back around quickly in time to see a small smile playing on his perfect mouth.

"Is there something urgent you need to speak to me about?" I ask with annoyance.

"Yes."

"Then would you care to get it over with and tell me?"

"I seem to have forgotten now."

I glare at him. "Isaak."

"Camila."

A rush of excitement shoots up my body. When it comes back down again, it settles between my legs. I can actually feel my center throbbing at this point. It's so intense that I'm worried Isaak will notice.

Which of course is impossible. Then again, Isaak sees things in me that I can barely see in myself. Who knows where the limits of his perception are?

Damn it, he's right. I do think too much.

"Would you care to wait in the room for me?" I ask. "I just have to dry myself off and get dressed."

I turn off the shower and slide the clear glass door open. I'm about to reach for the towel when he stops me with a curt, "No."

"No?" I repeat.

"Leave the towel. I like you wet."

The blush on my cheeks is fierce, but Isaak only smiles a little wider and pushes himself off the door with his bent leg.

My hand tightens around the towel. I'm about to draw it to my body, but he reaches out and takes it from me. He throws it carelessly to the opposite end of the bathroom.

"You're an ass," I say as he saunters closer.

"So you've told me. Multiple times."

"Don't you value privacy?"

"Mine? Yes. Yours? Not so much."

I roll my eyes. "Why are you here, Isaak?" I ask again.

He doesn't answer immediately. His eyes run once more over my body. My nipples are painful, and if this continues any longer, I'm almost certain my wetness is going to start seeping down my thighs.

"I'm here to tell you that the meeting has been set and agreed to."

His eyes are fixed on my nipples at this point, so it takes me a moment to register his words. "What meeting?"

Isaak lifts his eyes to mine. "The meeting you requested to have with Maxim."

I freeze with shock. "You contacted him?"

"Yes."

"Oh," I breathe. "Wow."

Never in a million years did I think Isaak would actually agree to this, let alone go through with it. I'm not sure if that's an encouraging sign or not.

Where has all his possessiveness gone? Where is the jealous rage?

"Where's this meeting taking place?"

"Right here. On my turf."

"Here?" I gawk at him.

"Not the bathroom, obviously," he teases.

I roll my eyes so hard they nearly get stuck in the back of my head. "I gathered that much, asshole."

He smirks and continues. "Maxim is required to come alone and unarmed. He'll be frisked at the gate and if he has so much as a sharpened pencil on him, he's going to be thrown right out on his ass."

"He… he actually agreed to all of that?"

"Without hesitation."

I stare at Isaak, both amazed and slightly disbelieving. Is this some sort of trick? I'm not sure who to distrust: Isaak or Maxim?

"Something wrong?"

"I… I just… didn't expect it to be so easy."

Isaak raises his eyebrows. "With him, or with me?"

"Give me back my towel," I tell him instead of answering.

"No."

I exhale with frustration. "You like saying that word a lot, huh?"

"People know what to ask for around me. And what not to ask for."

"I'm not about to put my life in service of your convenience, Isaak. I'm not going to change to fit your mold of me."

"What makes you think I have one?"

"Please. Men like you always do. You want me to be the quiet, passive, obedient wife. You want me to follow you around and service your every need."

It's an unfortunate moment to do it, but my eyes drop down and land on his crotch right when I say those words.

He gives me a knowing smile. That sexy, infuriating, lopsided smile he uses when he's really trying to disarm me. It's frustrating that, after everything, it still works so well.

I take a step back, but all that does is offer him an ever better view of my naked body.

"Don't think that anything has changed between us just because of what happened yesterday."

He feigns innocence. "What happened between us yesterday?"

"Stop it," I say, trying to move around him.

He grabs my arm and pulls me back to my previous position. Then he puts himself between me and the towel he's casually discarded on the floor.

"Isaak…" I warn.

"I told you: I like you wet."

As he says it, he reaches down between my legs and pushes two fingers against the folds of my pussy. He does it so fast and so smoothly that he's already inside me before I have the chance to move away.

I gasp as he forces me against the shower cubicle glass and passes a soft thumb over my clit.

"Hmm," he growls in my ear. "Apparently, you don't need any help getting there, *kiska*."

I gnash my teeth at him, but the effect is lost because at the same time, I involuntarily grind my pussy down against his fingers. His self-satisfied smirk gets wider.

I wish I had the willpower to resist this man. There's one thing I know about Isaak now: he's not about to force himself on me if that's really not what I want.

Except that I've never really been able to convince myself of that. I want him no matter what. Come hail or snow or hell or high water.

I don't know how to use his favorite word against him: *No.*

"Isaak… stop it," I say with a tremor. "Please stop touching me."

It's not wholly convincing, but I'm hoping it's enough to get him to back off. That's step one. Just a few inches of distance between us so I can think. So I can breathe.

"Why?" he growls, leaning in a little closer until all I can see are his too-blue eyes. "Would you rather Maxim touch you like this?"

My eyes flare with anger. It's so immediate and so intense, that even my desire for him takes a backseat. I put my hands on his chest and push him off me as hard as I can.

He doesn't so much as budge.

"You fucking asshole," I hiss.

He laughs. He fucking laughs in my face, with his fingers still knuckle deep inside me. And then he starts moving them.

A moan bursts through my lips as he presses me harder into the glass and finger fucks me until I've forgotten how fucking angry I am. At least momentarily.

He brings me towards the edge of an orgasm, and right when I'm on the cusp of coming, the sadistic bastard pulls out. I tumble down hard off the high without ever quite reaching the peak.

I'm even more furious because of it.

Isaak looks me dead in the eye while he sucks my juices off his fingers.

Then he walks away casually, as though this was his plan all along.

"What are you going for here, Isaak?" I demand.

I want to follow him, force him to look me in the eye and answer my questions. But my knees are weak and I know that if I try to walk right now, I'll fall. So I cling to the counter and yell desperately, angrily, hopelessly.

He turns to face me slowly, but he doesn't bother giving me an answer just yet.

"Is this just another game you're playing with me?" I ask. "Or is this your way of asserting dominance? Marking me before your cousin walks in here?"

He stands there silently.

"You're just a jealous animal, marking your territory."

He smiles, completely unfazed. "Maybe."

I grind my teeth and find my legs again to walk forward, suddenly completely unconcerned with my nakedness.

"It doesn't matter how many times you fuck me," I tell him. "You will never own me."

"No?" he asks. "That sounds like a challenge."

It's meant to piss me off. It works—on some level. But something in his face has another effect on me entirely.

Maybe it's because his eyes seem to burst. There's something fierce and demanding and aggressive about them right now. Like there's a storm raging inside him and he's trying to rein it in.

I know the feeling.

And apparently, so does my body.

I push him backwards and he goes easily this time. I don't even care that he's orchestrated this argument so perfectly, that he's issued a challenge that I can't back away from now.

I start stripping him of his clothes aggressively. He just stands there, all six foot-four of him, watching my every move. He doesn't try to help me. He doesn't say a word.

But I feel his eyes on me the whole fucking time. It pisses me off just as much as it turns me on. And I realize that's the curse the two of us are bound by.

My mouth fills with saliva the moment I free his hard cock. It almost slaps me in the face when I bend to pull his pants down his legs. He kicks his clothes away and I get back on my feet.

I slam the toilet seat shut and sit him down on top of it. The moment he's seated, I straddle his lap, aim him at my center, and then slam myself down on top of his cock.

He slides into me seamlessly. Perfectly. Inevitably. Same as he always has.

That's the other half of the curse.

His fingers find my ass as I start riding him. I'm so turned on at this point that there's no possibility of taking it slow. I don't have a plan or rhythm. I just crash my hips against him hard, taking him as deep as I can.

The pressure starts building almost immediately, but all that does is encourage me to ride him harder. I keep my hands fastened around his neck while he squeezes my ass possessively.

And somewhere in the middle of all that frenzied fucking, our eyes meet.

The electricity that passes between us is charged and unresolved and filled with the kind of heat that you only read about in books.

I'm powerless against it. I feel my heart shudder with warning.

You're going too far, Cami.

But I can't stop looking at him. And he can't stop looking back. Neither one of us looks away for even an instant.

Even when my body starts to complain, I ignore it and keep dropping myself on top of him again and again. Over and over, until the whimpers fly free from my lips and I don't actually care if every single person in this mansion can hear what he does to me.

"That's it, *kiska*," Isaak groans. I can tell from that timbre in his voice that he's close.

He removes one hand from my ass cheek and clamps it to my right breast. One squeeze and tug of my nipple is all it takes to send me cascading over the edge of my orgasm.

Is it possible to feel two opposing things at the same time?

To be both terrified and completely calm?

I decide it doesn't matter at this point. I'm going to take Isaak's advice and stop thinking. Because honestly, it's too late now.

I've already fallen down the rabbit hole.

Wait, no—not fallen.

"Fallen" implies that I didn't have a choice.

I didn't fall into Isaak Vorobev's world.

I jumped.

16

ISAAK

"He's here."

The first thing I notice is that Bogdan's usual smile is nowhere in sight when he steps into my office room.

The second thing I notice is how tensely he's holding himself. Like he's ready to pull out his weapons any second.

I get to my feet and round my desk to stand in front of my brother. "Where is he?"

"Waiting outside. I told him I'd get you."

Even his tone has changed. It's deeper, more guarded. He's warier than ever.

I, on the other hand, feel fucking fantastic. I smirk to myself, knowing what an insult it is to Maxim to be left outside the house like some common vagrant off the street.

"Has he been frisked?"

"Yes," Bogdan says regretfully. "Vlad did it himself."

We head out of my office together. "Where were you for that?" I ask as we walk. "It's not your style to give up the honors."

"Overseeing security," Bogdan says. "Maxim's men have been stationed a few miles out from us. It'll take them only ten minutes to get here. Five, if they fly."

"Which they will," I say without concern.

"Are we anticipating a fight?"

I shrug. "Maybe, maybe not. Either way, we're ready."

As we pass a window, I spy Maxim standing outside in the circular courtyard. Half a dozen of my men stand around him in a loose semi-circle. They've given him a wide berth, but their presence is just as menacing as I've intended.

Maxim's expression is controlled, but he's overcompensating. I can see even from here how tense he is. His eyes jump from side to side, waiting for something to go wrong. He's wearing a dark blue button-down and a pair of unnecessarily tight suit pants.

He runs a hand through his hair, and for a moment, I see a flash of the boy I used to spend time with when we were young.

It's gone almost instantly.

I can no longer reconcile the man he is with the innocent child he used to be. If I did, maybe there'd be hope for him.

But as it stands, this will only end when one of us is dead.

"Where's Camila?" Bogdan asks.

"In her room. I told her I'd come and get her when he was here."

"I can do it," Bogdan suggests.

"No," I say firmly. "I want to speak to her beforehand."

Camila wasn't far off the mark when she accused me of marking my territory. I need to make sure everything is set up perfectly before I'll allow Maxim to get anywhere near her.

"I still can't fucking believe you're allowing this," Bogdan mutters.

"She needs closure. And I want to get the measure of the man."

"You've already done that."

"I need to know how far his feelings for Camila run. He's risked a lot in coming here today."

It says a lot about how similarly we think that Bogdan doesn't suggest taking Maxim out where he stands. There is honor in our Bratva, but it has to come from the top.

I plan to be better than the man who made me.

I walk out into the courtyard with Bogdan by my side. Maxim's eyes snap to my face and narrow into slits.

"Cousin," he says coldly.

"You dressed up for me," I remark. "I'm flattered."

"Where is she?"

"In my bedroom."

Maxim doesn't miss the implication. He grits his teeth and his eyes dance with anger. "Where is she really?"

I smile a little wider. "What makes you think I'm lying?"

Wisely, he decides to drop the subject. True or not, nothing can be gained from fighting with me now. Especially when he's completely outnumbered.

"Bogdan," I say, gesturing my brother forward. "Frisk him."

"That's already been done," Maxim growls.

"But not in my presence."

Again, he grits his teeth, but again, he says nothing. He's forced to stand there and spread his arms wide while Bogdan checks him for weapons.

Bogdan takes longer than necessary, and when he's done, he gives Maxim a shove from the back so that my cousin stumbles forward towards me.

"I expected to be treated with respect when I came here," Maxim scowls at me. "But I suppose that was too much to expect from someone like you."

Before I can open my mouth, Bogdan is at Maxim's throat, wrenching him from behind into a chokehold.

"Listen to me, motherfucker: you're lucky you're not dead already. My brother had you. He let you live because you made a gentleman's agreement. He held up his end of the bargain, even when you didn't."

To his credit, Maxim stays calm and composed. "You expect sympathy, after what your father did to mine?"

"How much longer are you going to hide behind the actions of dead men?" I demand, my voice drowning out everyone else's. "Does it even matter anymore? My father is dead and so is yours. The only thing we can claim are our own actions."

Maxim shakes his head. "Spare me the lecture. I'm here to see my fiancée."

The words are definitely possessive, but more than that, they're meant to anger. I walk forward and grab Maxim by the collar.

This time, fear flashes across his eyes. I revel in the satisfaction of seeing him under my fucking foot.

"She's no longer your fiancée," I remind him. "She's my fucking wife." I twist him around and shove him forward. "Keep walking until I tell you to stop."

He looks back over his shoulder. "You promised me safety."

"Did I? I can't recall. My memory comes and goes."

His shoulders stiffen. "If I'm not back in two hours, my men will descend on this property and kill every single fucking person on the grounds."

"If I chose to kill you, Maxim, your corpse would be ash in the wind by the time your men got within the fucking zip code."

"You'd really go against your word?"

"You expect something from me that you yourself didn't stick to?"

"I was trying to avenge my father's death," he hisses.

"You did that by killing my father," I remind him.

"It won't be right until I've taken back my birthright."

"Jesus, not this fucking thing again," I say, rolling my eyes.

He trips on his way towards the hangar, and I laugh unreservedly. The bastard can only growl at me, giving the illusion of dominance, even though I can see through the façade.

He doesn't want to appear weak in front of me and my men.

It's probably another one of the reasons he agreed to all my conditions. Quite apart from earning an audience with Camila, he's hoping to repair his reputation in the eyes of the men who matter the most.

It's important for your men to respect you. But it is absolutely imperative that your enemies respect you.

I push him towards a little shed space next to the hangar. It's a single room that I've used for different purposes over the years.

Sometimes, it serves as a cell to hold an enemy. Other times, it's a storage space when we're moving high-risk products on the black market.

Today, it's going to be the meeting place for Maxim and Camila.

I open the door and gesture for him to go inside.

"She's not in here," he says suspiciously. He knows as well as I do that most men who walk into this room don't ever emerge alive.

"I'm going to go get her now," I tell him. "But before I do, I want to know one thing."

"What?" Maxim asks suspiciously.

"What did you hope to accomplish by coming here today?" I ask.

He's silent for a long moment. "You've been a worthy adversary all these years, Isaak," he says, turning his back on the door.

"I wish I could say the same."

He decides to ignore that. "I can understand why you consider yourself the superior leader. But you got a head start on me. And I didn't intend to let that last. So of course I pursued Camila. You can pretend she's just a way to stick it to me. But you forget, cousin: we grew up together. As much as you know about me, I know as much about you."

"Your point?"

"I have a history with Camila that you can't touch. I was with her for a long time."

I nod as the pieces click together. "You think you can convince her to leave with you."

"She's mad at me. Understandably so. But the feelings are still there."

"Don't project your state of mind on her," I snap. "Even if she was in that place once, she's not anymore."

An edge of doubt shimmers in Maxim's eyes. He's worried that he's overestimated Camila's feelings for him.

"So then you don't have anything to worry about, do you?"

I smile, but I can't help but be impressed. He's manipulated the situation perfectly, in such a way that I can't shrink from the challenge he's posing. If I cancel the meeting now, I look like a coward.

But I'm very fucking sure of my path.

"If she chooses me, will you respect her choice?" Maxim asks.

I smirk. "I have never forced any woman to be with me against her will. If Camila chooses you, she can leave with you."

That's exactly what he wanted to hear. And it makes me wonder: why is he so fucking confident in his chances?

Because for him to take a risk like this one, he must have some kind of trump that he thinks will seal the deal for him.

Time will tell what that is.

"Then the next hour will decide things, cousin."

I'm done with this bullshit banter. "Get inside," I tell him harshly.

The moment he's inside the shed, I shut the door on him and start heading back towards the house. Bogdan falls into step beside me as guards step up in front of the shed doors.

"Are you sure about this?"

"The *mudak* thinks he has me. I have to prove him wrong."

"This is out of your control, though," Bogdan points out. "This is up to Camila."

I glance at Bogdan. "Do you have so little faith in my charms, brother?"

Bogdan stops short and gives me a sheepish shrug. "You better hope your charms have worked on her. Camila isn't as easy to manipulate as other women have been."

I give Bogdan an unconcerned expression and head inside.

He's completely right about Camila, though. She's the most stubborn woman I've ever come across in my life. I would be fucking pissed—if I didn't respect her for it.

I push my way into her room without bothering to knock. She jerks to her feet. Clearly, she's been waiting for me. My eyes sweep over her body, and irritation colors my features as I walk over to her.

"What the fuck is this?" I ask, fingering the thin strap of the pretty powder blue dress she's wearing.

She slaps my hand away. "It's a dress, Isaak. I'm sure you've seen them before."

She's annoyed, but I can tell she's self-conscious, too. Because she knows exactly what's ticking me off right now: she's made a fucking effort.

For Maxim.

"It's an interesting choice," I say, circling her like a predator circles prey.

She stands still, trying to determine whether fighting is the best way to handle my current mood. "I just put on the first thing I saw, okay?"

I stop in front of her, examining the slight flush on her cheeks. I raise my hand and graze her jaw with my fingers. "And you decided to leave on the makeup you had on from the night before? Oh, wait… you weren't wearing makeup last night."

She shrugs away from me and puts some distance between us. "Can you please not pick a fight with me right now?"

"Someone's nervous for their big date."

"Are you jealous or just territorial?" she demands. "I suppose it doesn't matter. They're only a hair's breadth from one another."

The dress is tight around her chest, but the cleavage still manages to be conservative. Still, the fabric clings to her body, leaving little else to the imagination. The cutouts along the ribs don't help.

"Stop it," she snaps.

"What?"

"Examining me."

"I'll do whatever the fuck I want."

She snaps her mouth shut, and I can tell it's taking all of her willpower not to bite back at me.

For a long moment, it's easy to get lost in this. In drinking in the sight of my wife. Just like it was easy to get lost in all the build-up, the preparation for what happens next.

Somewhere along the way, I'd completely lost sight of the actual intent: which is that I have to lead Camila into a room with Maxim and then close the door on them.

For all my confidence… I can't control what will happen when that door snaps shut.

"Is he here?"

"Yes."

I scrutinize her expression, but other than apprehension, I can't pick up on anything else. I can't deny that she looks fucking beautiful, though. She's left her hair loose and relatively untouched. Her makeup is subtle at best, but it still irks me that she chose to put any on at all.

"Let's go," I say brusquely.

She follows me out of the room in silence. The entire way to the warehouse shed, her head moves from side to side as though she expects to run into Maxim at any moment.

"This is the first time you'll be seeing him since you found out the truth about him," I remark.

She nods slowly. "Is it stupid that I think I'm going to walk into that room and see a different man?"

The question is so innocent, so nerve-wracked, that I can't bring myself to be cruel or curt. "It's important that you see him for what he really is. Not Alex—he never existed. There is only Maxim Vorobev."

We reach the shed. Bogdan is stationed right outside. He walks forward and gives Camila a reassuring smile.

"If he tries anything at all, don't hesitate to call on us," he reassures her. "We'll take care of him."

She looks slightly alarmed by that. I realize that it hasn't even crossed her mind that something so confrontational could go down.

"I… I'm sure that won't be necessary," she stammers. But Bogdan's placed a kernel of doubt in her head now.

"You ready?" he asks.

She nods.

I walk her towards the door. The possessive beast in me roars for satisfaction. For primal claiming.

I've never said no to that inner monster before.

Today is not the day I start.

I act on instinct. Grabbing Cami by the arm, I spin her around and shove her back up against the very wall that Maxim is behind right at this moment.

She gasps, and the sound is barely out of her mouth before I'm sealing it in with a harsh kiss. I delve past her shocked lips, hot, heavy, aggressive.

Camila is tense, but she returns the kiss feverishly. It's what her body knows how to do. When the beast in me comes to eat, she offers herself up for the feast.

Despite this…

Despite Maxim…

Despite everything…

That has been the same from the very beginning.

When I pull away, her eyes are raging with uncertainty and confusion. I back off, never breaking eye contact, but she stays plastered against the wall. I'm aware that we're being watched by every single one of my guards, including my brother, but I don't give a fuck.

Let them watch. Let the whole world watch.

Cami is mine.

She straightens after a moment and clears her throat.

I walk forward and pull open the door. The room is bare except for two chairs and a single overhead light, just an exposed bulb on a wire.

Maxim is facing away from us. At the sound of our entry, he turns and looks.

His eyes lock on her immediately. I hate the way recognition and affection flare like fireworks in his eyes before he wipes them clean.

"Go on," I tell Camila.

Then I'm forced to stand there, denying every instinct in my body, as she walks towards him.

17

CAMILA

I can feel the ghost of Isaak's kiss still reverberating through me like an electric shock. It jerks me out of my head, where I've been living for the last god-knows-how-many hours, wondering what the hell is going to happen when I see Alex again.

I look at Isaak. His eyes are intense and stormy, the blue of his irises awash with emotions I can't quite place.

I'm not stupid—I know the kiss wasn't about love or hope or anything so storybook dramatic and foolish. It was just him trying to remind me who I belong to now.

I ought to fight back against that. I should've done it from the start. But Isaak Vorobev does things to me that no one else alive can do— make me want to submit.

So despite my heart hammering at my ribcage like a warning that I should've slapped him across the face and ran from his kiss, I found myself instead slipping into it. Giving myself up to him.

And loving every fucking second of it.

I slide my eyes over to the man in the shed. Alex, Maxim, Maxim, Alex—I don't even know anymore.

But it's him alright. The man who approached me in that library almost two years ago.

The same man that had pursued me furiously and refused to take no for an answer.

The same man that asked me to marry him amidst a sea of daffodils and roses.

Alex. That's the name that I associate with all those memories. But it's not Alex at all. The man standing just a few yards away with his hands clasped behind his back is Maxim Vorobev.

"Go on." Isaak's voice pushes me into the shed.

Then the door snaps shut.

And we're alone.

The light overhead is harsh enough to cast Maxim's face in sharp shadows. But I recognize him anyway, of course. His light blue eyes, his flowing blonde hair. His aristocratic nose and chin. He's a good-looking man, just not in the same way that Isaak is.

He's lost a little weight, I observe, as I take in his neatly pressed button-down shirt and the dark pants that seem a tad bit too tight.

The observation makes me want to laugh, but I'm present enough to realize that it has less to do with his pants and more to do with absurdity of this moment. Nothing feels real.

"Cami…" he whispers.

I flinch when he says my name as though he knows me. As though he's been waiting so long to say it.

He takes a step towards me and I back off immediately. He raises his arms and holds his ground.

"I'm sorry," he murmurs. "I don't mean to scare you."

"Scare me?" I repeat with a frown. "I'm not scared of you."

He considers that a moment, trying to read my mood, my current state of mind. Trying to find the Camila that he thought he knew. Thought he could manipulate.

I wish him the best of luck with that. Hell, I can't even find the old me. The last few months have changed everything.

I feel like a totally different person. So I can only imagine what Alex… fuck, what *Maxim* must be seeing when he looks at me now.

"You look… you look stunning," he says softly. "But then, you were always a beauty."

"Right," I acknowledge with a sarcastic nod. "And that's the reason you approached me, wasn't it? That's why you pursued me so relentlessly."

He sighs. "I wish you had found out a different way."

"Found out?" I say harshly. "Please, don't pretend like you were ever going to let me in on your master plan."

"Can I explain?"

I shrug. "What would be the point?"

"The point would be helping you understand my perspective. My story."

"It's kind of egotistical of you to think that I'd even care at this point. Scratch that: it's extremely egotistical."

He tenses, his expression teetering between uncertainty and impatience. "You listened to his side," he points out. "It's only fair that you listen to mine."

That gives me pause. "Fine," I say. "Go right ahead. But keep in mind: one single lie, and I'm walking out of here forever."

He nods solemnly. "Understood."

He takes a deep breath. I can tell he wants to get closer to me, but he's resisting the urge in order to respect my boundaries.

I can't help but compare to the man waiting outside. Isaak would never have allowed me that courtesy. He would have forced himself into my personal space and broken down my walls until I had no defenses left.

"It's true I came after you for no other reason than I wanted to get back at my cousin. Hit him where it hurt. He claimed that you two were strangers the night the restaurant was attacked."

I find it amusing that he refers to the worst night of my life that way. "The night the restaurant was attacked," as opposed to "the night I attacked the restaurant."

"He was telling the truth," I say.

Maxim's eyes knot together. That's all it takes to make me realize that he still doesn't really believe it.

"That night," I emphasize, "was the first time Isaak and I ever laid eyes on each other."

His frown deepens. "I watched the two of you the entire night… I saw the chemistry between you…"

"The whole night?" I ask.

"Well, part of the night," he concedes.

I nod. "Right. Because if you'd really been there the whole night, you would have seen that I was on a date with another man, and Isaak was dining with some other people. He left them to come save me from my horrible date."

Maxim sighs. "Whatever. It doesn't matter, Cami. Don't you see? My cousin has never approached a woman before. He usually just has women come to him. The fact that he even felt the need to approach you meant you were important."

"And you decided to take advantage."

"I was trying to avenge my father, Cami," he says, almost pleadingly. "Isaak's father killed mine. Vitaly killed his own brother to steal a title that was never his to take."

His tone is begging for understanding, but I'm not sure I can give it to him today. Maybe not tomorrow, either. Or ever.

"I was a pawn in your game."

"Yes," he says without shying away from the fact. "You were most certainly a pawn… at first."

He emphasizes the last two words. He keeps his eyes on me and lets those words linger in the air between us for a long time before he continues.

"I never expected to actually develop feelings for you."

"Don't," I interrupt, turning from him.

"Cami, I'm being honest here. Just look me in the eye and you'll know."

But I can't look him in the eye. Because whatever we had—whatever I *thought* we had—is broken. And I'm more and more convinced that what we had was never real in the first place.

I clung to a powerful man because I saw him as my only way out of a six-year nightmare.

Admitting that to myself feels like a betrayal.

But real truths hurt.

"Are you going to address the kidnapping?" I ask coldly.

He knows exactly what I'm talking about. It's obvious that he had hoped to avoid this topic altogether.

"Cami…"

"You kept me chained in a dank cellar for days. Then you had that… that awful woman come in to try and scare me into giving her information about Isaak. Information I didn't have."

"I miscalculated," he admits, dropping his eyes for a moment. "And like I said, you were just a pawn to me at that point. But it changed, Cami… Once I got to know you, it all changed."

"How did you even track me down?" I ask. "I was in the program for years when you walked into my life."

"I have friends on the inside," Maxim answers. The answer is just vague enough to still be secretive.

I turn my back on him and wrap my arms around myself. It suddenly feels cold in here.

I expected lies. I expected obfuscation. What I really didn't expect was to be confronted by so many old memories of us together, back when his name was still Alex.

Back when I had hope that I'd be reunited with my daughter again.

"Cami, please," says Maxim. "I know I betrayed you over and over again. I should have told you the truth and come clean. Then, at least you would have been prepared when Isaak entered the picture. It was my mistake and one I intend never to repeat."

I look over my shoulder at him. "You sound like you're asking me for a second chance."

"What if I am?"

I snort with disbelief. "You can't be serious."

He circles around and plants himself right in front of me. "I am a hundred percent serious, Cami. Why do you think I'd risk everything to come here today? Why do you think I'd come alone and unarmed, right into the lion's den? I'd risk it all for you. I'm here because I wanted to show you that."

"Isaak is a man of his word," I hear myself say as if it's another person's voice coming out of my mouth. "You came because you knew he wouldn't go against his word if he'd granted you safety while you were on his property."

Anger flits across Maxim's eyes. I wonder how much more he's suppressing for my benefit.

"Isaak?" he scoffs. "Isaak is not a man of his word. He's a snake, just like his father was before him."

"You're a little biased."

"And you've been brainwashed," he insists. "Cami, have you forgotten all our time together? Have you fallen out of love with me so easily?"

He sounds so forlorn, so broken by it, that it tugs at my guilty conscience.

How do I explain to him now that I wasn't as in love with him as he believes? Not even as *I* believed? Can it really be love if you can fall out of it so easily?

"Al—Maxim… everything is different now."

"Alex," he says with a deep sigh. "You were going to say Alex, weren't you?"

"I thought I'd made the transition in my head," I admit. "But seeing you now, all I see is Alex."

"That's just it, Cami: I want to be that man again. I want to be Alex for you. Some days, I wake up and I feel as though the persona I created for you is who I really am."

The sincerity in his eyes is what gets to me. It could still be an elaborate act, but it's hard to believe in the moment. It's like when you wake up from a pleasant dream, and for one brief moment, you can convince yourself that falling back to sleep will turn that dream into reality.

It's a self-delusion, though. The oldest trap in the book.

"Cami…" he croons, his fingers brushing against my arm.

I look down at the spot he's touching me, but I can't bring myself to feel much of anything. There's just a whole lot of confusion.

"I lied to you about so many things, Cami. From the beginning. But I never lied about my feelings. When I said I loved you for the first time, I meant it."

His words catapult me back to that day. We'd been in his penthouse apartment and he'd woken me up with breakfast in bed. I had just stuffed a huge bite of syrup-soaked pancakes into my mouth when he said it for the first time.

All I remember was feeling relieved that I couldn't speak immediately. Because I had no fucking idea what to say in return.

"I'm not sure it matters anymore, Maxim," I say, using his real name deliberately.

"Please don't say that. Please."

He grabs me and pulls me into his arms. I have to drop my hands, but they stay awkwardly at my sides. I know I shouldn't feel so guilty, but I can't seem to help it. Isaak's kiss still burns on my lips. Being in Maxim's arms feels… foreign. Wrong.

He must be able to sense that, because he pulls back. He doesn't release me, just holds me at arms' length so we're looking at each other.

"Cami," he whispers, "please… I just want you to be safe and happy."

"What if I told you I was both those things now?"

His expression freezes with shock. "You're lying." I try to shrug out of his hold, but his grip is strong. "You're just mad at me for lying to you," he says. "That's all this is. I know you love me, Cami. I know it."

I have nothing to give him.

"You've just forgotten… You've forgotten what we had. What we can still have…"

He leans in without warning and his lips brush against mine before I realize what's happening. I jerk away from him and back away.

"No… no, that's not what I want."

He's trying hard to control his anger, but he's slowly losing the battle. His face is souring by the second. Darkening. Glowering. "He really managed to get inside your head, didn't he?"

I grit my teeth. "Is it so hard to believe that I could have made certain conclusions on my own?"

"I know Isaak. He's skilled in deception."

"Yeah? Must be a family trait."

He bristles at that, but he doesn't reply. He just stands there, trying to calm himself down. It strikes me how different he is from Isaak. Maxim's emotions are always so close to the surface. But even in the hardest of situation, the most volatile of fights, Isaak maintains an eerie calm that forces the other person to unravel.

I realize now what a skill that is.

"Maybe I'm being unfair to you," I say, breaking the tense silence. "You're not the only one who kept secrets."

He frowns. "What are you talking about?"

"I have a child, Maxim." I say the words quickly, before I can lose my nerve.

A part of me wants to acknowledge my daughter at long last. But another part of me knows it might be the only way to force Maxim to let me go.

I have a child with his sworn enemy. Somehow, I don't think he'll love me enough to accept that. I don't think he's capable of it.

I close my eyes and brace myself for his anger.

Instead, he steps forward and takes my hand.

"Cami… I know."

My eyes wrench open. I feel all the shock I was expecting from him. "Uh… what?"

He nods. "I've known for a while now."

"But—"

He smiles. "I have my ways, Cami. Isaak's not the only powerful don here."

"You… knew?" I say again, still stuck on trying to process that.

"Of course I did."

"How long have you known?"

"Long enough," he replies vaguely.

"Isaak's the father," I say, waiting for a reaction.

He tenses, but his expression doesn't falter. "I suspected as much."

I can tell he's trying really hard to control his expression. Even his body language feels carefully orchestrated. As though he's aware that I'm dissecting his every move.

"Are you still going to stick with the story that you and Isaak were strangers that night?"

Ah. So there it is. He still thinks I'm lying, and considering the current topic we're discussing, I can understand why it would be hard to believe my story.

Then again, who can believe a connection like that unless they experience it themselves?

Every time I look back on that night in the restaurant, the details of certain moments stand out like a foghorn in the darkness.

I don't just remember snippets of our conversation. I remember Isaak's gestures, his smell. The look in his eyes when he was admiring me.

I can still feel the way it felt being so close to him. That heady feeling of knowing a man like him could be so enamored with a woman like me.

I knew in my bones from that very first moment that I didn't belong in his world. But he was drawing me in with every look, every touch, and I couldn't help falling forward just how he wanted me to.

I've read about that kind of thing my whole life. Love at first sight, that lightning bolt of feeling that cleaves your world in two.

Reading it is one thing.

Feeling it is something else entirely.

"I know it seems hard to believe," I stammer. "It's hard for me to believe, too."

Maxim hasn't moved. "Cami, I want you to know it doesn't matter to me. You have a child with him? I don't care."

"How can you not?" I demand. "He's your mortal enemy."

He smiles. "And you're the love of my life. This trumps that."

In another reality, I can see myself swooning at those words. I can see myself falling into his arms and being happy that I'm there.

But as it stands, I feel my heart constrict uncomfortably.

He doesn't seem to understand: it's too late. Isaak has worked his way into my head and my heart. It's made me realize that he was there all along.

"Maxim…"

He doesn't let me finish. He moves closer and grabs my hand. "I'm the only one who can protect you. I'm the only one who can keep you safe."

I try and move back, but he's gripping my hand a little too tightly. "Maxim, please…"

"You can't trust him, Cami," he insists, refusing to let me speak. "The only one you can count on is me."

"You don't—"

"Ask him where your daughter is," Maxim cuts in.

I stop short. "What?"

"Your daughter," he says again. "Ask him where she is."

I frown. "I don't understand."

"She's no longer with your sister, Cami. Someone took her. Care to guess who?"

18

CAMILA

Isaak has her.

Isaak has my daughter.

Isaak has Jo.

Looking back on it now, it all makes sense. I'd seen a child at the window of the west wing. Isaak had refused me any calls to my sister. I'd overheard Bogdan asking Isaak if he was going to tell me something.

Oh God. Oh God. Oh God.

I turn away from Maxim as the shock and the betrayal wash over me relentlessly. Isaak had taken her. He'd taken her like he'd taken me.

It was hard enough for me and I'm a grown ass woman.

But my baby... she's only five years old.

"She must be so scared," I whisper out loud.

Maxim's hand lands on my shoulder and I recoil away from him, feeling territorial about my space now. He doesn't push the issue. He drops his hand and looks at me sympathetically.

"I can help you, Cami. If you just let me, I can get you both out of here. Safely."

He stresses the last word, implying that staying here would be dangerous. At the moment, I'm inclined to believe him.

"Why? Why would he do this?"

"He's just like his father, Cami," Maxim says, grabbing both my arms and giving me a light shake. "He's manipulative and cunning and ruthless as fuck. He has no moral compass—"

"And you do?" I ask bitterly. "You're not exactly the Dalai fucking Lama, Maxim."

"I get it. You're mad at the world, and you have every right to be. But this is serious, Cami. We're talking about your life here. Your daughter's life."

I shake my head, trying to clear it. But it just keeps getting heavier and heavier. I feel like I'm drowning.

"He's going to use the girl to control you," Maxim continues. "He's going to use her as leverage to make you give him whatever he wants."

Would he do that to his own child, though?

I'm extremely aware that I'm too biased to properly answer a question like that. Even now, after everything that's just been revealed, I keep looking for justifications for him.

"He's probably got her hidden in some horrible location," Maxim suggests. "Waiting to reveal her at just the right time."

My eyes snap to his. Apparently, he doesn't know that Jo is right here on this property. Because now, I'm convinced she is. I remember the day that Isaak showed me his huge hangar.

Afterwards, when we were walking through the mansion, I'd caught him off-guard in that part of the house. He'd been in a strange mood, a mood that had prompted him to ask me tons of questions about motherhood. About Jo.

"Do you really think he would hurt her?" I ask.

"I don't know. I wish I could tell you confidently that he'd never hurt his own flesh and blood. But he's tried to kill me numerous times."

"That's different," I hear myself say. "You've tried to kill him numerous times, too."

A flash of anger flits across his eyes. "He's the one who took the first shot."

I'm almost tempted to correct him, but really, why bother? Why go to bat for a man who's been keeping a secret from me? A secret that he has no right to keep at all?

I try and remember to breathe, but everything in me feels like it's turned to stone.

"Cami…"

Maxim's fingers graze my cheek and I jerk again. He gives me a hurt look, but I can't bring myself to care. Where has it gotten me, trusting all these men?

They've only disappointed me, betrayed me, or both.

I have only myself to rely on.

I think about all the heroines that came before me, Jane Eyre and Elizabeth Bennet and my daughter's namesake. Sure, they may be fictional, but I believe and I have always believed that their real-life counterparts have existed.

That they still exist.

Maybe, if I'm brave enough… I can be one myself.

"Camila, I'm trying to help you."

"*Help me?*" I scoff. "The only reason you know me at all is because you were trying to use me."

"And I haven't denied that," he says quickly. "But I'm telling you now, what I feel for you is real. And if you come with me now, not only will I give you the life you deserve… I will make sure your daughter gets the life she deserves, too."

He definitely knows how to make an argument. For a moment, I find myself falling into the trap.

"Maxim, he's not going to let me just walk out of here with you," I point out.

He gives me a smile that's bordering on self-satisfied. "Actually, that's exactly what he'll do."

"What do you mean?"

"Just before you came in here, Isaak and I had a conversation. We came to an… agreement."

I grit my teeth and wait for the rest. Somehow, I know already that what he's about to say is going to piss me the hell off.

"If you choose to walk out of here with me, he's going to let you. The decision will be yours."

Yep.

I was right.

It does piss me off, but not in the way I expect.

"And those are my only choices?" I demand. "Pick one man or the other?"

Maxim's eyebrows knit together. "I—"

"Of course the two of you would talk and decide that my only options are you or him," I snap. "What if I don't want either one of you? Did that ever cross either of your sociopathic brains?"

"You need security," he says. "And I can provide you with that."

"So can he."

"But can you trust him?"

I laugh with irony. "Are you kidding me, *Alex*?"

"If you remember correctly, you gave me a fake name, too."

"I had a legitimate fucking reason for doing that," I snap. "And if you remember correctly, I told you the truth the moment it was getting serious between us."

"That's just my point! We got serious with each other. I fell for you and you fell for me."

He tries to move closer, but I'm not willing to let him near me anymore. I need space. I need my bruises to heal. I'm tired of the same old wounds getting pressed again and again.

"Be angry with me if you want. But trust me. Choose me and I'll get you out of here. Then we'll get your daughter back. Together."

He's really fucking good, I'll give him that.

"Maxim—"

Before I can give him my answer, the door flies open and Isaak storms in. It's the first time I've seen them together, standing only a few feet apart.

Maxim is almost as tall as Isaak. Even their builds are similar, though Isaak is broader in the shoulders and more built than his cousin.

Maxim's face is like Isaak's reflected in a rippling pond. The similarities are there, but they're subtle, blurred. Isaak is sharp and unrelenting and crisp. Maxim is a muddled imitation of him.

The moment they're in the same space, the atmosphere in the room shifts instantly. Tangibly. Like it's tightening, shrinking, all the available space condensing down and drawing the three of us closer together.

I take a deep breath, but it does nothing to alleviate the heaviness in my heart.

I can't help but stare at Isaak, wondering how he could spend all this time with me—how he could talk to me, smile with me, fuck me—and not once mention that he had my daughter under the same fucking roof.

I can feel the knife in my back. It hurts more than I could have ever imagined.

"Time's up," Isaak says coldly. "Maxim, time to go."

Maxim glances at me with a confidence that strikes me as insulting. He turns back to Isaak. "She's made her decision."

Isaak's blue eyes land on me. Why the hell does he have to be so heartbreakingly beautiful?

"And what is your decision, Cami?" he inquires.

Somehow, his confidence strikes me as less insulting. Probably because where he's concerned, my feelings have always been so close to the surface.

Not that he wouldn't have broken into my head if he had to.

"Cami…"

I glance between the two formidable men I'm trapped between. The impossibility of this moment is not lost on me. It feels surreal, and not in a good way.

"I have made my decision," I say, pushing both men out of my head, and focusing only on the one constant love of my life. "I'm choosing Isaak."

Maxim's eyes ripple with disbelief.

He had never been certain of my affection for him. He had never been certain I would choose him. But he had placed all his hope on the fact that I would choose Jo.

And he's absolutely right about that.

When it comes to choosing, I choose her. Every single fucking time.

But for all his planning and scheming, Maxim didn't know one tiny little detail that changes everything: my daughter is on this property.

And while she's here, there's no way I'm about to leave it.

I'm not choosing Maxim.

I'm not choosing Isaak, either. Not really.

I'm choosing my child.

"Y—you can't be serious," Maxim stutters.

"I'm sorry," I say, shaking my head, hoping he doesn't give anything away. "I'm sorry, Maxim. But I have to stay."

He moves forward, his hands reaching for me, until Isaak's arm flies through the air and latches onto Maxim's shoulder to root him in place.

"That's far enough," Isaak growls. "She made her choice. You made a deal."

"Don't fucking touch me," Maxim growls, shoving Isaak off.

Isaak looks unconcerned as he turns his head to the side and nods for his guards to approach through the open door.

Maxim ignores them to focus on me.

"Cami, please don't do this. You have options… You have a way out."

"I don't want a way out," I say softly.

He can't understand my reasoning. I can see the struggle in his eyes. But it's clear that he's understood one thing: he's badly miscalculated.

The moment Isaak's guards grab him, he starts struggling fiercely. Ignoring him, they pull him out of the shed and drag him towards the gates. The whole time, he keeps eye contact with me.

"Cami, please! You have to listen to me. He can't be trusted."

I can feel Isaak's eyes on me, studying my every move. I don't move my face at all. I just stand there, staring off after Maxim like it means nothing to me.

I hold my position, even after he's been dragged off past my line of vision.

"Camila," Isaak says gently, placing his hand on the small of my back.

I have to do everything in my power to keep my body from reacting to his touch. I want to shake him off me and scream accusations in his face.

But I have to be smarter about this.

"Are you okay?" he asks.

I don't even know how to begin answering that question. But I decide to go with a variation of the truth.

"It was… complicated."

"He tried to convince you to leave with him?"

"Yes."

"What else did he say to you?"

I shrug. "Nothing important."

I haven't looked him in the eye since his men dragged Maxim off. I know I probably should, but I can't bring myself to muster up enough strength.

"I... I think I want to be alone now," I say softly.

He drops his hand from my back. I feel just as much relief as I do disappointment. I'm not sure which one frightens me more.

"Okay. I'll get you back up to your bedroom."

"No," I say a little too fast. "That's not necessary. I know the way."

"I know you do, but—"

"Isaak," I say, cutting him off. "It's fine. I'm a big girl. I can take care of myself."

There's a frown in his eyes. It's edging into coldness. "What did he say to you in there?"

I shrug. "He told me this and that. He tried to convince me that he was the better choice. Basically, he told me a bunch of lies. But I'm not falling for anyone's lies. Not anymore. Not ever again."

19

ISAAK

She's not herself.

She walks and talks and reacts. But she's not really there. She's working off a set of pre-programmed responses that leave me feeling like I'm talking to a life-size doll.

Of course she insists that she can get up to her room on her own. But I don't take no for an answer. Because there's something very fucking wrong.

"Are you sure you're okay?" I ask, trying one last time to get her to open up to me.

She shakes her head.

I'm about to turn away when she stops me. "Isaak?"

"Yes?"

"I want to speak to my sister."

Her tone is tense and clipped, but her eyes betray the desperation she's feeling right now. I wish I could do something to alleviate some of that need… but I'm not about to change my plans for that.

"Not now."

Her expression hardens. "Why not?"

"Because Maxim and his men are probably attempting to track any call we make from his location."

"You have untraceable lines," she reminds me.

"I do... but even experts make mistakes. And Maxim has been in this house. I'm not taking any chances."

It's funny how weak my arguments are, but I offer them anyway. With all the confidence that I was taught would be my secret weapon if I mastered it.

She's not buying it, but she's not pushing back like she usually does, either. What the fuck has that son of a bitch filled her head with?

"When will I be allowed to speak to my sister?" she asks.

"When it's safe."

I'm aware it's a frustrating answer, but I can't predict the next few days. And until I have a solid plan in place, I'm not making promises I can't keep.

She opens her room door and walks inside. The rigidity of her posture tells me exactly how she's feeling. When she turns to me slowly, it's with a carefully controlled expression.

"Goodnight."

I can't help myself. "Camila, whatever he told you, it's not true."

"Do you know what he told me?"

"I will when you tell me."

"Does it matter?" she asks with a nonchalant shrug. "He's lying, right?"

"You seem very affected by the conversation."

"Wouldn't you be, too?" she asks. "After coming face to face with the person you were going to marry, only to discover that that person is a complete stranger?"

"I'd never be in that position," I say without thinking.

I don't mean it as a reprimand, but that's exactly how it comes out. She doesn't really react. Her expression stays stagnant.

"You're right," she says with a nod. "You'd never be in my position. You're always the one pulling all the strings."

I want to keep pressing. I see smoke in her eyes, and where there's smoke, there's fire. I ought to go hunting for the source.

But I force myself to wait. She needs to open up to me in her own time, when she's ready. I have no doubt that she will. This is just Camila's M.O. She runs hot and cold, teetering on the brink of extremes.

Sometimes, I wonder how she has the energy to keep all the emotion going.

"Goodnight, Camila."

She gives me a nod and closes the door on me. Feeling strangely dissatisfied, I head to the west wing of the house.

I turn the corner to find Mama walking toward me. I notice paint stains on her hands.

"Busy day?"

"How did it go?" she asks, ignoring my question.

"I'm not sure yet," I admit. "She seems… shaken."

"Of course she's shaken. Not only did you let him into the house, you gave them complete privacy. God knows what he told her."

"She's too smart to fall for his shit."

"Can you be sure of that?" Mama asks. "Because you haven't exactly been completely honest with her, either."

I exhale with frustration. "If you mean Jo—"

"Of course I mean Jo," she snaps. "That child needs some stability, Isaak. It would help if she could see her mother."

"I'm working on it," I snap right back. "This is a fucking delicate situation."

"Which could have been avoided if you'd just told Camila from the beginning."

"Jesus Christ, she wouldn't have listened then."

"And you think she'll listen now?"

I glare at Mama until she looks down, cowed by the intensity in my eyes.

"Do you think I do anything without having a good reason for it?" I press. "She needs to understand that I call the shots here. She thought she could keep my child from me. I need to show her that comes at a price."

"So that's what this is about?" Mama asks. "You're trying to teach her a lesson?"

I narrow my eyes. "She needs to know who I am."

"I think she already knows," Mama says coolly. "But for the record, I think you're going about this all wrong."

I roll my eyes. "You want me to play nice? Try and win her over?"

"It might be the smartest way forward."

"It's fucking weak," I snap.

"You're confusing Camila with one of your lieutenants," Mama says. "She's not an enemy whose fear and respect you need to earn. She's the mother of your child. And she may very well be the mother of your future children, too, if you play your cards right."

"That's just it," I growl. "It's not for me to play my cards right."

Mama sighs. She gives a resigned nod. "That's right. Because there can be no compromising for the don. Your father was the same way."

"Don't start that shit again."

"Isaak—"

"I'm done with this conversation. I'm only here to see my daughter. Who's with her?"

"Bogdan," Mama replies. "We're relieving the nanny until she's done with lunch."

I move around her and head straight for Jo's room. Before I even reach it, I hear her high-pitched giggle. Then there's another laugh, deeper and full of mirth.

Unable to keep the smile off my face, I stride into the room.

Bogdan's on all fours and Jo's on top of him, riding him like an elephant. "Faster, Bogie! Faster!"

"We really have to talk about that name, Jo."

I laugh. "I think it suits you perfectly."

Bogdan straightens up and Jo slides off his back. She looks at me with a cautious expression, but I can see the tentative smile at the corners of her mouth.

"Hey, kiddo," I say, moving onto the carpet. "Having fun?"

Her face breaks into a smile. "Bogie was being the pony and I was riding him."

Bogdan rolls his eyes. "I thought I was a camel."

"That was before."

"Oh."

Jo puts her hand on his shoulder as he talks and I note the ease with which they interact with one another. She's still not as free around me. But then again, I haven't put in the time that Mama and Bogdan have.

"Have you been painting?"

Jo nods vigorously. "You wanna see?"

"Of course."

She runs off towards the corner of the room to her little white table. There's a bunch of pictures sitting on the table to dry.

"She's quite the artist," Bogdan tells me. "Honestly, I think she may have some real talent."

When Jo brings her artwork over to me, I'm impressed to discover that it's not bias talking. Bogdan was totally right—the girl is talented. Her paintings are colorful and vibrant, and there's even some technique behind the finger-drawn shapes.

"Wow, Jo. This is pretty damn great."

She giggles and slaps a hand over her mouth.

"What?" I ask. "What did I say?"

"*Damn*," Jo repeats. "That's a bad word."

I frown. "I don't think so."

Bogdan snorts with laughter. "Apparently, her aunt has a whole list of bad words that the kids aren't allowed to say."

"Yeah," Jo says with another vigorous nod. "Like 'stupid' and 'ugly.' Those are bad words too."

I'm itching to correct her, but I decide not to mess with a rule that I'm fairly certain will make sense to anyone outside of my sphere of reality.

I didn't exactly have the most normal childhood in the world.

"Okay, I'll keep that in mind."

"Can I see my aunt soon?" Jo asks suddenly.

I find it interesting that she seems to know that I'm the person to ask. Perceptive. *Definitely my kid*, I think, pride coloring every facet of the thought.

How quickly things shift. I'm not prepared for it. But I am getting more and more ready to embrace it all.

"Not quite yet," I say as gently as I can. "But soon."

"Soon?" she asks.

"Yes."

"What about my mommy?"

"Soon."

She frowns as though she has less trust in this answer. "Soon?" she repeats again.

"Yes. Soon."

"You know where Mommy is?"

"I do."

"Tell me," she says.

Bogdan wags his eyebrows at me, clearly amused and impressed by the authority in Jo's tone. She's definitely got Camila's fire. Fuck, she's probably got mine as well.

"She's not far from here, actually. But we need to give her a little time."

"Why?"

"Because it's going to take her a little while to come around," I say, phrasing my words carefully.

"Oh. She doesn't want to see me?"

Her face falls instantly, and disappointment taints the glow in her eyes. I feel the urge to pull her into my arms, but I resist.

One, because I don't want to scare her.

And two, because I honestly don't know how to maneuver a gesture like that.

"Of course she does. You are the only thing that your mommy talks about."

"Really?" she asks, her face lighting up instantly.

"You're her favorite person in the world."

"So she'll come soon?"

"Definitely."

"Okay," she says, seemingly satisfied with that. "Excuse me."

I frown as she gets to her feet. "Where are you going?"

She blushes a little when she replies. "I have to pee."

She skitters over to the bathroom as Bogdan chuckles under his breath. "She's a character, that's for sure."

"*Blyat*'," I groan. "I have to tell her soon."

"Jo?"

"No, idiot. Camila."

"Oh. Well, yeah. You should have told her ages ago."

"Don't you start."

Bogdan smiles. "Mama already read you the riot act, huh?"

I nod. "She's fucking passionate about it."

"She's fallen in love with Jo already."

"I don't blame her."

"She seems pretty drawn to you," Bogdan points out. "I'm impressed, really. If I were five and faced with you, I'd want to run in the opposite direction."

"Fuck you, *sobrat*."

There's a little gasp from right behind us and I turn to see Jo standing there, staring at us with wide eyes. "You said another bad word!"

Bogdan starts laughing, while I try damage control.

"Um, I didn't say what you thought I said…"

"Yeah-huh. You said 'fuck.'"

Bogdan laughs harder, and I can't help admiring the clarity with which she pronounces the word. It's damn near professional.

"Um… okay, I did. My bad. It slipped out."

"That's no excuse," she says with a hand on her hip.

Bogdan actually snorts gracelessly, while I try to ignore him. It's hard to keep a straight face looking at Jo, too. With her lips pursed and her hip cocked, she looks like the spitting image of her mother when she's pissed.

"You're right. I'm sorry."

She smiles and softens. "That's okay. But don't use bad words, okay? You're smarter than that."

I raise my eyebrows. "Is that what your aunt says?"

"Not to me," she smiles. "But to Uncle Jake sometimes. And Pete."

"I'll try and do better."

Her smile gets wider and she walks over to me and pats my head. "That's a good job you're doing."

Her attempt at adult conversation has Bogdan cackling like a hyena. I roll my eyes at him and refrain from punching him in the stomach.

We play for a while. By the time I walk out of the room, I've managed to shake off the lingering gloom from Maxim's meeting entirely.

I'm about to head down the hallway when I hear footsteps. I know instantly they're hers. I round the corner and she comes to a standstill in front of me.

"Isaak."

"Camila," I say. "What are you doing here?"

She hesitates. "Um…"

I resist the urge to look back over my shoulder. Bogdan is still with Jo, and the two of them together have a tendency to get loud.

I need to get her out of the west wing as fast as possible, but I also need to be subtle about it.

The fact that I've caught her here twice now is starting to trouble me. Either it's just a coincidence, or else she's suspicious about something.

It's always possible that Maxim could have tipped her off. But how could he have known about Jo?

The only mole I can think of right now is Eric fucking Keller. The old man had seemed both sincere and concerned when we'd last met. But the best kind of moles are the ones you least expect.

"What are you doing here?" I ask.

She meets my gaze and her green eyes are sharp. Ready for another fight, my beauty. My body tenses, anticipating what's to come. My cock rises with excitement. Apparently, anger and desire aren't so far apart.

Her eyelashes flutter and my dick goes rigid.

"I was looking for… you," she says softly.

20

CAMI

His eyebrows rise. I cringe internally.

It's not the words themselves. It's what they imply.

That I need him. That I want him. That I can't be left alone for five minutes without searching for him.

It makes me feel weak. Camila Ferrara, professional damsel-in-distress.

"You were looking for me?"

"Um… yeah."

"Why?"

I take a deep breath, trying to make my excuse convincing. It's imperative that he doesn't suspect that I suspect. My plan hinges on him staying in the dark.

If he knows that I know about Jo, there's every possibility that he might move her to a different location. And if that happens, I'll never be able to find her.

"I… I guess I just didn't want to be alone," I say, settling on a truth I can't avoid.

He considers that for a moment. "Let me show you the wine cellar."

"The what?"

"Alcohol has a way of making you forget thoughts that won't leave you alone. You look like you could use some."

I chuckle. "Fair enough. Lead the way."

He steers me in the opposite direction. I resist the urge to look back over my shoulder. As we head towards the staircase, I'm pretty sure I hear a high-pitched laugh.

A laugh that's heartbreakingly familiar.

Jo.

But quite apart from being sad, I feel my heart lift. If she's laughing, she can't be so bad off here, can she? It still doesn't take away the sting of Isaak's betrayal, but it's a comfort to me all the same.

I fall behind him as we walk. Mostly so I'm free to ogle his broad shoulders to my heart's content. It strikes me that I shouldn't want to ogle him at all right now.

Or ever.

But my eyes still scale down his tall, athletic form.

He's a beast of a man, but there's finesse there, too. He's not brutish in his build. He's beautiful. He's what I imagine a Greek god would look like.

"You're staring."

I actually jump. I'm so shocked that even my blush is held hostage by the way he calls me out. He hasn't looked back at me once. And it's not like we've passed any mirrors.

"I... I wasn't."

But I don't even manage to convince myself.

"I can feel your eyes on me, *kiska*," he says.

"Someone has an ego."

He smirks before looking back ahead. "Given the way you're gawking at me, I'd say it's with good reason."

Great. As if he needed the self-esteem boost. I roll my eyes and try to act as though he's being ridiculous, but I know there's no real point.

He knows.

He knows everything.

I decide that there's a way I can spin this to my advantage. Flirting with him is only going to lull him into a false sense of security.

If I can relax him enough, maybe he'll talk. Maybe he'll tell me about Jo. And if that fails, then maybe all that wine we're about to consume will do the job for me.

Plausible? Sure, why not? But somehow, it feels like a long shot. Even under the influence of alcohol, I'm not sure Isaak is the type to ever lose control.

He's abnormal that way, free of weaknesses and vices that cripple other men.

His father cut those things out of him.

"Hey."

I look at him, realizing that I've stopped on the last stair.

"Coming?"

I swallow and follow him into the room. This place is dark, but there are peaks of brightness cast by the sharp gold lights hitched up onto the wall. As I round the corner, I see a double-height shelf staring back at me, filled with rack after rack of dusty wine bottles. Behind it, another dozen or more shelves stretch into the shadows, each similarly stocked.

"Wow," I breathe. A smoky scent hits me the moment I step through the archway.

Isaak slides the glass door shut behind us. All I can hear is the sound of each of us breathing. I take a seat on one of the massive ivory armchairs that sit next to each other on the right side of the room and admire the wine display.

"How much is all this worth?"

He gives me a smile.

"What? Is that a rude question to ask?"

He selects a bottle from the nearest rack and saunters over to the massive oak table on the left side of the room. He grabs a couple of glasses from a cabinet that I can't see and pops the cork.

"I haven't done the math in a long time," he says, pouring out two glasses. "But safe to say it's a big number."

"A million?"

He shrugs.

"Two? Five? Ten?"

"Something like that."

You'd think I wouldn't be impressed by his wealth anymore. I've seen his manors, his cars, his clothes. But for some reason, this is making my jaw drop. "Should you be opening that bottle? Isn't it enough to, like, finance a small country?"

Isaak laughs. In this closed space, it's the most beautiful sound I've ever heard. Then again, it sounds like that everywhere. "Wine is meant to be drunk," he says. "To be enjoyed."

"How expensive is that one?"

He answers without looking at the bottle. "This is a Jeroboam of Chateau Mouton-Rothschild. 1945," he says. "It costs around three hundred and ten thousand dollars."

"Jesus, Joseph, and Mary."

Isaak pours carefully, then fills a glass and walks it over to me. "Drink," he orders calmly. "Enjoy."

I watch him twirl the wine in his glass a few times as he sits down next to me. He looks so calm, so practiced, so confident. I've always felt like I'm just making shit up as I go when it comes to wine. But Isaak exudes expertise from every pore.

I watch as he sniffs. Sips. Closes his eyes and savors.

I'm fixated on that pouty bottom lip of his and the flicker of his tongue—so much so that he almost catches me staring.

Again.

"Are you going to try it?" he asks, eyes still closed. "Or are you just going to stare at me the whole time?"

I flush with color and curse how fucking transparent I'm being right now. I can try and justify my behavior by claiming my ulterior motive, but honestly, that's not the reason I'm doing it.

Isaak just breaks my brain like that.

I look at my glass and take a sip. I try to do it the way he did—hold it on my tongue, really letting those flavors seep into my taste buds before swallowing.

It's luxurious, that's for sure. I've always thought tasting fine wine could be described as drinking liquid velvet. It's a poetic phrase, but in this case, I feel it's more than appropriate.

I get hints of coffee, spice, and... fruit?

"Wow," I say. "That's… interesting."

"Do you like it?"

"I do," I say, staring at the wine because at least it means I'm not staring at him. "It's hard to pin down, though. There's a hint of something I can't quite put my finger on."

"Black fruit," he says immediately.

"Oh. Yes, duh. That's definitely it."

I take another sip and swirl it around in my mouth. The liquid seems to get richer as it sits on my tongue. When I glance at Isaak, his eyes are fixed on me.

It strikes me suddenly that drinking wine can be a very sensual experience. But then again, it might be less about the wine and more about the man I'm drinking it with.

"Now who's staring?" I counter.

He smiles. A sexy, seductive smile that defeats the purpose of me calling him out. He's shameless in his desire. Always has been.

"And I make no excuses about it," he says. "I enjoy staring at you."

"You do?"

"Don't play coy," he says immediately. "It doesn't suit you."

He's right. It doesn't, and I don't know why I tried. When I look down again, I realize my glass is almost empty. I compare our glasses immediately and realize his has barely been touched.

I frown.

"Something the matter?"

"No," I say, a little too quickly.

"It's not a competition, you know," he tells me. "Unless you're trying to get me drunk."

"Why would I be trying to get you drunk?"

He arches one eyebrow. "You tell me."

I shrug, and I'm proud of how I carry it off. "I've got nothing to hide." I manage to keep the bitterness out of my tone. But I'm not sure about my face.

Which is why I decide to take that moment to finish the tiny splash of wine at the bottom of the glass.

"How about a refill?" he offers.

He raises the bottle, but I eye his glass.

"I'll wait until you catch up."

He grabs his glass and throws back the priceless drink like it's a cheap shot in a dive bar. "There," he says. "How about now?"

I nod and he pours us both more wine. I vow to go slowly this time around, but it's hard with Isaak. Every time he looks at me with that seductive gaze of his, I feel the need to divert by drinking.

But all that does is undermine the reason I agreed to come down here with him in the first place.

"Tell me a secret," I blurt out when the silence gets too stifling.

He regards me with a cool expression. I'm not sure if he's wary, weary, or just amused. "A secret?" he repeats.

"Yeah. Something I don't know."

He glances off to the side as though he's trying to think. He's good. Really good. But I'm onto him now.

"The secrets I have will mean nothing to you."

I will myself to stay calm. "Give me something. Anything."

He takes a big sip of wine. "It might make you hate me."

I tense. "Tell me anyway."

He's going to tell me. He's going to say Jo's name, say she's here. My body is buzzing with anticipation. I'm actually more excited than I am angry. Because once he tells me... he's going to have to let me see her.

"... Maxim's assumption turned out to be accurate."

I do a double take. "I don't understand."

"His accusation that my father killed his... it's true."

I stare at him for a moment, letting that sink in. "Your father really did kill his?"

"Yes."

"To... become the don?"

"Yes."

I straighten a little. "And you denied it this whole time."

"Only because I believed it was a lie," Isaak explains.

His eyes are hooded, but I know him well enough now to know that he's trying to hide his discomfort, his regret. Maybe even some deep-seated disappointment.

"How did you find out?"

"My mother admitted the truth to Bogdan and me recently."

"Wow..."

He nods and finishes his second glass of wine much quicker than the first. I wonder if that's exactly the reason his tongue is starting to loosen. I lean in a little closer, but the unwieldy armchair I'm sitting in doesn't really have much give. I'm not as close as I want to be. Not intimate enough for the deepest secrets to wriggle their way free from the shadows.

"That must have been hard to wrap your head around," I say carefully. "Especially because of the way your father preached loyalty."

His eyes snap to mine. I see the naked surprise in them. He hasn't expected me to understand. Certainly not to this extent.

"Right… That's exactly how Bogdan and I feel."

"Hypocrisy is an easy trap to fall into," I suggest.

He nods thoughtfully, his hand still absentmindedly twirling his wine glass. How much has he had? I've lost count—along with my own alcohol intake.

There's no question I feel a little light-headed and woozy.

But it's the kind of feeling that makes me feel lighter, bouncier, more open to everything.

I'm also aware of just how beautiful his jawline is. Of the way his dark hair, slightly overgrown at the moment, curls softly at the back of his head. His blue eyes are deep and winding, a maze I would want to get lost in if I had the courage.

His gaze finds mine. For the first time, I neither turn away or blush. I hold his confident gaze with confidence of my own. The atmosphere prickles, little darting ropes of energy ensnaring me and coaxing me towards him.

"You're not giving him back the Bratva regardless, are you?"

Isaak shakes his head. "No. What my father did was disloyal, but there's no escaping the fact that he saved the Vorobevs from certain ruin."

"Would that have been so bad?" I ask.

He raises his eyebrows. "Do you know what ruin means in the Bratva?" he asks calmly. "We don't just pack up and go out of business. It means we die. Brutally."

I frown. "You're exaggerating."

"I'm not. Men who are loyal to a family, to a Bratva? They can't be allowed to live. Their enemies would never allow it. And if that's true for the lieutenants, it's certainly true of the people who share the blood of that name. If we had been ruined, our enemies would have come for us. And they would have bled us all dry."

I shiver at the thought that there could have been an alternate reality where Isaak doesn't exist. What would that reality have looked like? It certainly would have changed the entire trajectory of my life.

I would have finished my horrible date with the handsy asshole whose name I can't even remember now. He would have walked me home and I would have tried to avoid kissing him.

Then I'd have gone on with my life. Gotten a job teaching in a good public school, somewhere close to Bree.

I might have met a man—a sweet, boring academic type who likes reading but doesn't drink too much. We would have dated a few years, gotten married, had children.

Jo would never have been born.

I'd have others, yes, but not her. Children with different variations of her face, her laugh, her aura.

And I'd have never known about Isaak Vorobev or the Bratva he was meant to rule.

"Where'd you go?"

I blink twice and remind myself that Isaak's right here, staring at me. "Nowhere important," I tell him.

"More wine?"

"No."

He sets his glass aside and settles into the stately armchair. His eyes rush down my body and then up again.

"Come here," he commands in a dark rasp.

His tone should piss me off, but it has the opposite effect. A shooting burst of desire scales down my core and lands between my legs. It settles there, forcing me to my feet like I'm a marionette and Isaak has full control of the strings.

He remains seated while I walk over to him and stand between his parted legs.

He pushes himself off the back of the armchair and places his hands on my hips. They glide down slowly, disturbing the fabric of my divided skirt. He pulls the string casually, his eyes fixated on my face.

I'm supposed to be down here for a reason, but his eyes are distracting me. It doesn't matter in the end… if I'm distracted, then so is he.

He pulls off my skirt and casts it off to the side. I'm glad I'd chosen to wear the black thong this morning. I'd opted for it only because of the skirt I was wearing. It was just a practical choice. But now, it seems calculated.

"Take off your shirt."

Maybe if I was sober, I'd find his commands demeaning. But as it stands, I want him to boss me around. I want him to bend me over and completely dominate me.

I want him to think I belong to him.

That's the only way I'll ever get free.

I pull off my t-shirt and throw it onto the ground between the armchairs. The bra I'm wearing is a conservative white lace design that doesn't show off much cleavage.

Isaak seems offended by that. He points. "Get rid of it."

I unhook the clasp from behind and slip it off my shoulders. His eyes fall on my nipples and they harden immediately. He reaches out and runs his fingers over both of them.

It's amazing how much my pussy pulses from his touch. He doesn't put any pressure on them, and still my body aches with shooting pangs of need.

Then he drops his hands.

"Turn around."

I do.

His hands run over my ass cheeks, and then he teases off my thong and gets rid of that, too. I'm completely naked now, standing in front of him, ready to be devoured, but I'm not at all self-conscious.

Apparently, the wine has really helped calm me down.

"Bend over."

I stiffen a little.

"Do it now," he orders in that rust-edged steel voice of his.

I lean forward until my hands can touch the ground. A second later, I feel a sharp pain on my right ass cheek. "Ow!" I cry, darting up right again.

I whip back around to see him smirking. My ass stings with the force of his slap.

But he offers no explanation and certainly no apology. He just unzips himself. His massive cock jumps out, throbbing and ready to fuck me.

"Get on top of me," he instructs.

"I want to taste you first," I murmur as seductively as I can while I start to slink to my knees.

Isaak catches me by the crook of my elbow to stop me from finding the floor. "No," he says sharply. "Not today. Get on top of me."

I hesitate again. His eyes offer me no mercy.

Then I shrug and relent. I stand again and straddle him. As I settle into position, his cock rises up and rubs against my slit. A moan escapes my lips. Isaak's eyes go bright with hunger.

"That's a good little *kiska*," he croons.

He grabs hold of my hips and pulls me down hard onto his cock. I'm not ready, and I'm certainly not prepared for the impact and aggressiveness with which he enters me.

I cry out as he fills me deep.

I'm panting lightly as I meet his eyes. He still looks so damn calm that it makes me feel like I'm just unravelling faster in comparison.

Then he jerks my hips back. Back and forth, making sure he's balls deep the entire time.

He's in full control—at first. But as I get my bearings, I decide that Isaak Vorobev has had his way with me for far too long.

I want to taste what control is like.

I take charge, grinding my pussy against his cock, savoring the deliciousness of having him so deep inside me. The moans build and multiply as I ride him. And any attempt to take things slow goes right out the window after those first few strokes.

He slaps my ass and teases my nipples as I ride him, spluttering and moaning the entire time. Then he grabs my nipples and twists.

"Come for me, *kiska*," he growls. "Come now."

And amazingly, I do.

Our eyes lock together and I spasm hard on his cock, filling the wine cellar with my uninhibited cries. I know when Isaak releases, too. His body jerks and his eyes waver, but more than anything, I can feel him drenching me from the inside out, mixing with my own wetness.

I collapse against his broad chest and rest my cheek against his collarbone. It feels so damn soothing that I can't get up. I can't seem to open my eyes, either.

I wait until his breathing and heartbeat slow. It's coming—the moment I've been waiting for. The reason I came down here, the reason I followed Isaak's orders, the reason I bent and stripped and moaned for him.

Because I want the secret in his head.

I take one more minute to savor the stillness and the silence and Isaak's smell and bulk all around me.

Then I steel myself.

It's time to find my daughter.

21

ISAAK

The dream is confusing—but then, dreams usually are.

Maxim is in it. So is Otets. At one point, even Uncle Yakov makes an appearance, reminding me how much I liked him when I was a young boy.

My father's face is black and puffy. He looks like raw meat that's gone bad.

I want to set out my list of grievances. I want to tell him everything he did wrong in life, but even though I'm aware I'm dreaming, his presence settles over me like a boulder I can't move.

He is still Don to me.

And his black face scowls darkly in my direction, reminding me of the power he exerted in life—and the power he still holds in death.

Maxim and Yakov fade away, their presence obliterated by the looming shadow that is my father. I can't find it in me to mourn either of them. Their deaths were fated the moment my father moved against them.

And I will finish the job.

Because even now, I cannot find it in myself to be disloyal to the memory of the man. False or not, liar or not, murderer or not—some bonds can never be broken.

I hear her voice call to me from beyond the shadows. Her sweet scent fills my nostrils, trying to pull me out of the depths of the underworld. Threatening to disappear if I can't find my way to the surface.

Even now, I can feel her warmth snaking up my body, but she's pulling away, trying to avoid the sins of the world I'm tied to.

A part of me wants her to be free, but the larger, wilder, more selfish part of me clings to her body. I'm not used to letting things go. I'm not used to the act of preservation. I have been taught to destroy. Destruction comes easy to me, so much so that I have learned to find beauty in it.

Her lips tickle my ear, my chest, reminding me of the fragile kind of beauty that I've always looked down on.

I never thought breakable things were worth saving.

Until Cami.

But my eyes are fixed forward, rooted on the dark shadow looming in front of me. I know he has no power anymore. I'm the one who holds the world in my hands.

But I have to throw off his memory to truly come into my own.

Her presence gets more and more faint, until I can no longer feel her at all. Her warmth and her scent are both gone.

And with them goes any light that remained.

I open my eyes. The dull glow of the lamps soothes the transition into consciousness.

It takes me only seconds to adjust and then I'm completely awake and completely aware. Her body was wrapped alongside mine at some point; I know that much. But she's no longer next to me, curled against my chest.

Her clothes are gone. None of her faint, flowery scent lingers in the air.

Fuck.

I dart to my feet and give the room a quick once-over. When it's clear she's gone, I bound upstairs, taking the steps two at a time.

I know already where she's gone.

I've been a fool to take her suspicions so lightly. I knew she was onto something, but I ignored it, hoping that the situation would resolve itself before she had a chance to discover anything on her own.

I should have told her down in the wine cellar. But I'd missed my chance because my cock had been talking too fucking loudly.

I run to the west wing, knowing she'll be there. On my way, I dial Mama. She answers almost immediately. I can hear Jo's voice in the background.

"Where are you?" I ask urgently.

"We're out," she replies. "I asked if I could take Jo out some place fun. And you approved it—"

"I know, I know. That's not why I'm calling."

"What's wrong?"

"Where are you exactly?"

"About fifteen minutes from the mansion. What's wrong, Isaak?"

"Divert," I tell her. "Take Jo for ice cream somewhere."

"She's already had ice cream."

"Jesus," I growl. "Then take her to the gardens. The southwest corner, where the honeysuckle grows. Keep her there until I come or call."

"She knows?"

"She suspects," I grimace. I hang up before she can ask anything else.

I slow to a quick stride down the hall, knowing that if Camila has found Jo's room, she'll have proof. Then she will know for certain. But as I walk down, I realize that the door to Jo's room is shut tight.

But the door preceding it is slightly ajar.

I open it silently to find Camila standing in the center of the empty space, looking around desperately.

"What are you doing here?"

She jumps. When she turns around, her expression is guilt paved over with determination.

"Nothing."

"Nothing?" I repeat. "Seems to me like you're looking for something."

She transitions quickly from fierce determination to innocence. But I don't buy it for a second. I have to admit, though: she's getting better at masking her emotions.

Apparently, I'm rubbing off on her.

"No. I just woke up and felt like exploring."

"You could have asked me to show you around," I point out. "After all, I know this place like the back of my hand."

"I didn't want to disturb you."

I give her a tight smile that says, *You're full of shit*. "There's nothing much in this wing," I tell her. "Just a bunch of empty rooms that I haven't decided what to do with."

"Empty rooms, huh?"

I nod. "There's nothing to see here."

"Can I look through the rest of the rooms?"

"You'd be bored," I say. "Unless there's something specific you think you'll find here?"

It feels like something of a Mexican standoff. She purses her lips as she studies my face, trying to figure out the best way to answer. If she admits to knowing that Jo is here, she's scared of the leverage she's losing.

"No," she says. "Nothing at all."

"How about a trip to the pool then?" I suggest, knowing it's on the opposite side of the spot I told Mama to take Jo.

"Oh. Sure. That sounds good."

I nod and lead her out of the room. She's forced to turn in the opposite direction and head down the broad corridor. She's missed Jo's room by one door.

I'd arrived just in time.

Once we get down to the bottom of the staircase, we turn to one another. The secret between us squashes out all the possibility that we had shared down in the wine cellar. It chokes out any sense of hope.

"I guess you have stuff to do, huh?" she asks.

"Trying to get rid of me?"

"No," she says. "Just wondering…"

"I do have some things to see to. Will you be okay on your own?"

"I don't need a babysitter," she says defensively.

I watch her walk towards the sliding doors that lead to the pool. I know she's not going to swim; she just wants to space to recover from her botched plan.

I pick up my phone and type Vlad a quick text.

Then I head towards the honeysuckle patch nestled into the very edges of the garden.

∼

I hear Jo before I see her. She squeals when she sees me and comes rushing forward, stopping just short of jumping into my arms. She has to crane her neck up to see my face.

"Whoa… you're so taller."

I laugh. "You'll be tall, too."

She frowns. "How do you know?"

I shrug. "Just a hunch."

She looks at me suspiciously. "I'll be as taller as you?"

"Maybe even taller."

Her eyes go wide. "Taller than Sam? And Peter?"

I laugh. "Definitely."

She turns and runs towards Mama, who's sitting on one of the benches next to the honeysuckle vines. "Babushka, did you hear that?"

Babushka?

I meander forward while Mama tries hard to avoid my stare. "I heard, sweetheart," she says, giving Jo an affectionate smile.

"Oh my gosh!" Jo squeals, spotting a butterfly. "Look, Babushka…"

"Why don't you see if you can get it to land on you?" she suggests.

Jo starts jumping as she tries to grab the butterfly. She proceeds to chase it around the garden while I turn my attention to Mama.

"Babushka?" I say. "Really?"

"She doesn't know what it means," Mama justifies.

"What does she think it means?"

"She assumes it's my name," Mama replies innocently.

"Jesus, Mother."

"She's my granddaughter, Isaak," she says, lowering her voice a little. "Am I supposed to lie to her about that?"

"She's not ready to know the truth."

She narrows her eyes at me. "And you're going to decide that, too?"

"I thought I made it clear before: I decide everything."

She sighs. "For God's sake, Isaak… it's time to tell Camila. Once you do, the two of you can explain things to Jo. Don't you want the child to know who you are?"

"Of course I fucking do," I snap. "But she's five. She's not going to understand either way."

"Children respond to love, Isaak. Just be there for her. She warmed to you so fast. I think that's a good sign. A hopeful sign for the future."

I glance towards my daughter. She's still pursuing the butterfly around the garden, giggling every time it flits out of her reach.

"That's what you would have been like, if you'd been allowed a childhood."

"Childhoods are for children. I was never a child."

Mama sighs and looks at Jo with regret. "Look at that little girl and tell me she doesn't deserve one. Tell me she doesn't deserve two loving parents."

I grit my teeth. "I will tell Camila."

"She already suspects the truth if she's searching the house for Jo," Mama points out. "What are you waiting for?"

"For her to accept that the Bratva life is not one you can walk away from."

"Still trying to teach her a lesson?"

"Many."

"Your father tried to teach me, too," she remarks. "And I hated him for it."

"And yet you kept his secrets," I point out.

She flinches at the accusation. "Yes, I did," she sighs. "Out of fear, not love."

"Whatever gets the fucking job done."

She shakes her head as if she can't believe what I'm saying, can't accept it. "You don't mean that."

I meet her gaze unflinchingly. "I do."

She nods sadly. She may not believe what I'm saying. But she believes that I believe it. "You remind me a lot of him," she says. "But you're better, Isaak. Stronger. Smarter."

"Your problem has always been that you see me as someone else. I am what I am."

"I see…" she sighs. Her expression turns soft. "I see a lot of your father in you." She runs her hands down over her face. "I'm sorry, Isaak. I know I let you down in many ways."

"Stop," I tell her impatiently. "I'm not interested in rehashing the past. I don't live there. The only thing that I'm concerned with is the future."

"I know. And your future is a little girl chasing a butterfly around the garden, my son."

"It's my decision to make."

"You don't have to do everything alone."

"Yes, I do. Being don is a singular path. There's only room for one man to walk it."

"That's what he thought, too," Mama says tiredly. "And he was wrong. A truly strong don is one who has a partner by his side."

"Don't think I can't see what you're getting at. Camila was not made for this life."

Mama rubs a knuckle through her tired eyes. "You don't have to be born into something to understand it, or to adapt to it. I'm speaking from experience."

"You walked into this world willingly," I remind her. "Camila didn't."

"You underestimate her."

"She reminds you of yourself, doesn't she?" I prod. "That's what you're taking up her side."

Mama shrugs. "Not particularly. I just think she's a good match for you. She fights back. That's a necessary quality for a Bratva wife."

"She fights back with me. And that's supposed to be a good thing?"

"Exactly," Mama says. "Exactly."

Before I can respond, Jo comes running up to both of us. "You told me you'd teach me Russian," she tells me.

"That's true. I did make that promise. What do you want to learn how to say?" I ask.

She hops up on the bench and slips her fingers through mine. I tense at the surprise gesture before curling my fingers around her tiny little hand.

"I don't know. Anything."

I sit down on the bench next to Mama and take both Jo's hands into mine. "Let's start with a promise."

"A promise?" she repeats, her brow furrowing in confusion.

"Yes, a promise. Like this: *Ya vsegda budu tam dlya tebya.*"

I will always be there for you.

Mama stiffens.

"I don't think I can say that," Jo says.

"It's okay," I tell her. "It's not a promise you need to make to me. It's one I'm making to you."

22

CAMILA

I'm coming undone.

I'd been so sure that Jo was in that room. But the signs suggested no one had ever lived in there. It was pristinely clean as usual, without even a stitch of furniture.

Of course, there was still one more room down the hall, but Isaak had caught me before I could get to it.

I have no idea why he's keeping me in the dark if in fact Jo is in this house. Is it just to be cruel? To prove a point? To use as leverage later on?

I stare at the too-still, too-blue waters of the pool. Nothing about it calms me down.

I end up back in the house. But instead of making a beeline back to the west wing, which is most probably guarded by now, I head to Isaak's office.

I have little to no hope that it's just left unlocked, but I have to try anyway. Staying still is going to be the death of me.

The door to his office looks intimidatingly secure, but I approach anyway. I try the handle and to my amazement, it swings open. I give silent thanks to any deities that may be listening and head inside.

His office matches his personality. Dark, austere, and mysterious as hell. I move forward cautiously, taking note of all the imposing cupboards and drawers and file cabinets strewn around the room.

I try a few but all are locked tight, which makes sense, considering the door was left unlocked. I'm not concerned with what he's got in his drawers, though.

I just need his phone.

And there it is, resting on the edge of his desk.

I take a seat in Isaak's massive chair and dial in Bree's number. It takes a moment, but she picks up eventually. It sounds like she's run to answer it.

"Hello?"

"Bree."

"Cami, fucking fuck, fuck, fuck, fuck!"

"Well, hello to you, too."

It feels so good to hear her voice, but I have to be strong here. I'm teetering on the brink of emotion and I'm scared that I'll tip over.

"Cami, please tell me Jo's with you."

I freeze. My body goes from hot to cold and then back again in a matter of seconds. Maxim was right. Isaak has her and he's purposefully keeping her from me.

"Cami…?"

I try and take a breath, but my lungs feel like they've turned to cement. I have to calm down. I knew deep in my bones that he had her. But to hear it proven is more shocking and more painful than I expected.

"Cami… oh God, oh God… you didn't know… you—"

"It's okay, Bree," I say quickly. "She's okay. Jo's with me."

The words come out before I've had a chance to think through the decision completely. But my instincts take over and as I speak, I skate through the reasoning in my head.

As mysterious, as scary, as intimidating as Isaak can be… something inside me says that he would never ever in a million years hurt Jo.

That certainty forces me to be calm.

It cajoles me into backing him, supporting him. Into covering for him so that my sister won't worry. So that if one day, they meet one another, Isaak won't have a black mark on the front of Bree's book.

"Wait, what? Jo's with you?"

"I'm sorry… Horrible moment for the line to duck out," I say easily. "But yes, Jo's safe. I don't want you to worry."

"The note you wrote me—"

What the fuck?

"—said that Jo was in danger and she needed to be removed."

"I know that sounded dramatic. But basically, yes. Maxim was closing in," I say, keeping my answers short.

I hate that I'm covering for Isaak right now. Despite how furious I am, I can't get away from trying to protect him. It's not solely for him, though.

Bree has spent six years worrying about me day and night. I don't want to burden her any more than I have to.

"Jesus, Cami. I was so scared. I mean, the letter came in your handwriting, but I was still terrified. Not that I had much of a choice. She was already gone and all I had was the note."

Is that how he'd done it?

I feel sick to my stomach imagining what Jo must have gone through, being snatched up by a complete stranger. Did they scare her? Hurt her? Drug her?

I have to stop myself from imagining the possibilities. It'll only make me sick.

"I'm sorry I didn't call and talk to you first," I tell Bree, choking through my disgust with myself. "But things were… difficult."

"Were the lines tapped?"

"Yes."

"Shit…"

"I'm sorry, Bree."

"Don't apologize; you wanted to keep her safe, I know that. But I'll admit—those first few nights after you took her… they were rough."

I cringe at the very thought of what she and Jake must have lived through. Jo may be their niece, but they've raised her since she was a six-month-old baby. They've been there from day one watching her blossom into this amazing little person. I can't imagine what it must have felt to go looking for her only to find a mysterious letter in her place.

"She must have been thrilled to see you," Bree sighs.

"I… yes… Bree? I'm sorry, I don't have much time—"

"Jesus, Cam. What the fuck is going on? I thought this guy could keep you safe. You sound more scared than ever."

"Not scared," I clarify. "Just stressed."

"Do you really believe Maxim would hurt you?"

"I don't know," I answer honestly. "But where Jo is concerned, I'm even less certain. He knows who she is, Bree. He knows she's Isaak's child."

"I can't imagine what you're going through. It doesn't feel real."

I take a deep breath and swallow my tears. "I wish you were here."

"Me, too, kid," she says. "Me, too."

"I hope I'll get to see you soon."

"I hope you're right, Cami."

I clutch the phone and jerk my head upright when I hear a noise down the hall. "I gotta go, Bree."

"Okay. Give Jo a kiss from me."

I hang up before she can get wind of the fact that I have sobs bottling up in my chest. The moment the line goes dead, I let my tears run free.

The plan is to get out of Isaak's office as soon as possible, but my legs feel rooted to the ground. And suddenly, I decide that I don't care if he catches me in here.

What's the worst he can do—kidnap my daughter?

I wait until the feeling seeps back into my legs. Then I get to my feet and start pacing until the bitterness slowly alleviates my blind panic.

I've circled around the room a dozen times before I come to a halt in front of the small bar set up in the corner of the room. No wine here, I note.

But there's a bunch of other really expensive shit. Tequila, gin, vodka.

I pick the biggest bottle of whiskey and saunter out of his office. I leave the door wide open because… because, well, fuck it. And fuck him.

Then I make my way to my bedroom. The moment I'm ensconced inside my own space, I crack open the bottle of whiskey and look around for a glass.

When one doesn't immediately jump out at me, I decide I don't need one after all. I throw the cork to the side and take a big swig of whiskey.

Its oaky bitterness burns my tongue and makes me cringe. Of course I've picked out the strongest whiskey on the shelf. The taste is unpleasant from the start, and it gets successively worse.

I don't care. Let it hurt. Let it burn. I keep drinking in the darkness until I've drained half the bottle.

When my head starts to spin, I put it down and admit defeat. I'm no match for the whiskey. Its effects are already making me unsteady on my feet. I feel as though my features are melting together.

I trip forward and almost fall right into the windowpane. I manage to steady myself on the sleek black frame and wait for the world to stop spinning.

That's when something catches my eye.

I notice Isaak's broad shoulders first. He's walking through the gardens towards the house. He's completely alone, but his expression seems calm, satisfied. He looks like he's in a good mood.

"Fuck you," I growl.

He stops short and for a bizarre moment, I wonder if he's somehow heard me, although I'm a story up and a hundred yards away from him.

Then I notice he's talking to someone outside of my line of vision. A few seconds later, the person he's talking to moves closer to him.

Bogdan.

The two brothers talk. I press my face to the window and watch them.

From a distance, they both look quite similar. They both have impressive builds and the same kind of coloring. But Isaak has a natural authority that he manages to exude even from this distance.

"You're projecting, Camila," I tell myself out loud. "Your feelings for him are clouding your judgement."

But try as I might, I can't make myself feel any different about him. He's manipulated me into falling for him and if that isn't enough, he's trying to take over my entire life. He's trying to take my daughter.

So why doesn't that stop my belly from burning every time he so much as breathes?

I will never win with him. He's an alpha, and he's not willing to share his crown. I'd always known that—some part of me had known it, at least. But somehow I'm only just now processing it. I'm only just now accepting what that will mean for me.

And for our daughter.

As the daylight fades, I retrieve the bottle of whiskey and take another swig. It's not as strong or as bitter anymore. It's very possible I've singed off the top layer of my tongue.

When the bottle is almost completely emptied, I resume my pacing. It takes several tries before I've mastered walking in a straight line, but what I lack in direction, I make up for in simplicity of thought.

It's time to be bold.

It's time to be brave.

It's time to stop hiding behind my feelings for him.

I walk out of my room and head downstairs, towards the kitchen. I don't meet anyone on my way there, but I do run into a maid wiping down the kitchen counters.

She jerks upright with a start when I walk in. "Mrs. Vorobev," she says timidly. "I'm sorry, ma'am."

"What are you apologizing for?" I snap.

It's like a train wreck. I want to stop myself, but I can't. All my impulse control has gone flying out the window, half a dozen swigs ago.

He wants me to be a Bratva wife? Well, then, I'm going to be a fucking Bratva wife.

"I… I… is there anything I can do for you?"

"Do you have any alcohol in here?"

She raises her eyebrows and that just pisses me off. "Save your judgement for someone who gives a shit," I hiss. "Where's the fucking booze?"

"I'm sorry, Mrs. Voro—"

"Stop calling me that. That is not my name."

The girl freezes, her eyes going wide with fear. She's young, I realize. Younger than me. She's prettier, too, and for some reason that pisses me off further.

"What's your name?"

"Samantha, ma'am."

"How old are you?"

Her blonde hair is shorter than mine. It's set in natural curls that I've always coveted. Her eyes are huge, Bambi-like, with effortlessly graceful lashes.

"I… I'm twenty-one, ma'am."

"I remember twenty-one," I say bitterly. "I was going to be a teacher. I was going to travel the world. I was going to live in France one day and eat croissants for breakfast every single fucking day."

I know I'm scaring her. I have to admit, it's a good feeling. Maybe I can't blame Isaak too much for throwing his weight around.

It's nice not be the doormat for a change.

"Who are you trying to impress?" I ask, moving in on her.

She backs away, her eyes flitting to the door. "Ma'am?"

"You're wearing makeup," I point out. "Who is it for?"

"N... no one, ma'am."

I narrow my eyes at her. "I'm the boss's wife, remember?" I ask, wondering how these words are escaping my lips at all. Wondering why I can't stop. Wondering what the hell is wrong with me. "You have to do what I say."

She looks like she's on the verge of tears.

"Are you trying to fuck my husband?"

Part of it is the alcohol. I'm not so drunk that I can't recognize that. But a part of it is something else entirely. Desperation combined with a certain element of helplessness.

Because no matter how much I want to, I can't seem to escape my feelings for Isaak.

"No, ma'am!" the girl gasps. "Of course not. I would never…"

I laugh, cutting her off. "He'd probably fuck you if you tried hard enough. I'm only his wife in name, you know. He doesn't give a shit about me."

The girl freezes, as though she's starting to realize what this is really about. "Ma'am… can I get you anything?"

I turn on the spot, wondering what I came in here for. Because I know I came in here for something. Something specific.

"Wait," I say. "It'll come to me in a moment."

She watches as I look around. This strange thing happens where I float up out of my body and I'm looking down at myself. I'm looking down at the cute blonde looking at me.

She's got pity in her eyes—and not much else.

Jesus, I'm being pitied by a twenty-one-year-old. A frightened, timid little girl who barely knows how the real world functions. Is this what I've been reduced to?

I wanted so much to be a heroine.

And somehow, I've ended up a cliché.

"Ma'am, how about some water?"

My eyes snap to hers, and I think we both realize that it was a mistake to ask me that. "What the fuck are you trying to say?" I demand. "Are you trying to accuse me of being drunk?"

"No, ma'am—"

"Why offer me water?"

"Because… it's what my mother taught me to do in these kinds of situations."

I cock my head to the side. "What kind of situations?"

"When… when a person seems… distraught."

The word lands right between my chest. She says it softly, but it feels piercing.

Am I distraught?

The more I think about it, the less I can get away from the word. It makes me wonder how I ended up here, in this lost and aimless place.

"I remember why I came in here," I tell her suddenly.

"What is it, ma'am?"

"I came in for a knife."

23

CAMI

I slip into his room in the dead of night.

He's kept one side of his blinds open. A beam of moonlight pours into the room and forms a perfectly circular pool on the hardwood floor.

The alcohol has settled into my bones now and everything feels so clear. It's like all my senses have been dialed up to maximum.

His massive bed looks even bigger right now. He's lying in the center of it, sleeping. I pad around the room, proud of the fact that I don't make the slightest sound.

Until I pass a mirror, suck in a sharp breath, and freeze at the sight of my own reflection.

I don't look distraught, exactly. But I do look desperate. Because really, only a very, very desperate woman would sneak into a don's room at night with a knife in her hand.

It's my only weapon against him. On any other day, I would have been nervous about that fact. But considering he's lying in bed naked and asleep, I figure I'm the one with an advantage.

I slowly step up to the side of his bed and stare down at him.

He's lying on his back, but his face is tilted away from me. I can still see the perfect angles of his face and jaw. I can see the straight line of his nose and the light stubble that's just starting to form on his chin.

The sheets are pulled up around his waist, but his chest is bare, revealing his rock-hard pecs and the eight-pack I've admired more than once.

He looks so damn beautiful. So damn powerful, even in sleep.

I stare down at the knife in my hand, wondering what happens next?

Do I raise my arm and come at him like an axe murderer? Do I make a tiny, precise incision across his throat? Do I just lunge and stab blindly like the desperate woman I am?

I don't really make the decision to climb onto his bed. More like my body makes it for me, and suddenly, that's what I'm doing.

The fact that he doesn't stir makes me feel bolder. I crawl a little closer until I'm at his side, only inches from touching him.

I look down at his face, and I feel my will falter.

What the hell am I doing?

The clarity I'd clung to only moments ago is long gone. I'm left with a whole host of emotions that I can't possibly wade through.

Because the truth is, I'm not capable of hurting another person. Not like this. And even if I was, I'm definitely not capable of hurting this person.

Jo, I remind myself. *He has Jo and he's keeping her from me.*

I repeat that in my head several times until the anger and resentment make my hand steady. I place the blade at Isaak's throat.

But before I can move it, his eyes open.

I freeze, terror ripping through my body. He doesn't blink his eyes open like a man who's just woken from the throes of sleep. He doesn't look confused or disoriented. He doesn't even look tired.

He looks wide awake, fully aware, and ready for a fight.

He's known I was here the entire time. As usual, he's just been humoring me. Waiting for me to get close enough before he springs his trap and catches me in its claws.

The difference is that this time, I've got a knife.

And he has nothing.

Not that he looks remotely concerned with that fact. In fact, the look in his eyes suggests… amusement? The blue of his irises is cast in darkness, so I can only see the twin pinpricks where his pupils reflect the ambient moonlight.

"What's the plan now, *kiska*?" he whispers.

Desire hurtles through me, the way it always does when he rasps his nickname for me like that. I'm at once disgusted and shocked at myself. Even in this situation, I can't seem to muster up enough strength to resist him.

His body does something to me. His eyes, his voice, his very presence —it reduces me to my most basic carnal self, and all I feel are hormones having their way with me.

I wade through it all, refusing to let my desire for him eclipse my need to protect my daughter. Jo's here. I need to get her out.

This is the only way.

"I'm done being your plaything," I tell him, trying to match his level of calm.

You'd think it would come naturally, considering I'm the one with the knife to his throat. But I have to really work to keep my voice from trembling.

"You've used and controlled me for long enough. I want out."

"And this is your way of saying goodbye?"

"Don't laugh at me."

"Who's laughing?"

"I'm serious," I tell him. "I'm done, Isaak. I'm fucking done."

"I hear you."

"So… you're going to let me walk out of here."

"No," he says, shifting his body slightly so it's angled towards mine. "No, I didn't say that."

"You realize I'm the one with the knife at your throat, right?"

He nods. "I'm aware."

I bring the blade closer. It's touching his skin now. I apply a little pressure so that he knows I mean business. "You feel that?"

"I do."

"I'm not bluffing here. I will slit your throat if I have to."

He smiles. It's equal parts infuriating and arousing. You can't help but admire a man who can maintain this level of indifference with a weapon threatening to end his life at the slightest slip of a hand.

"Okay." It's almost like he's placating me.

"Where's Jo?" I hiss.

He doesn't look in the least bit surprised. I'm prepared for him to deny it altogether.

Instead, without missing a beat, he says, "She's here."

"Here?"

"You heard me. She's right here, under the same roof as you and me."

"The west wing."

"Yes."

"So I was right. I wasn't imagining it."

"No. You were not."

I stare down at him, taking in the fact that he doesn't look in the slightest bit apologetic. "How could you?"

"You denied me access to my own child," he says coolly. "You hid her from me for her entire life. I had every right to take her back."

"She's not yours."

"She most certainly fucking is," he snarls, showing a flare of emotion for the first time. "I am her father. She is mine."

There's possessiveness in his tone. I recognize it—it's the same way he sounds when he calls me his wife.

"I don't want this life for her."

"Unfortunately, that's not something you can decide. She is Bratva. She was born Bratva and that entitles her to the privileges you denied her by keeping her from me."

"Privileges?" I snap. "Do those privileges include a full security detail because you're at risk of being kidnapped or killed at every turn?"

"The Bratva comes with its' risks, yes."

"They're risks I don't want my innocent fucking five-year-old to have to deal with."

"There's no point in being naïve, Camila," Isaak tells me. "Do you imagine that keeping her separate from me is going to guarantee her safety?"

I frown.

"Maxim knows about Jo, doesn't he?" Isaak presses. "He's the one who told you she was here."

I don't deny it.

"You don't think he would hurt her if it meant getting back at me?" he asks. "You can give her back to your sister and keep her away from me. Go for it. That still wouldn't make her safe. Our enemies know about her now. It's too late for a normal life, Camila. For either one of you."

My hand is shaking now. The blade grazes against the skin of Isaak's neck twice, but he doesn't seem at all concerned.

"I… I… I still… have to get her out of here."

"Have you thought this through?"

"Yes," I lie.

"Camila."

"What?" I snap. "Stop saying my name like that."

"You reek of whiskey."

"I'm perfectly sober."

It's not exactly the truth. But it's not a total lie, either. I can feel the alcohol draining from my system even as speak. There's never been a more sobering conversation than this one.

"Really? You don't look comfortable."

"I haven't been comfortable since you entered my life."

His hands land on my hips and I tense. My eyes slip down to the way his fingers curl around my waist. "It's a little awkward talking in this position. Care to let me up?"

"No."

"Very well," he says with a sigh.

He grips my hips and before I can protest he lifts me up and forces me on top of him. I'm straddling him now, my thighs gripping his hips.

Fuck… he's hard.

I choose to ignore that. My hand falters at his throat, but despite the pain in my arm, I keep it there still. I can't deny that this position is a lot better—at least as far as the burning knot of desire in my stomach is concerned.

I'm directly on top of him now, looking down at his upturned face. He looks even hotter from this angle. His hands refuse to budge from my hips.

"That's better," he says, unconcerned about the fact that the knife is still at his throat.

"Why would you do this?" I sigh. "She's a little girl. She's five years old. She must have been so scared."

"It was unfortunate, but you left me no choice."

"Are you blaming me for you abducting your own daughter?"

His shoulders rise and dip in the lightest of shrugs. The knife at his throat doesn't really afford him a lot of room to maneuver. "I gave you the option of making the introduction."

"And when I said no, you decided the best thing to do would be to just… take her?"

"It was only going to be a matter of time before Maxim made a move on her. I couldn't risk that."

"Don't bullshit me," I snap. "You were trying to teach me a lesson."

"That too."

"You bastard."

"Bogdan is the one who went to get her. He tranq'd her and brought her here. Mama was with her when she woke up. She was scared at first—but she's happy here, Camila."

I shudder and try to ignore the mental image of Bogdan shooting my daughter with a tranquilizer gun. "You really expect me to believe that?"

"She misses her aunt and uncle," Isaak tells me. "She talks about her cousins a lot. She even asks after you. But she gets along well with Mama and Bogdan."

"And you?" I demand. "Has she met you?"

"She has," he says, but he doesn't offer any more information.

How was their first meeting? I'm dying to know, but I refuse to ask. He seems to know that because there's a barely-there smile playing around the corner of his lips.

"Does she know who you are?"

"No."

"What have you told her?"

"That her mother is coming to see her soon," Isaak tells me. "And that she's being kept here until you come for her."

I frown. "What does she think I'm off doing?"

"Important things," Isaak says. "Brave things. She already believes you're some sort of superhero. It wasn't a hard story to sell."

I can't deny that that makes me feel slightly better. Not about the situation in general, but about how Jo might see me. I've struggled with my absence in her life all these years. And I've assumed she's struggled with the same thing.

It's not even close to the truth, but the fact that Isaak has tried to protect my image in her eyes means something. Not enough to make me forgive him—but something.

"That doesn't even begin to make up for everything you'd done," I tell him.

His cock presses against the V between my thighs, and I have to bite down on my bottom lip to keep the moan from escaping.

"I know."

"Then why aren't you apologizing?"

"Because if you gave me another chance at it, I wouldn't do anything differently."

I press the knife into his throat in anger. When I pull it back a moment later in shame, I realize I've left a small cut. It's just pierced the skin. Just enough for one tiny ruby-red bead of blood to trickle down the curve of his neck.

"You want to revise that answer?"

"No."

What will it take to see fear in his eyes? What will it take to bring him to his knees? I'm starting to think that it's not possible.

He's staring death in the face, and he doesn't even flinch.

I can feel my resolve start to falter. So before I can throw in the towel completely, I barrel forward for the sake of my daughter.

"I'm going to take Jo and leave," I tell him. "And you're going to let us."

"I'm afraid I can't do that."

I grit my teeth, praying for the forces of the universe to give me the strength I need. A strength that will match his own.

"Then I will kill you right here, right now. If you don't let me take Jo and go, I will slit your throat."

His darkened eyes spark with the dimmest of fires. I'm not sure if that's disbelief or admiration. I choose to believe it's the latter.

"Will you, though, Camila?"

"You don't think I can do it?" I demand.

"I think you're capable of lots of things," he says solemnly. "But not that."

"I will," I insist. "I'll do it."

"Okay."

"That's all you have to say?"

"You want to kill me?" he asks. "Then go ahead. I won't fight back. Slit my throat, Camila."

I blink at him in disbelief. His expression is deadly serious. I'm watching for the punchline, but none is forthcoming.

"Do it, Camila," he urges. "Kill me."

24

ISAAK

Her eyes go wide. She's terrified, but she's trying to hide it behind a veil of ruthlessness that she doesn't have.

She presses the knife into my neck. It's not painful; I've suffered far worse without blinking an eye.

What *is* painful is the erection that's currently buried between her thighs. She's only too aware of it, but she's trying hard to ignore it.

My hands are still on her hips, egging her on, trying to push her limits, even as she tries to dial back.

The whiskey is my friend tonight. She's consumed enough of it to make her believe that this was a good idea. But now that she's sobering up, she's starting to realize just how out of her depth she is.

It's not in her nature to back down, however. Which just makes my erection throb that much harder.

"Kill me, Camila," I say again.

"You don't mean that."

"I mean every word of it."

"You're just going to lie there and let me do it?"

"Yes," I tell her. "And you're the only person in the world I would allow this privilege."

"The privilege… to kill you?" she says, balking.

I smile. "The only way to kill me, Camila, is if I allow it. So here we are. I'm allowing you to kill me. Are you going to waste the opportunity?"

"Are you really so confident that I won't?"

I grip her a little tighter and grind hips upwards into hers. She knows exactly what I'm doing. Her eyes flash.

"You're underestimating me," she says. "What if I do kill you?"

"Then I'll be dead," I shrug. "What would it matter?"

"I don't understand you."

"What don't you understand?"

"You're the man who refuses to die."

"I refuse to die at the hands of my enemies," I correct. "But I don't mind dying at your hands. In fact, I'd say that's a pretty good way to go."

Confusion flickers across her expression. She's trying to decide if I'm manipulating her or not. That's slightly irritating, but I suppose I can't blame her.

But the fact is, I mean every single fucking word I'm saying.

Still doesn't mean I believe that she'll actually go through with it.

"I never imagined the angel of death would be quite so beautiful," I remark.

Her eyes blaze with green fire. "You think flattery is going to get you out of this?"

"Has life really jaded you to the point where you won't accept a compliment?"

"I'm trying to kill you," she snaps. "Doesn't seem like the appropriate time for that sort of thing."

I have to try very hard to keep the laughter from breaking through. "I'm aware of that, Camila. Am I disappointing you with my reaction?"

She narrows her eyes. "Any last words?"

"Would you be opposed to letting me inside you while you kill me?" I ask. "That would truly be a glorious death."

"You're a fucking asshole," she hisses.

"Right. Too much to ask."

Her eyes flicker down to my bare chest. I can see that her eyes are dilated. Even in the dark, her desire for me is palpable.

And my desire for her is currently stabbing her between the legs.

We're both showing all our cards now.

"Well, go ahead then. The suspense is waning."

She grits her teeth and redoubles her grip on the knife. But she doesn't make the killing blow.

I smirk. "You can't do it, can you?"

Her chest rises and falls desperately. "I… I'm not a murderer."

"Is that the only reason?"

She frowns. "What the hell is that supposed to mean?"

"It means I know the real reason you can't go ahead with this."

"Don't—"

"You're in love with me."

She pulls back a little and it alleviates the pressure against my neck for a second. I don't change my expression as I stare up at her.

Her blonde hair falls to the tops of her breasts in wild curls. The whiskey scent clinging to her skin is another turn-on. In fact, it might be my new favorite drink.

She looks like a sad avenging angel.

Even the knife in her hand is making my balls turn blue.

"I am not fucking in love with you," she growls.

"Oh, I think you are."

"Even your ego can't be that big."

"It is," I tell her calmly. "But that's a separate issue completely. My ego doesn't change the fact of the matters."

"Since you're in love with yourself, I suppose it makes sense that you would think everyone else was in love with you, too."

I smile at her attempt to turn this around on me. I thought she'd know me well enough by now to know that it's not going to work.

"Okay," I say, issuing the challenge with relish. "Then prove me wrong. Kill me."

"Isaak—"

"You have a knife at my throat, Camila. I'm completely in your power. Do with me what you will." But even as I say it, I can't help but grip her hips a little tighter, reminding her of my hold on her. "Go on."

"You're only saying that because you know I won't."

"Then let me help you." I grab her knife-wielding hand and press it against my neck. Her eyes go wide when she realizes what I'm going to do. Immediately, I feel her resistance, but I'm much stronger than she is.

"Isaak!" she gasps.

I force her hand to my throat and cut into my own flesh. I pierce the skin, and I can feel it split apart. If I push a little harder, I'll slice my own throat.

"No!"

"This is what you want, isn't it, Camila?"

"You're bleeding, Isaak. Stop. STOP!"

I release her hand and she pulls it away from my throat, taking the knife with her. Her cry echoes around the dark bedroom. She looks terrified as she stares at the blood running down the side of my neck.

It's only a flesh wound. I wouldn't even put a bandage on it, but Camila looks positively shell-shocked.

"What the hell is wrong with you?" she gasps with disbelief.

"I'm not afraid of death, Camila. I never was."

She stays limp on top of me, her eyes wide and afraid and drenched in panic. I press myself upright. When I reach for the knife, she doesn't fight me as I pluck it gently from between her fingers.

I lean to the side and abandon it on the bedside table. When I straighten up again, she's inches from me, her bright green eyes searching for something that makes sense to her.

"Listen to me," I whisper, placing my fingers underneath her chin and forcing her eyes to mine. "It's okay."

"I… I was supposed to come in here… I was supposed to… to…"

"Shh. Stop thinking about what you're *supposed* to do," I say. "That'll never get you anywhere. Think about what you *want* to do."

Her eyes are locked on my face. She's trying to reconcile her principles with what she's feeling for me. Because apparently, the two don't get along in her head.

I'm not about to help her justify anything. But I'm sure as hell not gonna let her out of my bed, either.

My arm wraps around her waist, pulling her into me. My erection is aching now, and I'm dangerously close to abandoning all self-control.

"No…" she whispers, but her voice is weak and unconvincing.

I flip us over in a sudden motion. She gasps with shock. I can't blame her. I don't give her any warning and I'm certainly not gentle.

But she did just walk into my bedroom with a knife. She's forfeited the right to expect tenderness. She's got me turned on to such a point, that I doubt I could summon up enough willpower to give it to her anyway.

I rip the clothes off her, tearing them into confetti and throwing the scraps off the bed.

"No… Isaak… stop…"

I grind my bare cock against her and she moans again. Her eyes roll back and her body shudders.

"*Kiska*, you've got to be more convincing."

She falls silent then. I can see the defeat in her eyes. I'm not going to get anymore fight out of her.

I grab her arms and pin them overhead as I start to press my hardness between her thighs. She jerks against me, biting down on her bottom lip to keep from crying out.

I smile inwardly, knowing that she's going to be screaming her lungs out in a moment. All that's left between us is a pair of sheer, lacy panties.

Those go the same way the rest of her clothes did.

Then there's nothing to stop us except for us.

And I don't think either one of us can stop what's about to happen.

The scent of my wife's sweet pussy fills my nostrils. I lay the length of my body on top of hers and suckle a nipple into my mouth.

Just like that, she loses her battle and cries out. Half in pleasure and half in pain. I don't let her recover before I thrust inside her.

She's dripping wet. Her thighs clench around my hips as she invites me in with every roll of her body. I fuck her relentlessly, like it's the last fuck we'll ever have.

Who knows? Maybe it is.

Within minutes, she's alternating between moans and screams that she can no longer control. All I can hear is the erotic sound of my hips slamming into hers. Her breasts jump violently with every thrust and her hands ball into fists.

I'm still gripping her wrists tightly, refusing to let them go. I like her like this—completely at my mercy.

And judging by the volume of her moans, she likes it, too.

She comes violently, writhing beneath me as her body erupts with goosebumps. But I don't stop and I certainly don't slow down.

This is her punishment.

This is what she gets for trying to escape me.

She gets to come again and again until she can't take it anymore—and then once more after that.

I pull out and flip her over. She gasps, her breath begging for some relief. But she's not going to get it anytime soon.

I force her onto all fours. As she trembles, I slam into her from behind. Then I grab a fistful of her hair and hold on to it like a pair of reins. I tug on the makeshift ponytail, forcing her neck to arch as her eyes stare up at the ceiling and guttural moans pour from her throat.

She groans tiredly, but I just keep fucking her, watching her ass cheeks shiver and shake with every thrust. When I can't hold on anymore, I pull out of her and twist her around again.

She's breathless, but I ignore that as I climb up her torso and shove my cock deep into her throat. Her eyes go wide in shock, but the naked lust is all I need to see before I explode down her throat.

It's a big load, but she takes it all, sucking me dry before my body finally goes still.

I remove my cock slowly and fall against the bed. Camila holds her position for a second longer, and then flops down beside me, keeping a small distance between us.

Her breasts shudder with the strength of her gulping breaths. I'm tempted to reach out and play with her nipples, but the time for that has passed.

She needs more from me now than just my cock, my touch, my dominance. Her eyes are hooded, filled with complicated emotions that she's trying to wade through.

I take the wrinkled sheet and pull it over her. She watches my every movement through hazy, lidded eyes as though it's hypnotizing her.

"Is this why you stayed behind instead of leaving with Maxim?" I ask. "You wanted to find Jo?"

She doesn't answer for a long time. "You already know the answer to that."

"And if it hadn't been for Jo?"

She sighs and turns her face up to the ceiling. I can see the curve of her breasts through the thin sheet and it threatens to make me hard all over again.

"I don't know, Isaak. I don't know anything anymore."

I nod and ponder that for a while. "Get some sleep," I tell her eventually. "Tomorrow, you can see her."

Her head jerks to me. "Do you mean that?"

"Yes."

She's still for a long time. Then I notice her breathing return to normal. Her shoulders seem lighter, even her movements come easier.

She closes her eyes.

And a moment later, she's sleeping.

25

CAMILA

I wake up all at once. For a moment, I don't remember why I'm buzzing with anticipation.

My body is sore, but the memory of why comes fast. And when it does, I'm almost embarrassed looking at the bed I'm lying in.

It's filled with memories of last night's furious, passionate, extremely confusing fucking.

I sit up, realizing that Isaak is not here. I'm alone in his room, and a part of me is glad. I need time to process and accept. I need time to sift through what's happened between us. What I did to him. What he did to me. What we both did to each other.

The whiskey was to blame for some of it. But the rest… the rest I have to take responsibility for.

The sheets fall off my breasts and pool around my waist. I'm still naked, lying in the bed of the man who abducted me and my daughter.

I'd feel ashamed if I weren't so tired.

My skin is flushed all over, like a pervasive bruise that leaves soreness but not pain. I notice that there's an imprint around my wrists from when he held me down last night.

I trace the line delicately, remembering that moment and everything that followed.

The way he had pressed himself on top of me. His broad chest, the lines of his abs cutting into my stomach as he fucked me like he was trying to brand himself into my flesh.

He didn't need to go through the trouble, though. He marked me permanently a long time ago.

The door swings open silently. I grab the sheets and pull them back up to cover myself. Isaak walks in, fully dressed and looking exceptionally calm and completely in control.

Have I ever seen him come undone? Lose control? Panic in the slightest? I'm not so naïve that I think he doesn't feel any of those things. I just know the cool façade he keeps has been trained into him so well that it never wavers.

It's effective.

"You're awake."

I have no idea what to say to him. Last night hangs over my head like a guillotine. And I know that at any point, it can come crashing down and cut my head clean off.

"I... I'm sorry. I overslept."

Have I overslept? I don't know the time. Judging from the light filtering in through the partially open blinds, it's at least seven in the morning.

"Don't apologize," he says, walking to the edge of the bed.

He doesn't sit down. Just stands there, watching me with his direct gaze. I look away and fuss with hiking the sheets up around my chest.

"I've already seen you naked," he says wryly. "More than once, actually. You can do away with the pretense."

I fight the blush on my cheeks as I ignore him and pull the sheet over my shoulders anyway. "I was drunk last night."

"Is that an excuse?"

"One of many."

He smirks. "You weren't so drunk that you didn't know what you were doing."

I raise my eyes and glare at him. "Are you an authority on what happens inside my head now?"

He shrugs. "Your eyes give you away, Camila. And besides, I would never have fucked you if you were that drunk."

"Right. Because you're such a gentleman," I say sarcastically.

His expression doesn't change. "You can either pick a fight or come see your daughter," he says grimly. "I don't have time for both."

Jo. I freeze instantly and stare at him. "You… you're serious?"

"Yes."

"Now?"

"Now," he confirms.

"Oh my God," I say, jumping out of bed so fast that I lose the sheet.

I'm standing here in broad daylight, naked in front of him, and I genuinely don't care. I don't even feel a stitch of self-consciousness.

Even when he steps towards me, his eyes trailing down my body, I hold my ground and let him stare.

He reaches out and grazes his fingers over my breasts. "You might need to put on some clothes first."

I roll my eyes. "Why? You seem to like me this way."

"Oh, I do. But it might confuse Jo a little."

"I'm getting dressed now," I say, turning on the spot until I spy my clothes in the corner.

To my surprise, they've been folded and placed neatly on a chair, though most of it is torn to shreds. Next to them, on the bureau, is a fresh outfit, clean and pressed.

"The maid was in here?"

He frowns. "What?"

"My clothes from last night are all folded up. And there's another stack of stuff here."

His frown turns annoyed. "I did that. I don't require a maid for everything."

Somehow, I find the fact that he did all that bizarrely endearing.

"What?" he asks when I don't stop looking at him.

"Nothing," I say quickly. "Nothing at all."

I get dressed in a hurry, then I run to the bathroom for a quick few minutes to get all the morning ablutions over and done with. When I go back into the bedroom, Isaak is by the door, waiting for me.

"Does she know she's seeing me today?"

"No." Isaak shrugs. "I thought we'd surprise her."

The statement settles and for a moment, I have this strange warmth spreading through my chest. It feels like the kind of thing that a couple would discuss.

"B…but… shouldn't she be prepared?"

"You're overthinking."

"Of course I am! I haven't seen her in the flesh for over two years now."

"You're her mother," Isaak says. "Trust me, she doesn't need to be prepared."

I open my mouth but nothing comes out.

"What is it?"

"I… I…"

I look down and shake my head. Isaak puts his hand underneath my chin and pushes my face up so that I'm forced to look at him.

"What is it?" he asks again.

"I'm… nervous."

He smiles, and that makes me narrow my eyes.

"What?"

"You realize you slipped into my room with a knife last night, right?"

"Shut up," I say, shaking off his hand.

He chuckles under his breath. "Be the heroine you were last night. Walk in there and hug your daughter. She doesn't care about the circumstances of your absence. She'll only care that you're with her."

It feels very ironic that I'm being encouraged and supported by Isaak on how to approach this situation with Jo. But I need his support. Even his presence feels like a tonic, washing away the shadows of my fears.

I want to move closer to him, as though his very proximity will give me strength. But I resist the urge. I rely on him far too much as it stands.

I take a deep breath and nod. "Okay. Let's go."

He leads me to the west wing. My eyes dart from side to side as we approach the last room along the corridor. The only one I didn't get to before Isaak caught me snooping.

I hear a bubble of laughter. It feels like someone's sent a spear straight through my heart.

"Go on," Isaak encourages me, gesturing towards the handle.

I grind my teeth and push open the door. At first, I only see Nikita. She's sitting on the large circular carpet, blocking the child sitting opposite her.

"Jo?"

Nikita turns and Jo pops her head out from behind Nikita.

"Mommy?"

She stands up.

Our eyes meet.

And it's like fireworks.

Books always rely on fireworks to describe a magically romantic moment between love interests. But what else could capture this moment so perfectly? The burst of surprise. The cry of pleasure. Color coming into a world that has been so, so dark for so, so long.

"Jo," I whisper again.

And then we dart to each other at the same time. We meet in the middle and she jumps into my arms and my baby is back with me just like that, and I can smell her and touch her and love her the way I haven't been able to for far too many years.

I hoist her onto my hips and twirl on the spot. "My Jo!"

"Mommy!" she screams. "Mommy, Mommy, Mommy!"

I don't know how long I twirl. I'm only forced to stop because my heart starts thudding dangerously fast in my chest. And even that I don't mind. Everything feels like it's in danger of spinning out of control.

That's fine. That's all fine.

Nothing else matters but this.

I pull back. "Let me look at you."

She keeps her hands around my neck as she gazes up at me, her blue eyes bright and growing more and more similar to the color of her father's.

"You're so beautiful, my girl."

"Mommy," she repeats again, unwrapping her hand from my neck and touching my hair. "You have such nice hair."

I laugh. "Not as nice as yours. It's gotten darker."

She smiles. "Aunty Bree says the same thing. Is she here, too?"

Of course she'd ask for Bree. She may call me Mommy, but my sister has been the only true mother she's ever really known.

It's only fair, so I try not to let that get to me. I won't allow anything to dampen this moment. I kiss the top of her head and set her down at last.

Only then do I realize that the room is empty. Nikita slipped out at some point and Isaak hasn't even entered. I suppose they're trying to give us some privacy. I appreciate the gesture.

I sink down onto the soft carpet and Jo settles in front of me, with her legs crossed in the same way. I clasp her hands in mine and lean in.

"How've you been, my baby?"

"I'm not a baby anymore," she says without any accusation or malice in her tone. There's only pride. "I'm almost six."

"You're completely right. You are almost six. You're so tall."

"Uncle Jake tells me that I might be taller than Sam."

I laugh. "I'll bet Sam doesn't like that."

"No, no," Jo says, shaking her head from side to side. "He doesn't. He says he'll be taller."

"We'll just have to wait and see, won't we?"

Jo smiles and nods. Then she looks around the room, realizing that we're alone. "Hey, where's Babushka?"

I frown. My knowledge of Russian is basically nil, but even I know that *"babushka"* is the word that children in Russia use to refer to their grandmothers.

"Babushka?" I ask, treading carefully.

Jo nods. "That's her name. I mean, her name is Nikita, but her other name is Babushka. I like it. It sounds funny."

"Do you know what it means?"

Jo frowns. "Not really, but I'll know soon. I'm learning Russian."

I tense, wondering how Isaak has managed to manipulate so much in such a short period of time. "Russian, huh?" I ask, trying to keep the worry from my face. "That's a tough language."

"Yeah, but I like learning new things. Aunty Bree says that knowledge is power."

I smile, because that's exactly the phrase that I used to use on Bree through my teens when she accused me of studying too much and neglecting my personal life.

"She's absolutely right. Knowledge is power."

I notice Jo's eyes flit to the door and I turn back to see who's just walked in. The moment she sees Isaak, her eyes go wide with brightness and she scurries straight to him.

I sit there in shock as she grabs his hand and reels him towards our spot on the carpet.

"He's teaching me Russian," she informs me.

Isaak's gaze passes over Jo before turning to me. Before he can say anything, Jo rushes on. "Isaak, where's Babushka?"

"Probably in the next room, sorting through the damage you two did yesterday."

Jo blushes. She drops my hand and then runs out of the room. I get to my knees and stare at her, wondering how she can let go of me so quickly when we've only just been reunited.

"You okay?" Isaak says.

The questions rubs me the wrong way. Or maybe it's the fact that I'm quickly realizing how little control I have over any of this.

"What damage did they do yesterday?" I ask sharply.

Isaak raises his eyebrows, taking note of my tone. "My mother took her shopping. They bought quite a few clothes."

"Jo refers to your mother as *Babushka*."

"She doesn't know what it means," he replies, still not taking an apologetic tone. "And before you grab the closest weapon, you should know that Nikita did it without consulting me."

"Why should she consult you if I'm Jo's mother?"

"Because I'm Jo's father. We have equal rights."

"Not as far as I'm concerned."

His calm doesn't break, but I see the ripple of irritation on his brow. "Then maybe you need to start compromising."

"Are you being serious right now?"

"What exactly is pissing you off?" Isaak says. "The fact that she's comfortable here, or the fact that she's already in the next room with my mother?"

How? How the fuck does he know exactly what bothers me? How does he know what's going on in my head at any given moment?

"This is not her home, Isaak."

"It is now."

I stiffen. "So that's the plan? You're going to keep her here indefinitely?"

He cocks his head to the side. "She's a lot safer here than she is with your sister."

"Says you."

"But my word counts."

"And mine doesn't?"

"You don't have the power of the Bratva behind your word, Camila," he says. "I do."

"So does Maxim."

I know I'm hitting below the belt, but I'm pissed and hurt. And I have no idea how to deal with either emotion apart from railing on Isaak.

"Is that right? So what's your plan, then? Take Jo and go crawling back to your fiancé?"

The word no longer fits with me. Maybe that's why he uses it at all—to hurt me. But I'm not ready to back down just yet.

"Maybe."

His eyes flare, but it doesn't break his façade of calm. "And you believe that Maxim is just going to raise my child as his own?"

"He might, if he truly loves me."

"And does he?"

I falter. "I… I think so."

"Are you going to risk Jo's life on 'I think so'?"

"He won't kill Jo."

Isaak rolls his eyes. "You are not Bratva. You don't understand. This life is lived in extremes."

"Jo is my daughter."

"And she means nothing to him," he retorts. "He killed his own uncle. You think he'd balk at the thought of killing Jo? She's your daughter, but in Maxim's head, Jo's *my* daughter. And that's a distinction that should matter to you."

I get to my feet. Isaak moves forward to meet my anger.

"What if you're wrong?" I say.

"I'm never wrong."

"You're fucking infuriating, you know that?"

He smiles, and I feel my stomach flip instantly. The anger turns to desire and I try to step away from him before this blows up in my face.

Before I can get away from him, he grabs me. He pulls me close, his eyes raking over my face as though he's searching for answers.

"I know you, Camila. You want me, but you're too fucking afraid to admit it. So you hide behind Maxim and that's easy to do because you don't actually give a shit about the man."

"You—"

"Deny it all you want," he growls, cutting me off. "I see through you, Camila Vorobev."

I go still in his arms. *Camila Vorobev.* Jesus. It's like the words of a spell.

My hands ripple with goosebumps. I can't even tell if I'm terrified or excited.

"You want to fucking come at me? Then come at me. But be prepared because I'm not going to pull my punches for your sake. You defend your feelings for Maxim only because you don't want to admit you never loved the man you promised to marry."

He sees my silence and knows what it is—confirmation that he's right.

"You wanna fight, *kiska?*" he asks in a low voice. "Then let's fight."

I'm expecting him to land the final blow, a parting line that will bring me to my knees.

Instead, I'm met with a kiss.

His lips crash down on mine and I gasp, my mouth parting ever so slightly. He's gripping me so tightly that there's no hope of escape.

Though I'm not even sure if escape is what I'm after.

Then I hear Jo's voice, and Isaak and I break apart just as she runs through the door, trailed by Nikita and Bogdan.

I watch them all, trying to hide my self-consciousness. I realize how similar Jo looks to all of them. They look like family. And that's when I realize something.

They *are* family.

In this room, I'm the odd one out.

26

ISAAK

She's definitely shaken. She watches everyone and everything with a wary expression.

The only time it softens is when she's looking at Jo. In contrast to Camila, Jo seems absolutely elated to have everyone around her. She asks for her aunt and uncle a couple of times at first, but then she relaxes into the group she has.

She's on the carpet now, trying to make Bogdan get on all fours so she can ride him like a donkey. He's been trying to distract her onto something else for the last ten minutes, but to no avail.

Camila is sitting a few feet away with her legs crossed. Her eyes are on Jo, and she smiles instinctively every time the child does.

"Jo, sweetheart, do you need anything?"

"No thank you," Jo says, glancing at her.

"Hungry?"

"Babushka already gave me breakfast."

"It's almost lunch time now."

"I wanna get on Bogie's back and ride him like a donkey," she insists.

I snort with laughter from the window seat. Bogdan throws me some fierce side eye. "Come on, Bogie," I taunt. "One lap around the room."

"Would you like to be the donkey this time?" Bogdan asks.

"Not particularly, no. Jo wants you."

Jo looks between us distractedly, but her focus shifts back on Bogdan. "Please?"

"Nooo!" he moans. "Anything but that."

"Why?"

"My knees hurt."

Jo frowns. "I'll get you knee pads."

My eyes fall to Camila. She's watching their interaction carefully. The slight smile on her face feels forced. I know her well enough to know that she's feeling out of place with Jo. But she doesn't know how to reconcile that feeling, so she's choosing to take it out on me.

"Don't be too hard on her."

I glance to the side where my mother sits. She's looking drawn and tired. The black lounge dress she's wearing washes her out a little. She hasn't made the usual effort with her appearance, but I decide not to ask about it. Conversations with Mama these days turn into more trouble than they're worth.

"Too hard on whom?"

"You know who. This can't be easy on her."

"What?" I demand defensively. "The fact that she knows her kid is protected and secure here? What a nightmare that must be for her."

"She hasn't seen Jo in a long time, Isaak," Mama points out. "Can you imagine coming face to face with your child after years, and feeling like you're no longer essential in her life?"

"I don't have to imagine it. I met my daughter for the first time only weeks ago. She's almost six years old."

"It's different for a mother. You didn't know Jo existed before a few weeks ago," Mama reminds me. "Camila's had to navigate a separate life from her daughter since the moment she was born. It's not easy…"

"How would you know?"

"Really?" she asks, looking at me with raised eyebrows. "The same thing happened to me."

I roll my eyes. "We were never taken from you."

"Weren't you?" she hits back. "We lived in the same house, I saw the two of you every day… but you stopped being my sons. And you became his."

"We are Bratva."

She nods, and exhales tiredly. "Yes, you are Bratva. And sometimes in the Bratva there's no room for women unless it's carved out by the men holding the reins. That was not done for me. I just want to make sure it's done for Camila."

When I look towards the carpet, I realize that Camila is looking straight at us. Can she hear our whispered conversation?

No, I think not. But she is smart enough to know when she's being discussed. Her eyes flicker to mine, and I can see the silent anger in them, lurking right beneath the brave face she's trying to put on.

"Camila and I… it's not a real marriage," I say, keeping my eyes on her.

Mama sighs. "Then maybe you should make it real."

I force my eyes from Camila's and turn to Mama. "Why are you encouraging this?"

"Because she can make you stronger. She can give your life the kind of balance that's necessary to be more than just successful in this world."

"What is more important than success?" I ask.

"Happiness, son."

She gets to her feet and heads toward the door. Jo doesn't notice her leave because she's still trying to bully Bogdan into being her donkey.

"My lovely," Camila calls, her tone growing warm and nurturing instantly. "Here, let me tie your hair back. It's getting in your eyes."

It's strange watching her mother Jo. It ignites a bunch of feelings that I don't expect.

It's not just the mothering. It's the fact that she's mothering *my* child. I think back on the night Jo was conceived. It feels like a lifetime ago and like yesterday at the same time.

The sex had been passionate. Wild. Animalistic.

And it created something amazing.

Jo walks up to Camila and turns around. I watch as Camila runs her hands through Jo's hair before tying it up nice and tight.

"There. All done."

"Thanks, Mommy."

"You're welcome, sweetheart. Do you want me to read you a story?" she asks.

"No, that's okay. Babushka will read to me. She does every night before I sleep."

"But... I can do it this time?"

I can hear the ache in her voice. This means a lot more to her than it does to Jo. She's bracing herself for a rejection, but she's silently hoping for more.

Jo considers that. "If Babushka is tired, maybe then you can read to me."

Camila forces a smile onto her face. "That sounds like a plan."

"Have you spoken to Aunty Bree?"

"I did recently."

"I want to speak to her, too."

Camila nods. "We'll definitely speak to her together. Okay?"

Jo nods. "Okay."

Then she turns and focuses her attention back on Bogdan. His eyes go wide and he pretends to be knocked out cold. Laughing, she runs up to him and jumps right onto his stomach.

"Ow!" he grunts.

Jo just laughs harder. "You're not sleeping!"

"I'm trying."

"No, no! No sleeping. It's daytime."

"Some people sleep during the day."

"No, they don't."

"Yes, they do."

"No, they don't."

"Yes, they do."

I tune the two of them out as Camila gets to her feet and walks over to the window seat. She sits down next to me where Mama was sitting only a moment ago.

"He's good with her," she says grudgingly.

"I know."

"How long has she been here?"

"A couple of weeks."

"Jesus."

"Look at her," I say authoritatively. "She's happy. She's safe. What more do you want?"

Her eyes rake over my face. "Let's not do this now."

"Camila—"

"She doesn't need me."

She makes the admission with a deep sigh that seems to shake her entire body. She wrings her hands together as she watches Jo and Bogdan play on the carpet.

"Of course she does."

She glares at me. "I'd appreciate it if you don't lie to me. It's condescending."

"I'm being condescending?"

"I would have thought you'd be aware of that."

"I'm always aware of what I'm being and when."

"I can't even follow that sentence."

"Then maybe we should stop talking," I snap.

She glares at me, and I see her expression seal up. So much for being patient. I just don't seem to have that gene inside me.

Jo comes running up to us, her eyes bright with excitement. "Bogie said he'd take me to the zoo to see some real-life donkeys," she says. "Can we go now?"

"Not now," I tell her. "But we can definitely go at some point."

"When?" she asks, clearly not liking my vague response.

I smile. "Soon."

She narrows her eyes at me. "Tomorrow?"

"We'll see, Jo. Go play with your… with Bogie," I correct myself just in time.

Her little shoulders hunch. Then she says carefully, *"Do skorogo."*

"Very good," I chuckle as Jo whips around and runs back to Bogdan. When I turn to the side, Camila is staring at me.

"What now?"

"What did she just say to you?"

"'See you later.'"

Camila frowns. "That's what she said?"

I nod.

"And whose idea was it to teach her to speak Russian?" she asks.

"Hers."

"Excuse me?"

"Excused."

She frowns. "You're telling me that my five-year-old just decided out of the blue that she wants to learn a foreign language that happens to be your mother tongue?"

"It wasn't out of the blue," I say. "She heard me talking in Russian, and she was curious about it. Said she wanted to learn. So I've been teaching her a little bit. That's all."

"That's all?" Camila repeats, because clearly to her, that's not all.

"She would have grown up speaking Russian if her birth hadn't been kept from me."

She narrows her eyes. "And how was I supposed to contact you, Isaak? It's not like you left me with a forwarding address or a number where I could reach you."

"How about six months ago?"

"Oh, you mean the day you hijacked what was supposed to be my wedding day and forced me into marrying you?" she asks. "That day? Sorry, I was a little preoccupied with the forced marriage part to think about telling you about the secret daughter part."

"And after the shock had passed?" I ask, ignoring all the sarcasm.

"I didn't know if I could trust you."

"When you were in danger, I'm the one you called," I remind her.

"I still wasn't sure I wanted Jo to have this kind of life."

"What kind of life is that?"

"A claustrophobic one. A trapped one. A controlled one. The kind of life where she's nothing more than a man's possession. Her father's property until the day comes when she gets to be her husband's property instead."

"She is not property at all," I snap.

"No? Then what is she?"

"My daughter," I say, and even I can feel my eyes flash. "She is Bratva. That means she will never be used or hurt or taken advantage of. She will be protected. She will be taught to be strong. She will call the shots her entire life, because what I can give her is more than just safety. I can give her power, the means to control her own fate, so that she never has to rely on a man if she doesn't want to."

Camila stares at me for a long time. Her expression teeters between uncertainty and bewilderment.

"You'd do that for Jo… but not for me?"

I look away from her. "Once Maxim is taken care of, you'll have the same choice."

"Which is?"

"Freedom. If you want it."

"And Jo?"

"Jo will stay with me," I tell her, standing up and effectively ending the conversation. "Like I said: she is Bratva. You are not."

Her face ripples with hurt, but I don't bother giving her comfort. She has to embrace certain truths if we're to accomplish anything together. Watching her leave will be difficult, but I'm not about to force a woman to stay against her will.

I gave her the choice before. I can survive doing it again.

"Isaak," Jo says, running to me and winding her fingers through mine. "Come play with me."

Camila sits on the fringes of our little group for most of the evening. She participates when Jo calls on her directly, but otherwise, she remains removed. As though she wants to make it clear that she's Jo's mother, but not part of the family.

I ignore her for the rest of the evening. She gives me the same courtesy. By the time night falls, Jo falls asleep on the carpet between Camila and me.

Bogdan left a couple of hours ago. Since then, we'd been using Jo as a human buffer. She's worked so well that we'd actually managed to avoid outwards aggression for as long as she'd been awake.

But now that she's asleep, it's seeping out again.

There's venom in Cami's eyes, made more palpable by the sexual tension that's lingered between us since that interrupted kiss from earlier in the day.

Honestly, that kiss needs finishing.

And she fucking knows it.

"We should get her into bed," Camila says.

I lift Jo gently into my arms and carry her to her bed. The moment I put her down, Camila moves forward, pushing me out of the way.

"Do you mind?" she asks irritably.

I back up a few steps and watch as she brings the covers over Jo's little body and tucks her in comfortably. No sooner has she wrapped the kid up like a toffee than Jo starts to stir.

"I don't think she needs to be swaddled," I say.

She glares at me. "I don't need your advice. I know what I'm doing."

But she clearly doesn't. Instead of admitting that, she doubles down and starts to bring the blanket more firmly around Jo.

The kid starts stirring more aggressively.

"Jesus," I mutter, pushing Camila aside and taking over.

I pull out the sheets and rest the blanket gently over Jo's waist so that her arms are free. She gives a sigh of relief and turns over. Within seconds, she's settled.

When I straighten and turn around, Camila's watching Jo sleep with wide eyes. Slowly, she moves them to me.

I can see all her uncertainty and insecurity brew together. There's a moment when I think she'll veer towards sadness, but she settles on anger instead.

"I think you should leave. She needs to sleep."

I raise my eyebrows.

"I'm not leaving her," she clarifies. "I'll sleep in here tonight."

"What are you guarding her from?"

"Anyone I have to," she snaps. She strides over and yanks open the door, motioning for me to leave.

I go to the exit, but I stop in front of her so that she can't close it. "You need to think about what's best for her," I say. "Think about it very, very carefully."

Her green eyes spark. "I know what's best for her. That's why I kept her apart from this shit—from *your* shit—all these years. And what was my sacrifice worth in the end? Not a damn thing. You plucked her out of her safe, stable life and plunged her right into the chaos of your world."

"This is her world, too."

"It didn't have to be."

"She deserves to know her family."

"She has a family."

"It's not either-or, Camila."

"It is to me."

"Then you're going to be disappointed."

Without even realizing it, we've come together. There's maybe an inch separating our bodies, and the hum of energy thrums between us like a live wire.

"You had no right to take her."

"The fact that I took her means you can be with her right now. You should be thanking me."

"Don't," she snaps. "Don't pretend like you did this for me."

"You're right. I didn't do it for you. I did it for me."

"To punish me?"

"No," I growl. "I did it because I wanted to know my own fucking daughter."

She stops short, her eyes flitting to Jo before she looks back to me. I see the tremor of guilt in her eyes. She's definitely conflicted… but she's also as stubborn as ever.

She has a right to be, perhaps, in this case. But I'm still not going to allow her an inch of leeway.

"No. You did it just because you could," she says softly.

She puts her hand on my chest and pushes me out of the room. Her hand lingers for a moment before she pulls away.

"But just because you can do something," she adds, "doesn't mean you should."

Then she closes the door on my face.

I'm so tempted to push my way back in, pin her to the wall and fuck her until her eyes are rolling back in her head. But I don't.

Because Jo's in there with her. And because I want the two of them to have tonight.

I turn away from the door and notice Bogdan standing there with a smug look on his face. He'd clearly seen the last few minutes of our hushed but heated exchange.

"It's no wonder you're hard all the time," he remarks.

"Fuck off, you little shit."

Bogdan laughs and heads off in the opposite direction.

But the truly annoying part is… he's completely fucking right.

27

CAMILA

I wake up an hour before Jo does.

I sit next to her bed and watch her sleep. It's borderline creepy, but considering I've missed so many of her mornings, I decide I'm justified in this instance.

She's just a beauty of a child. I don't think I'm biased in thinking so, either. Anyone looking at her can see how pure, how delicate her features are.

The more I look at her, the more I see of Isaak in the twist of her nose, the arches of her eyebrows, the lines of her face. She *is* him, in miniature, and it's spookier than I expected.

Sighing, I sneak back to my room for a few minutes to grab a couple of things. When I return, Jo's stirring. I slide under the sheets and wrap my arm around her.

She blinks her eyes open and gives me a squinty glare laced with confusion.

"Hey, baby. Good morning." She still looks confused. "It's me, Mommy."

"Mommy?"

"Yes, honey."

Slowly, as the sleep shifts off her eyes, she sits up and looks at my face. "I didn't dream you?"

My heart feels like it's soaring and breaking at the same time. "No, my sweetheart. You didn't dream it. I'm right here."

"You slept with me?"

"I did. You don't mind, do you?"

I'm slightly nervous about her answer, but she gives me a sweet smile and shakes her head. "No. Next time, maybe we can ask Aunty Bree to sleep with us, too."

I hide my disappointment behind a smile.

It's not that I begrudge my sister and daughter their bond; I just wish there was a little more room for me in Jo's heart. The memory of yesterday comes back in full force, along with all the feelings it conjured.

Jo had been excited to see me, but after the initial reunion, she'd seemed to relegate me to the background of her life. As though she wasn't sure how to deal with me in real time.

I sat on the fringes and watched her play with Bogdan, who she's already got nicknamed. And she'd even played with Isaak.

Of course Isaak's interaction with her was much more dignified than Bogdan's. I'm very annoyed and slightly impressed that he's managed to manipulate even the nature of his relationship with Jo in such a way that he's not forced to pretend to be a donkey if he doesn't want to.

Just another instance of Isaak getting his way.

"Mommy?"

"Hm?"

"Can we go down and see where Isaak is?"

I give her a smile and try to understand how he's accomplished this at all. He's not exactly the cuddliest of people. And yet somehow, he's managed to make an impression on Jo.

All without telling her who he really is.

"Jo?"

"Yes, Mommy?"

Every time she says that, it pulls at my heartstrings. I feel guilty for being such an ungrateful bitch. So what if Jo didn't cling to me like she does with Bree?

It will take time. I've been away all of her life. I can't just expect things to fall back into place, because there was never an established place to begin with.

I left before Jo and I could develop a connection of our own.

It'll come. In time. In time. In time.

I tell myself that again and again as I walk Jo to the bathroom.

"Mommy?"

"Yeah?"

"No, you asked me something."

"Oh right. Right. Um, I wanted to ask you if you, uh… liked Isaak?"

She's standing in front of the sink with her toothbrush. She looks at me in the mirror. "Yeah, I do. He's really tall."

I laugh. "Is that the only reason you like him?"

"I also like his eyes."

"Yeah, they're a very pretty color, aren't they?"

She frowns and puts her toothbrush down on the counter before turning to me. "No, I mean he has nice eyes."

I stare at her. "Aunty Bree taught you that?"

"Yeah," Jo replies, with a nod before turning back to the mirror. "Aunty Bree tells me to look for kind eyes. They're the people who'll help."

I smile, remembering that we'd learned the phrase from our grandmother before she'd passed away. When I started dating, I'd asked Bree for advice and she'd told me she had only one piece of advice for me.

"Look for a man with kind eyes, Cami. Then you'll be set."

Had I looked for kindness in Maxim's eyes when I first met him? No. I hadn't even remembered that bit of advice. I'd lived by it in high school. And then I'd gotten older, more jaded, more reclusive. I spent years with my head buried in books and I'd stopped looking people in the eye.

Until Isaak.

"Mommy, what are you thinking?"

"Sorry," I mumble. "Why don't you use the toilet and we can go downstairs?"

"Okay. Can I have some privacy, please?"

"Oh."

I stare at her in shock for a moment. Then I realize she expects me to back out of the bathroom. She seems so young to me still. I have to remind myself that she's almost six.

"Of course, honey. I'm sorry."

I hurry out of the bathroom and she closes the door on me. I feel strange. A walking cliché, a bird without her wings. I've waited so long to be reunited with Jo—and now that I'm here, she doesn't need me.

I'm forced to shake off the self-pity when Jo walks back into the room, all dressed in a pink dress that's clearly new and clearly expensive.

"That's a beautiful dress."

"Thank you," she says brightly, clearly having hoped for a compliment. "Babushka bought it for me when we went shopping. She says the color suits me."

"It does. But I'll bet any color suits you."

"Not yellow."

I raise my eyebrows. "Not yellow?"

She shakes her head. "Sam says I look like a banana when I wear yellow."

I laugh. "What's wrong with that? Bananas are great. I love them."

Jo gives me a little giggle and slips her fingers into mine as we head down the staircase together. It gives me just a little bit of hope.

If she's young enough to want to hold my hand, maybe she still needs me.

Maybe I'm not too late.

Maybe there's still hope.

∾

When we arrive in the kitchen, breakfast has already been laid out. It's an elaborate spread, far more than I'm used to. Fresh croissants and danishes, a smorgasbord of scones, yogurt and cereal and bowls of crispy hash browns, sizzling sausage, thick bacon slabs.

"What would you like, honey?" I ask.

Jo pops onto a chair and surveys the spread. "Bread and butter."

"That's it?"

"Uh-huh."

I butter her two slices of toast and hand them over with a glass of orange juice. Then I ask the maid for a cup of coffee and grab myself a chocolate croissant.

"Where's Isaak?" Jo asks, biting into her buttered bread.

It's more than a little annoying that Jo seems so attached to him already. How has he managed to win her over in so short a period of time? She's known me her entire life, and I'm struggling right now because it doesn't feel that way at all.

"He's busy, darling. He probably has big, important stuff to do."

"That's right," comes a deep voice. "I do."

"Isaak!" Jo jumps off her chair and runs to him. She hits him with a hug around the waist and he runs his hand through her hair.

"Morning, kid."

"Good morning, Isaak!"

He hoists her up and settles her back into her chair. "Is that all you're eating?"

"Yeah."

"Suspicious of the rest of the food?"

"Sus… suspitious," Jo repeats, clearly liking the sound of that word. "Yeah… yeah."

Isaak grabs a strip of crispy bacon and pops it on the side of her plate. "Try that. It's delicious."

Jo looks put off by the darkened cut of meat. She wrinkles up her nose and shakes her head. "I don't want to try it."

"If you don't try it, you'll never know how good it is."

"Aunty Bree has it at home sometimes," Jo says warily.

"But have you tried it?"

"No."

Isaak nods to her plate. "Eat up. You'll need a big breakfast before we head out today."

Her eyes go wide with excitement. "We're going out?!"

I glare at Isaak, hoping to get his attention. He very pointedly ignores me.

"You wanted an outing today, didn't you?"

"Yeah!"

"Alright then, where would you like to go?"

"I get to choose?"

"You get to choose."

She squeals and claps her hands together, clearly delighted. "I know where I want to go."

"Let's hear it."

"The aquarium!"

Isaak doesn't so much as blink. "Then that's where we're headed. But first, eat up. No bacon, no aquarium."

Jo looks down at her plate and considers the bacon for a moment. Then she picks it up and raises it to her mouth. She takes a tentative bite and then another, bigger one.

"Hey... it's good. It's really good!"

Isaak smiles triumphantly. I grind my teeth in irritation. It all comes so easily to him. Every aspect of his world. Even this, something he never dreamed he'd be doing.

I don't know whether I want to jump his bones or break them.

"Bread and butter is also a good breakfast," I say sourly.

Isaak meets my eyes and his smile only gets wider. "Jo, why don't you try this after you're done with that? It's a chocolate croissant."

"Okay," she says happily.

I get up and head towards the kitchen island with my cup of coffee. After a moment, Isaak joins me.

"Is there a problem?" he rumbles.

"Do you have to be so controlling with my five-year-old?"

"First of all, she's my five-year-old, too. And secondly, which part of encouraging your child to have a full breakfast is controlling?"

"It… it's just the way you did it."

"How did I do it?"

"You manipulated her. You… you bribed her."

"Yeah, I think that's the first chapter in Parenting 101. *How to Bribe Your Kids.*"

I shake my head and change the subject. "What is this trip?"

"What do you mean?"

"I mean, what's your motive?"

He raises his eyebrows, and his expression turns deadly serious. "I'm planning on stealing all the rarest fish in the aquarium so that I can sell them on the black market. Premium sushi is all the rage these days."

I glare at him. "That's not funny."

He smiles and shrugs. "Stop asking me stupid questions, and you'll stop getting stupid answers."

"I'm not playing *Happy Family Field Trip* with you," I snap.

He looks supremely unconcerned. "Fine. Then you can stay behind and explain to Jo why you'd rather spend the day here alone."

My heart plummets as I realize that there's no way out of this. "Damn you."

Isaak merely lifts his mug to his lips and smirks.

∾

After breakfast, the three of us pile into one of Isaak's more modest cars and we head off to the aquarium. I try to resist, but I can't help stealing little glances at him the whole way there.

It just feels a little... weird, to say the least.

Going to such a normal place with Isaak feels a little bit like we've entered the Twilight Zone. He's going to stick out like a sore thumb.

Two hours later, my assumption has proved to be true.

But not in the way I thought.

Isaak sticks out, but he's not awkward or conscious in any way. He walks around, holding Jo's hand and giving her extra little tidbits that not even the information cards offer.

There's a species of jellyfish that are biologically immortal.

Dolphins have two stomachs.

And apparently, stingrays are closely related to sharks.

I didn't know any of this. But Isaak does. Don't ask me how. As we walk through each display, each tank, each room, he reads out the information cards to Jo and then tacks on another little morsel that has her eyes going wide and her jaw dropping in delight every time.

He seems completely at ease. I guess I shouldn't have expected anything less.

But he does stick out. His height, the breadth of his shoulders, his blue eyes, his handsome face. I counted a dozen different women openly checking him out before we even made it through the first exhibit space.

He doesn't seem to notice that I haven't said a word to him since we left the house. Or maybe he just doesn't care. But I'm starting to realize that the silent treatment is wearing more on me than it is on him.

"Jo," Isaak calls. "Come on."

"Where are we going now?"

She's been a ball of energy since we got here and she shows no signs of powering down any time soon. Which is a good thing, I suppose, because neither does Isaak.

One of the aquarium managers leads us through a darkened path that opens out into a bright space framed by fake rock and a massive pool in between.

I hear the clap of laughter and I know immediately that we're in the presence of—

"Dolphins!" Jo screams. "Oh my God!" She sprints forward and grabs Isaak's huge hand in both of hers. "Can I touch them?"

"You can do more than that," he says. "You can get in there with him."

Jo looks positively entranced as she turns to me. "Did you hear that, Mommy? I can get in with the dolphins!"

I put on my brightest, fakest smile. "I heard, baby."

"You can get in, too, ma'am," the aquarium manager offers courteously. "We have diving suits in all sizes."

"Thanks, but I think I'll sit out here and watch."

Isaak doesn't even glance my way as he leads Jo to the changing rooms. When they re-emerge, they're both decked out in full diving gear.

It's freaking annoying how good Isaak looks. His every muscle is accentuating by the tight, unforgiving material. No one looks good in head-to-toe Spandex.

Except for Isaak Vorobev.

They clamber into the tank with the employee diver and I watch for about an hour as Jo pets and plays with the two dolphins who are brought out to us.

I stare at Isaak almost as much as I do Jo. By the end of the hour, my smile is coming in more naturally.

She's sacrificed so much in her short life, even if she doesn't know it. Maybe Isaak is right: maybe she deserves a father. And not just any father, but him. The kind of man who can offer her things like this.

Maybe I'm not enough for her on my own.

I shake away the dark thoughts clouding my head as the employee helps Jo out of the tank. She and Isaak waddle off to change back into their clothes.

When they re-emerge, we head back into the main body of the aquarium. Literally the second we step back amongst the public, I spy a pair of young women gawking up at Isaak and giggling sheepishly behind their hands.

"Jesus," I say, rolling my eyes.

"What's the matter?"

"Nothing," I say with a shrug. "Just wondering if we should get a display case for you, too."

His smile is a little too knowing. "Does it bother you when other women check me out?"

I snort. "Hardly."

But I'm not sure I'm doing a very good job of being convincing. Rather than stay for the standard Vorobev Inquisition, I charge ahead and stick close to Jo as we finish circling through the last few displays.

When we're done, I look up and realize Isaak isn't trailing us like I thought he was. Matter of fact, he's at the far end of the tunnel, chatting with a woman I don't recognize.

She's my age, give or take, and she's pretty. Very pretty. Strawberry blonde hair and the kind of petite-but-curvy frame that drives men wild.

"Mommy, who's that?" Jo asks, following my eyes.

"Just some woman who's bored, sweetheart. Why don't you go watch the crabs? Then we can head outside again. Stay where I can see you."

Jo goes without argument. I storm over to Isaak and his new bimbo.

I hear the back end of their conversation. The woman flips her hair with unnecessary vigor as the walls seem to echo with her laughter.

"It's impressive that you know so much about ocean life," she says flirtatiously, touching his arm. "I heard you telling your daughter about whales before."

We did the whale exhibit two hours ago. Has this woman been keeping tabs on us since then?

"I read a lot," Isaak says calmly.

I wouldn't call him a flirty personality. His voice doesn't change; his mannerisms don't shift. He's just unfailingly confident through everything he does.

Including this.

"Excuse me," I blurt, pushing myself right into the conversation.

The blonde turns to me with disappointed eyes. She must've clocked who I was a long time ago. "Oh, hello! You must be Isaak's friend."

If I could shoot venom out of my body like one of the stingrays we'd passed earlier, I would do it now.

"Friend?" I repeat. "No, I'm not his friend. I'm his wife."

I know the minute the word leaves my lips that I'll pay for this later. But at the moment, it's worth it to see the look on her face as her hopes falter and die.

"Oh. I didn't realize."

"Isaak," I say, glancing towards him, "Jo's tired. She wants to go home."

"I'm sorry, Annabelle," he says, while I roll my eyes behind her. "It was a pleasure talking to you."

She gives him a sad wave before we head over towards Jo. I can practically feel the smugness rolling off him. Which is exactly why I do everything I can do avoid his eyes.

"She was nice," he says simply.

"Shut up."

He chuckles.

"Next time," I add, "maybe you could avoid chatting up some gold-digger while you're supposed to be spending time with your daughter."

He looks at me with raised eyebrows. "You've spent the last few days telling me that you're not my wife and Jo's not my daughter. What changed in the last five minutes?"

I start to retort but fall silent when I realize I don't actually know how to come back from that one. How does he always manage to trap me so simply, so effortlessly?

"If there's something you want from me, Camila… you'll need to say so."

"I don't want anything from you," I snap, just as Jo comes up between us.

"Where to next?" she asks before Isaak can respond.

He meets my gaze for a moment longer before looking away. It's a good thing, too—another couple of seconds and his stare would have burned a hole in my face.

"Home, kiddo," Isaak says, swallowing her hand in his.

She doesn't so much as blink when he says that. Because now, for Jo, home is where Isaak is.

Where the hell does that leave me?

28

ISAAK

The atmosphere between us has been tense for days now, but it hits an all-time high as we sit in the car, pretending to be a real family.

"We should be home in half an hour."

I can probably get us there in fifteen. But I'm taking the long route. Even with the discomfort of all the tension, something about having Camila and Jo this close… it makes me feel something.

I just can't quite put my finger on what.

"Home," Cami whispers.

I brace myself for some catty remark to follow, but nothing comes. She didn't even say it with her usual feisty passive-aggressiveness. In fact, she seems almost… calm. Eerily so.

"It's your home, you know," she says, keeping her voice low, reminding me that Jo's asleep in the back seat. "Not mine."

"I think that's up to you."

She's quiet for so long that I assume she's done talking. Then: "You were great with her today."

I'm not expecting that. "Thank you," I say sincerely.

"Seriously. All those hours walking around, talking about ocean stuff, answering her questions…"

"Which part of that surprised you?"

"Your patience," she admits without hesitation.

"I can be patient when I try to be."

"Clearly, you've never tried with me, huh?"

"Are we fighting again?"

She sighs. "No. I don't want to fight today. I'm too tired."

I glance at her, noticing how subdued her green eyes look right now. She's got her arms wrapped around her body again.

"Are you cold?"

"No," she insists. "No, I'm not cold."

"Camila—"

"She doesn't need me," she blurts. The words wrench from her as though I'm holding a gun to her head.

She pointedly avoids my eyes, but I see her cheeks burning red. It's obvious how much it cost her to say that out loud. To me, no less.

"Why do you say that?"

"Oh, come on. You were there yesterday."

"I was, and I don't know what you're talking about."

She glances towards me. "She may call me Mommy, but she doesn't see me as that."

"She's five. Her version of normal is different. That's not necessarily a bad thing."

"Isn't it? Somehow, I always assumed that I'd be able to come back one day and things would just… fit together. I'd be her mom and she'd be my kid and we'd be like two peas in a pod. We'd be happy."

"She's happy now," I point out.

"I'm not naïve. I know she's settled here," she admits. "But that's exactly my point. She seems to connect with you, your mom, your brother… everyone except for me."

"Is it possible that maybe you're expecting a little too much from her?"

She frowns. "What do you mean?"

"I mean that she's five and, like you've already said, she's used to not having you around. She should be taking the lead from you, not the other way around."

"You mean I should be trying harder?"

"It's not a matter of trying harder, Camila. Just be there for her. Be with her. Without expectations. Stop expecting her to run to you, to grab your hand, to ask for your help. Just make yourself available to her, and eventually, she'll turn to you of her own accord."

Her expression grows contemplative. "Is that another lesson from Parenting 101?"

I drum my fingers on the wheel. "I had no expectations walking in to meet her the first time. I just wanted to see her. I stayed on the fringes and watched her. I didn't push, and I didn't ask too much. Eventually, she became curious about me."

"It's different for you."

"How so?"

"You haven't been dreaming of being reunited with your kid for almost six years. You can have different expectations, because your sense of responsibility is different."

My expression turns cold. "You assume that just because I found out about Jo recently, my sense of responsibility towards her is less than yours?

"You're a man."

"Is there a point forthcoming?"

She glares at me, her green eyes piercing. "Nothing matters more to you than the Bratva," she says. "You think that makes you so different from so-called 'normal' men? It doesn't. It's just a different version of the same thing. Men put themselves, their goals, their careers ahead of everything else. They focus on ambition as opposed to family."

"Oh, I see," I growl. "The Bratva means more to me than Jo."

"You've made that admission yourself before."

"I don't believe I was talking about my daughter."

"Does she need to be mentioned specifically?" Camila asks. "I don't know that she does."

"Jesus, Camila. Get off your high horse."

She looks at me with naked shock, startled.

"It's clear you haven't understood a fucking thing I've said to you."

"What have I missed?"

"Everything. Absolutely everything."

She considers my expression for a second. "Care to explain it to me then?" she asks softly.

"Why?" I snap. "You've already made up your mind about where I stand. I'm just a savage, no more than an animal who takes what he wants when he wants it."

She raises her hackles, arms over her chest and jaw clenched tight. "You want me to think different?" she counters. "Then be different."

"I am what I am."

"And I'm supposed to understand that, aren't I?" she asks. Her voice cracks ever-so-slightly. "I'm supposed to understand you, but you don't owe me anything where my feelings are concerned. Did I get that right?"

"Your feelings?" I ask as we hurtle through the gates of the compound. "I'll start acknowledging your feelings when you start admitting to them."

We're here sooner than I would like, and since I'm not prepared for this conversation to end, I make sure the doors stay locked when I park.

It's unnecessary, though, because Camila doesn't even seem to register the fact that we're back at the mansion or that I've parked the car.

"Don't fucking turn this around on me," she hisses, her eyes darting to Jo to make sure she's still sleeping.

"It is already about you, so why shouldn't I?"

"I'm allowed to be pissed that you stole my child!"

"*My* child," I correct harshly. "And I took her because you kept her from me for far too fucking long."

"That's not an excuse."

"I'm not giving you an excuse; I'm giving you my reasoning."

"Your reasoning is ridiculous."

"You're ridiculous," I snap.

She falls back against her seat as though I've slapped her. Her chest rises and falls and I can't help but admire the cleavage I can see peeking out through the V neck of her tight white t-shirt. I notice that her nipples are hard and poking out through the thin fabric. I decide to be a gentleman and refrain from pointing that out.

I refuse to let her rile me up. Instead, I lean back in my seat and look at her calmly. "You want to have an honest conversation, Camila? Then let's be honest."

She frowns.

"You were jealous today."

Her eyes go wide when she realizes how I'm planning on cornering her. "Isaak…" she stammers, looking away.

"Come on," I press. "What was with that whole display?"

"Jesus. It was hardly a 'display.'"

"Answer a single fucking question honestly, Camila. For once, just say the truth, as you mean it, as you feel it. What do you want to be? Are you my wife or not?"

She tries to avoid my eyes, but there's nowhere for her to hide. "What do you want me to say to that?" she rasps hoarsely.

Jo stirs in her sleep. Scowling, I gesture for Camila to get out of the car. I step out before she can get her car door open and stalk around to meet her on her side.

I wait until she turns to me, her face blazing with guilt, resentment, anger. She meets my eyes and I can see the defeat edging into them.

"I was jealous, okay?" she says. "Is that what you wanted to hear?"

"It's a start."

She grits her teeth furiously. "I know it was stupid, because I have no real right over you. We're not a couple, no matter what that piece of paper says. But… but… I got fucking jealous. I did. I can't deny that."

I nod.

"But why were you even talking to her?" she explodes at me.

I have to retain my smirk. Though it's a very satisfying feeling to know that she's still insecure about a random conversation I was having with a stranger who means nothing to me.

Not that I didn't know exactly what I was doing when I'd encouraged the pretty blonde with the calculating eyes.

"She came up to me," I say innocently. "She started a conversation."

"She was hitting on you! You were supposed to be spending time with Jo—"

"Don't," I interrupt. "I spent every moment of today with that kid and you're harping on the two minutes I decided to pay attention to someone else? Grow up."

She starts to splutter, "Are you ser—"

But I cut in again. "Or is it more about the fact that I wasn't paying attention to you?"

"Fuck you," she spits. "Fuck you, fuck you, fuck you."

"Why were you jealous, Camila? Why does it matter if you don't care about me?"

She shakes her head and tries to turn from me without answering.

I grab her hand and twist her around so that she has nowhere to run. "Come on. You're the one who's demanding honesty from me. Give some to get some."

"Why should I? I never get it from you!"

"You want me to be honest with you?"

"Yes."

"Fine," I say without letting her go. "The truth is, I don't want Maxim anywhere near you or Jo."

"Jesus, I already knew that, Isaak."

"What you don't know is that, for a moment there, I was worried that you'd choose him."

She stops short. We both do. The only sound is our mingled breath coming hot in the cool air.

Cami's eyes search my face for signs of a trap. "Are… are you serious?"

I don't look away. "Why would I lie?"

She shakes her head. "You were worried I'd choose him?"

"You have a history with him. I wasn't sure how deep your feelings for him ran."

"I have no feelings for him, Isaak," she says after a long pause. "Not anymore."

"I know that now."

She looks down, then to the side, and then up again. Anywhere but at me. Her hands hang limply like she doesn't know what to do with them anymore.

"You… you were jealous, too?" she asks tentatively. Hopefully.

"Of course I fucking was."

"You hid it well."

I shrug. "All part of my training."

A small smile edges into the corners of her mouth. "I wasn't aware that your training extended to marital relations."

"Now you have jokes?" I scoff. "What happened to the white-hot rage?"

"Sorry. I'm just… surprised, I guess. I never expected an admission like that from you."

"Don't get used to it."

She rolls her eyes. "Being human doesn't make you any less strong, you know?"

I laugh bitterly. "Tell that to my father."

"I would if he were around," she says immediately.

"I'm not sure you would. He was a scary man."

She scoffs. "If I can handle you, I can handle anyone."

"You're delusional if you think you can handle me at all."

"Is that a challenge?" she asks, taking a step towards me.

I smile. She returns it. My cock jumps to life and she seems to realize the underlying sexual tension that's just sparked between us. Well, really, it's always sparking between us. But sometimes the heat becomes too much to ignore.

"I would never choose him over you," she whispers. "I would never choose anyone over you."

I reach out and tuck a loose strand of her hair back behind her ears.

"Today was a good day," she tells me.

I nod. "It was."

"Is there a reason you know so much about ocean life?"

"The same way you know so much about literature, art, and history. I read."

"When do you find the time?"

"I don't sleep."

She smiles. "Figures. Too tough for sleep. Very on-brand."

I chuckle again. "How would you feel about inviting your sister and her family over one day?"

The question catches her off-guard. She just stares at me for a long moment before she finds her words again. "Um… my sister? You want to invite her where?"

"Here."

"Here as in here-here? To the mansion?"

"Camila…" I say tiredly.

"You… you would do that?"

"She's your sister. She's Jo's family. And she is the woman who raised Jo. From what I can tell, she did a damn good job of it too."

Her eyes are bright with naked gratitude. "Isaak… that would be perfect. Perfect."

"I figure I might as well make an attempt at undoing the damage I've caused to my reputation by taking Jo."

She bites her bottom lip, and my cock perks up a little more. "Uh… yeah. I covered for you."

I raise my eyebrows. "You did?"

She nods. "A little white lie."

"Why?"

"Does it matter?"

"Camila."

"Don't make me say it."

"I think you know me well enough by now to know I'm going to make you say it."

She sighs. "I was trying to protect you, okay?"

I smile, knowing exactly why she would want to shield the more unsavory aspects of my personality from her sister: because she wants Bree to like me.

"Will you wipe that look off your face?" she snaps.

"What look?"

"That smug fucking smirk."

She tries to turn away from me, but I pin her between me and the car. "Where do you think you're going?"

"We have to get Jo inside," she says with a noticeable little gulp.

"She's comfortable," I growl. "It can wait."

Then I lower my lips down to her neck.

Her body goes limp the moment I touch her. My hand finds her breast and I feel her up while my kisses leave a trail of heat along her neck and jawline.

"Isaak…" she moans.

"You're mine, Camila," I whisper to her, pinching her nipples between my fingers through the fabric of her dress.

I pull away for a moment so I can look into those jade green eyes of hers.

"You hear me? Mine."

Her lips are raw, her eyes misty with desire. "I hear you."

29

CAMILA

"This is so much fun!" Jo squeals as she runs around the garden.

I'd asked to have our breakfast laid in one of the circular little nooks strewn across the garden. This particular one has a stone table and bench built in, so it was perfect.

I expected Jo and me to have a little heart-to-heart while we ate. But she took one look at our surroundings, said to heck with breakfast, and started exploring. She scampers back over periodically for a bite of bacon—a newfound favorite, ever since Isaak bewitched her with the stuff—before going back in pursuit of a butterfly or a caterpillar or some particularly grim looking marble bust covered in ivy.

Which means I've been sitting here alone, contemplating the last twenty-four hours and all the things I wish I could take back.

Also, the things I wouldn't take back. Like the moment I'd interrupted Isaak's "talk" with that blonde girl and referred to myself as his wife. I don't think I'd change anything about that.

"Mind if I join you?" comes a sudden voice.

"Nikita," I say in surprise. "Sure, please, sit down."

She's dressed impeccably today, as usual, in emerald green pants, long and flowing, and her blouse is a draped white confection that almost comes down to her knees. It's artsy and graceful and suits her perfectly.

Even the touch of gray coming in around her temples is refined and elegant. I could live ten lifetimes and still not figure out how to mimic her ever-present poise.

She sits down opposite me just as Jo comes running up to the table again.

"Babushka!" she cries, diverting her trajectory and going straight to Nikita. "Are you going to eat breakfast with us?"

"I'd like to. Do you mind?"

"No, I like it."

Nikita leans in and places a gentle kiss on Jo's forehead. As wary as I am of Jo assimilating to life here, I can't help but soften at the way everyone treats her. Like a precious object. Even Nikita's kiss is filled with affection.

Suddenly, it makes sense why Jo settled here with these people so easily. How can you not, when you're the recipient of so much love?

"Is this your plate?" Nikita asks her, pointing to the half-eaten piece of buttered toast that sits beside a bed of fresh berries.

"Uh-huh. I'm walking and talking."

Nikita smiles, and it makes me realize I've never actually heard her laugh. Not a real, full, uninhibited laugh. It's almost like she's lost the ability.

"Walking and talking?"

"Yup," Jo says, taking a big bite of her toast. She pops a strawberry into her mouth and runs off in the direction of the pond. "Be right back! I'm talking to the frogs."

"She's adventurous," Nikita observes as Jo goes to kneel by the water's edge.

"Alarmingly so," I chuckle, keeping a careful eye out. "What would you like to eat?"

"Just some coffee, if you'd be so kind. I like mine strong."

I pour her a cup and she gives it a tentative little sip before sighing and looking out over the gardens.

I eat my avocado toast and observe Nikita silently. I can imagine what she must have been like in her heyday. Beautiful, sophisticated, charming. She would have made a worthy Bratva wife. The kind of woman any don would be proud to have on his arm.

"You're staring."

I nearly jump. Apparently, she has her son's ability to observe everything even when it seems her attention is focused elsewhere.

"Sorry," I mumble.

"Go ahead."

"I'm sorry?"

"Ask me whatever it is you wanted to ask."

I blush. "I was just wondering what it was like for you. Like, entering this family."

She gives me a knowing nod. "It started with promise. I was very excited to marry Vitaly."

"So he didn't kidnap you then?"

I'm not trying to be facetious or accusatory, but it certainly comes out that way.

Nikita just gives me an understanding smile. "I can understand why you might imagine that's how all Bratva dons find their wives. But it's more the exception than the rule, I'm afraid."

"So I'm one of the lucky few?"

Nikita ignores that. "My father was a businessman in St Petersburg. I lived there until I was seven years old. After my mother passed away, he moved us here, to America. As soon as we landed, my father got to work. He made contacts. At the time, there was only a small Russian community and it was mostly controlled by one significant name."

"Vorobev," I guess instantly.

She nods. "His business suffered on its own. It took the help of the Vorobevs to give him a leg up. But that partnership cemented a friendship between my father and Vitaly's."

"Oh. So it was an arranged marriage sort of situation?"

"In a way," she answers. "We were thrown together in the hopes that something would materialize. The first night we met properly was at Yakov's wedding."

"Who's Yakov?"

"Vitaly's older brother."

"Maxim's father," I whisper.

She nods again. "I watched the splendor of that marriage. I watched Svetlana walk down the aisle in her gown. She was beautiful. And the groom looked so happy. I was young enough to buy into the fairytale. But really, I fell prey to the pretty picture. I saw only the beauty and the wealth and the security of marrying into the Vorobev Bratva. Vitaly was handsome and charismatic. Between those things, how could I not swallow the lie?"

"Did he woo you?" I ask. Based on what Isaak's told me about his father, I can't exactly imagine it.

"Not in the traditional way," Nikita admits. "Bratva men tend to woo their women differently."

"A casual kidnapping to get the blood going?" I joke.

She smiles—an open, sincere smile that just barely reaches her eyes. "I suppose it's adjacent to that method." I raise my eyebrows, and she continues, "In that the woman really doesn't have much of a choice, once he's decided that she's the one he wants."

"And Vitaly decided on you?"

"I don't say this with pride or ego, but when I was young, I was very beautiful."

"You're still beautiful," I assure her. It's easy to say because it's true.

"You're kind," she says, but I can tell she gets no real pleasure from the compliment. She's past the stage where her looks are of any consequence to her. It occurs to me suddenly that maybe she even resents them, for garnering the attention of a man who so dramatically changed the course of her life.

"A few months later, I had my own wedding," Nikita continues. "It was not as grand or as big as Yakov's. As the younger brother, that was only fitting. But at the time, I thought it was perfect. I was so happy on that day. I was proud to be his wife."

I nod. "For a while, right? But it changed."

Nikita sighs. "I was not a person to him; I was his property. He used me when it suited him and discarded me soon after. He entertained his whores in our bed and disrespected me in front of his men just to get a laugh."

I can see the depths of her humiliation etched in every line on her face. And for the first time, she does look old to me. She looks affected by all the years she's lived. Scarred in ways I can see and ways I can't.

"I knew I could never leave him. If I tried, he would kill me. So I stayed and I decided to find solace in my children. But…"

She trails off and exhales again. Another deep, cavernous sigh laced with lingering pain, lingering loss. "I was a fool to think that my children were my own. Just like me, they were his property. They always were. I thought at the very least, I would get to keep one. Bogdan would be mine. But no… he was taken, too."

"You make it seem like they were stolen from you and never returned."

"That's how it felt. We lived under the same roof. But they were governed by different rules. They answered to their father. They were taught by him. They had nannies and tutors. They had him. What did they need me for?"

"Love?"

She raises her eyes to mine and smiles. "I was struggling, Camila," she says softly. "I barely knew how to love myself. How could I love them? Especially when they belonged so fully to him."

I struggle to understand what she's trying to tell me. "But surely… you loved them?"

"Oh, God yes," she says, her eyes going wide when she realizes I've misunderstood. "Of course I loved them. I love them both. They are my sons. But I never got to shape them or raise them or nurse them through the harder moments of their lives. I was kept at a distance."

"Why?"

"Because Vitaly was raising leaders. Dons," she explains. "He wanted to weed out any softness in them. He wanted to make sure I wouldn't corrupt them with my weaknesses."

"Your weaknesses being what: compassion, empathy, affection?"

"All of the above."

"Then he did them a disservice."

She shakes her head. "He never understood something: you can't weed those things out of people. No matter how hard you try. Nature matters so much more than nurture sometimes. Vitaly assumed that because his relationships were transactional, that it would be the same for his sons. He never saw it coming."

"Which part?"

"The bond that my sons have with each other. Isaak protected Bogdan at every turn. It's the reason he was able to have some semblance of a childhood."

I think of those scars on Isaak's forearm, and I feel my heart tighten at the image of a ten-year-old standing in front of his little brother like a human shield.

"Isaak stood up to Vitaly."

"For Bogdan, yes. He did it time and time again. Vitaly realized that if he pushed, he would lose the battle. But he chose to focus on the fact that Isaak, at such a young age, was strong enough and brave enough to stand up to him. It bodes well for the day when Isaak would take over."

"There is no one stronger than Isaak," I say softly.

Nikita smiles. "He'd like to hear you say that. Vitaly would, too. But don't be fooled by his shiny armor, Camila. Every single person needs someone to help them carry their burdens. Even I did."

The way her expression changes tips me off immediately. It feels like we've been circling around something hidden for a long time and I'm only just now realizing what she actually came to talk about.

"Who did you choose to help you carry your burden?" I ask, choosing my words carefully.

She smiles like a teacher whose prized pupil understands the lesson. "A man who was kind to me."

She says it in every way but with her words: *I had an affair.* Probably with someone close to Vitaly, if I had to guess. One of his lieutenants, maybe. Someone sworn to protect him and his family.

"That was bold of you," I say without judgement.

Nikita shrugs. "Not really. I was desperate. Blind with loneliness and hopelessness. I wanted an escape. I needed something to cling to. Life was not worth living, if it meant living in Vitaly's shadow."

"Were you in love with him?" I ask, wondering if I'm overstepping.

But Nikita doesn't seem to mind. "Very much," she says softly.

I can sense the urgency of her feelings, even now. I wonder how many years she's spent keeping these things to herself. How hard that must've been. How alienating.

"Did Vitaly ever find out?"

"No. He didn't, and I took that secret with me to his grave. Until now."

I look at her in shock. "You mean I'm the first person you've told?"

"Yes."

"Why?"

"You're an outsider, too, just like I was."

"You're not encouraging me to have an affair, are you?" I ask, trying and failing to make a pitiful joke.

"Oh, I know there's no such risk."

I frown. "And why is that?"

"Because you love my son," Nikita says confidently.

I consider denying it, but I don't want to ruin this conversation by punctuating it with a lie. There's something to be said about honesty. It can build bridges, close distances. Make friends.

We're interrupted when one of the maids enters the garden. "Ma'am," she says to me. "Your sister and her family are here."

Nikita rises to her feet. "I'll give you some privacy."

"You don't have to leave."

She smiles. "That's kind of you, but I don't want to intrude on your reunion. I'm sure I'll meet them another time."

With that, she picks up her cup of coffee and glides out of the garden through a path that leads away from the house. I get to my feet and glance around for Jo, but she's out of sight for the moment. I can hear her tromping through a nearby hedge.

Before I can call for her, Bree turns the corner.

I stand there in shock, staring at my big sister for the first time in over two years. It takes me an absurdly long time to remember how to use my words.

"Bree!"

"Oh, Cami!" she cries.

We run into each other's arms in a pretty good imitation of a romantic movie scene. We hug each other tight as I try to fight back the tears that are threatening to flood my cheeks.

When we finally pull apart, I realize Bree lost the fight with her own tears.

"You big softie," I accuse her, reaching up to wipe away her tears.

She laughs. "Becoming a mother does it to you. Where's Jo?"

"Don't worry, she'll be here. She's off exploring the gardens."

"Cool! Are there any dinosaurs here?"

I turn around and catch sight of Jake and the boys. I run forward and embrace each one, astonished at how much Bree's sons have grown in the last couple of years.

It makes me feel old. Makes me remember just how long I've spent apart from them.

Bree shakes her head. "Cami, this place... It's amazing!"

Jake looks at me with wide eyes. "'Amazing' doesn't even begin to cover it. This is full blown luxury. You've been living the high life, huh?"

I shoot my brother-in-law an annoyed glance. "I wouldn't put it quite like that. But yes, it's definitely comfortable here."

"AUNTY BREE!"

Everyone jumps when that elated squeal peals through the air. Jo hurtles straight to Bree and leaps into her arms. I can't even find it in me to be jealous because it's such a joyous moment.

After she's done hugging her aunt, she turns her attention to her uncle and cousins. Bree slips back to my side and we link arms like we used to do as kids.

"This feels pretty surreal, doesn't it?" she remarks.

I nod. "You have no idea."

"This place really is spectacular."

"I know."

Bree glances over at me. "Are things as amazing as they look?" she asks, her tone changing.

I take a deep breath. "It's... complicated."

"Okay, fair enough. I figured you'd say that. Tell me this: do you want to be here?"

I bite my bottom lip. "Actually, I do. For right now, I think I do."

She smiles. "Is it because of him?"

I don't say anything, because I know she can see it all in my eyes. She nods slowly and tightens her grip around my shoulders.

"Of course it's complicated," she says. "Love always is."

30

ISAAK

"How many?"

"A small contingent. Seven men in total."

"How far from our safehouse?"

Bogdan checks the monitors. "A couple of miles."

"Fuck," I groan, slamming my fist down on the table. "This is not the only movement we're seeing. Two days ago, same thing at our Maple Valley safehouse. And a few days before that, same thing at Cedar Hurst. They're connected."

"We can contain it."

"That's not what I'm worried about," I say. "He's planning something."

"So are we."

"The fucker orchestrated that meeting with Camila because he had an ace up his sleeve. Now, he's forced to resort to the back-up plan. I know Maxim—that's going to make him desperate. Desperate men do reckless things."

"And reckless people make mistakes."

"Sometimes," I say firmly. "Sometimes, they're content to make fucking chaos."

"It's a good thing you thrive on chaos, then," Bogdan points out.

At another point in my life, I would have agreed with him. I still do, in some respects. But everything has changed now.

"I can't afford to anymore," I say softly. "I have Jo to think of."

Bogdan watches me carefully. "And Cami."

"Say what you want about Otets, he was right about one thing: sentimentality makes you weak."

Bogdan raises his eyebrows. "That's the old dad wisdom you're summoning up right now? Seriously?"

"Think about it: he had no weaknesses. Not a single one, because he didn't allow people to affect him. Even you and I… we were his sons, but did he ever once treat us like we were anything more than projects?"

"And that's what you want for Jo?"

"I didn't say that."

"You seem to be implying it."

I roll my eyes. "Don't be a smart ass. I'm just saying, I can understand why he would want to keep his relationships—"

"Cold and unfeeling?"

"Call it what you want. He was strong because of it."

"And he was still poisoned and murdered," Bogdan points out. "As strong as he was, it didn't save him."

I can't argue with that.

"Jo and Cami, they're good for you, *sobrat*. They'll give your life purpose. Otets never had any outside of the Bratva."

"He would argue there's no purpose outside the Bratva."

"Because he loved no one and no one loved him."

"Really?" I ask with raised eyebrows. "Not even you?"

"I feared him. And I respected him… Or at least I did before I knew he was a fucking hypocrite who murdered his own brother."

I nod. "It's hard to wrap my head around even now. He preached loyalty so much."

"That's not why I'm pissed."

I frown. "Then why?"

"He killed his brother, Isaak," Bogdan says softly. "I could never kill you."

I smirk. "I know that. You haven't beaten me in a single fight your entire life."

He doesn't laugh. "When I think about the kind of man who could kill his brother…" He shakes his head. "That's not a man I could ever respect. That's not a man I could ever love."

"You're a better man than I am, Bogdan."

It's his turn to smirk. "Hardly. But since I don't want to argue, let's just say I am the better man."

I laugh and this time, he joins in. It reinforces the bond we have as brothers, to do something so simple as laugh together and clasp my hand on his shoulder. The Bratva is stronger because of this. Because of us. How could Otets not see that?

For the first time in my entire life, I feel pity for the man who made me.

And I feel relief that he hadn't managed to destroy every last breath of humanity I have left in me.

I have Bogdan to thank for that. Mama, too.

And, of course, my wife and daughter.

"We still have to kill Maxim," I say, getting the conversation back on track.

Bogdan nods. "Definitely."

"Keep an eye out on all this movement," I tell Bogdan. "Inform me if there's a breach. And inform all our safehouses. Double up on the men there. If there's an attack, I don't want them to be caught off-guard."

"Got it, boss."

I clap him on the shoulder as I head towards the door.

"Time to meet the family, huh?" he taunts. The mischievous spark is back in Bogdan's tone as he twists around in his seat to look back over his shoulder at me.

I roll my eyes. "They're Jo's family."

"Legally speaking, that makes them yours. You wanna impress them?"

I glare back at him. "Since when have I ever tried to impress anyone?"

"There's a first time for everything."

"Not with this."

I'm about to leave when he stops me again. "Isaak."

"What?" I snap, wheeling around once more.

"Is that really what you're wearing?"

I slam the door closed, but it still doesn't drown out his laughter. I head straight for the gardens, wondering what the next hour will be like.

I've been through every situation in the book. But somehow, this one feels a little alien.

The kids notice me first. Jo comes running up to me and grabs my arm. She swings from it like a chimpanzee and wheedles me towards the adults, who are seated around the picnic table with drinks in hand.

"Aunty Bree, Aunty Bree!" Jo squeals. "This is Isaak. He's Mommy's friend. He's teaching me Russian."

"Is he now?" Bree asks, getting to her feet and offering me her hand.

Bree's a little shorter and fuller than Cami, and she looks older. Partly because the high-waisted blue jeans and loose-fitting blouse enhance every aspect of her mom vibes.

But she's attractive in her own right, and she definitely shares similarities with Camila. A certain wryness about her smile. A flash in her eyes I recognize.

Her husband, on the other hand, is long and lanky. He looks like a caricature of a cartoon character with his round glasses and his awkward handshake. But something about him seems painfully genuine. I decide I like him already.

"It's nice to finally meet you, Isaak," Bree says carefully.

"And you." I nod, sitting down next to Camila.

Bree watches my every move. Her eyes flit between Camila and me, picking up on everything from the tiniest little brushes to the most fleeting of glances.

I can sense how nervous Camila is. Her usual fire has been tamped down by the tension of the moment.

"This place is amazing," Jake says.

I give an inward sigh at the small talk, but I force myself through it for Cami's sake. "Thanks."

Apparently, my one-word answer throws him for a loop, because he turns to his wife for help.

"So, Isaak… we don't know what exactly you do for a living."

Camila goes ramrod stiff next to me. I have to hold back a laugh. "This and that, really," I say vaguely. "It would probably bore you."

Bree smiles brightly. "Not at all. I'm interested."

"Well, I have several businesses in the States and abroad."

"What kind of businesses?"

"Don't worry, they're all legal. Well, most of them."

For a moment, she looks confused. As though she doesn't know whether to laugh or not. Jake makes the decision for her by giving a little snort of amusement.

"So you're teaching Jo Russian?" he says, not-so-subtly changing the topic.

"She asked to learn. So I'm teaching her."

"You know, it's not wise to start something if you're not going to finish it."

"Bree," Camila warns.

She smiles pleasantly. "Just saying. I read it in a parenting book a while ago."

"Bree," Camila says again in exactly the same tone, clearly trying to diffuse the situation before it escalates. "You know, I remember Jo saying she wanted to show us the marigolds on the other side of the garden."

Jake gets to his feet immediately. "Let's go check them out. She's been dying to show us around."

Bree throws Camila a stern glance but allows herself to be dragged off by her mild-mannered husband. They head towards the children. Camila stays behind with me.

"Well, that was awkward," I say immediately.

She exhales sharply. "Can't you make more of an effort?"

I raise my eyebrows. "I did."

"How?"

"By showing up in the first place."

She narrows her eyes. "Seriously?"

"What do you want from me?" I ask. "I don't do small talk."

"Well, newsflash: that's how people start conversations in the real world."

"Sounds fucking boring."

She glares at me, and just like that, the fire's back. I lean into it, because I like getting her riled up.

"You wouldn't be happy there," I tell her. "In fact, you'd be fucking miserable."

"Where?"

"In the so-called 'real' world."

"Maybe that's what I want," she snaps.

I raise my eyebrows in disbelief. "To be miserable?"

"To be *bored*," she hisses. "To have a normal life. To have normal, mundane, boring problems like everyone else."

I roll my eyes. "Forgive me for not believing you."

She doesn't take the bait. "You can make more of an effort," she says again instead.

"To what end?"

"To win over my sister," she blusters. "To get her to like you!"

I shrug. "I don't need to be liked."

"Fucking hell, Isaak. *I* want her to like you. I want them all to like you."

The moment the words are out of her mouth, she blushes fiercely. I watch the way the color spreads across her face, brightening her eyes and making my cock spring to life.

Given the circumstances, that's fairly inconvenient.

"You know what?" she says angrily. "Never mind. Go back to your exciting, chaotic, dangerous life. I'm probably boring you right now anyway."

Before I can respond, she stalks off.

I lean back and sigh. If this is what people in the real world mean by family drama, I could do without it. But I suppose they might consider murder, betrayal, and intrigue to be a little bit more concerning.

To each their own.

I have to admit, though: seeing Jo play with her cousins makes me feel a little lighter. The boys are good with her. The older one is definitely the more protective one. The young one's way of showing affection is annoying the hell out of Jo. He also keeps glancing back at me, as though he can't quite figure out if I'm real or not.

"This must be strange for you."

I turn to Bree, who's materialized at my shoulder, and give her a half-smile. "Which part?"

"Meeting us," she explains.

I expect her to take the seat opposite me, but instead, she sits right next to me. She doesn't even keep much of a distance between us.

"I wouldn't say it was strange."

"Unwelcome, then?"

"Are you trying to get me in trouble?"

She smiles. "I'm trying to figure you out, Mr. Vorobev."

"I'm afraid you'll be disappointed."

"Why, because there's nothing much to figure out?"

"Because the only way anyone figures me out is if I let them."

Camila has noticed the two of us sitting here. She's quite a distance away and still, I can feel the anxiety rolling off her. But it's not surprising. The girl thinks too much.

Bree has apparently noticed the same thing.

"She's probably trying to figure out a subtle way to come over here and interrupt this conversation."

I smirk. "I'm not sure if she's worried about you or about me."

Bree shoots me a glare. "She tells me everything, you know."

"Not everything."

I have to admit, she has a very impressive glare. Completely devoid of fear. I can't help admiring it.

Then she sighs. "Well, I can't say I don't understand," she says, mostly to herself.

I frown. "What exactly do you understand?"

"Why she managed to get involved in this whole… situation," Bree says, casting me a side glance. "There's something about confidence.

Add that to a handsome face and any woman would have a hard time resisting."

I smile. "Are you hitting on me, Bree?" I ask. "Because I'm flattered, but I don't think it's appropriate in front of the children."

She almost smiles. "Camila has never been one to fall for the best-looking guy," she says abruptly. "It's never been about that for her."

"And you're an authority on Camila, are you?"

"I'm her big sister," Bree says with the same kind of confidence I relate to. "I've known her for her entire life. I mothered her through most of it. And when some asshole plunged her into a world she wasn't prepared for… I was the one she chose to raise her child."

Well, well, well. Big Sister fights dirty.

I like her all the more for it.

"People change, Bree. Maybe Camila is not the same person you remember."

"Actually, she's exactly the same person," Bree tells me. "That's what worries me."

I raise my eyebrows, waiting for the threat that I know is coming. I'm not used to getting them from so diminutive a figure as the woman sitting beside me, but Bogdan was right in one regard: there's a first time for everything.

"She doesn't fall easily, Isaak," Bree continues. "But she has with you."

I listen intently, unwilling to take my eyes off the slender figure in the distance whose eyes keep flitting to me every few seconds.

"So if you hurt her in any way, I will make you pay for it."

I drag my eyes off the curve of Camila's ass and look back at Bree. "You're threatening me?" I ask with amusement.

"You probably feel tempted to laugh right now. Go ahead if you want. It doesn't make the threat any less real. I will make you pay if you hurt her."

"And how do you intend to do that?" I ask mildly.

"Haven't figured that part out yet," she says candidly. "I just know I will."

I smile. "You know what? I believe you."

"She doesn't know how worried I am about you. About Jo. I'm keeping my feelings to myself because she's been through enough. And for the first time in a while, she actually seems… settled. Happier. And she deserves to be."

"I hear you."

"Do you?" she asks. "Because this is not a game to her."

"It's not a game to me, either."

Bree nods. "Okay then."

"Are you giving me your seal of approval now?" I ask, trying to suppress my smile.

She snorts. "Not by a long shot."

"That's okay. I like a challenge."

"Yeah, I bet you do."

"Yup," I say with a crisp nod, "definitely flirting with me."

She snorts with laughter, just as Bogdan comes around the corner with his face drained of color. My expression shifts instantly.

"Excuse me, Bree."

Before she can respond, I walk over to Bogdan.

"Bad news?" I ask.

He shakes his head in dismay. "It's not good, Isaak. Not good at all."

31

CAMILA

"Did Isaak say where he was going?"

Bree gives me a pointed look. "Honey, I think you know better than I that he's not the kind of man who's going to be offering explanations as to where he goes and what he does."

I sigh and sit down next to her. "It's nice to have you here."

"Is it?" she asks. "Because you seem a little on edge."

I shoot her a glance. "I'm not on edge."

"Cami…"

"What were you and Isaak talking about before?"

"Oh, you know, landscaping and interior design." I give her a pointed look and she smiles. "Are you worried about something I might have said, or are you worried about something he might have said?"

"I'm not quite sure," I admit.

She laughs and loops her hand around mine. It takes me back again. To when we were little girls with embarrassing parents and the only solace we found was in each other.

But back then, we'd lived in a little patch of dry land in the Midwest and our parents' idea of an outing was a family barbeque out in the neighbor's backyard. Inevitably, the gossip was boring and the food was bland.

It's a very different view right now. Jo's sitting on Jake's shoulders as they walk around the glistening pond, and the boys are playing with the football they've brought, tackling each other onto the pristine grass and laughing.

"You worry too much," Bree tells me.

"Can you blame me?"

"Not in the slightest. But sometimes you need to avoid worrying, even if it's justified."

"How the hell am I supposed to do that?"

"By trying."

I roll my eyes. "Oh, of course. Why didn't I think of that?"

Bree bumps her shoulder against mine. "You know, when I had Peter, I was a nervous wreck."

"Yeah, I remember."

"You remember some of it, not all of it. I saved the majority of my freak-outs for Jake."

"Really? Not me?"

She laughs at the look on my face. "Does that upset you?"

"A little bit," I say. "I thought I was your best friend."

"You are. But so is he."

"Wow. This changes the way I look at him now. A competitor."

Bree just laughs. "The point is, I went crazy overboard with all my worry. And after a couple of sleepless nights, Jake sat me down and told me that I needed to try to stop thinking so much."

"What were you worried about exactly?"

Bree shrugs. "Having a child in a dying world. Raising him in a society that's motivated by greed and money and judgement. I worried about him being bullied in school. I worried about him falling down the stairs. I worried about everything and anything I could think of. Until Jake held my hand and told me that all the things I was worried about… they were probably gonna happen."

I frown. "That doesn't seem comforting."

"That's what I thought—at first," she says. "He told me that Peter was probably going to go through his share of bullying in school. He would probably be bought in by consumer culture and chase money like everyone else in our neighborhood. He'd probably end up with anxiety or depression at some point in his life and the planet was going to die sooner or later, and his generation would be the one to deal with the major fallout of climate change."

"Yikes. Sounds like quite the pep talk."

Bree laughs. "Actually, it was.

"Explain that to me."

"He was trying to get me to see that you can't predict the future, honey. And you can't change it even if you could. Things will happen. And even if the specific things you worry about don't happen, other things will. You can only prepare your children for what's to come, instead of worrying about shielding them completely from all the woes of the world. Because in that, you will fail."

I sigh. "You think I should prepare Jo, instead of trying to protect her?"

"Listen, this is freaking Bratva we're talking about. I think you definitely need to protect her. But preparing her is also a good idea."

"I suppose I should start by telling her who Isaak is, huh?"

Bree shrugs. "You can start to think about it."

I pick at my lower lip and brood for a moment. "Do you like him?" I blurt out.

Bree glances at me. "Is it important to you that I do?"

"Of course."

"Would it change anything if I said I didn't?"

"Hm... probably not."

She nods. "Good. Yes, I like him."

"Wow, that was assuring."

Bree smiles and pulls on my arm a little tighter. "I gotta say, he is extremely handsome."

I laugh. "Yeah. I know. Don't let him hear you say that, though."

"I mean, the first time I saw him, I was trying really hard not to swoon. Even Jake took one look at him and went, *'Damn.'*"

I burst into laughter. "He did not!"

"Ask him. I kid you not, that's exactly what he said."

"I will ask him."

"Go right ahead."

Once the laughter dies down a little, Bree's expression grows more serious. "As beautiful a man as he may be... it matters more what kind of man he is."

"I know."

"I had a ten-minute conversation with him, Camila. That's not enough to get the measure of a person. You'll have to tell me."

"Before I do, I want to know what your first impressions of him are."

Bree nods. "Okay, well, first of all, he's hot. Did I mention that?"

I laugh and shove her shoulder.

"Like, seriously fucking hot."

"Got it."

"Second of all: he showed up, Camila," she says, her tone going soft.

"You're giving him points for that? It's bare minimum effort."

"Oh, come on! You think he showed up for any other reason apart from you?"

"Jo."

"Jo," Bree repeats. "Yes, probably. But it was mostly for you. Jo wouldn't have cared."

"I don't know about that. Jo loves him."

"She does seem quite fond of him."

"She is indeed. They've already got their own secret language."

"Hate to break it to you, honey, but Russian's not a secret. It's been around for a while and anyone can learn it."

"Somehow, I don't feel like I have the right."

"What?"

"I don't even know, really… Would it be presumptuous of me to learn?"

"I have no idea what you're talking about right now."

I sigh. "What I mean is, it might seem a little bit like I… I want to be a part of his family if I start doing things like that."

"Are you still playing hard to get with the man?"

I snort. "I wish."

"Honey, correct me if I'm wrong but you're legally married, are you not?"

"Well, yes," I say, blushing. "But… once Maxim has been, y'know, dealt with…"

"Yes?"

"… Isaak isn't going to force me to stay with him."

"Oh," Bree says, her eyebrows rising. "Oh."

"Yeah."

She studies my expression carefully. "But you don't want to leave him, do you?"

I shake my head imperceptibly, because somehow saying the words feels like defeat.

"Does he know that?"

"No."

"Then maybe you should tell him."

"Why?"

Bree looks at me in surprise. "Because… because it's the truth."

"I don't know, Bree. Will he even want me around once Maxim's taken care of?"

"You're the mother of his child."

"Two people don't need to be together to raise a child."

Bree sits back a little. I can tell she's thinking carefully about her response. "I agree with that," she says at last. "But if those two people have feelings for each other, I think it's a smart choice to stay together."

"What makes you think he has feelings for me?" I ask. "I mean other than the fact that he *'showed up'* to a garden party at his own house."

She laughs and swats my hand away. "We sat here for ten minutes talking, and for nine and a half of those minutes he didn't take his eyes off you."

I'm not gonna lie, it feels good to hear her say that. Bree knows it, too. Her eyes flash with mirth.

"I am scared, Bree," I say softly. "I'm so fucking scared."

"Of course you are," she says at once. "This is an intimidating world to be a part of. But I gotta say… it suits you."

"It doesn't always feel that way. What if I don't fit in?"

"You make space for yourself in it. If that's what you want."

"Maybe I do. I don't know everything I want. But I do know…"

"You want Isaak in your life."

I nod. "Yeah. That."

"Falling in love doesn't mean you betrayed your values, Cami."

"Doesn't it?" I protest. "I'm giving up everything for a man. How is that not betrayal?"

"What exactly are you giving up?" Bree questions. "A life on the run, a transient existence away from your family? At least now you have safety and security."

"Because of a man."

"A man you love. A man who loves you back."

"He's never actually said that to me. I doubt he ever will."

"Why?"

"He'd consider it a sign of weakness."

Bree frowns. "Cami, if you're not really happy here, you always have me and Jake. You come back home and you can stay with us for as long as you want to."

"Thank you. That means a lot to me."

"It's not a hollow offer."

"I know."

I lean my head on her shoulder and wonder where Isaak is now. Where he had to rush off to so abruptly. I wonder, if I decide to stay with him, will I spend the rest of my life in a state of panicked worry?

I take a deep breath and remember what Bree just said to me: I can't control the outcomes here, so why waste brain space worrying about them?

I turn my gaze to Jo and watch her laugh.

And in that moment, I stop worrying. Just for a little while.

∽

A couple of hours later, once the sun has set and we've all moved inside, Bree gets to her feet. "Time to go, kiddos."

"No!" Jo laments, grabbing a hold of her hand.

"It's past your bedtime, little munchkin," she says, touching her fingertip to Jo's nose. "And we'll come back again to see you."

"Soon?"

"Very soon."

Jo seems to be satisfied with that. Her eyelids are pretty droopy anyway and I realize that Bree's right. It got late when I wasn't paying attention.

"Aunt Cami?"

I turn to Sam, who's practically at the height of my shoulder now.

"Yes, sweetheart?"

"Who was that man that Mama was talking to earlier?"

"Um, his name is Isaak."

"Is he a Marine?"

I smile. "Not quite."

"He looks like G.I. Joe."

Peter scoffs immediately. "He does not. He looks more like a superhero undercover."

Sam rolls his eyes. "Like your boyfriend, Captain America?"

"He's not my boyfriend! I just think he's cool."

Bree and I exchange a look and I have to try really hard not to laugh. "If you boys want, next time, I'll introduce you both to him and you can ask him yourself. How's that?"

Peter looks a little nervous, but Sam is immediately excited. "Great! Can we come back tomorrow?"

"No," Bree says immediately. "But soon. Now let's go."

Once I've seen Bree and her family off, I carry Jo up to her bedroom and tuck her in. Her eyelashes flutter as she looks at me and she doesn't even ask for a story.

"Can Aunty Bree come again?" she murmurs sleepily.

"Of course."

"And Uncle Jake, too?"

"Mhmm."

"And Peter?"

I smile. "Peter and Sam as well."

She frowns. "Does Sam have to come?"

"Jo!"

She giggles under the covers. "I'm only joking you."

I kiss the top of her head and start humming under my breath. Within two minutes, she's sleeping soundly, completely tuckered out by her excitement-filled day. I'm jealous—the excitement has me wired, not sleepy.

I slip out of her room and head straight to Isaak's office. One look tells me he's not there and he hasn't been for a while.

I count up the number of hours he's been away. It feels like forever. Maybe Bogdan or someone else might know where he is, but when I try to find someone, I come up empty. The house feels eerily abandoned.

Feeling strange, I end up in Isaak's room, pacing up and down, jumping at the slightest noise.

Two hours later, I'm still sitting on his window seat and he's still not here. It isn't until nearly three in the morning that I hear heavy footsteps.

I want to get up, but I'm so tired and my legs feel heavy and numb, and before I can move, the door swings open.

"Camila?"

I forget about the pins-and-needles in my leg and stare at Isaak. He doesn't look hurt, but he looks exhausted. And pissed, and a whole host of other things besides.

"What are you doing here?"

"I... I was wondering where you were."

"So you came to my bedroom?"

"Why did you leave so abruptly this morning?"

He removes the jacket he's got on and I notice streaks of blood across the white shirt. "Oh my God!" I gasp, jerking myself up to my feet and ignoring the complaints in my legs. "You're bleeding."

He pulls the shirt off his shoulders and discards it on the back of a chair.

For the first time, I'm more concerned with checking him for wounds, rather than ogling his extremely defined set of abs.

"It's not my blood," he says matter-of-factly.

"Oh," I say, calming down a little. "So you're not hurt."

"No."

Now, I feel a little silly for coming up here at all. I should have just stayed with Jo in her bedroom. But for some reason, I'm not ready to leave yet.

Against my better judgment, I ask, "What happened?"

He raises his eyebrows. "You want to know?"

"Yes."

"It's not a nice story."

I bite my lip. "I want to know anyway."

He walks over to me, shirtless and completely confident in that fact. Not that I can blame him. He doesn't sit down, just leans against the wall, his body slanting to one side casually.

"Maxim hit one of our newest warehouses. He set fire to one side and attacked the other. He massacred every single person in there."

I shudder as my stomach roils. "Oh my God."

"Twelve in total. Four people were burned to death. The rest had their throats slit. They were strung up like pieces of meat."

My gut churns again, but I asked for this story.

"They were all fucking civilians," Isaak growls. "Employees hired out to work in this warehouse and move goods. They had no fucking idea who they worked for."

"Isaak, I'm sorry…"

His eyes find mine. He's furious, but that fury is not directed at me.

"You're sure it's Maxim?"

"He wrote a message for me on the floor of the warehouse," he says. "*I'm taking back what's mine.*"

"That… that's what he wrote?"

"Yes. He wrote it in the blood of the men and women he killed today."

I can feel the blood drain from my face. I realize in this moment just how naïve I still am. Because, before now, I would never have thought it possible that Maxim could be capable of something so monstrous. So cruel.

"I'm going to make him pay for this," he snarls.

He's about to turn away from me when I grab his hand. "Isaak, you're in no fit state to do anything right now. You're exhausted."

"I'm fine."

"Your eyes are bloodshot, you haven't slept, you haven't eaten. You're not you. You need to make the decision tomorrow when you can think clearly."

He narrows his eyes at me. "Are you trying to postpone his death?"

"No, you stubborn bastard," I snap, refusing to let go of his arm. "I'm trying to keep you from acting hastily and making a mistake. If you go in like this, you could get hurt."

"Would you care?"

The question hangs between us for a moment. And I know there's no way I can get out of answering it. I stare at him for a moment.

It feels like there's only one way to answer this question.

I move closer to him, wrap my hand around his neck, and bring his face down to mine.

32

ISAAK

I was gearing up for a fight. Not a kiss.

But then, Cami and I are always a breath away from either fighting or fucking. It's a coin toss as to which way we're going in any given moment.

Her fingers tremble against the back of my neck, holding me close. My hands linger on her hips. Her lips are gentle at first, but the longer she stays locked in my arms, the hungrier she seems to get.

I slide my hand between us, running it over her breasts. Her nipples are hard, desperate to be touched. She moans as I roll her right nipple between my fingers.

Then I push her down against the window seat and start undoing my pants. She watches me with wild eyes, wet with desire.

I hold her gaze the entire time I'm undressing. Her eyes land on my cock the moment I pull my pants off. She sits up and reaches for me as I walk to her.

As soon as I'm within arms' reach, she bends to grab my cock. She strokes tenderly a few times, and then sucks the tip of my dick into her mouth.

"Fuck," I moan as she starts playing with my balls.

My vision blurs, distorts. All I can see is her gorgeous blonde head bobbing up and down as she takes me deeper into her mouth.

I can't decide what to focus on. My anger at Maxim is still there, burning beneath the surface. I can't forget the words that were sprawled out across the warehouse floor. I'd told Camila part of the message.

But not all of it.

I'm taking back what's mine…

Including her.

She should probably know what a fucking piece of shit her ex-fiancé is. But I want to protect her from the worry. I want to protect her from sleepless nights filled with nightmares of his leering, cackling face.

She's here now. She's safe. And I'm going to make sure that motherfucker will never touch her again.

I repeat that vow to myself as she swallows me whole.

She turns her eyes up towards me with my cock deep inside her throat. Our eyes lock, and the urge to come is so strong that I almost lose the fight then and there.

I grit my teeth and stop pumping my hips into her mouth. Taking deep breaths, I let the orgasm recede. It's not time for that yet.

Then, when I'm in control once more, I start fucking her mouth slowly.

Her eyes go wide as I gather up her hair between my hands. But she keeps her gaze on my face the whole time, as though begging for more.

Her hands flutter against my ass, and when I ramp up the pace, she clings tightly to me. Her moans are muffled by my throbbing cock.

I push myself to the edge, and then I pull out before I go too far.

"Enough of that," I growl. "I want all of you."

I pull her up to her feet as she tries to catch her breath. While she's still trembling, I strip her of her clothes until she's standing naked in front of me. Then I run my hands over her body—tenderly, delicately. I cup her breasts, squeeze them gently in my hands before stepping back and circling her like a lion circles his prey.

She stands deathly still. "Good girl," I murmur. "That's a good little *kiska*. Stay right there and let me look at you."

As I round her, I graze my fingers across her plump ass, giving it a little smack before finishing the rotation. I can see the desire burning deep in her eyes.

But she's holding back. She's not touching me, because she wants me to be the one to touch her. For all her fight, all her feistiness when it comes to sex, she likes being dominated.

Not that I didn't already know that.

I take her in my grasp and hoist her up around my waist. She grips my shoulders as I walk her over to one of the larger armchairs.

I sit down in it and push her knees to either side so she's straddling me, positioned right above my rock-hard dick. Her hands trail down my chest, down the grooves of my abs, the downward sloping V of muscle above my hips.

Taking my erection in my hand, I aim it at her dripping wet pussy. "Sit down on my cock like a good *kiska*," I snarl, my voice so low it's felt as much as heard.

She uses her hands on my shoulders to lower herself down.

Slowly, slowly, slowly, the head of my cock parts her folds and then sinks into her. One blissful, agonizing inch at a time. Cami's eyes flutter in their sockets. I keep a tight grip on her hips as I drag her down onto me. Drag myself into her.

And then, what feels like a fucking century later, our hips meet flush. She sighs like she's been waiting for this moment her whole life.

I bite the inside of my cheek until I'm bleeding to force myself to think of something other than how good it would feel to erupt inside her right now.

Not yet. Not fucking yet.

"Come on, baby," I encourage. "Ride me."

Camila starts to wind her hips up and down my length. She looks like she's already about to burst at the seams.

We pick up tempo as we go. Each stroke a little faster, a little harder, a little deeper than the last. Her body gives way to draw me in. My cock gets harder. Our breath comes faster.

Her breasts bounce in front of my face, so I let go of her hips to snare one in each hand and run a teasing thumb across the hard peaks of her nipples. Her eyes roll back in her head at the added sensation.

"Harder," I growl, slapping her ass harder. "Harder."

"Yeah, Isaak," she moans. "Yeah, right there, right fucking there…"

The air is slick with heat. Moisture rolls off my body. Same as hers. I watch the little beads of condensation form along her breasts as I thrust up into her from below.

She cries out wordlessly, her hair flying wildly around her face.

In one particularly violent thrust, her hazy eyes meet mine, and I can tell she's close. Very close. She pushes up on her knees again and grabs the head of the chair I'm sitting on to give me space to maneuver.

Then I start pounding into her from below, hitting every single spot inside her.

She makes sounds I've never heard her make before. Like this time is different than all the times that have come before it. Fuck, maybe it is. Maybe we crossed some bridge today.

Or maybe it's just the animal in her finally coming out to face the animal in me.

God knows I feel like a fucking animal. Like a savage, vicious predator, no trace of humanity left in me. I want to come on her face, down her throat, on every inch of her body.

I want to mark her with my scent just so that every fucking man who lays eyes on her knows exactly who she belongs to.

When she comes, her body shivers violently. Her walls clench around my cock, squeezing out my orgasm in tandem with her own.

There's no time for me to come anywhere other than inside her.

The moment her orgasm finally relinquishes her, she falls onto me, limp and quivering in the aftermath. I tap-dance my fingers up and down her spine and catch the perspiration clinging to her skin. It takes several minutes before her breath and heartbeat fall back into their natural rhythm.

Then, abruptly, Cami pushes herself off me.

Her gaze roams around the room, looking everywhere but at me. It annoys me so much that I grab her chin and force her to look at me.

"Something wrong?"

She blushes. "No."

"Then why do you look guilty?"

She sighs. "This is not what I came to your room for."

"No? Then what did you come for?"

"I was worried about you."

"There's no need to worry about me," I tell her, though I am touched she would admit that out loud. So far, she's been highly protective of her feelings, especially the ones that have anything to do with me.

Maybe I was right. Maybe we made some kind of imperceptible progress.

"You're not invincible, Isaak."

"Wrong."

She looks at me and shakes her head. "If only that were true," she says with piercing longing in her tone.

"Careful," I say gently. "If you keep talking like that, I might get the impression that you're in love with me."

She smiles. "Please. You already made that assumption months ago."

"Assumptions are not truths."

"Is there a difference in your head?"

I smile and palm her ass. With a groan, she starts to clamber off me. But before she can get far, I stand up, still buried inside her, and walk us both to the bed like that.

I lay her down on her back on the sheets. Then, carefully, I pull out. The evidence of our lovemaking is smeared all over her thighs. I pluck a few tissues from the nightstand and carefully wipe her clean.

She balances herself on her elbows and watches me. "Thank you," she murmurs, eyes hooded.

I meet her gaze and smile. Then I collapse onto the bed next to her. We lie like that for several minutes before she breaks the silence.

"Sam thinks you're G.I Joe."

I turn to the side and catch her profile. "What?"

"G.I. Joe," she smirks. "Like, the soldier. Big tough guy. Very macho."

I snort. "Really?"

"Really. Peter is convinced you're more like Captain America."

"Jesus. That goody-two-shoes? Tell him to pick again."

She laughs. "Not your kind of superhero, huh? Which one would you say you are, then?"

She flips onto her side to look at me. I can't help but stare back. She's a beautiful woman. But she's most beautiful like this… with her hair loose, her face make-up free, her skin flushed from frenetic fucking.

"You know I'm no superhero, right?"

A ripple passes over her eyes. She nods silently. "I know."

"Does that bother you?"

"Sometimes," she admits.

"I can't change that about myself."

"I don't know," she says with a small lift of her shoulders. "I think anything can change if you decide it can be done."

There's unapologetic hope in her eyes. Right now, I can't bring myself to kill it.

"What are you going to do?" she asks.

I know what she's talking about, and I find that, weirdly enough, I want to talk to her about this. It's not the kind of subject I've ever discussed with anyone other than Bogdan and my lieutenants.

But somewhere between all the fighting and the fucking, something has definitely changed. Blossomed. Something comfortable and familiar.

"I'm going to have to answer in kind," I say grimly.

"With blood?"

"Yes."

There's no point beating around the bush. She knows it already; she just needs to hear me confirm it. And I'm not about to lie to her about what the Bratva is.

We're not a bunch of superheroes running around trying to save the world. The Bratva is about power, not peace. And sometimes, power requires blood to be spilled.

"Did learning the truth about your father change anything for you?" she asks softly.

"Killing his brother was a betrayal," I say. "Not just to Yakov, but to the Vorobev Bratva as a whole. But in many ways, he did it for the Bratva."

"Are you justifying what he did?"

"No, I'm just stating a fact."

"You can't know his motives."

"I knew my father," I say firmly. "I saw him for what he was."

"If that were true, why didn't you see that he was the one who killed your uncle?"

I look at her sharply, but she meets my gaze without flinching. Maybe what Bogdan has been bleating about this entire time has been true all along.

She is my perfect match. The only woman that has ever provided me with enough of a challenge to keep me interested. To keep me involved.

Maybe that's why I hadn't been able to walk away that night at the restaurant. Something in me recognized something in her.

Six years later and it still can't let go.

"You may have a point. But both things can be true at the same time. I missed a few things, but at the core, I knew him. And for him, the Bratva was everything. It was the end-all and be-all of his existence. And he couldn't bear to see what Yakov was doing to it."

"Which was what?"

"He was splitting it up and selling it off like junking a used car into scrap metal. He was weakening our position and leaving our men exposed. In danger. Everyone associated with the Vorobevs became a target."

My fists tighten behind my head as I remember those violent days.

"We lost thirty-seven men in the weeks after Yakov sold an entire portion of our stock to a foreign investor. Bratvas thrive on their business acumen. But at the end of the day, it is not truly a business. You can't just liquidate and move on. You can't sell and walk away. You live and die by the Bratva. No other routes. No other options. That is our way."

"It sounds like he wasn't interested in being don."

"I don't think he was."

"Then why not hand the reins over to someone who did want it? Like your father?"

It's a good question. But I still don't have the answer. All I have are guesses and assumptions and a whole host of memories that are tainted by the truth I learned after his death.

"I can't begin to understand why either of them did what they did," I tell her honestly. "But I'm here now and I have to deal with the fall-out."

She's silent for a while. Then: "Isaak?" Her tone is shaky, filled with trepidation, but there's a determination that transcends even that.

"Yes?"

"This is purely a hypothetical situation, so please don't read into it. But I want to know: what if you were to hand the reins over to Maxim?"

I can see why she might think the question would start another fight. In any moment before this, it probably would have.

But lying next to each other in bed like this… it feels like we're finally occupying common ground after months of fighting from separate corners.

"What would I do then, Camila?"

She shrugs. "You could live your life," she says tentatively. "You could build a family, maybe. Raise them away from all the violence and danger."

Her eyes are filled with unspoken vulnerability. She's trying to keep her tone detached, but I hear the tremor. I hear the fear. I hear the fragile hope.

I wish I could give her the reassurance she craves. A promise that we might be able to have a future that doesn't involve the Bratva.

But she's still speaking from the perspective of an outsider looking in.

She still doesn't understand the all-consuming nature of the world I was born into.

"I can't be anything else, Camila. In all the ways that matter, I am my father's son. And I will live and die by the Bratva, just like he did."

She turns her face to the ceiling to try and hide the disappointment in her eyes, but I catch it in the heavy sigh as her chest rises and falls.

"Even if I tried, Camila, there will be no clean break for me."

She frowns. "What do you mean?"

"I mean Maxim will never let me walk away. Even if I promise never to come back, never to challenge him for the title. He will not rest until I am buried. And until all my heirs are buried with me."

I notice the goosebumps erupt across her skin. I have no choice but to let that terror sink into her.

She needs to understand just how much of a threat Maxim poses to me.

To us.

To Jo.

She takes a deep breath. "I… I should go back to Jo's room. I want to be there when she wakes up in the morning."

It's an excuse, but I don't stop her as she pushes herself off the bed. She needs room to breathe.

I sit up and watch as she gets dressed. She throws me only a half-hearted smile before she heads towards the door.

It's a quiet, peaceful retreat, as far as she and I usually go.

But I fucking feel it in my bones.

This one hurts.

33

CAMILA

"Hello?"

Marcy's tone is infallibly cheery. Not at all what I was expecting, really. Then again, in more than six years of knowing Eric, I've never actually heard the sound of his wife's voice.

"Hi, is Eric there by any chance?"

I'm expecting the next question, but I still cringe when she asks it.

"Can I know who's speaking?"

"Um, my name's Cami. Camila."

"Cami?"

"Yeah, I'm, uh… a friend of Eric's."

I don't want Marcy thinking Eric's having an affair or anything, so I add, "He was actually my agent at one point."

"Camila?" she says again, as though she's met me before.

"That's me."

"Well, isn't this something! I've heard a lot about you."

"You have?"

I can practically hear the smile in her voice. "Oops, I don't think I'm supposed to say that."

I can't help but laugh. "I've already forgotten what you said."

"Thanks, dear. Hold on, I'll put Eric on." She pushes the receiver away from her mouth before she yells for him, but it still comes through loud and clear. "ERIC!"

Their comfort with each other translates even through the phone. Just the way she says his name speaks volumes. A part of me is envious of it.

A second later, I hear scratching noises as the phone changes hands.

"Camila?"

"Hi Eric."

"Jesus, are you alright?"

"Of course I am. I'm fine, Eric."

"Thank God," he breathes. "I was so worried I'd made a mistake by letting you go off with him."

"You didn't," I assure him. "I'm safe. And… so is Jo."

"Jo?"

"She's with me now, Eric."

"Oh my God," he says. "Cami, I'm so happy for you."

I smile. "Thanks."

"Not exactly according to protocol, but whatever. Protocol can get fucked at this point, I guess." He chuckles. "How's it been being reunited with your daughter?"

"It's been… oh, you know, amazing. Challenging, but amazing."

He catches the tone in my voice at once. "Challenging, huh?"

I feel myself blushing even though I know he can't see me squirming in shame. "She doesn't exactly run to me for things. She finds it easier running to Nikita."

"Nikita?"

"Isaak's mother."

"Wow, so it's a family affair then?"

"I wouldn't say that."

"What are you if not family, Camila?"

I sigh. "That's the problem, Eric. I don't really know."

"Hey, kid, listen… it was always going to be an adjustment for you. No matter which way you swing it."

"Speaking of swinging it… what did you tell the agency?"

"That you chose to leave our protection of your own accord."

"And they believed it?"

"Well, I had the paperwork," he admits, sounding a little guilty.

I laugh in amazement. "How in the world did you manage that?"

"I already had it all drawn up and ready for when you were planning on leaving after your marriage. I just fudged the dates a little bit."

"Damn, Eric. You're a regular old maverick. Didn't think you had it in you."

"God, stop, I'm begging you. I feel guilty enough as it is."

"Don't be. It was the right thing for me, being here."

"With Isaak, you mean?"

"Yeah. I guess, yes."

"And he's been treating you well?"

"I mean, sure."

Eric pauses for a moment. "That doesn't sound very convincing."

"It's just complicated. And I'm not sure I should be talking about this with you."

"You're mortally wounding me here, Camila. I thought we were friends."

"We are! We definitely are."

"Then why shouldn't you confide in me? Unless... he's controlling what you say?"

I rush to reassure him. "No, no, no. No, he's not. He knew I was going to call you today and he didn't say a word."

"But was he happy?"

"Eric," I say with an ironic laugh, "come on. This is Isaak Vorobev we're talking about. He's not exactly the 'happy' type."

"Hmm..."

"What?"

"I'm just trying to figure it out. The commonalities. Like, what is a sweet summer child like you doing with the Lord of Darkness over there? What do you two talk about? What do you do when you spend time together?"

I smile. "Mostly just really raunchy, deviant sexual escapades."

He splutters into a cough. "Dear Lord!"

I crack up as Eric proceeds to yell at me. "Sorry, sorry, I'm only kidding."

"Well, the heart attack you just gave me feels very real indeed. Okay, I think this is a good place to end this conversation."

"Oh, boo, don't be such a prude."

"You do sound a lot better," he laughs. "Happier."

Hearing him say that makes me realize something: that I actually am happy. At least as happy as you can be knowing that the father of your child is about to start a full-scale war with the man who you were going to marry.

Damn, my life is complicated.

Something occurs to me out of nowhere. "By the way, whatever happened with Andrew?"

"He threw a hissy fit when I showed up at HQ with your signed papers. Claimed I'd forged them."

"Did anyone take him seriously?"

"A few, but they were drowned out by the rest. I've been in the agency a long time. And my friends had my back."

"Politics, huh?"

"You said it."

I smile. "Catch up again sometime soon?" I ask.

"That sounds good."

"Maybe you can bring Marcy. She sounds lovely."

"Marcy," he sighs.

In the background, I hear her cry out good-naturedly, "Are you gossiping about me, Eric Scott Keller?"

"I hear you two are the ones gossiping about me," I tease.

He blanches. "She told you? I love that woman to death, but God, she can't keep a secret to save her life."

"Um, excuse me, you're the one who's been telling her stuff!"

"You gonna make me feel bad about this now? Just what I needed: two women teaming up on one poor old man."

I laugh. "Poor old man, my ass. You're gonna outlive us all. I'll talk to you soon, okay?"

"Be safe, Cami."

"Will do. You, too."

I hang up and lean back in Isaak's massive black leather chair. It's clearly been built for him, because I feel as though I'm being swallowed by it.

"Nice chat?"

I stifle a scream and lurch upright as Isaak walks into the office.

"How long have you been standing there?"

"Last five minutes," he says without bothering to hide it.

"Wonderful. Didn't anyone ever tell you that eavesdropping is not polite?"

"My house. My office. My phone."

I roll my eyes. "Does that mean you want your gigantic chair back?"

He smiles. "No. You look good sitting in it."

"Do I?"

"Like a queen in her throne."

It's funny how easy things have been since yesterday morning. Almost too easy. I keep waiting for an argument to break out.

But so far, nothing.

I'm trying to enjoy the moment, but I can't help worrying about everything that's to come. I haven't even begun to think about the aftermath of this battle with Maxim.

If Isaak wins—which I have to believe he will—what then? We skip off into the sunset together and be a family?

Somehow, I can't see that happening.

I don't fit into Isaak's world. And he's not even going to attempt fitting into mine.

"Where'd you go?" he says suddenly, drawing my attention back to the present.

I pull my eyes to his and shake my head. "Nowhere."

He narrows his gaze at me. He doesn't even have to say a word to make me start blushing and stammering.

"It's nothing," I say, trying to find a believable lie. "I was just thinking about the last few years. How much Eric helped me."

"Eric, huh? Hmm…" He seems to accept that, although he does seem mildly suspicious. "What exactly did you tell him just now?"

"Just wanted to reassure him that I'm doing alright."

"And he believed you?"

"Well, he asked a couple questions. Wanted to know, like, what we talk about. What we do."

"And you told him about our raunchy, deviant sexual escapades."

I look at him with a start and then realize he heard the last part of my conversation. I burst into laughter. So does he.

He saunters around the desk and leans against it, just out of arms' reach. Grinning mischievously, I scooch the chair closer to him so I can wind my fingers through his.

"Well, it's not untrue," I say with a wink.

His eyes float down to my breasts. Heat spreads from my nipples right through the rest of me. Usually, there's an argument that precedes any sexual interaction we have.

But it's different this time.

It's easy.

Like Marcy yelling Eric's name, there's something calm and comforting for me to slip into, to nestle myself amongst.

This. Him. Us. It's easy, it's natural, it's perfect—when we let it be.

His hand falls against my hip and I lean into him. I grip the edges of his desk and he leans down and presses his lips to mine.

He kisses me for a long time. Delicately at first, just the grazing of his lips. Then a flicker of tongue, and more, and more, until we're hungrily making out, my hands around his neck.

He scoops me up in one huge arm, turns, and deposits me on the desk. He never breaks the kiss, not even for a moment, as he pushes up my blouse and starts fondling my breasts.

Then: "Mommy?"

I whip around and yank my shirt back into place. Jo is standing in the doorway with her head tilted to the side in confusion. "Mommy, what are you doing on the table?"

I push myself off it and try not to be too obvious in adjusting my blouse. "I was just, uh, taking a seat, honey."

"On the table? That's weird."

Isaak just smirks from the sidelines, without making any attempt to help me. I decide to just ignore the whole situation.

"What are you up to?" I say desperately.

"Babushka told me that you were in here making a call," Jo says. "I wanted to talk to you."

I have to bite back a laugh. She has her hands folded in front of her waist and her politest voice on. Already a shrewd negotiator at five years old. "Yeah? About what?"

"About going outside," she says, sneaking a shy glance at Isaak. "Can we go to the aquarium again?"

"Again?" he rumbles. "We saw all the fish already."

"Somewhere else, then?" she asks hopefully.

She looks up at him with her big blue eyes, and for the first time since I've known him, Isaak doesn't look so aloof.

"Kiddo, I wish I could. But today is not a good day."

Her face falls immediately. His falls with it.

Apparently, Isaak has finally found the one person who can make him feel bad about doing things his way.

"Why not?" she protests. Her lower lip is starting to tremble.

"Because I'm busy today."

"Doing what?"

"Yeah, Isaak," I chime in. "Doing what?"

He throws me a glare. "I have a few meetings I need to be at, Jo. But don't worry, I'll take you out another day."

"Tomorrow?"

"We'll see."

"What does that mean exactly?"

I have to resist the urge to laugh. Watching him deal with Jo is oddly fascinating. A little endearing. And, annoyingly, also a major turn-on.

"It means I'll try my best to take you out tomorrow."

"Promise?"

"Jo, some things I can't promise."

"Please?"

He sighs. "Oh, for fu—for crying out loud. Alright."

She claps her hands together. "Yay! Tomorrow. You promised." Then she turns to me. "Mommy, can we play in the garden now?"

"Sure thing, honey. You can head on out there. I'll follow you out in a bit."

Having whipped us all into shape, she runs off. Isaak straightens up and clears his throat.

"That was efficient," I tease.

He rolls his eyes. "She's five."

"Oh, okay. So you just gave in out of the kindness of your heart."

"Shut up," he mumbles as I laugh louder.

He walks around to his desk and already I can feel the air shifting, growing colder, steelier. I can sense he's getting into business mode. "You're really planning an attack on Maxim?"

"You always knew I was."

I nod and swallow. "Just… be careful."

He smiles. "Is that concern I'm hearing?"

"Shut up," I repeat back to him.

His laughter follows me out of the room. I force myself not to look back. He will win the fight. I'll see him again.

This is not the end of the story.

~

I find Jo in the garden by the pond. Nikita is sitting on one of the stone benches a few feet away. As usual, she seems lost in thought. I sit down next to her, but she doesn't so much as acknowledge my existence for the first few minutes.

"She's a wonderful kid," Nikita says out of the blue. "So much like me when I was a little girl."

"Yeah?"

Nikita nods. "I grew up without siblings, too, so I liked to play in the garden a lot. I made all the animals I found my friends."

"Well, hopefully, Jo won't always be an only child."

I speak without thinking, and the moment the words are out of my mouth, I regret them. Especially when Nikita turns to me with a pointed look.

"I… I didn't mean it… that is… I wasn't—"

"Take a breath, Camila," Nikita smiles. "Even if you did want to have more children with Isaak, why should you be embarrassed of that?"

I open my mouth, but I realize I don't really know what I want to say. "Isaak and I… I'm not sure how realistic it is."

"Why? Because you're from different worlds? Successful marriages have been forged on much less. And unhappy marriages have been broken on much more."

I raise my eyebrows. "Careful. I might think that you're encouraging me."

She gives a soft smile and watches Jo chattering to the tiny baby frogs hopping around on the lily pads floating in the pond.

"How do you do it?" I ask on impulse.

"Do what?"

"I don't know… Like, watch all this happen. What do you do when you know your sons are in danger, but there's no way to stop them and no way to keep them safe?"

She takes a deep breath. I can feel decades' worth of her worry in that one exhale.

"Bratva men consider themselves strong," she says. "They consider themselves brave and resilient and powerful. And they are all those things. But it's still nothing compared to the strength and resilience of the Bratva women. Some of them fight right alongside their men. They play the game like all the men that surround them. Other Bratva women stay at home and wait to hear if their side has fallen or prevailed. That takes strength, too. To be sidelined, to be kept out of all the decisions but still have to bear the consequences."

She turns to me. Her eyes are bright, fierce.

"If you decide to be a part of this life, Camila, you're going to have to become a lot stronger."

My eyes fall to my lap. "I'll only be a disappointment if I try."

"Why do you say that?"

I shrug. "Isaak's world still feels like a novel to me. Some fictitious universe where the good guy always wins. But it's not, and he doesn't. It's just all too real. I'm not sure I can handle it."

"Oh, I don't know about all that."

I arch my eyebrows. "Do you know something I don't?"

She gives a little shrug. "Well, I will say that as 'normal' as you claim to be, you still seem to crave adventure. You chase excitement."

I shake my head. "I think you've got me mixed up with someone else."

She smiles. "Think about it, Camila: how did you and Isaak meet?"

My cheeks color as I think about that night. How Isaak coolly and calmly sent that handsy dirtbag running for the hills. And then, of course, everything that followed. The drinks. The laugh. The bathroom.

The explosion.

Nikita doesn't wait for me to say anything out loud. "And tell me this: how did you end up here in Isaak's home again?"

We both know the answer to that: I'd ended up here because I'd called him.

She's still not done. "And how did you end up engaged to Maxim?"

That one stumps me for a moment. I stop being defensive and I think about my motives. My *real* motives.

Yes, Maxim had pursued me furiously. But I've never had a problem saying no before. I could've done it then.

I still remember Maxim's smart suits, his cocky confidence, his obvious power and wealth. They weren't the reasons I had said yes.

But the truth wasn't so far off.

The truth is, I accepted him only because he was a pale imitation of the man who plagued my dreams and my nightmares.

"He reminded me of Isaak," I whisper.

Nikita puts her hand on my knee and gives it a gentle pat. It's so out of character for her that I do a double-take. "Self-awareness is the first step, Camila."

"First step to what?"

"Happiness."

"And what if even that doesn't work?" I ask with trepidation.

"Then at least you'll land where I have."

"Where's that?"

"Acceptance."

34

ISAAK

"It's done," Bogdan says, walking into my office.

"All the safehouses have been fortified?" Vlad asks.

"Yes."

"Warehouses?" I ask.

"Done and done."

"What about our properties?" I ask. "We have two clubs in the city that need extra protection."

"I've doubled up on the security, and everyone entering will be frisked on their way in."

It's hardly foolproof, but it's better than nothing. I turn my eyes back to the monitor in front of me. All I can see are a bunch of colored specks dotted around the screen.

There hasn't been movement for the last twenty-four hours.

"Well?" Bogdan asks, craning to try and see the monitor himself.

"He hasn't fucking moved," I growl. "Not since the attack on our warehouse."

"Seriously?"

"He's been holed up in his fucking fortress. Nothing seems to go in or out."

"You think that's a good sign or a bad one?" Bogdan asks.

"Everything is bad where Maxim is concerned."

"What's our move?" Vlad asks. "If he doesn't leave his compound, then—"

"Then we take the fight to him," I say. "It doesn't really matter. The only thing that changes is the location where he dies."

"He'll have the home court advantage," Vlad points out.

"Good. He'll need a few advantages if we're going to keep this fight interesting. I wouldn't want to be bored."

Vlad and Bogdan exchange a smirk. I know they're both excited at the prospect of an imminent battle. They're seasoned enough to know the risks, but young enough that the adrenaline has already started pumping.

I can relate to the feeling, but I still find myself somewhat removed from it all.

I'm not sure if that's age speaking, or just the weight of responsibility on my shoulders. Vlad and Bogdan are my righthand men; they bear the brunt of a lot of the decision making.

But the buck starts and stops with me.

It's not something I've ever spent a lot of time thinking about. It just *was*. Like breathing or walking.

But my perspective has changed in the last few months. It doesn't take a genius to figure out why that is.

Jo. Camila.

Realizing I was a father has forced me to face my own mortality. I could die in this fight. It's not likely, but it's certainly possible.

What would happen to Jo if that were to happen? What would happen to Camila?

"Heyo, we have movement," Vlad says suddenly, jabbing a finger at the screen.

I circle back around my desk so I have a better view. A double-click of the mouse takes us from the GPS overview of the city to a live security camera feed aimed at Maxim's compound. The footage is grainy at best, but it's better than nothing.

On screen is a vehicle. A chromed-out, tinted black monstrosity.

"Bulletproof," Vlad mutters, eyeing the details. "Whoever it is, is important."

I squint at the screen, trying to catch the person inside the car. I zoom in, but the pixels split apart, distorting the image and giving me nothing more than nonsensical digital snow.

"Who's coming to visit?" Bogdan asks out loud. "Do we know if he has a mistress?"

"No serious mistresses," Vlad says immediately. "I've been doing a deep dive into his contacts, both social and otherwise. There's a blonde whore in the West Valley he's particularly fond of. He visits her a couple of times a month, but not lately."

For some reason, it offends me that he picked a blonde woman at all. I wonder if he imagines Camila when he fucks her.

"Other than that," Vlad adds, "there's no steady woman in his life."

"Apart from his mother, you mean."

All three of us look up to see Nikita standing at the threshold of my office room. She walks in without an invitation and takes one of the armchairs in front of my desk.

"If anyone is entering his compound at this stage of affairs, it's going to be her."

I look at Bogdan. "Do we have eyes on Svetlana?"

"No."

"That's a mistake," Mama says instantly. "The woman should be watched."

"She's not a player," Bogdan argues.

"Bogdan, don't be one of those men who constantly underestimates someone because she happens to be a woman," Mama scolds.

It's a surprise only because she's never sharp with Bogdan. She usually reserves that tone for me, not that I usually give a fuck.

"I'm not," Bogdan says defensively. "But come on, Mama, Svetlana has never had skin in the game."

She raises her eyebrows and looks at him with a piercing gaze that I don't really recognize. Not from her. She never wears her emotions on her sleeve like this.

"Svetlana has *always* had skin in the game. You don't think she wants her only son to be the leader of the Vorobev? She has always been ambitious, and I'm willing to bet that's only gotten worse with age."

"Okay, even assuming you're right about that, what does it matter? What can she do?" Bogdan asks.

"Maxim doesn't have a head for politics," Mama asserts. "He's not strategic or cunning. But Svetlana is all of those things and more. You can bet that, if there are plans being made, Svetlana is the one controlling their trajectory."

"Okay, so we kill the old bitch first," Bogdan says with a shrug. "Then we take down Maxim."

I pay close attention to Mama. Her face is etched with worry and her lips are pursed in a way that tells me she wants to say something that she's probably not going to say in the end.

"Mama?"

"Hm?" she says, meeting my eyes.

She's distracted, lost in thought. She's been doing a lot of that lately: turning inwards to wrestle with ghosts only she can see.

It's a sign I should've recognized a long time ago.

"Is there something you're not telling us?"

Bogdan and Vlad turn to her immediately. She handles the weight of their scrutiny with calm. "Nothing that would change things now," she says wearily.

I frown. "What the fuck is that supposed to mean?"

"It means that anything I have to add wouldn't help you in this fight."

"Is that your way of telling me you *are* hiding something from me?"

She gets to her feet, tall and poised like the Bratva queen she has always been. "It's irrelevant now, Isaak."

She strides for the door. I'm tempted to go full don on her and order her locked in here until she spills what she knows.

Instead, I let her leave. I exhale with frustration the moment she's gone.

"What the hell was that about?" Bogdan asks.

"I don't actually give a shit," I say, grinding my teeth together. "We can deal with our mother's cryptic riddles once we've handled Maxim."

"Sounds like a plan to me," Bogdan agrees.

"We're not making a move today, but make sure the men are ready anyway," I tell Vlad. "When things start to happen, they will happen fast.

"Got it, boss."

He leaves soon after. Bogdan and I head out of my office towards the gardens where I know I'll find Jo and Camila.

"Things have been going well between you two, huh?" Bogdan asks, wagging his eyebrows at me.

"Can you stop being a child for one fucking second?"

"Eh, nah. Maturity is for the birds."

I give him a grudging smile. "Have one of the men bring one of the Audis around. I've planned something special for Jo today."

"The carnival thing?"

"Yeah."

"Sweet."

"You're coming with us."

"Ooh, lucky me." He actually sounds excited.

I roll my eyes. "Just to be clear, you're my muscle."

That dampens his cheer. "Seriously, you're making me the bodyguard?"

"Suck it up."

"Will you buy me a corndog at least?"

"There's that maturity again."

Bogdan only laughs as we enter the garden. Cami and Jo are sprawled out on a lawn blanket surrounded by stacks of books. They're both wearing nearly identical sundresses and it's the cutest fucking thing I've ever seen.

And that's saying something considering I've never used the word "cute" for anything in my life before now. But what else am I supposed to call it?

Jo jumps to her feet and comes flying towards both of us. For a moment, I think she's going to attack Bogdan first. But at the last second, she veers right for me. A little too accurately, in fact—her elbow smashes me in the groin and I have to bite back a groan of pain.

"Hey, kid," I grimace, patting her head while Bogdan cackles.

"You promised me we'd go out somewhere today!" Jo reminds me, keeping her arms firmly around my waist.

"Did I? Doesn't sound like something I'd say."

Her jaw drops. "Yes, you did! You did, you did, you did!"

"Hm. If you say so. Guess I have no choice then."

She throws her fist up in the air. "Yay! Can Bogie and Babushka come too?"

"Bogie's coming with us," I say, earning a dirty look from Bogdan. "But Babushka might be tired."

"She's never too tired to spend time with me."

"Oh yeah? How did you figure that one out?"

Jo shrugs. "She told me."

Somehow, that tiny, innocuous little comment is enough to blunt my current annoyance towards my mother. Say what you want about the woman; there is no question that she loves Jo.

"Okay. You can ask Babushka to join us," I sigh.

"Yayyy!" Jo screams again before running off to corral her grandmother.

Who she still doesn't know is her grandmother.

I've been wondering about that lately. As far as Jo knows, I'm just a friend of her mother's, and Nikita is just *Babushka*, a funny name that means nothing.

Which was fine when she first came here. But now, it's starting to grate at my patience a little.

It feels wrong.

Maybe that's why I'm quiet the entire drive to the carnival. Bogdan sits up front with me, while Mama, Camila, and Jo sit in the back. Every so often, I catch Camila looking at me in the rearview mirror.

The carnival is a festive mishmash of games, rides, and shows. A Ferris Wheel looms over a merry-go-round, trick shot booths, happy families shooting water guns and trying to blink towers of bottles over to win a stuffed prize.

Jo, of course, is overwhelmed and excited. She bounces around on her toes, pointing at different things and generally freaking out, not sure which direction she wants to run in first.

"Calm down, honey," Camila says, running her fingers over the top of Jo's head. "We'll get to each thing, but you've got to pick something and tell us what you want to do first."

She slips her hand into Mama's and looks longingly over at the cotton candy stand. "Can I get some of that?"

Camila sighs. "Of course. Sugar is at the top of the priority list. As you wish, princess, let's go."

Jo scampers over to the stand with Mama. Bogdan follows close behind. He may bitch and moan about shit sometimes, but he takes his job seriously. Especially when I make a request of him.

"You've been quiet," Camila says suddenly from my righthand side.

"I'm always quiet."

"More so than usual."

"Have you been watching me?"

"Maybe," she says with a smile that's bordering on a blush.

"I've just been preoccupied with a few things," I explain. "That's all."

"Care to share them with me?"

"Why?"

She raises her eyebrows, but despite my tone, she doesn't seem to take offense. "I don't know, because we're… friends?"

It comes out sounding like a question.

I laugh. "Friends?"

She blushes an even deeper shade of rouge that makes the green in her eyes come alive.

"Friends works," she says with a shrug, trying to play off her own embarrassment.

"Do you fuck all your friends the way you fuck me?"

She actually stops short at that one. Her jaw drops and she stares at me with wide eyes. It's really fucking amusing.

And it's succeeding in distracting me from the chaos I'm about to plunge myself into.

"I… that's…"

"Mommy!" Jo cries in amazement, running up to us with a stick full of fluffy pink cotton candy. "Look what I got!"

"Saved by the kid," I murmur under my breath.

Cami hears me, but she doesn't respond. Just smiles pointedly and turns her attention to Jo. "Whoa, that's a big stick of cotton candy for a little lady!"

"It tastes like strawberries and cream."

"I'll be the judge of that." Camila helps herself to a piece and nods. "Hmm, yeah, that's good."

"Can we go over to that side? I heard someone say they're having a puppet show."

"Lead the way," Camila says.

I'm fully aware that her enthusiasm has less to do with the puppet show and more to do with avoiding any reply to my statement about just what exactly a "friendship" entails.

And yet somehow, Camila and I end up falling back while Bogdan and Mama keep a close eye on Jo. Her eyes keep flitting around the fair, landing on every single woman who looks at me.

"Don't worry," I say, reading her mind. "As far as I'm concerned, you and my mother are the only women here."

"Don't be an ass," she mumbles. But there's that blush again.

We pass by a house of mirrors and a huge stall hawking a jungle's worth of stuffed animals. Jo extorts a promise from Bogdan to buy her the stuffed lion on our way out before we end up sitting on a bench in front of the carousel. Bogdan helps Jo jump up onto a cock-eyed-looking elephant with ears that are far too big for his head.

When I point that out, Camila just gives me a look. "That's Dumbo."

"Certainly looks like one."

She gives me a little punch on the arm. "Dumbo, as in the Disney character."

I blink. "Am I supposed to know what any of that means?"

"You should," she says seriously. "You're a dad now. You've got to know about Dumbo. Elsa and Anna. And Olaf as well."

I raise my eyebrows. "I'm terrified."

She laughs at my slightly shell-shocked expression. "I bet Bratva battle seems a breeze compared to parenthood, huh?"

"Fewer shady characters to worry about," I agree with a smirk.

We languish in the silence for a moment before I finally say the thing that's been running through my head all day long.

"I think it's time we told Jo who I am."

Cami freezes. But it doesn't take long for her to slump forward and a sigh to come whistling between her teeth. Like she was prepared for this subject to come up.

"I've been thinking a lot about that lately, too."

"And?"

"What if I asked for a little more time?"

"What purpose would that serve?"

"I don't know. It would give her time to process and accept, maybe."

"How can she do that before she knows the truth?"

"It's a lot for a five-year-old. That's all I'm saying."

"She's strong," I say simply. "She gets that from you."

Cami looks up at me in surprise. I swear I see the glimmer of a tear in the corner of her eye before she sniffles and turns away.

"You're the big, strong Bratva don," she mumbles. "Who's to say she doesn't get it from you?"

I shrug. "There are different kinds of strength, Camila."

She smiles sadly. "Funny. I had a similar conversation with your mother not long ago."

It's still strange to me that the two of them have developed such an easy rapport in such a short period of time. Camila has managed to integrate herself into my family in a way I never managed to.

Not that I was working towards the goal much. But still—something about it is admirable.

She turns back to me slowly. A decision looms in her eyes.

"We can tell her," she says quietly.

I raise my eyebrows. "I expected more pushback."

She sighs. "That was my first instinct."

"Surprise, surprise."

She ignores that. "But you are her father and she deserves to know that. She's been without me for so long as it is. It would be wrong of me to deprive her of her father as well."

I nod. "We'll tell her together."

The corners of her mouth tilt upwards. I wonder if she's fixated on the feeling that the word "together" brought up. It certainly does something for me.

"Mommy! Isaak!"

"Hey, cutie," Cami says. "Did you have a good ride? Where to next?"

"I want Babushka to take me on the big wheel," she says. "Can I go?"

Camila bites her lip and nods. "Go on. Have fun."

With a clap of her hands, she's off. We watch as Mama grabs her hand and forces her to slow to a quick walk while Bogdan follows behind them after throwing me a wink.

"I have to say," Camila tells me, "you stick out in the outside world."

"No shit," I agree, catching another look from a passing couple.

"It's a compliment."

I snort. "I don't need fucking compliments. Never did."

"Right, of course. Sometimes, I forget I'm talking to the mighty Isaak Vorobev. You don't need anything from anyone, do you?"

I grab her hand and pull her up to her feet. "That's not true," I remark slyly as I pull her through the crowd. "There are some things I need. From one person in particular."

I can practically feel her pulse racing in her fingertips as she follows me blindly through the crowd.

"Isaak, where are we going? Where are you taking me?"

"Somewhere where we'll have only each other's stares to contend with," I tell her. "And once we're there, I'm going to tell you exactly what I need from you."

35

CAMILA

"The house of mirrors?" I ask as he pulls me towards the entrance.

"All the better to see you in," he chuckles darkly.

It's mostly a joke, but one part isn't—this Little Blonde Riding Hood is about to get devoured by the biggest, baddest wolf in existence.

As we step up to the entrance, the crowd fades away. No one is here besides a dour-faced carnie who waves us in. Suppressing a smile, I cling to Isaak's hand as he tows us into the darkness.

It's cooler in here than it was outdoors. The light glints off a few shards of mirror in this first little antechamber. Half a dozen doors open up onto hallways that wind into the depths of the building.

Isaak strides to the left-hand door like he knows where he's headed.

"Where exactly are we going?"

"Somewhere quiet."

We step through the door and he pulls it shut behind us. I turn around and my jaw drops immediately.

There are mirrors everywhere: above, below, left, right. We're walking on mirrors and looking up at mirrors and no matter which direction I turn, I see two, ten, fifty versions of us.

"This is weird," I murmur.

Isaak glances back at me. "I guess normal people like to make excitement where there is none."

"Hey, everyone gets their thrills a different way. Most people like their thrills risk-free."

"Do you?"

I pause before answering that question. I would have answered immediately a few days ago: *Hell no.*

But after my chat with Nikita, I have to think about it.

In so many ways, she saw what I've turned a blind eye to. So much about the last six years was completely out of my control. But some things happened that were solely my decision.

And just as she's pointed out, I hadn't made the safest choices. I justified and rationalized and excused the things I picked.

But when it came down to it, I picked danger.

Again.

And again.

And again.

"If you have to think that hard," says Isaak, "I think we know your answer."

I sigh. "I'm trying to figure myself out."

"You haven't done that already?"

"No, asshole. It's a work-in-progress." I punch his arm and my knuckles actually hurt. "Jesus, are you made of stone or something?"

He smirks seductively. "Parts of me, maybe."

I roll my eyes and suppress a giggle as he pulls me into another room.

Whereas the mirrors in the first place were all flat and standard, the ones in here are bent and curvy. There's a fat Camila and an impossibly skinny one, one where my head is on Isaak's shoulders and his head is floating in space.

"I take back what I said before. *This* is super creepy."

I raise my hand. All of my reflections follow suit. Isaak comes up behind me, his eyes raking up and down the mirror images.

When he steps up beside me, the two of us are reflected back and forth between opposing reflective surfaces. A hundred, a million of us, stretching on forever into the receding distance. It's creepy, yes—but also kind of awe-inspiring, in the strangest way.

"Is this what infinity looks like?" I whisper. It feels like the air has chilled further.

"There's no such thing as infinity," Isaak growls. "There's only here and now. Nothing else."

"Is that why you're so fearless?" I ask. "Because you're not worrying about the future?"

He nods. "Why worry about something you can't influence? I choose to spend my time focusing on what I can control."

"I've noticed."

He smirks. "Mock me all you want. My stakes are higher. If I lose control—even for a second—people die."

I frown. "That's not an exaggeration, is it?"

"No, *kiska*, it's not."

I exhale deeply, trying to wrap my head around what's to come. I realize I'm falling into the trap, thinking about things I can't change. But I'm not sure I have Isaak's discipline.

"I don't know how you do it," I tell him.

"I'm a different creature than you, Camila," he says. "From the moment I was a thought in my mother's womb, my future was mapped out for me. Even before my father became the Vorobev don, I was always going to be someone. I was always going to be Bratva."

"So you don't regret it then?" I ask. "You don't wish it could be different?"

He raises his eyebrows as though the very thought of regret is a foreign concept to him. "Regret gets you nowhere."

"I wish I had the same perspective you do."

"Do you?"

I look away to try and keep the blush from tainting my cheeks. "I just… I wish I didn't live in my head so much."

He smiles. "We all have our coping mechanisms."

"What's yours?"

He considers that for a moment. "Alcohol."

I snort. "Typical."

"Fighting."

"Predictable."

"… And you."

I stare at him, wondering if I'd heard that correctly. In my peripheral vision, I see all the identical Isaaks crowding towards a blonde girl who looks completely thunderstruck.

Nothing in here feels real, so it's not even that startling when I suddenly seem to be floating outside of my body. If anything, it's kind of pleasantly objective. I'm just a spectator now, staring at a man and a woman all alone in a hall of mirrors. Looking at each other like they're the only thing in the world that matters.

The man is gorgeous. Sin incarnate. Dark and stormy and impossibly huge.

The woman is—well, I suppose it's only slightly narcissistic to say she's pretty. Her golden blonde hair is lush and curly; her green eyes are certainly bright, certainly eye-catching. But there's still a trace of fear in her eyes. Hesitation in the set of jaw.

She looks like a fragile bird who's finally beginning to understand that she can fly—but she's still afraid to look over the edge of the abyss.

When I force my eyes away from the mirror, I find Isaak staring at me with a soft smile on his lips.

"Isaak?" I whisper.

"Yes?"

"I'm scared."

Everything is so quiet. So still.

"Of what?" he asks.

I swallow. "Everything."

"What difference does that make?" he asks. "Fear is a natural part of life. No one can escape it. It shouldn't change what we do."

"You've never been scared in your life," I point out.

He smiles. "I'm human, too, Camila."

I reach out and touch him with a single trembling finger. "Sometimes, I'm not so sure about that."

His smile gets wider, distractingly beautiful. And yet, I still notice when he wraps one hand around my hip. He squeezes me possessively, and without even thinking about it, I step forward into the circle of his arms.

"When I was seven years old and I realized that Bogdan was going to get his hand sliced if he didn't stand up to Otets… I was frightened."

I shiver. "Surely he wouldn't have actually—"

Isaak stares down at his own arm. "Oh, he would have done it. Without batting an eye."

My fingers dance over the scars gently. This is maybe the first time ever I've felt so free to touch him the way I want. Our proximity gives me easy access, yes. But it's more than that.

I'm comfortable with him.

"You were scared?"

"Yes."

"But… not for yourself."

He shrugs. "I don't get scared for myself."

"You're in dangerous situations all the time."

"I told you before: death… it's not something I run from."

"Why the hell not? If there's anything to run from, it's that."

"Because if you're constantly worried about death, you're never going to get to live."

"Wow," I drawl. "They should put that in a fortune cookie."

He grabs me around the waist and pulls me against his groin so I can feel his erection. "Careful, *kiska:* you keep talking like that and you're going to get punished."

Desire burns through me at the threat. It strikes me that the only reason I'm able to feel that desire at all is because I feel safe with him.

Isaak Vorobev makes me feel safe amidst the danger.

"I'm the only person in the world that you're not a threat to," I whisper. "That's what you said the night we met."

He chuckles. "You remember."

"Of course I remember. I remember everything about that night. Especially that."

"It's true."

"Why?"

He looks perplexed for a moment. "Why what?"

"Why is it true?" I ask. "I was a complete stranger. You didn't know anything about me. Why say something that insane?"

He shrugs. "Instinct."

"Come on, Isaak. You weren't interested in anything more than fucking me that night."

"I was interested in talking to you, too."

"Just so that you could convince me to sleep with you."

"Is that really what you think?"

"Well, what am I supposed to think, Isaak?" I ask. "I'm supposed to believe that of all the women you could have had, you chose me because you just knew instinctively that I was special?"

"Why aren't you satisfied with that answer?"

"Because it's unrealistic."

"Or maybe you're just jaded."

"I'm not going to argue with that," I concede. "But both things can be true at the same time."

"You obviously don't see yourself very clearly," Isaak tells me. "You don't see what I see."

"And what's that?"

Instead of answering right away, he steps behind me and pivots us both to face the biggest mirror in the entire display. He points at our reflection. Him dwarfing me. His eyes, dark and furious with lust and longing and maybe even love. His hands on my hips, his breath on my neck.

"You tell me," he growls.

"Isaak…"

"No? Then I'll tell you what I see. I see a lioness. A fierce protector who's waded through hell to keep her daughter safe. I see an angel. I see a Bratva queen. I see my wife."

Between each sentence, he presses another soft kiss into the curve of my throat.

My breath catches in my chest. I'm feeling too many things to contain them. I'm going to burst if I can't find an outlet.

Fortunately for me, making me explode is exactly what Isaak has in mind.

His fingers find the strap of my dress and slide it delicately off my shoulder. I want it—so fucking badly. But I catch his wrist.

"We're in a public place!" I protest weakly.

"So?" He looks supremely unconcerned.

"What if someone walks in?"

"They can watch," he growls. "The whole fucking world can watch if they want to. Not a single one of them can keep me away from you."

He stares right into my eyes as he says it. And when I can't find the words to fight back, he knows the truth: I want this as badly as he does.

My pussy throbs painfully as he reaches around from behind to unbutton the pale-yellow dress I'm wearing. He shimmies it down my shoulders, down around my waist.

I step out of it and turn to look at him.

He doesn't say anything for a long time. He just stands there and stares at me in my bra and panties like it'd take a fucking army to make him look away.

"Take off your bra."

I obey without a word. The moment my breasts spill free, I look down at the massive bulge in his pants. I swallow back and hold my ground.

"Panties next."

I shimmy out of panties and toss them back where my dress lies.

Standing naked in a carnival house of mirrors is probably one of the more surreal moments of my life. And yet… I don't feel self-conscious in the way I thought I would.

The way Isaak is looking at me prevents me from feeling anything other than desire.

"Fuck, you're beautiful," he whispers, and the words seem to echo all around us. "Come here."

I take one step towards him. And then we suddenly reach a point—at the exact same time, like we're perfectly in sync with each other—where this whole waiting game, the whole idea of patience and denial and delay, delay, delay? It's not fucking feasible anymore.

If we don't consume each other right this goddamn second, I don't know how I'm going to go on living.

He grabs me, flips me back around to face the mirror, and frees his cock. He's in me in a heartbeat, one slow thrust that fills me up fuller than I've ever been before. I bite my lip to stifle a cry and plant a hand on the mirror to keep from crumbling beneath him.

There's nowhere I can't look, because I'm everywhere. We both are.

And watching him fuck me is the sexiest moment of my life.

I watch greedily as Isaak starts to fuck me faster. There's no easing me into anything. He fucks me like he has every right to it, to all of me. He fucks me like it's the end of the world and he has only a few minutes left.

His muscles flex and contract with every thrust. My ass is going to be black and blue tomorrow, but I don't care.

I just want him deep, deep, deeper. I want to chase this feeling until it crashes over me.

Everything feels heightened. Multiplied times two for every reflection of us. Until it's all too much and I'm coming, I'm coming—

And then I hear footsteps.

"Some… someone's… fuck… coming…"

But it's too late to stop. Isaak comes inside me and I finish my orgasm as he does, spluttering from the lips and spasming hard on his cock.

As soon as I'm freed, I scramble to my clothes.

Panting wildly, I grab my clothes and run behind Isaak for good measure. I ignore my bra and panties completely and pull on my dress in a panic. It's a good choice, too, because as I'm buttoning up the dress, the door of the mirror room bursts open.

I relax a little when I realize it's Bogdan in the doorway.

I manage to hook up one more button before I realize that something is wrong. His clothes are torn and he's bleeding from the arm, the ribs, the nose, the lip. But all of that pales in comparison to the expression on his face—sheer fucking terror.

"What happened?" snarls Isaak.

He shakes his head. "*Sobrat*, I'm so sorry. Mama was found unconscious by the Ferris Wheel. They fucking jumped me. And they…"

Isaak understands everything that's happened a moment before I do. He walks forward in two furious strides. "Bogdan, where is Jo? Where the fuck is my daughter?"

My stomach feels like it's about to drop right out of my body. The sheer terror that grips me is so acute that I can't feel my extremities.

"I'm sorry," Bogdan says again. "They… they took her, Isaak. They fucking took her."

36

ISAAK

The silence is deafening as we drive back to the mansion.

We each sit in our own silence, every shroud a different color, tainted by a different emotion.

Mama's silence is filled with grief, loss, and a touch of confusion. She only came to minutes ago while we were on the road. They'd taken her out with chloroform.

They'd saved the muscle for Bogdan. His silence is drenched in regret and guilt.

Camila's silence, on the other hand, is burning with anxiety, filled with a fear that I can feel even with the distance between us.

And my silence is stewing in anger. A rage so deep and so volatile that I'm trying to figure out what to do with it. Because before I take my rage to Maxim, I need to let some of it out now—before I combust.

This is the closest I have ever come to losing control.

This is the closest I have ever come to swerving off the road and fucking burning my life to the ground.

Somehow, I let myself get distracted. Maxim swooped in and took advantage. I glance at my brother and he tenses immediately. He knows the fire raging beneath my brooding.

"Isaak—"

"Don't."

The word slashes through the air. I know everything's he's about to say and I'm not fucking interested.

I can't bring myself to look at Camila's face. She turned into a ghost the moment Bogdan said the words that broke through our little bubble of bliss.

And she's not coming back to the land of the living any time soon. The last time I looked at her, her eyes were glazed over. She looked in my direction, but I knew she was looking through me, not at me.

The only thing she was seeing was her five-year-old screaming for the safety of arms she was familiar with.

Bogdan's phone starts to ring and he answers it immediately. "Yes, tell me. Uh-huh… yes… yes… yes."

He sighs and lets his hand fall in his lap like it's the heaviest thing in the world. Which tells me exactly what he's about to say before he says it.

"Both teams have scoured the entire carnival," Bogdan tells me. "She's gone."

"Of course she's fucking gone," I snap. "He wasn't about to kidnap her and then keep her there."

Bogdan doesn't even flinch at my tone. He takes the anger and the blame because he's no coward. I try and remind myself of that fact to distract from how badly I want to land a punch at his nose and finish what his attackers started.

It's not his fault, though. Not truly.

It's mine.

The moment we're in my compound, the gates snap shut and I'm out of the vehicle. I don't look around and I don't wait to be spoken to. I storm straight into the house and straight into the room with the bar.

I think I'm craving a drink, but once I've taken a massive swig from the whiskey bottle on display, I realize alcohol is not going to do shit right now.

All the adrenaline coursing through my body is eating up the whiskey until there's nothing left but a gnawing hollowness in my gut.

How could I have been so fucking blasé about our outings?

Of course Maxim was keeping tabs on us. Of course he was watching. Somehow, I'd let myself underestimate him. And the loss of my daughter was the cost.

My hand tightens around the glass in my hand and I fling it across the room with all the strength I can muster. It slams against the French doors and shatters.

That's what gives me the satisfaction I was searching for in the whiskey.

Clinging to that fleeting feeling, I grab another bottle and hurl it across the room. Once I've started, I know I can't possibly stop.

Not when there's so much left to be destroyed.

I've destroyed half the room when Bogdan walks in. He stays by the door, wary of the next thing I'm going to break.

"Isaak!"

I ignore him and upend the coffee table. Imported from Milan a few years ago. Damn near priceless. *CRACK*—ruined.

"Brother!"

I turn to him, my chest rising and falling in sharp succession. I know what I must look like: a desperate man who's fallen off the deep end.

But that's exactly what I am. So be it.

I have no desire to attempt to calm down. This is the fury that I will wield to meet Maxim Vorobev and end this little dance we've been locked in for far too fucking long.

It's time I take him out.

Vorobev blood be damned—the bastard is going to die.

"ISAAK! Please." I turn to face my ashen-faced brother, chest heaving with exertion. "I know I fucked up," he says. "You want to hurt me? Go ahead. I deserve it."

He walks across the room, stepping over the furniture I've upended, and plants himself in front of me.

"Hit me," he says.

"Don't fucking tempt me."

Bogdan shakes his head. Despite his stoic face, I know he's desperate for a reprieve. He wants forgiveness. Even as boys, he could never stand it when we were at odds with one another. Some things never change.

"I should have been more vigilant," he whispers. "I took my eyes off them for two seconds."

"TWO FUCKING SECONDS IS ALL IT FUCKING TAKES!" I roar.

He hasn't ever seen me like this. Hell, *I* haven't seen me like this. It feels oddly cathartic to bellow like a feral animal. After years of honing the art of deadly silence, the ability to let my voice run wild is a welcome change of pace.

"I know," Bogdan says. "I should have done more. I should have been prepared. I should have—"

Before he can finish, I grab him by the collar and wrench him towards me. Our noses are only inches from another but I want him to look me in the eyes.

"They have my daughter," I snarl. My voice breaks. "They have Jo!"

"I'm going to get her back," Bogdan insists. "I swear to you, I will get her back."

I release his shirt in disgust and turn my back on him. "No. It's clear now that I have to do shit on my own. So I will get her back. You just stay out of my fucking way."

I expect him to leave the room. He knows how to read my moods. He knows better than to linger.

But he doesn't go anywhere. "Do you think I don't care about that little girl just as much as you do?" Bogdan asks.

"How much you care about her is irrelevant."

"*Sobrat*, I—"

"Stop!" Camila intercedes, stepping into the room.

Her eyes flash around, taking in the shambles that used to be a dignified sitting room. She maneuvers her way around the wreckage that litters the floor and comes to stand between us, her eyes sharp and filled with an agony that is painful to witness.

"Turning on each other is not going to get my daughter back," she says.

Her tone is remarkably calm. She's steady when she speaks, with a new steel in her eyes when she glances between Bogdan and me.

"It happened. They took her. She's gone. Now, we have to focus on getting her back."

I know she's right. But it feels good to break shit.

"Isaak," she says, turning to me. "We need a plan."

Those words coming out of her mouth have a strange effect on me. I'm both impressed and turned on by them. There's new strength in her that I haven't seen before.

But this strength has no place in my sphere.

The don's strength is all that matters.

Before I can answer, Mama walks in. She still looks a little unsteady on her feet, but some of her color has returned.

"I found something," she says.

"What do you mean?" Bogdan asks, moving forward.

She produces a piece of white paper, crumpled at the edges. "I found it just now," she explains, "in my pocket."

I grab the note before Bogdan can reach for it. There's only one sentence, scrawled in a familiar handwriting:

It's time you paid for what you stole from me.

My hands clench into fists. I crumple up the note and throw it onto the floor among the glass. "It's payback time alright," I mutter.

"More threats?" Bogdan asks.

I don't answer. Instead, I head straight out of the room. I'm aware of footsteps behind me, but I'm so consumed with my plans that I don't realize they're Camila's until she calls my name.

"Isaak!"

"What?" I snap without slowing down.

She follows me right into my office. "What's the plan?"

"It's forming," I tell her icily.

"Okay, well, whatever it is, I'm coming with you."

I grimace. I've expected those words since the moment I saw the new hardness in her gaze.

"No."

She stops short. "No?"

"That's what I said. You're not coming with me."

"She's my daughter, too."

"Irrelevant. You won't have any clue what to do in a situation like that."

"All I need to do is get to Jo."

"And you think that's going to be easy?" I demand. "You think you can just show up at Maxim's compound and ask nicely to have Jo back?"

"I can try."

"Don't be fucking naïve. It doesn't suit you."

"Stop it," she says, "stop treating me like a stranger. It's me you're talking to."

"You're not a stranger, Camila," I snap back. "I know exactly who and what you are: a fucking liability. Which is why I'm saying no."

She flinches back, but the determination only glows brighter in her eyes. She moves closer to me and jabs her finger into my chest.

"I know you, too, Isaak Vorobev. You do this. Say something cruel to push me away. Well, guess what? My daughter's life is at risk here, so nothing you can say will make the slightest bit of difference. You want to call me a coward, a whore, a liability? Go right ahead. I'll take every single insult you throw at me. Because there's nothing I wouldn't do for Jo."

She probably has no idea just how magnificent she is in this moment. I can't help but stand there and watch her. The way her eyes clash with her hair. The way her beauty seems all the more pronounced because of the newfound confidence in her eyes.

But I can't tell her those things. I can't tell her how she's the best parts of me. How Jo is the best parts of both of us. I can't tell her I need her, I love her.

Because my father taught me long ago that weakness gets you killed.

"Thanks for the speech. The answer is still no."

She stiffens hard at first, then steels herself and dives right back into the fight. "Isaak, if I'm going to be a part of this life, then you're going to have to include me in it."

I shake my head. "You're going to be a part of my life. But the Bratva is not for you."

"You can't do that."

"Watch me."

I press a button that has a direct line to my men. It's a silent trigger, so Camila doesn't even notice it. She's too pissed off anyway.

"I can try talking to Maxim," she's saying.

I snort derisively. "I'm sure that will go wonderfully."

"We do have a history."

"That history was shot to hell the moment you decided to stay with me," I point out. "You made your choice, Camila. And he's not going to forgive you for it. Why do you think he took Jo in the first place?"

Her eyes go wide. "Do you think… do you think he'll hurt her?"

The honest truth is that I don't know. But telling Camila that will just break her.

"He needs her for leverage," I say instead. "He won't do anything to her just yet."

I can see tears pricking in her eyes, but she doesn't let them fall. "Isaak, we have to get her back."

"Like I said, I'm working on it."

She takes a step closer and puts her hand on my arm. "Please," she begs, "let me help you."

Over her shoulder, I notice two of my men enter the room silently. They stand their ground, waiting for my instructions.

"I said no."

"Why?" she protests. "Because I'm a civilian? Because I'm a woman?"

I shake my head. "I'm not keeping you here because you're a woman. I'm keeping you here because you're *my* fucking woman."

Then I give the men a nod. They come forward as one and grab her.

Her eyes go wide as she realizes what's happening. She starts to thrash in their arms. "No, no, you can't do this. Isaak. ISAAK!"

"Take her to her room and lock her in there," I instruct the men.

They drag her away as she screams. But it doesn't touch me. Not in the slightest—because I know that while I'm away she's going to be safe.

And that's one less thing I need to fucking worry about.

37

CAMI

"No, no, NO! Let me go, you fucking bastards!"

The two guards gripping my arms don't say a word. Their faces are masks of stone. I struggle hard, but that only forces them to grip me tighter.

I notice a tall shadow pass in the corner and I crane my neck back. "Wait," I say desperately. "Wait! Bogdan. Bogdan!"

He doubles back and approaches me at a slow pace. One look at his face tells me that I'm barking up the wrong tree. I try anyway.

"Bogdan, you've got to get them to release me. They'll listen to you."

His eyes flit across the two guards and then he shakes his head. "Their orders have come directly from Isaak, Camila. There's no way I can overrule him. Even if I could, they wouldn't listen."

"Jesus, then punch the lights out of them."

He looks guiltily at me. "I'm sorry."

"You won't even try to help me?"

"Isaak wants to keep you safe, Camila."

"They have my daughter, Bogdan!" I scream. "And I might be able to help get her back."

He just shakes his head again. "Exposing yourself to Maxim is not a good idea. Not only will he have Jo, but then he'll have a good chance of getting you, too."

"Talk to Isaak then," I plead. "Talk to him and convince him to bring me with you."

He sighs. "I'm sorry, Camila."

"Don't be fucking sorry," I cry. "Help me!"

"I'm on thin ice with him already."

"So you're not even gonna try?"

Bogdan gives the guards a final nod. "I can't do anything, Camila. He's made his decision."

I start to scream again—no words this time, just anguish—as the guards continue to carry me through the mansion towards my room. Bogdan turns the corner and disappears.

"Coward!" I scream after him.

When we reach my room, they escort me inside and retreat quickly. The lock clicks shut, the kind of ominous thud that says, *You're never getting out of here.*

I run at the door anyway and slam my fists against the hard wood. It doesn't so much as shudder. Like everything else in this cursed fucking house, it's completely unyielding.

But since when has that ever stopped me?

I keep slamming my palms down on the wood, if only because I need something to do. Some way to let loose the pain churning inside me.

When the tears come, my strength leaves. I can't seem to stop them. I end up at the window, watching the men ready the vehicles and prepare for the mission to get Jo back.

I should be down there with them. Instead, I'm up here, locked in a room and forced to watch as other people go off to try and save my daughter. People I don't know, people who don't know my daughter.

I notice Isaak then. His presence is all-consuming. He commands attention immediately. Most of the men are tall, and yet Isaak stands out amongst them.

He talks to a few of the lieutenants overseeing preparations. I notice Bogdan and Vlad among them. Then, at some unspoken signal, they start climbing into the bulletproof vehicles.

"God..." I mutter to the glass windowpane.

Isaak heads to the passenger side door of one of the Jeeps. As though he can sense me watching, he turns around and looks up, directly at my window.

Our eyes lock. Despite the distance, I feel the connection between us stretch and tighten and pulse and shimmer.

Even when I'm pissed at him, I can't escape my feelings.

I can't stop worrying about him.

I can't stop loving him.

"Don't die," I mouth to him.

He gives me a nod and gets into the vehicle. The gates swing open and in perfect synchronicity, the vehicles whisk out, one after the other.

The moment the last vehicle is gone, the gates close. A large contingent of men steps up to survey the gates and double-check the locking mechanism, then they disperse to man the borders of the compound.

I know they're here for me. There's no other reason Isaak would leave behind such a large number of able-bodied soldiers if he weren't concerned about the possibility of the mansion being hit while he was away.

I find no solace in that thought, though. I have no interest in being safe. Not when Jo and Isaak are directly in the path of danger.

If anything happens to either one of them…

I fall forward and rest my forehead on the plush cushion of the window seat. My tears drip down onto the material, staining it and turning the pattern dark like blood.

I don't know how long I stay like that, with my head bent in submission as though I'm praying for something. Hell, maybe that's exactly what I should be doing.

Don't let them—

Please make sure they're—

But the words are too hard to say.

That's when I hear the door lock click open. I bolt upright as Nikita walks into my room. She shuts the door behind her and comes over to me.

"Oh, child," she sighs when she looks at my face.

She reaches for the box of tissues and offers me one. I pull a couple out and wipe away the tears and grime on my face. Nikita sits down on the window seat next to me and places the box of tissues between us.

"I don't know how you survived all those years," I say bitterly.

"It was different for me."

"How?"

"I didn't love my husband."

"Never?" I ask. I didn't think it would, but talking feels good at the moment. It's better than being trapped inside my head with never-ending nightmares and *What ifs.*

"I had the potential to love him… if he had been a different kind of man," Nikita admits. "But he was never interested in that. In me. He wasn't interested in a partner. He didn't want anything from me other than children."

"How did you survive it?"

"Some days, even I don't know."

I shake my head. "This is not like every other battle Isaak's fought," I say. "Jo's life is at stake if he makes a mistake or overplays his hand."

"My son knows what he's doing, Camila."

I shake my head. "Maybe so, but that doesn't mean I don't know anything. I could have helped."

She strokes the back of my hand tenderly. "He didn't leave you behind because he thought you'd get in the way. He left you behind because he wanted to keep you safe. He feels responsible enough for losing Jo. I don't think he could bear losing you, too."

I bite down on my lip. "What about me, though?" I protest. "Don't you think I feel the same way about him? Do you realize how hard it was for me to watch him get in the vehicle and drive off? Does he?"

"I do, actually," she says. "I imagine it's the same kind of awful as watching both your sons drive off to war."

Her words sober me a little. I'm not the only one suffering right now. "I don't want this life for Jo."

"Isaak will do what he swore to do, Camila. Take comfort in that. Neither he nor Bogdan had any choice in where their lives were headed. They were always going to be children of the Bratva. But Jo has two parents who will fight for her. That makes all the difference."

Another fat tear slips down my cheek. "She must be so scared…"

"She's half Isaak and half you," Nikita says, patting her hand on my knee. "She's strong and resilient enough to survive this."

"She's five," I point out. "She shouldn't have to be anything other than happy."

"The world is unfair," Nikita says. "Children are forced to grow up long before they should have to."

Some note in her voice forces me to look at her.

She looks… older. Her expression is pained and I realize suddenly that she's trembling all over. The first crack in her façade I've seen in a long time, maybe ever. I think about how much time she's spent with Jo in the last few weeks, and I realize that she's as scared as I am.

She's just doing a better job of hiding it.

Maybe she's putting on a brave face for me. Maybe this is just how she deals with every difficult situation that's thrown her way. You'd never known that only a few hours ago, the woman had been knocked unconscious and her granddaughter stripped away from her by bloodthirsty enemies.

"I'm sorry," I say. "I… I haven't even thought about how difficult this must be for you."

"You never get used to it. But you learn to endure it."

"I don't think I can ever learn that."

"Trust me: if you love him enough, you will."

I sniffle and dab at my eyes with another tissue. "Nikita, can I ask you something?"

She nods. "Ask me anything."

"How do you know if you love a person enough?"

She looks out the window as her eyes go hazy with memory. "When you're prepared to do anything to be with them," she says. "Even if it means your life."

I nod. "You're talking about the man you fell in love with."

"Yes."

"If your husband had found out…"

"He would have killed us both. I suppose, in the end, he did kill him anyway."

I freeze. "Wait—did he find out?"

She shakes her head. "Not quite. He wanted to seize control over the Bratva, and Yakov was simply in his way."

It takes me several seconds to dissect that sentence. Not just because of the easy way she delivers it, but because of the shocking truth it contains.

Yakov.

"Are you telling me what I think you're telling me?"

She takes a deep breath. "I've kept the secret so long. It feels good to say the words out loud now. It feels… freeing."

I just stare at her. Her beautiful, austere features have relaxed. She doesn't look so tired anymore. Definitely not as old. It makes me believe that all the pain etched into her features is a result of the secrets she's been carrying all these years. The gravity of hiding something so huge.

And now that she's let that weight fall from her shoulders, she looks like she could soar.

"Your secret lover was your husband's brother?" I ask. "Maxim's father?" I know I sound dumb and obvious, but it feels important to say it out loud.

She nods. "It's the main reason Svetlana hated me."

"She *knew?*" I gape at her.

"She suspected. She always knew that Yakov had a soft spot for me. She just didn't know how deep it went. Not until the end, anyway."

I stammer without really forming a word. I'm truly not judging her. I'm just trying to wrap my head around this information. I've only ever heard secondhand stories about Yakov, and I scramble to try and recollect what they were.

How did Isaak describe him? A weak leader, but a better man that his father was? I wish I'd been paying closer attention now.

"I had an affair with my brother-in-law," Nikita says, like it's important for her to say it out loud, too. I'm impressed at the fact that there's no guilt, shame, or regret attached to her tone. Just honesty. Fondness, even. "It started innocently enough. We lived in the same house. And he was… he was so different than Vitaly."

"How?"

"When he looked at me, he really *saw* me," Nikita explains in a hush. "He was interested in my opinions. He liked discussing books with me. We started talking, we became friends…"

It makes sense. She was trapped in a lonely, unhappy marriage. Of course she'd find solace in the one man who saw her as more than a possession.

"What about his wife?" I ask.

Nikita sighs. "I'm not going to pretend as though I thought much about her," she admits. "I wish I could say even now that I felt guilty. But she and I, we were never really friends. The day I married into the Vorobev, she decided to make me her enemy. And when she started noticing how kind Yakov was to me, she got insecure. Cagey."

"Was it real?" I ask softly.

It's a personal question, but I figure that she's the one who chose to tell me about this hidden part of her life. Maybe a part of her is done keeping secrets.

Maybe she wants to surrender the truth to the world and be judged for it, come what may.

"Yakov and I?" she asks.

"Yes."

She smiles. It tells me more than words ever could. "It was so real that it made us think we had a future together," she says.

"Really?"

Nikita nods. "I suppose it was another reason Yakov started dismantling the Bratva and selling it bit by bit."

"Oh my God," I breathe. "You were going to run away together?"

"We didn't have a definite plan," she admits. "It was such an impossible thing we were trying to do. But Yakov was determined to step back from the Bratva at some point."

"Why didn't he just hand it over to Vitaly then?" I ask. "He must have known that his younger brother had bigger ambitions."

Nikita sighs. "That was the whole reason he came up with that plan in the first place. He wanted to stamp out the power of the Vorobevs so that if Vitaly did take over, he wouldn't be able to come at us with the full force of the Bratva behind him. Vitaly would be too busy picking up the pieces to worry about where his wife had disappeared to."

"Were you planning on taking the boys?" I ask.

She smiles, but this one nearly shatters my heart. "We were so naïve. We were planning on taking all three."

"Maxim, too?"

Nikita nods. "Yakov refused to leave behind Maxim. Since I couldn't imagine going without Isaak or Bogdan, I understood. In fact, it made me love him more."

"Oh, Nikita," I say, putting my hand over hers. "I'm sorry…"

She shrugs. The gesture is heavy with old pain. "It was a foolish, naïve plan. It would never have worked. But Yakov was enough of a dreamer to believe in it. And I was young and in love. It seemed to me that he could move mountains if he chose to."

"You're sure that Vitaly never knew about the two of you?" I ask.

Nikita nods confidently. "He never knew. If he had, I'd have been drawn and quartered. And Yakov would have suffered a much more gruesome death. As it was, he was poisoned slowly. Over time. It was done so subtly that even I didn't suspect until the last possible moment. And by then, it was too late."

I shake my head in dismay. "I can't imagine what you must have gone through."

Her eyes grow filmy with the memory. "His death was the worst day of my life. His funeral was the second-worst. I had to stand on the side and watch Svetlana play the grieving widow. I should have been standing where she was. She may have had the title of his wife. But I had his heart."

"Did you ever confront your husband about what he did?"

Nikita gives me an ironic smile. "I don't have the type of bravery that you do, Camila. I didn't yell and scream and accuse. I didn't display my pain and anger. Doing that would have only made him suspicious. I did fight back, though. I fought back in the shadows, when he wasn't paying attention."

I frown. "I don't understand…"

"I had to wait years," Nikita tells me. "I had to time it just right. But after Maxim started pushing back, questioning the way his father had died, I decided it was time I had to act."

"Nikita..."

"He was so confident in the collar he had strapped around my neck that he never once thought that I might bite back. I played the dutiful wife and he ate the food I gave him, drank the cocktails I mixed for him. When he started to exhibit symptoms, he didn't once question why he was experiencing the same thing that killed his brother."

My jaw drops. I stare at Nikita, trying to reconcile the calm, reserved woman I know with the femme fatale who had murdered her husband in revenge for her lover.

"I... I thought... Isaak told me that Maxim had Vitaly killed?" I ask.

"Oh, he certainly tried," Nikita tells me. "He had deployed a man to do exactly that. I just beat him to it."

Goosebumps prick my skin. Why hadn't I seen it before? This woman is cunning and dangerous, even more so because of how unassuming she is. How easy to overlook.

"Do Isaak and Bogdan still think Maxim is responsible for their father's death?"

Nikita nods. "The mole Maxim planted in the house was blamed for Vitaly's passing. But the credit was never his to take. It was mine. Only mine."

I continue gawking at her. She's *proud* of how she killed Vitaly. She's proud of the fact that she's been able to keep the secret for so long without anyone suspecting her.

Part of me is awestruck.

Part of me is terrified.

"Nikita," I say, putting my hand over hers. "I appreciate everything you've been through. But… your sons deserve to know the truth."

She sighs. "I thought you might say that."

"Is that why you told me?"

"Maybe," she acknowledges. "Maybe."

I press forward. "I don't know what this will change, but I do know that Isaak and Bogdan are out there now because they think Maxim killed their father."

"That's not the only reason."

"No, I know that. There's a whole host of things forcing their hand. And I can only claim to understand a few of them. But Nikita, if this information has the possibility of changing something, then you need to share it with everyone. Not just me."

"Maxim and Svetlana are not going to listen."

"You avenged Maxim's father. You avenged Svetlana's husband. Don't you think that'll make a difference to them?"

She gives me a soft smile. "There's still a lot of naïveté in you, child."

I sigh. "I know I'm probably the most clueless person in this house right now. Maybe a few months ago, that would have driven me crazy. But you know what? I don't care anymore. If being naïve gives me the ability to hope, then I'm happy to jump down that rabbit hole. Hope is too precious of a thing to lose."

I get to my feet and hold out my hand to the woman.

"They won't let me out of this house, Nikita. Not without you."

She blinks. "You want me to let you go?"

"No—I want you to come with me."

38

ISAAK

"Detonate."

The moment I give the command, the entire south section of Maxim's compound goes up in a cacophony of debris.

I'd had my men scour the area before we'd planted the bomb. There's only a handful of his followers in the south section. But I know for a fact that Jo's not there. It's the safest place to destroy without compromising her safety.

Besides, the intent of the explosion is not to cause death. It's simply to make a statement.

Isaak Vorobev is here.

And this time, I'm not fucking around.

The alarm is raised immediately, but my men and I don't wait for the smoke to clear. We pour into the compound with our weapons drawn.

I've killed four men by the time we manage to walk out of the haze of dust floating all around, tainting the ether. I can't see Maxim anywhere, but I have no doubt he'll show up.

He hasn't left this compound in days. There's nowhere else he could be.

I watch as Bogdan and Vlad cut their way to the front of the line. Bogdan is fast and sneaky with his attacks, exploiting every angle at his disposal to cut a wide swathe of death. Vlad is a straightforward fighter who gets his way through brute force.

I do whatever gets the job done.

That's not ego talking. It's practice. It's the training style that was carved into me, literally and metaphorically. It's never enough to be strategic and cunning. It's never enough to be brutal and strong.

You have to back up brains with brawn. You have to be everything at all times.

My father wasn't a man who made small requests.

It takes us fourteen minutes to fight through to his gardens. I take a spiteful pleasure in mowing down the ludicrously ornate animal-shaped topiaries dotting the courtyard. I hope they were expensive.

The topiaries offer about as much resistance as Maxim's men do. It's pitiful how quickly they're slaughtered or surrender. In no time at all, we're at the doors of the house.

The mansion looms over us. Windows look down from both the east and west wings. If he had half a brain, Maxim would've had snipers stationed at every one of those vantage points, ready to force us back under cover.

"Maxim!" I bellow into the air.

As my voice rings around the grounds, my men gather around me, leaving only the fringes of our group taking care of the traitorous stragglers who don't know when to give up.

I glance towards either side of me. "Don't shoot at the house," I order. "My daughter is in there somewhere."

Two seconds later, I spot movement.

I redouble my grip on my gun. I count twenty, thirty, forty men streaming past the windows upstairs with guns in hand. The thunder of their boots shakes the ground.

"He's got at least forty men at his back," Vlad says grimly.

"We have to assume there's double the number in and around the house," I say.

There were fifty Vorobev men at my back when we started. No more than five or six have suffered injuries in the initial onslaught. I'm not worried about being outnumbered, though. I could assemble an army of street rats and still come out on top.

But this is the first fight I've ever been in with real fucking skin in the game.

Yes, I lost men, but they knew exactly what they'd signed up for. I'll give them honorable funerals and make sure their families receive distributions of cash for the rest of their lives.

That is my duty to them.

This is different.

Maxim has my child. And I'm very aware that, despite my superior numbers and the fact that my men are ten times more skilled, he has the only leverage that matters.

The thunder of boots grows louder. The doors burst open.

And then, sauntering down the stairs comes Maxim.

His men form a ring around him. I make it a point to step in front of my soldiers to ensure the contrast between us is obvious.

Cowards hide in the back.

Kings lead from the front.

"Maxim," I drawl. "Kind of you to join us."

His eyes dart to the ruins behind us. I've probably destroyed half an acre of his property and it rankles him. He's trying to come off as detached, but I sense his distraction, his anger.

Even from here, I spy beads of sweat forming across his forehead. His eyes dart around, taking in my men and the numbers at my back.

He doesn't look nervous, though. He's smart enough to know he still has the upper hand.

"You were a fool to come," he replies.

"Why?" I ask. "I'm going to win."

I have no evidence to back up that claim, but if all else fails, confidence can push you through. I make sure to meet his eyes. He needs to know that I will not falter when it comes to a fight.

Maxim shakes his head. "Are you forgetting one very important fact? I have your daughter."

"Do you imagine that hurting Jo will help you win Camila back?" I ask. "Because I assure you, that's not going to happen."

Maxim shrugs. "I'll spin a story. She'll believe me."

"She doesn't fucking love you," I snap. "She never did."

"Then why did she agree to marry me?"

I smile slowly, making sure to speak as clearly as possible so that Maxim's men can hear too. "Isn't it obvious?" I say. "She couldn't have me… so she picked the knock-off version."

His eyes ripple with anger and his fists tighten at his sides. His men glance at each other, wondering if they're about to get an order to attack.

"Did you come here just to taunt me, cousin?"

"I came for my girl."

"How admirable," he seethes. "How fucking noble of you."

"Where is my daughter, Maxim? I won't ask you again."

He opens his mouth to retort.

But then a new voice slices in from beyond my line of sight. "She's out of your reach."

Maxim looks behind him as his men part to allow the speaker to pass. A woman walks through the gap in the ranks and stops at Maxim's side.

Svetlana has aged, but not willingly. It looks like she's scrapping and clawing to cling to her youth. Her hair is dyed a dark, unnatural brown that contrasts sickly with her pale skin. I see the telltale tension of plastic surgery in her face, her lips, her jaw.

Strangely enough, I see shades of Mama in her features. They aren't related by blood, so it's not genetics marking the similarity.

Maybe this life just takes its toll on those who live it.

"Svetlana," I acknowledge.

"You want your daughter?" she asks, dispensing with the pleasantries.

"That's the whole reason I'm here."

"If you want something, then you have to be willing to give us something in return."

Us. The word stands out. It tells me a lot about who might be pulling the strings behind the scenes.

Or maybe that assumption is giving Maxim too much credit. Maybe she's pulling the strings out in the open and everyone fucking knows it.

"Maxim, I didn't realize that your mother was the reigning don here."

The annoyance in his eyes burns bright—but I'm fairly certain that this time, it has nothing to do with me.

"*I* am the fucking don," he snarls, taking a step forward out of the shadow of his men.

I bite back a grin. Nothing has changed. He's still so easy to goad. So easy to manipulate.

Svetlana seems to realize the same thing. She grabs his arm and tries to whisper something I can't hear in his ear. But before she can finish speaking, Maxim shakes her off and pushes her back.

He speaks low, just like her, but his words carry over to me. "Don't fucking interfere," he snaps to his mother. "This is my fight."

I notice the sharp spark in Svetlana's eyes. She doesn't like being talked down to.

Her shoulders brace upwards as she tries not to lose face. Mama was right about her. She is the more dangerous one of the two. Which means, when it comes to the fight, she'll need to be taken out just like her mangy son.

I don't relish the thought of killing my own aunt. It's not the code I've lived by my entire life. But sometimes, tough choices need to be made.

Maxim clears his throat and speaks up. "You want your daughter, then I want something in return."

"Yeah," I jeer, "your mommy just said that."

Maxim's jaw tightens with fury. "Return what's mine."

"And what would that be?"

"My Bratva. And my fucking fiancée."

I laugh in his face. "You are dumber than I thought you were. How stupid do you think I am? I gave you terms once before and you destroyed any chance at accepting them by attacking me."

"Those weren't terms. That was a fucking exile."

"It was generous, considering what I had planned for you."

"And yet here I am."

"By my mercy," I say. "I could have killed you that day. I chose not to."

He scoffs. "I fought you off."

Bogdan steps forward, clearly riled up by the conversation. "I was fucking there. I walked in to find you under my brother's grip. He could have snapped your neck in two seconds. He should have, but he didn't."

"Stop bleating, little lamb," Maxim hisses. "Your opinion is not wanted today."

"Careful," I warn him. "I'm not here to play nice. So you better watch your tongue when you speak to my men."

Maxim nods in fake sympathy. "Always the protective older brother. It's heartwarming, actually. Which one of you should I kill first? I think the little brat will be much more fun to watch suffer."

The whole time we've been speaking, I've been keeping an eye on Svetlana. Her eyes are alert and frenzied. Cunning. She's wary of this devolving in front of her.

She knows as well as I do: Maxim cannot be trusted to win.

"If you don't cooperate," she interrupts suddenly, "you will never see your daughter again."

Maxim gives her a cursory glance. I seize upon his hesitation. "You want the Bratva?" I ask. "You'll have to win it by blood. That's the only way to prove you're worthy."

"And Camila?" Maxim asks.

I raise my eyebrows. "Do you imagine that Camila is some whore I bought at auction? She's a woman, Maxim. Not a piece of property to be bartered or sold. If you want her, then she needs to choose you."

"Pah! You've brainwashed her."

"No." I shake my head. "I've set her free."

"Fuck you," he spits. "Always so high and fucking mighty."

His men shuffle and murmur. The tides are turning. Everyone can sense it.

Everyone but him.

"I never influenced her decision, you know," I muse. "Even when you came for her at that safehouse… she called me."

Maxim's eyes are twitching furiously now. "You think you are a hero," he snarls. "You think you are a god. But your daughter is inside with a gun to her head, cousin. How does that look from your high horse?"

"It will all be over soon," I tell him grimly.

He's not finished. He spits on the ground and takes another stride forward, away from the security of his men. "You're the son of a killer. Did you know that? A sneaky, murderous little backstabber in the night. Poison—is there a more cowardly way to end a man's life? His own brother! Do you know what your father did?"

He wants that to hurt. He wants to wound me so badly I lose sight of the bigger picture.

Instead, I shrug. "I know."

Maxim stops short. "You… you know?"

"I found out recently," I admit. "Which is exactly why I made you that offer during what was supposed to be a gentleman's tête-à-tête. It's also the reason you're standing here today. If it weren't for the fact that I owed you a blood debt, you'd be dead."

The shuffling amongst his ranks continues. I can sense the unease like a storm cloud. I intend to use it to my advantage.

"I told you time and time again, Maxim: it's about strength, and you are in your soul a weak man. I am not responsible for my father's actions. I was only a boy when he moved against Yakov. But when I knew the truth, I paid off his blood debt by sparing your life when I could have ended it. This is my Bratva now. It's time you accepted that."

"It is not your fucking Bratva."

"You want to prove you're strong enough?" I ask, stepping forward and laying the final piece of my trap. "Then fight me now. Win it and it's yours."

"No, Maxim," Svetlana says immediately. "He's trying to trick you."

But there's no stopping what's happening now. It's coming like an avalanche.

The ending of all this bloodshed.

Just a few more drops to spill.

"You want to fight me, cousin?" Maxim asks, his jaw setting with determination. "So fucking be it."

"Maxim—"

"Silence!" Maxim roars over Svetlana. "Or I will fucking remove you."

His mother goes quiet immediately, but I can see the anger and humiliation in her eyes. Beautiful.

Smiling triumphantly, I move forward, flexing my muscles. Our men form a large circle around us. My men form one half, and Maxim's men form the other. Svetlana falls back a little, but I glance at Bogdan and Vlad and gesture towards her.

I don't have to speak to make sure they understand me. I already know they do.

Keep an eye on that one.

Maxim steps out into the empty space. He's huffing and puffing. He doesn't know what to do with his anger like I do. How to bottle it. How to channel it. How to break it over your enemy's head when the moment is right.

I'm getting ready to do just that—when I hear something.

A voice raised in panic, trembling with uncertainty... and all too familiar.

"Wait!"

My men look behind their shoulders. I can't see what's happening—until two of them part to allow the new arrivals to walk into the center of the ring.

39

CAMILA

It's like the inner circle of hell in here.

There's no literal fire, but I can feel the heat of tension, anger, testosterone, bloodlust. I can feel the burn of a hundred stares and in the middle of it all, two titanic egos igniting one another to rage hotter and hotter and hotter.

My eyes fall to Isaak. I physically need to make sure he's alright, that he's still standing. The minor scratches and stains on him don't look too bad, though. If anything, they make him look better. Fiercer. Deadlier.

Then I turn towards Maxim. My ex-fiancé is standing directly opposite Isaak, looking as though his worst nightmare has taken shape in front of him.

I feel a pull of pity for the man. How could I not? I spent some of the longest and loneliest months of my life waiting for someone like him. And then, when he came into my world, I spent more months imagining the life we might have together.

I no longer have any guilt associated with accepting his proposal, though.

Yes, I was using him.

But he was using me right back.

I'd like to say we're even. But judging from the look on his face, I don't think he feels the same way.

"What the fuck are the two of you doing here?" Isaak growls.

"We were sick of being left behind," I snap. "Also, your mother has something she needs to say."

A woman dressed in black steps out from behind Maxim. I don't recognize her face, but her voice and her manner feel eerily familiar. I just can't put my finger on why.

"Well, if Nikita has something to say," she seethes, bitterness and loathing tainting her faintly accented English, "then I suppose the world must stop to hear it."

"Svetlana," Nikita says with a small sigh. "What a pleasure."

Oh, fuck. So this is Maxim's mother. Yakov's wife. The woman whose husband Nikita had had a years-long affair with.

The bitterness makes sense then.

She's definitely attractive. But in a different way than Nikita. They're both thin, dignified-looking women. But Nikita's beauty is softer and more obvious. Svetlana's beauty has a sharp edge that's further marred by the hate in her eyes. A sort of craven soullessness. A sheet of ice where a heart should be.

I scan the ranks of men just behind her—and gasp in shock as I see a face I recognize.

Everyone turns to me. Isaak's questioning gaze bores into the side of my face.

"Andrew," I whisper.

"Andrew?" Isaak repeats. "As in…"

"My agent," I say. "The one who was assigned to me after Eric was forced off my case. Oh God…"

Maxim glances back at Andrew and smiles. He doesn't have to say it for us to understand: he likes the fact that this is coming out now. It makes him look shrewd, cunning. Like he is the kind of don who has planned painstakingly and thought three steps ahead of his enemies.

"Andrew was always my man," he says haughtily. "He played his part to perfection."

"I don't know about that," I snap. "Everyone hated him. He was an unpleasant little prick."

Andrew grimaces in irritation. He was always touchy about his height.

Something else suddenly occurs to me. "That's how you knew how to find me in London." I turn towards Maxim. "Andrew tipped you off as to where I was."

"Very astute," he drawls sarcastically. "Such a smart little girl. And you know what? Finding you was the hardest part. Getting you to bed was easy. Getting a ring on your finger was even easier."

I have to breathe through the lash of anger. It's obvious what he's doing: goading me, pushing my buttons to draw a reaction. I hate that it's working.

But even as I try to tame my emotion, my eyes keep slipping towards his gaunt-faced mother.

Why the hell does she seem so damn familiar to me?

And then it hits me. I never saw her face properly. But her voice… that, I never forgot. It's stayed with me all these years.

She was my first introduction into the world of the Bratva.

She was the first person who spoke to me in that cell, after days of agonizing silence.

"You," I say, turning my gaze on her. "You were the woman who spoke to me after my first abduction… You kept me in that cell for days."

She doesn't bother denying it. "Yes, that was me."

I shake my head. "What was the point?"

"The point was to use you to get to me," Isaak interjects through gritted teeth. "They assumed that taking you would give them the leverage they needed to force my cooperation. It backfired, though. Didn't it, cousin?"

"What were you planning on doing with me, Maxim?" I ask softly.

He's not meeting my eyes. That sends a shiver down my back. Why won't he look me in the eyes?

"Cami," he mumbles, his tone going soft. "You know me. We were planning a life together. You know that I would never harm your daughter."

He's subtle, but I get the message loud and clear. *I have your daughter. Cooperate… or else.*

"Where is she?" I ask, my voice trembling just a little.

"She's safe," Maxim says. "But she's been asking for you. Come with me now and I'll take you to her."

Isaak tenses next to me. "She's not going anywhere with you."

"Please, Maxim," I say. "Just give her back to me."

"Give her back?" he repeats. "No, I can't give her back. But I can take you with me."

"Is that the choice?" I ask.

"That's the choice."

Nikita steps forward, buying me some time. "Before any decision is made, there's something I need to tell everyone."

Her eyes are fixed on Svetlana. Two cords of violent tension bisect the air—one rippling between Maxim and Isaak. The other between their mothers.

Talk about family drama.

"And why would any of us be interested in what you have to say?" Svetlana snaps. "You're nothing but a whore you chased after a man who wasn't yours."

I can tell immediately that this is the first time that Isaak or Bogdan have been confronted with this new possibility. Both their eyes flit to Nikita, waiting for her to deny it and defend herself.

"Mama," Bogdan says in a low voice. "What is she talking about?"

"Of course your boys don't know," Svetlana says with a laugh that's dark and murky. "You were always good at pretending. I'm the only one who saw through you."

"I know how you feel, Svetlana," says Nikita wearily. "And I'm sorry you suffered for it. But Yakov was never yours. Not in any way that mattered. A signature on a piece of paper means nothing."

Isaak's eyes miss nothing. His gaze dances between Svetlana and Nikita with growing realization.

"We were going to run away together," Nikita explains. "Yakov and I. We were going to disappear one day. And we were going to take the boys with us."

Svetlana's eyes go wide at first before narrowing in rage. "You were going to take my son?"

"You hated him," Nikita snaps. "He was a pawn to you. An heir you could control. Whereas we… we wanted him to know what it's like to be loved. To show him that the world can be a beautiful place."

Her voice is pure fire. For the first time since I've met her, she actually seems alive.

Nikita looks at Bogdan. Then she turns to Isaak. Her expression softens. "I'm sorry, my sons. I wish I had told you both sooner. I was just… scared. I was a coward."

"Fuck," Bogdan says, running a hand down his face.

"That's not all," I say. "Nikita, you need to tell them the rest."

"There's more?" Bogdan gapes.

His shock and disappointment is painted across his face. But Isaak's mask of composure never drops. Even now, even when the foundation of his world is breaking apart, he never forgets his training.

Nikita takes a deep breath. "Isaak, you killed one of Maxim's men the day Vitaly died."

"The fucker who killed him," Bogdan answers before Isaak.

"No," Isaak says suddenly.

And I know he's figured it out. It's the reason he's been so quiet this whole time. While everyone else reacts, Isaak processes. He reads the nuances between every sentence, between each expression.

"No, we killed the wrong murderer," continues Isaak. "He was planted to kill Otets. But someone else beat him to it. Isn't that right, mother?"

She doesn't break eye contact when she nods.

"I am the one who killed Vitaly Vorobev," she says. "I killed my husband."

The silence feels claustrophobic. A hundred violent men held sway by the secrets of two old women.

A war pinned in place by love that's stayed hidden for years.

"Mama…" Bogdan's voice is filled with shocked awe. He's staring at Nikita as though he has no idea who she is anymore. "Mama… it… it can't be true."

She looks at him with a resigned expression. "It's true, my boy. I'm sorry, but it's true."

"Why?"

She shakes her head. "I loved Yakov. And I always knew I would avenge his death. It took years, but in the end, I did exactly that. I took his life the same way your father took Yakov's: one drop of poison at a time."

Svetlana steps forward, her lip curled into a sneer. "And you think this information changes anything? Are we supposed to be grateful to you?"

"I am still the fucking rightful don," Maxim snarls. "No matter who you spread your legs for."

Bogdan flinches noticeably, but Isaak doesn't budge. He senses something coming. One more bombshell of truth. I can feel it, too, like an encroaching storm on the horizon. But I can't quite make out the shape of it just yet. I only know that it's coming.

Nikita turns to address Maxim directly for the first time. "You think your claim to the Vorobev Bratva is legitimate because you are the oldest son of the oldest son."

"Yes," he snarls. "Do you need me to draw you a fucking chart?"

Nikita glances to Isaak for a moment. My instincts start to tingle hotter.

It can't be…

"You are wrong."

Maxim bristles. "What the fuck are you talking about?"

"Isaak is not Vitaly's child. He is Yakov's. The oldest son of the oldest son. He is your brother. He is your don."

I keep my eyes trained on Isaak, but even now, his mask doesn't falter. I'm the only one who can see the subtle shift in the clench of his jaw. The only one who sees what is happening inside him.

The only one who knows what this means.

"Liar!" Svetlana hisses.

Maxim looks absolutely dumbfounded. He looks at Nikita, then at his mother, then finally at Isaak.

"Don't listen to her, Maxim. Don't listen to any of them!" Svetlana says desperately, clenching his arm. "It doesn't fucking matter. Take what you want! That's what a real don does."

Then, as chaos threatens to swallow us all…

Isaak makes his move.

40

CAMILA

I can't take my eyes off him.

He's always projected power. Strength clings to him like a second skin. But this time, it's different. He's angry, but he's completely in control.

Maxim is almost exactly his height, and yet, the man seems to shrink back a little as his cousin steps forward like an avenging fucking angel.

"I spared your life once before," Isaak intones. "And I'm prepared to spare it one more time."

Maxim's eyes go wide. "What do you mean?"

"I mean that this changes everything."

He glances at me, and I know he's thought of me before deciding on making this offer. I only hope that, whatever it is, Maxim will be smart enough to take it.

"You and I… we're brothers," he says. "And I was taught that family trumps everything else."

Svetlana's lip curls, but she's not looking at Isaak at all. She's got her gaze fixed on Nikita.

"Stand down now, and I will let you live in exile," Isaak says. "Stand your ground, and you will die along with the rest of your men." He takes a slow, steady breath to let his words sink in. "You are no don, Maxim. You enjoy the lifestyle of the rich and privileged. You enjoy the pursuit of power, but won't have any idea what to do when you have it."

"Those are self-serving words," Svetlana snaps.

"Not really. Nothing will change for me."

"Unless you die," she retorts.

"But he won't," Nikita says, stepping forward. "He was born for this. He was always going to be the don."

That seems to be the last straw for Svetlana. I see it in her eyes: she can sense defeat on the horizon. Before that happens, she's determined to get what revenge she can.

She yanks the gun from Maxim's holster, aims it directly at Nikita, and pulls the trigger.

"No!" I scream.

I lunge towards Svetlana. But she's too far and I'm too slow.

The gun fires.

Nikita drops to the ground.

I hear someone scream again. It might even have been me, but I don't know. I don't know anything anymore.

I find myself on my hands and knees as all hell breaks loose, scrambling toward Nikita's slumped form. Another gunshot rings out. Who fired, I don't know. Who was hit, I don't know.

Before I can get to Nikita, someone grabs me by the neck and reels me back. For a moment, I think it's Isaak, but then I recognize the dusky scent. He's still wearing the same cologne he used to use when we first met.

"Maxim!" I cry, trying to pry his hand off me.

He ignores me. I feel something cold and hard press against my temple. "Stop now!" Maxim yells. "OR I will fucking blow her brains out."

The chaos recedes almost instantly. Everyone freezes—and slowly, the picture before me comes into focus.

Isaak is standing a few feet away from his mother's unconscious body. Bogdan is on his knees next to her. I look to the side and realize that Svetlana is lying on the floor, too.

But unlike Nikita, whose chest is rising and falling, it's painfully obvious that she's dead.

Light smoke pours from the barrel of Bogdan's gun. I know immediately that he's the one who made the killing shot.

I can't say that I feel anything at the sight of blood pooling around Svetlana's head. Not pity or remorse or even justified anger. Just… nothing. She was barely human. A hollow space where a soul should have been.

"Don't you fucking touch her," Isaak growls to Maxim.

"I told you, cousin," Maxim snaps. "I'm not going to give up that easy."

If the sight of his dead mother is eliciting any feelings, he's certainly a master at hiding it.

"Please, Maxim," I whisper. "Just give me back my daughter."

"She's within your reach," he tells me. "If you come with me and stop making such a fuss."

Only then do I realize that I'm struggling, trying to resist his grip on me. I stop immediately and twist around so that I can look up at his face.

"I'll come with you," I say without missing a beat.

"Camila, don't trust him!" Isaak calls to me. "He's not going to let Jo go just because he has you."

Desperation radiates from Maxim. He tightens his grip around my upper arm, but I barely feel a thing. I look at Isaak and shake my head apologetically.

"I'm sorry, Isaak… but I can't risk it. I have to get her back."

"If any of you motherfuckers follow us into that house, I will shoot her," Maxim threatens.

He nods to his men and we back up slowly into the house. I notice Vlad say something to Isaak, but he holds up his fisted hand.

He's letting me go.

The moment we're in the house, Maxim turns around and pushes me towards the staircase. "Upstairs," he growls in a voice I've never heard from him before.

Five or six of his men accompany us upstairs. All of them have their weapons drawn. One is Andrew. He sticks close to my side with a leering smirk on his face like he's relishing all of this madness.

Maxim pushes open a door just past the landing and gestures for me to walk through. Then he turns to Andrew. "Stand out here and warn me if any of them get in the house."

I rush inside the room and look around desperately.

"Mommy?"

I turn around and find Jo cowering in the corner of the room between the wardrobe and the bed. The *pop-pop-pop* of gunfire downstairs terrifies her. It terrifies me, too, if I'm being honest.

But that doesn't matter. None of it does. This—my baby girl in my arms—that's the only thing I care about anymore.

"Jo!" I gasp. "Come here, baby."

She scrambles to her feet and runs to me. I grab her and pull her close, making sure to bury her head in my chest to drown out the noise.

"It's okay," I whisper. "It's okay. Mommy's here now."

"I'm scared."

"I know, darling," I tell her. "I'm scared, too. But we're together now. That's all that matters."

The door opens. Maxim storms in.

I pull Jo close to me and shake my head. "Don't touch her."

"Careful," he warns me. "Or your dear mother-in-law is not the only one you're going to be burying."

Goosepimples dot my flesh as I try to recognize the man in front of me. "What happened to you, Maxim?"

"What happened?" he repeats. "*You* happened. Fucking Isaak happened. Do you even remember that you used to love me?"

I blink back my tears, scared of what to say when he's so volatile. "Maxim, I'm sorry. But… but I don't think I ever loved you."

His eyes go wide.

"I'm not just saying this now. I always felt it. I just… I needed someone to help me get out of that nightmare… and you…"

"I was your way out until you found one you liked better," he growls. "Window shopping for a fucking white knight husband. How charming."

I'm holding Jo's head close to my chest. My hands are over her ears, but I'm not sure how much of this she's taking in.

"Please, Maxim, I'm sorry. But you and I were never end game."

"And he is?"

"I… I don't know."

"Liar," he growls. "I can see it in your eyes. The way you look at him. The way he looks at you."

His eyes fall to Jo. I tremble right alongside of her. He brandishes the gun in his hand carelessly, and I try to shield Jo just in case it goes off.

God knows *something* is going to happen soon. Maxim looks like he's coming undone. It's a direct contrast to Isaak's glacial control to watch rage purpling his features and twisting his jaw.

He glances towards the window, and that's when I realize that the gunshots have mostly subsided. The sound of fighting becomes distant. Subdued.

I stand my ground. Maxim walks to the window and glances outside.

"Well… good news for Isaak," he snarls.

Relief floods through me.

But it curdles and dies almost instantly when he turns to me. "But bad news for you," Maxim finishes. "I'm not about to die today, Camila."

I nod and swallow. "Okay."

"Because if I did, I'm afraid I'd have to take you with me. You or that kid you're clutching."

Cold, painful fear flushes through my body. "Please, Maxim…"

"Don't," he interrupts. "Pleading with me is not going to work this time. If I don't get out of here alive, then neither will you."

I glance down at Jo's dark head. She still has that innocent, childlike smell that I used to long for at night when I was thousands of miles away from her.

I know what I have to do next.

I just don't know if I have the strength to do it.

"Take me with you," I hear myself say.

Maxim does a double-take. "What?"

"Isaak won't hurt you if you have me with you. Use me to get yourself out of here. That way, neither one of us has to die."

He narrows his eyes. "What's the catch?"

"Let Jo stay here… with Isaak."

He considers that for a moment. "You'd leave her behind?"

"Yes."

I'll do it for Jo. For my baby girl. I'll do what I've done once before: leave her behind so that she can have a better life than the one I'm able to offer.

Even if we can't ever be a family, at least she'll have her father. At least Isaak will have her.

It's the most I can give either one of them now.

"You don't want her, Maxim," I tell him. "We'd have to leave the country, and you don't want to be saddled with another man's child, do you?"

That seems to get through to him. He nods crisply like a business decision has been made. "Fine," he says. "I'll leave the kid, and you help to get us out of here."

I nod.

Satisfied, he opens the door and gestures for me to lead the way. His men part to let me go out ahead of all of them.

Maxim joins me at the threshold of the door. I can hear the sounds of Isaak's troops amassing on the other side.

"I have your wife, Isaak," Maxim calls out. "I have your daughter."

Jo's head jerks up towards me. "Mommy, what is he saying?"

I lift her up in my arms. "Nothing, baby. Don't listen to him."

She buries her head in my shoulder. I cling hard to her, trying to internalize this moment before I have to let her go. Is it possible that this will be the last time I see her?

It's a cruel end to the journey I've been on these past several years, but—

I freeze as I remember what I have in my pocket right now. Something Nikita gave me on our way out of the compound to come here. The last words she ever spoke directly to me.

A woman should never be without a way out, she told me when she pressed it into my hand.

The knowledge of what's in my pocket gives me renewed courage. Fresh hope.

Maybe there's a way I can save Jo, as well as myself.

Maybe there's an alternate ending to this tragedy.

Maybe we can all make it out together.

"I want a vehicle," Maxim yells. "Right fucking now, or I'm going to be handing you a pair of bodies."

He grabs my arm and pulls me out of the house. My eyes land on Isaak, who's frozen in place a few feet away. Bodies litter the ground. I keep my hand on the back of Jo's head to press her face into my chest.

"Don't look up, okay, baby?"

"Okay," Jo replies, her voice trembling with tears.

"If the vehicle is not here in a minute, I will use this gun," Maxim vows.

I can feel his men at my back, but I decide not to worry about them now. Seconds later, a vehicle is driven up and parked between Isaak's men and Maxim's small, straggling group.

He tries to pull me towards the jeep, but I resist him.

"No, you promised me," I say. "Jo."

"Jesus," he growls. "Put her down then. Let the brat run to her father."

"Jo," I whisper to her. "Baby, I'm going to need you to go to Isaak now."

She pulls her face back just enough to look at me. "No, I don't wanna leave you."

There are tear tracks staining her cheeks, and it makes my heart break. "I know, love. I know. But Isaak has to get you out of here."

"Back home?"

"Yes."

"Will Aunty Bree be there?"

"I will make sure she is. Trust me, my darling. I love you." I straighten up.

Isaak watches the whole exchange with careful eyes. "Camila…"

"Isaak, this is the only way. Just trust me, okay?"

Bogdan moves forward and grabs Jo. I don't even have a chance to truly savor her weight in my arms before it's gone.

Then Bogdan is retreating back into the ranks with my baby in his arms…

While I do everything I can not to fall apart completely.

Isaak takes a step forward, but Maxim points his gun directly at me. "That was the bargain, Isaak. You get the girl. I get the woman. We'll be leaving now."

"That is my wife," Isaak growls.

"Not anymore," he says, grabbing my arm. "Now, she's going to be my whore. You got what you wanted. You got the Bratva. But I'm not leaving empty-handed."

Pleased with those parting words, he steers me towards the jeep.

That's when I strike.

I'm not even really aiming. My hand shakes desperately as I swing through the air. But I make sure the blade pierces his flesh. I bury it in his stomach, and as his eyes go wide with shock and pain, I kick at his groin for good measure.

Andrew's eyes meet mine. He raises his gun to my head.

But before he can shoot, another gunshot goes off. He looks down and I watch as the blood blossoms across his belly. He drops a moment later.

Good fucking riddance.

I feel as though the air has been knocked out of me as someone grabs me around the waist and yanks me to a side. When I look up, I'm staring into his blue eyes.

"Isaak…"

"Are you okay?" he asks urgently.

"I… I think so."

His eyes scour my body, looking for any signs of injury.

"Did I kill him?" I ask.

Isaak glances over his shoulder. "Not quite."

"Then you can finish the job for me," I say.

He nods once and walks over to Maxim's body. The other Vorobev is spitting blood as he stares up at his cousin.

"I gave you two chances to leave," Isaak says in the voice of an executioner. "Two chances to live. You spurned them both."

Maxim can only gurgle at this point. I want to look away, but I can't seem to. His remaining five men are corpses now. They surround him in a morbid ring of broken bones and crimson blood.

"But family still means something to me," Isaak says. "And you are my brother. So instead of giving you the drawn-out and painful ending you deserve…"

He points the gun at Maxim's head.

"I will give you a clean death."

He shoots. I jerk at the sound. Maxim's body twitches once, then goes limp.

And only then do I allow myself to feel relief.

It's over. It's over. It's all fucking over.

I get up, turn, and run towards Bogdan, who's still holding Jo. She reaches out to me and it's the most beautiful thing I've ever seen, my baby needing her mother. My girl in my arms.

"It's okay, darling," I tell her as she cries. "Mommy's here now."

I feel Isaak come up at my shoulder.

"Isaak's right here, too," I assure her. "We're both here. And we're never, ever going to leave you again."

EPILOGUE: ISAAK
TWO MONTHS LATER

"Nikki!"

The puppy just barks happily and keeps running.

"She runs fast for a chubby little bugger," I sigh.

Camila slaps my arm. "Hey!"

I laugh. "Well, look at her. You're feeding her too much."

"She's got a healthy appetite!"

"You mean you and Jo spoil her."

She gives me a guilty look. "Maybe a little."

"A lot."

Camila sighs. "It's been good for Jo to have a distraction. Especially after…"

She trails off as though saying the words out loud will be too painful for me. She's been treading on eggshells about Mama's death.

I think she's worried that something might trigger me belatedly. I can understand why she thinks that. For someone as emotive as Camila, expressing grief is natural. And healthy.

For me, it's… completely the opposite.

Even when I feel it, it's a dark hole deep inside of me. It's not buried, just… controlled.

"You can say her name, you know," I say. "I'm not going to start weeping."

She gives me a curious little side glance. "I know it must be painful for you."

"The damn dog is named after her, Camila," I point out. "I'm fine."

Naming the dog "Nikki" after my mother had been Jo's idea, of course. She had taken the death the hardest of all of us. Understandably so.

The dog was step one on the road to finding peace with everything we went through together.

Step two was telling her who I really am.

Step three was moving all her things from Bree's place to here.

"Mommy!" she yells. "Papa! Come on!"

She'd started calling me Papa almost immediately after we'd sat her down and had the conversation with her. She'd looked between us silently. And for a long time, I thought she was disappointed.

Then she's hugged us both. And that was that.

To be honest, it was a little anti-climactic. I was prepared for hysterics. Instead, I got what she's given every hardship in her young life: a smile and acceptance.

She has strength that I can only begin to guess at.

Which is not to say that it's all sunshine and rainbows. She's suffered in ways we might not appreciate for a long time. As her parents, I know Camila and I are not going to get a free pass. The questions will come when Jo is old enough to think of them.

But for now, we get to enjoy this. Family. Being together. Simple as that.

"You never talk about her," Camila says, as she slips her hand through my arm.

"Because there's nothing to say."

"Don't you miss her?"

"Sometimes."

I'm not sure if there's a whole lot of truth in that statement, but I know it's the answer that Camila expects to hear. It's not that I didn't love my mother.

I just didn't know her. Not truly.

So the love I felt for her was... detached. Removed. It felt more like a biological responsibility than a conscious choice.

I'm a cold bastard, in large part due to the cold bastard who raised me. But I've evolved enough to know that that's not what I want for my children.

I can break a cycle that once threatened to consume me.

"I miss our conversations," Camila admits. "She let me in, you know?"

I smile. "I'm glad you got to have a relationship with her before she went."

Svetlana's bullet had pierced Mama's spine and paralyzed her. We'd rushed her to the nearest hospital, but by the time we got there, she slipped into a coma.

She'd lingered unconscious for a few days before finally passing on.

I felt it once that day—the sharp sting of loss and the gnawing regret that made me feel guilty for not doing enough to understand the woman who made me.

But in the moments before her death, she looked so damn peaceful that I couldn't help feeling as though she'd been waiting to go for a very long time. Maybe she'd even been longing for it.

She'd unburdened herself of her secrets. It was time to leave then. It was all okay.

She left behind a bit of a mess, to say the least. Bogdan and I are still processing the bombs she dropped that day. But in the grand scheme of things, none of it changed a damn thing.

Not within the Bratva.

Not for my men.

And certainly not between Bogdan and me.

We don't recognize the term "half-brothers." We have never been that and we never will be. He is and will always be my brother.

Cami and I catch up to Jo, who's sitting by the pond with Nikki flopping around on her lap. Jo giggles happily and I watch as Camila's eyes go soft with tenderness.

"Sweetheart," she says, "we should go back inside now. Aunt Bree will be here in a few minutes to pick you up."

This is the first weekend she's going to be spending with her aunt and uncle since she came to live here. She's been excited about it all week.

"Okay!" Jo chirps, getting to her feet.

The puppy runs towards us and starts nipping at my ankles before performing the same routine on Camila.

"This dog needs to calm down."

"Papa!"

I can't say a fucking thing about the dog. Not one word of discipline. If Jo doesn't jump down my throat, Camila does. Honestly, some days, this little shit gets more attention than I do. She's gonna be a terror when she gets big enough to start doing real damage.

Laughing, Camila scoops up the chubby golden retriever and cradles her as we make our way back to the house. Jo skips on ahead, but when Nikki starts to whine, Cami begrudgingly sets her down.

The dog immediately rockets off after Jo, tail wagging so hard I wonder if she's about to take flight.

"Those two are going to be inseparable," Cami sighs.

"Going to be?" I ask.

She smiles. "I think it's a good thing. It's not like she has siblings to play with." I give her a look and she blushes immediately. "I didn't mean it like that."

"Maybe you should."

The blush gets deeper, but she says nothing. Lucky for her, Bree arrives then, with both boys in tow.

The older one is still a little shy around me—awestruck, I think—but the younger one worships the ground I walk on.

"Can't we stay a little bit, Mom?" Sam asks. "I want Uncle Isaak to show me his car collection."

Bree rolls her eyes. "You've already seen it."

"Not the whole garage!"

"Another day," Bree insists.

I ruffle the kid's hair. I've taken a liking to both her boys. They're very different personalities, and in some ways, they kind of remind me of Bogdan and myself.

You know, if we were normal kids who were raised by normal parents.

"Aw, come on, Mom!" Sam complains.

But Bree steadfastly ushers all the kids and the puppy into the backseat. "Have a romantic weekend, you two," she says, giving me a wink as she gets into the front seat.

"I'll call tonight, sweetheart," Camila promises. "I'll call before you go to bed."

"Bye, Mommy!" Jo waves from the back seat. "Bye, Papa!"

The moment the gates close behind them, I wrap my arm around Camila's waist and steer her back into the house. "Finally," I mutter, "some peace."

"Stop," Camila says, giving me the evil eye. "You're going to miss her."

"Of course," I admit freely. "But now it's our time to do whatever we want."

"Are you referring to the conversation we've been putting off for almost two months now?" she asks bluntly.

"Which conversation is that?"

She rolls her eyes. "The one where you ask me what my plans are?"

I take her hand and pull her towards me. Her body hits mine, and I adjust a little so she can feel my erection. "What are your plans, Camila?"

She glances over my shoulder, but it's mostly just so she can avoid looking at me.

"I've been doing a lot of thinking…"

"That's dangerous."

"And…" She gulps a little as my cock sticks her in the thigh.

"And?"

"Isaak, I just don't know what my place would be here."

"Your place is by my side, Camila."

"I'm never going to be the obedient wife," she reminds me, rebellion burning in her tone.

I chuckle. "No, I didn't think so."

"And you're okay with that?"

"I don't have much of a choice, do I?"

"Well, you can always replace me with someone else."

I snort. "I can't abide any other woman."

"Is that a fact?"

"Camila," I say, pulling her chin to me so that she's forced to look me in the eye. "I have been with a lot of different women in my life."

Her expression clouds instantly. "I hope you're going somewhere with this…"

I smile. "I can't remember their names now. Or their faces. I never wanted to wake up next to any of them. They were just placeholders. A stop gap on the way to finding you."

She raises her eyebrows. "That's the most poetic thing you've ever said to me."

I laugh again. "Don't get used to it."

She laughs. "Too late. I want more."

"Goddammit."

I reach up and start fondling her breasts, knowing that no child or puppy is going to run up to us and interrupt the moment.

"You're getting distracted," she chides.

"How can I not? Have you seen yourself?"

"Isaak," she laughs. "I want to be here with you. And not just because we have a daughter together. I would want you regardless."

"I love you, too."

"That's not what I said."

I wink. "It's what you meant."

"Jesus, so cocky."

"I am cocky about you, Camila. You know why?"

"Why?"

"Because you fell in love with me from the moment you saw me. Just like I fell in love with you. Everything that's happened since then is just noise. Variations on the theme."

Her face splits into the most magnificent smile.

She disentangles herself from my arms and takes a few steps back to look alluringly out of the glass patio doors. Then she starts undressing slowly.

"I guess there's nothing else to do but… swim."

She discards each piece of clothing. I take in her naked body with starving eyes. She's a work of fucking art.

She doesn't walk towards me though. She turns and sashays through the door, out to the pool deck. Without ever looking back, she dives into the water, the picture of grace.

My cock is a fucking weapon at this point.

When she comes up for air, she pushes back the hair from her face and gives me a coquettish smile. "What are you waiting for, Mr. Vorobev?" she teases.

I waste no time undressing before I dive in after her.

Epilogue: Isaak

As the water settles, she swims over to me and wraps her arms around my neck and her legs around my waist.

"You know, there is one more thing left to figure out."

She frowns. "What's that?"

I slip my hands down to her ass and give her cheeks a little squeeze. "Legally, you're a Vorobev."

She tenses slightly, wondering where this conversation is going.

"But you were forced to sign on the dotted line. I didn't give you a choice."

"Where are you going with this?"

"I'm trying to tell you that I'm giving you a choice now. To sign on the dotted line. To stay married to me. To do it in front of all our friends and family."

She smacks my bicep. "You're serious?"

I nod. "Never been surer. I think it'll be good for Jo. She needs to see something official. Something concrete to feel truly secure."

Camila nods. I can already see her imagining the day. She's looking past me and into the future. Her green eyes shine like emeralds.

"Isaak," Camila sighs, looking back at me and placing a kiss on my lips.

"Yeah?"

"I want you to ask me."

I smile. "Camila Ferrara Vorobev… will you marry me?"

EXTENDED EPILOGUE

Thanks for reading VELVET ANGEL—but don't stop now! Click the link below to get your hands on the exclusive Extended Epilogue so you can see Isaak and Camila's family growing (+ the cutest puppy in the world)!

DOWNLOAD THE EXTENDED EPILOGUE TO VELVET ANGEL

MAILING LIST

Sign up to my mailing list!
New subscribers receive a FREE steamy bad boy romance novel.

Click the link below to join.
https://sendfox.com/nicolefox

ALSO BY NICOLE FOX

Vorobev Bratva

Velvet Devil

Velvet Angel

Romanoff Bratva

Immaculate Deception

Immaculate Corruption

Kovalyov Bratva

Gilded Cage

Gilded Tears

Jaded Soul

Jaded Devil

Ripped Veil

Ripped Lace

Mazzeo Mafia Duet

Liar's Lullaby (Book 1)

Sinner's Lullaby (Book 2)

Bratva Crime Syndicate

Can be read in any order!

Lies He Told Me

Scars He Gave Me

Sins He Taught Me

Belluci Mafia Trilogy

Corrupted Angel (Book 1)

Corrupted Queen (Book 2)

Corrupted Empire (Book 3)

De Maggio Mafia Duet

Devil in a Suit (Book 1)

Devil at the Altar (Book 2)

Kornilov Bratva Duet

Married to the Don (Book 1)

Til Death Do Us Part (Book 2)

Heirs to the Bratva Empire

Can be read in any order!

Kostya

Maksim

Andrei

Princes of Ravenlake Academy (Bully Romance)

Can be read as standalones!

Cruel Prep

Cruel Academy

Cruel Elite

Tsezar Bratva

Nightfall (Book 1)

Daybreak (Book 2)

Russian Crime Brotherhood

Can be read in any order!

Owned by the Mob Boss

Unprotected with the Mob Boss

Knocked Up by the Mob Boss

Sold to the Mob Boss

Stolen by the Mob Boss

Trapped with the Mob Boss

Volkov Bratva

Broken Vows (Book 1)

Broken Hope (Book 2)

Broken Sins *(standalone)*

Other Standalones

Vin: A Mafia Romance

Box Sets

Bratva Mob Bosses (Russian Crime Brotherhood Books 1-6)

Tsezar Bratva (Tsezar Bratva Duet Books 1-2)

Heirs to the Bratva Empire

The Mafia Dons Collection

The Don's Corruption

Printed in Great Britain
by Amazon